MARY ELIZAB

THE CONFLICT

Volume 2

Elibron Classics
www.elibron.com

Elibron Classics series.

ISBN 1-4021-9106-5 (paperback)
ISBN 1-4021-1791-4 (hardcover)

This Elibron Classics Replica Edition is an unabridged facsimile of the edition published in 1903 by Bernhard Tauchnitz, Leipzig.

COLLECTION

OF

BRITISH AUTHORS

TAUCHNITZ EDITION.

VOL. 3662.

THE CONFLICT. By M. E. BRADDON.

IN TWO VOLUMES.

VOL. II.

THE CONFLICT

BY

M. E. BRADDON

AUTHOR OF

"LADY AUDLEY'S SECRET," "VIXEN," "LONDON PRIDE," ETC. ETC.

COPYRIGHT EDITION

IN TWO VOLUMES

VOL. II

LEIPZIG

BERNHARD TAUCHNITZ

1903.

THE CONFLICT.

I.

THE joy which Walter Arden hoped to feel in the sight of familiar things, the quiet fields and hills and woodlands, the sober old homesteads and cosy villages between Southampton and London, and even in his own library, was lessened by the state of physical prostration in which he landed from the American liner that brought him from New York. Throughout the homeward pilgrimage by river and sea, by rail and steamer, he had been carefully tended by Alick Mackenzie and Archer Stormont; but the rallying power which he had shown immediately after the healing of his wound had failed mysteriously before the band left Dawson City in the steamer for St. Michael, carrying their fortunes with them in strong iron-bound chests. Mackenzie hoped that restful days on river and sea would have restored his strength; but the listlessness and apathy continued, and he was in weaker health when he landed at Southampton than when he left the gold-fields. The motive power of existence seemed broken; and when his friends had seen him established in his old rooms, with his old servant in attendance upon him, he sank down into a languid endurance of life, caring for nothing, hoping for nothing. Even his books had lost their charm, nor could the old or the new things in literature—neither the book beloved of mankind for two thousand years, nor the book that had taken the town by storm yesterday—bring him relief from the haunting memory of those last months on the Yukon, and the mysterious change in Michael Dartnell's character.

His landlady ministered to him with an almost maternal tenderness, employing all the resources of her culinary art to tempt an invalid appetite, but with scant success. Her mourning-gown told him of her sorrow, even before her trembling lips broke into speech.

"Oh, sir, there is no one in the little parlour now—the room that we made so pretty, with your kind help. I keep the door locked, and no one goes there but me, to dust the furniture and air the room. The pretty things are all there; her bust of Byron, and his portrait that Lady Mary gave her, and her books, and the flower-vases. I put a few flowers there every Sunday; for, though it may be foolish of me, I can't help thinking that her spirit may haunt the room where she spent so many quiet hours."

"Was she long ill?"

"No, sir; I think I may say she was never ill. I thank God for that in the midst of my sorrow. She suffered neither sickness nor pain; she just drooped and drooped, all through last autumn, and seemed a shade weaker every day. I had the best of doctors for her, thanks to your kind sister, who came to see her ever so many times, and took her in her own carriage to her own physician; but he didn't pretend he could do anything to lengthen her life. He gave her a prescription, and she took the medicine, and seemed to rally just a little; but she was fading away all the time. Her life was ebbing from her slowly and gently, like the tide going out."

"Did her mind seem stronger towards the last?"

"No, sir; she was always the same, except that those dreadful thoughts of hell-fire and fiends and the bottomless pit seem to have left her. She was happy in her pretty romantic way, as she used to be before that trouble came upon her. She would talk of Byron, and shed tears over his early death, when he was fighting the Greeks—or fighting for the Greeks, was it? Poor child, how she adored his lordship! She had his picture propped up beside her bed in the last days, when she was too weak to hold up her head, and she died in her sleep, without so much as one troubled sigh, with her face turned towards his face; and I wondered if his spirit knew of the love of one simple low-born girl, given to him more than seventy years after they laid him in his grave."

"I'm afraid your life must seem sad and empty since your loss, my dear Mrs. Berry," Arden said gently.

"Oh, Mr. Arden, I feel as if my heart, and all the hopes I ever had in this life, were locked up with the pictures and books in that little room. If I had only this life to think about—well, I believe I should just walk down to Westminster bridge, in the dead of some dark night, and drop quietly over the parapet. One drowned woman more or less would make no difference in this big city. But I look forward to the life to come, when I shall find my poor ruined girl again among the souls of the redeemed, whose sins are washed white in the blood of the Lamb. I cannot fly in the face of my Creator, Mr. Arden, and forfeit my hope of life eternal, and reunion with my girl."

The fervour of her words, and the exalted look in the poor plain face, touched him deeply. Yes, this was the only possible consolation for the bereaved, the sure and certain hope of reunion in the life to come.

He remembered Rachel's words, "What could I say to them, how could I comfort them, if I did not believe in the life after death?"

Arden called in Carlton House Terrace on the day after his return. He had just strength to get into a hansom and let himself be driven where he wanted to go, looking with uncaring eyes at the houses and the people he passed, and with the dreamlike half-alive feeling of extreme weakness.

Disappointment awaited him. Mr. Lorimer was in Central America; Mrs. and Miss Lorimer were at Harrogate. He went back to Jermyn Street feeling that the town was empty of all human interest.

Lady Mary Selby called upon him on the following day.

"Mrs. Berry told me you were coming home on the *Boston*," she said; "but I think you might have written to me before you left Klondyke. Only one shabby letter in more than two years!"

"I had so little to write about."

"So little? In a life of adventure!"

"Would you have relished descriptions of snow-mountains and lakes? I know you care only about people; and there were no people, from your point of view, between San Francisco and the Yukon."

"You might have written about yourself."

"I had nothing satisfactory to tell you."

"Then your expedition has been a failure?"

"Something of a failure."

"No gold?"

"Gold? Oh yes, plenty of gold. I believe I am richer by a quarter of a million or so."

"A quarter of a million! Do you call that failure? Why, my husband is quite jubilant when he has made a quarter of a million, as he did the week before last, by the boom in mineral oils."

"I know. He calls it another milestone on the road to a modest competence. I have heard him. But I did not go to the North-West for the sake of the gold; I went to forget things."

"And have you forgotten?"

"Nothing."

"I'm glad you have not forgotten Rachel Lorimer"

"If you love me, you ought to be sorry. But it was something to find that she is still Rachel Lorimer."

"And will be to the end of the chapter, I believe, unless you can make her change her mind."

"I cannot hope to do that, unless I could change my mind."

"And is your mind still the same?"

"Yes; the light that shines into her life has not come into mine."

"How can you hope for it if you won't even go to church?"

"You think church would convert me—to sit in a row of close-packed human beings, and listen to the pious banalities of a popular preacher, to hear fifty-two sermons a year, of which perhaps two would appeal to my reason or touch my heart."

"If you went to hear the right preachers, you would end by being convinced."

"My dear Mary, if Rachel's perfect life cannot convince me, there is no hope for my salvation; not even in a miracle. But tell me about yourself. You look younger and handsomer and happier than when we parted."

"Yes, I am happier. I have been enjoying my trivial life. The only way to be happy is to be trivial—to enjoy the present moment, and to value the things one has. My parties were among the most successful of the season. I had the best home and foreign royalties, and all the pretty people, and all the clever people—I mean all the people who have done things within the year—books, or pictures, or flying-machines, or scientific discoveries."

"And how do you come to be in town in October?"

"Oh, the usual business—to buy things. We have been on Selby's Moor, and we came from Scotland in his motor-car. There were three break-downs, and I had to stand shivering on a lonely highroad while the wretched thing was mended. I shall travel by rail in future. If one has to wear ugly clothes and goggles, the motor isn't good enough. Picture a honeymoon couple!—'the bride's going-away toilet was a mackintosh coat and smoked spectacles.'"

"How long shall you be in town?"

"As long as I find London the pleasantest place in the world. But I want to hear more about you, Walter. You are looking dreadfully ill. You must have worn yourself out in that horrid Arctic region."

"No, no; the Arctic region is not to blame."

"What was the matter, then? You are looking ten years older than when you left England. There must be some reason."

"Yes, there is a reason. I have been through tragic experiences, things I cannot talk about—yet awhile."

"I won't worry you. But I hope you will see my pet doctor, who will set you right very soon."

And Lady Mary urged the merits of the last fashionable physician, the man whom everybody insisted upon as the one infallible healer.

"You must see him at once—to morrow morning. You must write immediately for an appointment."

"My case is not so desperate. I am suffering from a kind of reaction, and I only want rest. Just to lie back in my chair half asleep, with a book dropping out of my hand."

"That is not enough. He will send you somewhere——"

"I shall ask him to send me to Harrogate."

"Ah, then you know that Rachel is there?"

"Yes; I was told she was there. But I hope she has not been ill."

"No. They are there for her mother's rheumatism."

"Then I would consent to Harrogate, if your physician should send me there. But I have no hope, Mary—no hope of anything better than to be Rachel's friend and helper."

Arden promised to consult the great man without delay, but on the next morning he was too ill to leave his bed, and his servant sent for the general practitioner who had the honour of attending Mrs. Berry's lodgers, whether lords or commoners, and who had been a kind friend to Lisbeth till her last hour.

He found the patient suffering from no specific disease, but in a state of extreme prostration, and with a good deal of fever. He ordered perfect rest and careful nursing—a trained nurse to assist Martin the valet.

Lady Mary came on the following afternoon, and insisted on a consultation with the oracle from Cavendish Square, to which the Jermyn Street practitioner politely assented, and had the satisfaction of finding his opinion confirmed and his treatment approved.

"Mr. Arden must have passed through great suffering, mental as well as physical," the physician said to Lady Mary, after the consultation. "I suppose you know that he has been badly wounded—a stab from a knife or dagger, which narrowly missed his heart?"

"No; I know nothing."

"Mr. Wellborough found the scar when sounding him. It must have been a severe wound, only just missing a vital point, and recent; certainly within the last six months."

"Can he have been fighting a duel?"

"No, no; the wound could not have been made by a small sword. The scar indicates the blade of a knife or dagger. Mr. Arden has had a narrow escape."

Walter Arden, Jermyn Street, London, to Douglas Campbell, Leith, Tasmania.

November 30th, 189-.

MY DEAR DOUGLAS,

I promised to write to you as soon as I arrived in London; but you know the proverb, *Mann denkt, Gott lenkt.* I have been in this house nearly two months, and for much of that time life has been a blank, or I have been dwelling in a world of my own, where all things were strange and incredible, and only within the last week have I again become a reasonable being, conscious of the world in which I live; conscious, and happy with an ineffable happiness, having by means of my very weakness and piteous condition won the prize which was denied to my passionate pleading in the days of my strength.

I will not trouble you with the details of my illness, for it was almost a repetition of the long period of fever and weakness which I suffered in the log cabin after my wound. Fever and delirium; long days in which life trembled in that fine balance with which the doctor weighs his patient's chances; and then a slow rallying, a gradual return to the consciousness of the life around me, in which the simple furniture of my bedroom ceased to present itself under all manner of horrible or grotesque shapes, and became again familiar objects—a wardrobe on the right, a dressing-table on the left, the sofa, the mantelpiece—all so commonplace and soothingly peaceful after the labyrinths in which I had lost myself, the catacombs where I had walked for weary hours clutching an expiring candle, the submarine ships in which I had panted for breath, the Siberian dungeons, the Thibetan monasteries. Only the common everyday world; but what bliss to find it again, after being lost among the spectral terrors of delirium.

That was my faithful servant quietly sweeping the hearth and replenishing the fire; and the comfortable-looking middle-aged woman standing by my bed was my nurse.

But the angel—who had looked down upon me sometimes, radiant with a divine light, in the midst of scenes of terror—where was she?

I asked what had become of the angel, but the nurse thought I was delirious still, and only murmured some soothing recommendation to take the prescribed nourishment, and try to sleep. I had no power to persist. I was weaker than an infant, and fell into a kind of half sleep, while the nurse arranged my pillows. It was the first sleep that brought me comfort since the beginning of my illness. I slept till the short winter day was done, and awoke to find my room lighted dimly by a pair of candles on a table at some distance from my bed.

There were two women in the room. One was sitting in the large armchair by the fire, in bonnet and mantle. I could not see her face. The other was sitting by my bed, bareheaded, the candlelight shining on soft brown hair and the loveliest eyes in the world.

"Rachel!"

Yes; it was Rachel. I stretched out my hand, and it was clasped in hers, and I heard a stifled sob before she spoke.

"Mother and I are so glad you are better," she said

quietly. "We have been to see you every day; but you did not know us."

"I knew that an angel looked down at me sometimes—that the gates of heaven opened for an instant, and that I looked and saw an angel, while I was lying in the depths of hell."

"Ah, now you are talking as if you were delirious again. There were two of your angels—mother was always with me."

"Dear, dear Mrs. Lorimer," I said.

She came over and sat by me, and held my other hand, and I lay thus between these dear women, mother and daughter, and I knew that all I had ever suffered of sorrow on earth was outweighed a hundredfold by the bliss that was granted to me.

Rachel loved me. The dear hand that clasped mine, with a warmer clasp than ever friend gave to friend, was my assurance of her love. It scarcely needed our quiet talk next day, when Mrs. Lorimer left us for a brief span, which she spent with my sister in the library, to convince me of my happiness.

I asked her if she would trust her life to me, if she would believe in my reverence for the religion she loved, because it was hers, and that no act or word of mine should ever attack her faith.

"I must believe, I must hope, and go on hoping, that in His own good time God will give you the faith that makes life on earth worth living——"

And then she told me how unhappy she had been when she knew that I had left England for the wild life on the Yukon, and that she had made me an exile, and had sent me to face hardships and dangers that might end in death. She had acted from a sense of duty. She had sacrificed her love for her faith; but when the deed was done, she repented, and began to doubt if she had chosen the best course, if a truly religious woman would not have accepted the risk from which she had recoiled, and devoted herself to the man she loved, trusting to the Divine guidance to bring him to the true faith.

"The faith that can move mountains will surely help me to lead one good man into the light," she said, with the simplicity which makes her belief in the spiritual world so lovely and so pathetic to an unbeliever like me.

She is mine, Douglas, this adorable creature whose presence has for me been like the coming of sunshine into a place of darkness. She will trust her life to me, and every hope, every desire, every thought of mine, will be centred in her. Henceforth her lightest wish will be my law. I shall live only to adore and to obey her. Her coming has routed all the brood of evil.

In ineffable, in unmerited bliss,

I sign myself your faithful friend,

WALTER ARDEN.

II.

Mr. and Mrs. Walter Arden had been married three years, and the only cloud upon their wedded happiness was the shadow left by the loss of their only child, a son whose life upon this planet had lasted something less than half a year.

"He is waiting for us in heaven," his mother said sometimes, when her husband surprised her in tears, and knew that they were shed for the one sorrow of her life.

A child under six months is hardly a sentient being to the indifferent observer. It is a creature to be cherished by an overpaid nurse, and wheeled about in a white chariot under an embroidered satin coverlet, and to be admired and gushed over by its mother's female friends, who would not recognise the thing they praise if they happened to meet it half an hour afterwards with somebody else's nurse.

But to one person upon earth—to the mother—there is a world of thought and meaning in those starry eyes; and every gesture of the delicate limbs, and every vague sweet smile on the roseate face, has its significance. Rachel had worshipped her infant son, not to the neglect of the unfortunate and the unhappy, for all the business of philanthropy had gone on uninterruptedly during his little life; but looking back on that brief span of exquisite happiness, which seemed a life apart, a life in which he was, she felt that all her thoughts had centred in her child, that she had made him her idol, to the forgetfulness of other women's children—the ill-nurtured, sickly little ones at the *crèche,* who, from her own point of view, had as strong a claim on her as her own very son—the claim of "the least of these," imposed upon her by her Saviour.

He had been taken from her. Was it a lesson for the unregenerate heart? She stood beside his grave with her husband, the grave in a rural churchyard, far from the smoke and din of cities, which was to be her own and her husband's resting-place in the days to come, the last home, amidst scenes of peacefulness and woodland beauty, which they had chosen for their beloved. She stood by the open grave, with Arden's hand clasped in hers, and her thoughts soared from the coffin and the clay to that new life which her child was living, and which to her seemed so much the more certain and assured because of this little life that had flickered into darkness here, to shine among God's populace of radiant faces, in the light of the Lamb.

In all their after-talk of the son they had laid asleep in the Berkshire churchyard, she never questioned her husband as to his faith in that celestial future where her missing treasure was to be given back to her. She spoke of her own hope as if it were a certainty; and only in the searching look of the lovely eyes did Arden see the doubt struggling with the hope that he too looked forward to the mystic reunion of spirit liberated from the bonds of flesh.

The sorrow was an old wound now, and the life flowed on in graciousness and peace, a life that meant incalculable good for others. Arden had associated himself and his fortune with all his wife's plans. She was his leader, his conscience, the better part of himself. If he could not be a Christian for her sake, he could at least be a philanthropist. They worked together. He understood all the business of charity, the accountancy, the supervision, all that needed a strong will and mind. He had a secretary who helped in the drudgery of correspondence and accounts, and the greater part of whose time was occupied in answering begging letters, or investigating the claims of the supplicants; but there was no part of the machine which his hand did not direct, no detail in which he was not personally interested.

When the question of her married home was mooted, Rachel proposed a house in one of the old squares, Bedford or Russell for choice, the largest house they could find, where there would be room for philanthropic tea-parties after Mrs. Bellingham's pattern, where she would be out of the way of the fashionable world and its laborious culture of futile pleasures.

But Mr. and Mrs. Lorimer overruled this selection.

"If those old squares were the kind of places I remember when I was a boy, guarded by iron gates, remote, melancholy, slow, I would make no objection to your living there," Lorimer told his daughter, "but the noises and the traffic of our obstreperous modern London have burst the gates and spoilt the quiet. The flavour of the Georgian century is gone. Students and old-fashioned people have fled from the neighbourhood in despair. If you want quiet, you must live in the West End."

Mrs. Lorimer put in her plea. She wanted her daughter near her. That was essential. So a small house was found in a quiet little street near St. James's Palace, and within five minutes' walk of Carlton House Terrace. The house was small, but the rent was immense. All the resources of modern architecture had been brought to bear upon a prim square house of the early Victorian order, and it had been made eighteenth-century, with shallow bow windows, small panes, beaten iron-work and copper decorations, and quaintnesses of every kind. It was like that house in Arlington Street, of which it was said the owner ought to live over the way in order to look at it. Happily, the house was neat and pretty within as well as a thing of beauty outside; and Rachel was a woman as well as a philanthropist, and could not help loving her dainty home, with its white walls and gay floral chintzes, Louis-seize cabinets and tables, and choice water-colours, the gift of her adoring father.

The house had been furnished by Mr. and Mrs. Lorimer with a lavish outlay that had seemed sinful to Rachel, who could never withdraw her mind from those martyrs of poverty in the dark corners of the great city. But she submitted to the will of those she loved, from whom she had received boundless indulgence, and by whom she had been allowed freedom that is rarely granted to a rich man's daughter. She accepted the pretty house with a warm gratitude, but she resolutely refused the diamonds which her father wanted to give her. She had her pearls which had been selected for shape and colour, two or three at a time, year after year, till the perfect necklace was complete. This necklace she loved for the love that had created it; but costliness in clothes or jewels in a general way was distasteful to her. A country vicar's daughter would have desired a more elaborate *trousseau* than Mr. Lorimer's heiress carried to her new home.

The cynical among her girl-friends declared that she affected this Spartan simplicity because she thought it accentuated her beauty, and was the only possible way of being original in a world where everybody of importance was dressed by the same people and with the same reckless expenditure.

"Her quakerish satin frock is more conspicuous in a crowd than all our furs and feathers," said one, "though it can't cost her more than fifteen pounds."

"She has found out the exact hat that sets off her profile, and she makes a virtue of wearing it all through the season," said another.

Mrs. Walter Arden did not abjure society. She had youth and health. She was happily married, and the long days spent in going about doing good left her with a reserve of bright thoughts and gaiety for the evenings. She had her opera-box, a gift from her mother, and she went to all the evening parties, where the clever people—political, literary, or artistic—were to be met. She was oftener seen as Mrs. Arden than she had been as Miss Lorimer, for she enjoyed the independence of a married woman's position, and the knowledge that she was no longer a mark for the fortune-hunter. The attentions paid her now must be offered without any hidden motive. She was safe in the haven of a happy marriage, and knew that somewhere in the crowd her husband was waiting for the hour that would bring them back to the quiet house and the dual solitude they loved.

When the question of his daughter's marriage settlement was mooted, Mr. Lorimer heard of Arden's Klondyke fortune with unqualified astonishment.

"I didn't think you were the kind of man to make your pile," he said frankly. "I fancied you too much of a dreamer to pick up gold even if you found your way to Tom Tiddler's ground. I could understand your being keen for the journey—your imagination fired by that restless chap, Stormont; but I expected to see you come home minus your travelling expenses, with a box of snap-shot films, and the materials for a book. *That's* all I expected for you out of the North-West."

"You see, I had better luck than I deserved."

"You mean that for once in a way personal merit was rewarded as richly as business capacity. Well, as you and our girl are a brace of philanthropists, I propose, with your leave, to tie up your two fortunes in such a manner that neither of you will have the power to chuck away the capital, while free to make East End ducks and drakes of the income."

"For my fortune, I lay it at Rachel's feet, to deal with as she pleases."

"At *my* feet, you mean, to deal with in a commonsense way for your mutual advantage. Rachel would throw the whole of it after the widow's mite."

"My dear friend, you must do what you think best. The money is there, valueless for me except as a means of carrying out Rachel's wishes."

"Yes, yes, I understand. Well, you can spend the best part of your income upon seaside camps and children's dinners; but I will take care the principal is under lock and key. You will bring two hundred and fifty thousand into settlement; I shall give Rachel the same amount. Your income from gilt-edged securities will be fifteen thousand a year. I hope that will be enough for a comfortable home, and for your 'poors,' as I heard an Orleans princess call them."

"Our 'poors' will rejoice in your liberality."

"And you and Rachel will not lapse into eccentricity, affect squalor, and walk about in patched boots, and ride in halfpenny omnibuses?"

"On fifteen thousand a year we can afford hansoms, and sound boots."

"Yes, as long as you remember that you are a man of the world as well as a Christian socialist."

Arden winced at the word Christian, averse to sailing under false colours; but he made no protest, remembering Lorimer's idea of Christianity, which was to do right things in the right way.

"Talking of socialists, what became of your East End genius, Rachel's favourite, the man of whom you wrote in your letters to my wife?" asked Lorimer.

"I am sorry to say he came to a bad end."

"A very bad end, I guess, by your face."

"Yes, it was bad, and very bad. The man changed—and disappointed me."

"I see the subject is painful. I won't ask for details. Does Rachel know?"

"She knows nothing except that the man is dead. I would not trouble her mind with horrible fancies."

"Horrible fancies?"

Lorimer echoed the words wonderingly, startled by Arden's pallor, and the pained look in his contracted brow and troubled eyes. The words and the look puzzled him, distressed him even.

"You must tell me more about this business another day, Arden," he said. "I hate mysteries."

The other day never came, for in Lorimer's busy life impressions pass quickly, and all things going smoothly and happily in his daughter's courtship and marriage, the lover and husband's devotion being above suspicion, he forgot that momentary doubt, the flash of fear that had been evoked by the strangeness of Arden's manner and speech on one particular occasion.

Commonsense ruled the house in Guelph Place; there was no touch of that eccentricity which Lorimer and his wife had apprehended. Mr. and Mrs. Arden spent about a fifth of their income upon themselves. Three thousand a year will go a long way in a family of two, where neither husband nor wife requires the stimulus of high play or extravagant clothes to give a zest to existence. Rachel's personal expenditure was trifling, but she liked to keep her sitting-rooms supplied with flowers, and those flowers of the freshest, and for this purpose two of her East End girls came to the house on alternate days bringing their baskets from Covent Garden, with the sweetest that the market could supply, bought advantageously in the early morning, not the rare products of tropical hot-houses, but flowers that had bloomed in dewy gardens under sunny skies, flowers fresh from the mother-earth that bore them.

There could scarcely have been a happier life than Rachel's since the passing cloud of sorrow, the one sad memory, the joy that was and is not, the sorrow common to all lives. For her there was so little leisure to brood upon that one sorrow. All her days were occupied, all her thoughts were busy in the labour to which she had devoted her life, the steady unintermittent work for others that had been going on since her fifteenth birthday, when she cast in her lot with Mrs. Bellingham, and became a sister of charity without the nun's habit. There could scarcely have been a happier home than the small house whose hours were measured by the big clock on the front of St. James's Palace; and those who knew Mr. and Mrs. Walter Arden intimately always cited them as a splendid example of harmony of mind and heart in married life.

"They certainly contrive to make the best of both worlds," said a young matron, whose married life was a notorious failure. "With Mrs. Arden's perfect health it is easy to go in for philanthropy. If I had her constitution, I could defy germs, and wouldn't mind doin' a little slummin' now and then. It's rather interestin'; and philanthropy always pays, don't you know."

"Oh, pays, does it? That's a new idea!"

"You see it gets a woman talked about; and that's not easy nowadays, when all the women in society are clever and most of them pretty. No doubt Mrs. Arden would have always ranked among the pretty people; but she's too much of a prude to go far in that direction. But as the lovely young philanthropist she has made herself a place in society. Joey Bagstock is deep, sir, deep!" concluded the lady, with a false laugh.

If there were women whose egotism and vanity took offence at Rachel's popularity, there were others, and some among the most exalted, who admired and loved her. Philanthropy has its social circle among the many circles in the whirlpool of society; and the Ardens had their particular set of friends and fellow-workers, who were all busied in the same ceaseless endeavour for the betterment of mankind. To the frivolous and sceptical, all their work was so much filling of bottomless pails, so much upward-rolling of stones that always rolled back again; but to the workers, in spite of failures and disappointments, there was the conviction of progress, the assurance that out of the many helped and comforted some at least had been better for that help and comfort, some death-beds had been smoothed, some young lives had been brightened, the conditions of life improved for many, and the battle valiantly fought against the three-headed monster, dirt, disease, and death.

In the world of philanthropy there was one man who rose above the ruck, pre-eminent, less for the largeness of his money gifts, though these were on a splendid scale as measured by his means, than by the fire of enthusiasm that informed every act of his life, and by a depth of religious fervour rare in this modern age of materialism and self-indulgence, an age in which the scoffer gives the tone to conversation, and homely, well-meaning men are ashamed to declare themselves followers of Christ, when schoolgirls with flowing hair and short petticoats pronounce themselves Darwinians, and ask if anyone can really believe the old-fashioned creeds that sustained their grandmothers, when the churches are full of women, and only the eloquence of some famous preacher here and there has power to attract a congregation of men.

Lord St. Just was a churchman of the school of Laud, with so strong a leaning to all that was grand and beautiful in the faith of ancient days that it was a wonder to some of his friends that he had not taken the final step and surrendered his will and his intellect to the Passive Obedience of the Roman Church.

He had stopped in that *via media* where Newman intended to stop, and deeply as he admired Newman and Manning, he had never felt the necessity that compelled them to leave the church of their fathers.

He came of one of the oldest families in Cornwall, where there had been St. Justs since the Conquest, and though there were houses that boasted a Saxon descent and a more remote association with the soil, few could show a lineage as unbroken, or a family record so free from stain or blemish of any kind. Always conspicuous in the field of battle, and devoted servants of the Sovereign, the St. Justs had been Tories and High Churchmen through every change in popular feeling, liberal landlords, bigoted politicians, hating a Whig and a Methodist, opposing Reform, and Catholic Emancipation, and the Repeal of the Corn Laws, but submitting to the inevitable with a good grace. More than one St. Just had made his mark in politics, and when Ambrose, the thirteenth Baron, took a double-first at Oxford, it was supposed that he, too, would make a figure in the public arena and maintain, or even enhance, the prestige of the family. His mother, who adored him, was moved when her friends told her of the career open to her son.

He was an only son, an only child, and his mother,

still remarkable among matrons for her beauty, had scarcely a thought or a hope that did not centre in this one existence. She had lived only for her son, since her husband's untimely death in the Ashantee War, where he had gone as a volunteer, exchanging from the household brigade to a line regiment in order to serve under Wolseley. Even before her widowhood, when the delicate boy was still in the nursery, her son had been paramount.

"My dear Ethel, yon know you can spare me," her husband said, when he pleaded for leave to join the expedition. "You will be so taken up with Ambrose's health that you will hardly know I am gone till you see me home again, with a scratch or two by way of distinction."

Lord St. Just distinguished himself in the brief war, and though seriously wounded, did not die of his wounds. Fever and climate gave him the *coup de grâce* while he was waiting for the transport that was to take him home. His widow mourned him long, and never even entertained the idea of a second marriage, though she was only six-and-twenty at the time of his death. She kept all admirers at a distance, lived in the old Cornish manor-house between sea and moorland, and devoted herself to her son. While he was in the nursery, and schoolroom, learning his rudiments with the village curate, she hardly left Cornwall; but when he went to Eton she took a furnished house at Maidenhead, in order to be near him, which she exchanged for a house at Woodstock when he went to Oxford. She was careful not to place any restraint upon his boyish independence in those happy Eton days. It was enough for her to be near him, to know that the river at the end of her lawn was the river on which he took his pleasure, that she might see his boat flash by and his hat waved to her at any moment, that he could run in to breakfast or luncheon when the whim seized him—that he was near. To hear the college clock strike, to drive by the cricket-field and see the lads' white flannels flash in the sunshine was bliss. To know that he was near her, and happy! What more could the maternal heart desire?

At Woodstock life was even happier than at Maidenhead, for the undergraduate had more freedom than the Eton boy. St. Just was able to take his friends to his mother's house, and she made little dinners for him, and got together the nicest girls she could find in the neighbourhood, and her house was a centre of attraction for the best set at Christchurch. And so her son grew to manhood, and his mother to middle age, and the lives of both had been cloudless, till there came the discussion of army or no army for Lord St. Just.

All his relations, except the widowed mother, were of opinion that he ought to be in the Guards. It was a family tradition. Every St. Just had to be a soldier. Blues, Life Guards, Grenadiers, Coldstreams, Scots Guards; no matter which regiment was chosen, there would have been a St. Just in it at some time or other; but the Life Guards for this young St. Just by all means. But this particular St. Just happened, in spite of family tradition, to have the bent of the student rather than the soldier. He had pluck enough to head a forlorn-hope or ride a Balaclava charge, had shown of what good stuff he was made in more than one life-saving adventure on the river, but he had no passionate desire for soldiering.

He had been among the reading men in his first and second year at Christchurch, but in his third year his mind had taken a new development.

Wider horizons had opened before him, and he had become the leading spirit in a little band of philanthropists, as earnest in their devotion to humanity as John Wesley and his companions at the same college in the early days of Methodism. Like that admirable man, young Lord St. Just was not exempt from the ridicule which usually attaches to any fervid endeavour to make crooked things straight; the normal idea being to leave them crooked, and not to bother oneself or anybody else; in short, never to "enthuse" about anything. But St. Just cared no more for ridicule than Wesley did; and he gave himself up, heart and brain and flesh and strength, to the work which it seemed to him good to do; and from the day he left Oxford his business in life was to help the suffering, and to raise the fallen. On all great questions affecting the good of the human race his voice was to be heard in the House of Lords. He had never willingly missed a debate in which the interests of humanity were at stake; and he made his mark early in his career as one of the most eloquent speakers in the Upper House. It may have been because he never spoke except when his heart moved him, and his mind was full.

St. Just was now in his thirtieth year, and there had been as yet no question of his marriage. He lived with his mother in the old family mansion in Portland Place, which had belonged to the St. Justs ever since it was built, a house large enough for entertaining on a grand scale, or for all the purposes of philanthropy.

There had been no brilliant gatherings, no dances or big dinners in the young lord's reign. The spacious dining-room had been devoted wholly to business purposes, committee meetings, and the rest, while a smaller room at the back of the house sufficed for hospitality, cosy dinners of eight or ten, luncheons at which artists and literary men were the salt that gave savour to the society of clerics and philanthropists. Lady St. Just entered with enthusiasm into all her son's schemes, believed as he believed, helped his work wherever a woman's help was wanted; and her lot would have been cloudless happiness but for one brooding fear in the background of her mind, a fear for the health and life of her son, the dread of hereditary consumption. It was on her own side of the house that the shadow had fallen. Her father and two of his sisters had succumbed to lung disease; two in the prime of life, one in the fair dawn of womanhood, lovely and beloved. At the time of her marriage, Ethel Challoner had been too young, and perhaps too thoughtless, to consider this family history a bar to wedlock, nor did any of her friends apprehend danger. She was a splendid specimen of girlhood, handsome, agile, full of life and energy, a star at lawn tennis, a fine horsewoman, seemingly everything that a man should desire in the mother of a stalwart race. People thought St. Just had made an admirable choice. Certainly there had been consumption in the family, but that could have been only an accident. There was nothing consumptive-looking about Lady St. Just's father, General Challoner, before his fatal illness. Some men are imprudent, come home from shooting in wet clothes, and sit about in the tea-room or the smoking-room instead of going straight to a hot bath; and the finer the man the more reckless of health, and the likelier victim to lung trouble.

It was only as the years went on and a certain chest weakness showed itself in her son that Ethel St. Just began to brood upon the family history, and to think that, with that taint in her blood, she had sinned in becoming a wife and mother.

Lady St. Just had never heard of the modern theory which denies the inevitableness of lung disease, and will only admit heredity in the transmitted type of abnormal sensitiveness, with organs adapted to receive the fatal infection. She kept her fears in the dark caverns of her mind, shrinking from them as from hidden monsters; and she had never ventured to discuss the subject with any of her scientific acquaintance, the men of experience and research who might have given her comfort.

It was natural that friendship should grow and ripen between people engaged in the same work and thinking the same thoughts. Modest and silent as Rachel's mission had been, Lord St. Just heard of the good she had done, and of her devotion to the cause which, to his mind, was the first principle of the Christian life, without which creeds were meaningless formulæ and many prayers profitless as the winds blowing through desert places. He had heard of Miss Lorimer's beautiful life; but as her work was local, and as she never harangued on platforms, or mixed herself with public movements, it was not till the third year after her marriage that he made her acquaintance, meeting her at an evening party in the house of a world-renowned painter.

"Father Romney has told me of your life work, Mrs. Arden," St. Just said, after their conversation had passed the preliminary stage of the year's pictures, and the last book.

"You know Father Romney?"

"He is my friend of many years, though we don't often meet. You see his work keeps him in the East."

"And your work is everywhere. Mrs. Bellingham has told me about you."

"That admirable woman! I do not see her half as often as I should like."

"She is my dearest woman friend, after my mother; and she is a kind of family connexion of my husband's."

"Will you ask me to one of your evenings, Mrs. Arden; so that I may meet my old friend? I have heard of your evenings."

"Oh, they are such insignificant little parties. Our drawing-rooms won't hold more than twenty people, and even then the rooms seem crowded—but all manner of good and clever people are kind enough to come, and I know Walter will be pleased to see you among them. We are at home every Thursday from ten to twelve."

He noticed that she said, "We are at home," where almost any other woman would have said, "I am at home." The plural pronoun had a pleasant bourgeois sound, indicating a Darby and Joan marriage, man and wife moving in the same groove, finding their delight in the same things.

Mrs. Walter Arden's Thursday evenings were popular among some of the choicest people in London, the workers with pen and pencil, men and women who had made their name in the world, politicians, well-known clerics, and here and there a fashionable butterfly, with brains enough to care for the things that do not belong to fashion.

Mr. Chudbrook Martyn, an Englishman with an Italian mother, polished, versatile, a poet and a painter, hovering between the worlds of art and of fashion, but an earnest worker all the same, was often to be found in the Arden drawing-rooms; Lady Hortensia Lambert, a woman of mind and wit, who loved art and letters better than the mode of the moment, the last society craze or the last society scandal, was also a frequent guest. Mr. Burton, the popular preacher of South Belgravia, the man who made people think about their sins, if he could not make them leave off sinning, was another *habitué*. The small rooms were on fire with intellect, a focus of ardent thought, at other parties to be found only in a state of diffusion, an ounce of brains in a gallon of rose-water.

Lord St. Just found an atmosphere in which he seemed to breathe the breath of life as he had never done before. He had the feeling of a man who has climbed a hill, and pauses near the summit to taste the freshness of the keen upper air. He felt strengthened, rejuvenated by his intercourse with Rachel and her friends. Never before had he met a woman whose beauty had so touched his imagination, whose character had so impressed him by its saintliness.

He knew many saintly women, toilers in the vineyard of the Lord, women who gave all their time and work and most of their means to the cause of humanity,

But, alas, few among these saintly ones possessed the charm of an attractive personality. Some of them were elderly, and the world had left them before they left the world. To meet a woman of remarkable beauty, in the bloom of youth, who had devoted herself with a joyous heart to a task that repels all self-loving women, was a wonder that impressed him deeply. He studied Rachel's character, reflected upon her life and the circumstances of her upbringing, until her image occupied the first place in his thoughts.

Then he awoke to a consciousness of his peril, one winter evening, sitting in a favourite church, on one side of the nave, while Rachel sat among the women on the other side. He awoke in a flash kindled by some words of the preacher—and knew that he had been giving too much of his mind and heart to a woman who could never enter into his life more nearly than she had entered already, as a friend and fellow-worker, the faithful and devoted wife of the husband she had chosen for herself.

Mrs. Bellingham had told him the history of that marriage, early in his acquaintance with Rachel. She had told him of that bitter day when the lovers parted, avowedly for ever, and when Walter Arden turned his face towards the Arctic Ocean in search of forgetfulness. She told him why he had been rejected, and how, after years of parting, and when he seemed on the point of death, Rachel had taken compassion upon him, and had given him her heart.

"She is so intensely in earnest that I wonder she could trust her life to an unbeliever," St. Just said gravely.

"One always hopes for the best when the unbeliever is a good man," replied Mrs. Bellingham. "I have a great regard for Walter Arden, and I was very sorry she refused him in the first instance; yet her refusal was the cause of his winning a fortune which he uses nobly."

St. Just set a watch upon himself after that sudden revelation in the church. His joy in life must no longer be counted by the hours he spent in Mrs. Arden's company. There need be no break, no lessening of friendship. It was in himself that the battle must be fought, and the hosts of Midian discomfited. They come, they come, in such strange forms, in a guise so unlikely to alarm. In dear society, in sweet friendship, in the radiance of an almost celestial beauty, which seems to exalt and ennoble the heart it moves, in the purest joys, the loftiest hopes, the enemies of man may be at work; and the victim of their subtle spells may awaken from his fond dream to discover hell where he thought he had found heaven.

St. Just appeared in Mrs. Arden's drawing-room less frequently, and tried to arrive at a more intimate acquaintance with her husband. They were both members of the Carlton and the Travellers, and met frequently. They were men of the same views and aspirations in the cause of humanity, both engaged in the same kind of work, and interested in the same things.

But on the spiritual side of life a great gulf yawned between the man whose hopes were fixed on the higher life, and the man who saw nothing but darkness and the grave.

St. Just was an enthusiast in religion. He belonged to that Oxford set which in the waning century had rekindled the torch of Newman and the Tractarians with a fiercer flame; men for whom the *via media* was no impossibility, but whose middle path closely skirted the great Roman road which leads straight to the Vatican; men for whom the beauty of holiness meant all that is exalted and far-reaching in a creed, all that is splendid, pompous, decorative in a church.

To the mind of St. Just the unbeliever, the man without God in the world, was a mystery. He could understand and pity the wretches given over to invincible ignorance—the heathens of London, on whom the light had never shone; but it was to him incomprehensible that a man of cultivated mind, mated with such a woman as Rachel, could shut his heart against the consolations of the Christian faith, and wilfully reject the one Divine hope which makes man's brief life on earth worth living.

As he became more intimate with Walter Arden, meeting him very often in hours of leisure, at their club, or in their philanthropic work, east or west, he discovered that Rachel's husband was the prey of some hidden care; and it was a wonder to him that such a man, so placed in life, so blessed by the love of an adorable woman, could be otherwise than utterly happy. He could think of but one solution to that problem. The man without God in the world could not know happiness. There was the something wanting, the promise of light behind the veil, without which all was dust and ashes.

One night, after they had been friends for more than a year, and had worked much together and become really intimate, St. Just ventured to touch upon Arden's gloomy mood. There had been a public meeting of some importance at Bethnal Green, and Arden had been present with his wife and St. Just. Rachel and Mrs. Bellingham had driven home together, and the two men had preferred the long walk westward, through streets which were for the most part silent. It was an exquisite summer night, and the great human hive seemed to lie hushed and tranquil under the stars.

"I don't like to see you subject to these fits of depression," St. Just said, after they had walked some distance without a word spoken by Arden, who had evidently not heard his companion's occasional remarks on the places through which they passed. "I have suffered from the same kind of thing myself. My doctor tells me it is only a question of health, what he calls being run down. I'm afraid you have been run down for some time past."

"No, no, it is not a question of health. I let other people think so; I tell my wife that it is so, rather than that she should suspect the miserable truth. I am not a happy man, St. Just. All things that make for peace on earth have been given to me; all things that make life dear; a wife I adore, the means of making the common lot better, of gratifying every good impulse, the knowledge that I am of some use in the world; all good things have been given me, and I have not found content."

To the deeply religious man the answer was clear.

"I think that is because you do not look for happiness in the right way, or in the right place," St. Just answered gently; and then he quoted an old-fashioned poet whom former generations revered—

"'He builds too low who builds below the stars.'"

"Ah, but I cannot build above the stars. My imagination will not carry beyond the things I see. The earth I know is Huxley's earth; the heaven I know is the astronomer's heaven. If there be anything in the infinite distance beyond Neptune—anything other than suns and systems, uninhabitable stars, immeasurable distances—anything in which we poor worms are interested, I cannot imagine it, or believe in it," he added gloomily.

"And therefore you are unhappy."

"No, not therefore. I was happy enough, reading my Darwin and my Spencer, six years ago. I was a creature without a care. St. Just, you are a good man; I know I can trust you with secrets I have told to none."

"Yes, you can trust me, as other men have trusted me, men whose secrets were hanging matters. But don't tell me anything unless you believe I can help you."

"You will sympathise with me, perhaps, if you can understand the unimaginable. I have but one friend to whom I ever open my mind, and he is on the other side of the world. I have written to him freely about myself, and he has sympathised and understood. But even to him I have not told what I am going to tell you."

"Make me your father confessor, if you like. You may trust me as if I were a priest."

"Six years ago it was my misfortune to come between a profligate and his prey. I could not save the girl; but I killed her destroyer."

"Murder!" said St. Just, in a horrified whisper.

"No; a duel—a fair fight, with seconds, everything *en règle*. He was physically my superior, and a fine swordsman. Happily for me—or, perhaps, unhappily—I was nearly as good, and fortune favoured me. In an onslaught which was more like the attack of a man-eating tiger than of a human being, he got the worst of it. He died cursing me; and he swore that I should never know peace, that in some form or other, or formless, he would pursue me; that when I was happiest, amidst the smiles of fortune, in the companionship of the woman I loved, his spirit should blast me."

"A wicked man's idle threat."

"Idle, yes! so I thought. But those words were spoken six years ago; and from that hour to this, except in certain blessed intervals, I have been a haunted man."

"And you killed him fairly? As a man of the world, you have nothing to reproach yourself with as to the manner of his death?"

"Nothing. Nor do I regret the fatal issue; since I freed the world of a wretch who lived only to do evil."

"And your imagination has been haunted by the dying man's curse. I can understand your feelings. To me the idea of a duel is horrible. The idea of a man, a sinner, taking upon himself to destroy his fellow-man, of set purpose, face to face, and eye to eye, is to my mind more terrible than unpremeditated murder, when the savage that lives in civilised man gets the upper hand."

"Yes, I know it is horrible, where the men who stand face to face are of the same nature; but this man was a monster of iniquity, and I felt myself a destined avenger. I told myself that if I killed him it would be an execution, and not a murder. No, St. Just; dreadful as it may seem to you, I have never repented of that act."

And then, in agitated phrases, pouring out his darkest thoughts, he told his friend of that haunting presence which made life a burden—the unseen, the ubiquitous, the thing which had neither shape nor name, neither sound nor substance, but which was always with him, in all his thoughts by day, in all his dreams by night.

He told of the scenes on the Klondyke, and the inexplicable change in the man he had trusted and almost loved, the rough, strong nature that his friendship had softened and refined, the radical artisan in whom he had acknowledged his superior in force of mind and will. He described those awful moments on the river, when, startled from his sleep, he saw a murderer's eyes glaring down at him, and knew that the soul looking out of those terrific eyes was not the soul of Michael Dartnell.

St. Just heard this strange story with pity and horror.

"Alas! my poor friend," he said, "superstition has always been one of the penalties of unbelief in God. Your imagination cannot conceive the mysteries revealed in the Gospel. The Incarnation, the Divinity of Christ, the Resurrection of the Dead, are to you unthinkable; and yet you are haunted by the idea that the wicked soul of the man you killed could live again in the form of your friend."

"Is the idea so strange? Is this doctrine of metempsychosis, which has been common to the savage and to the philosopher in innumerable ages, so incredible to you, the Christian—you who believe that the soul still lives, invisible, untraceable, impalpable to human sense, while the form it once governed lies in the dust, and goes on living, where and how you know not? Granted the after-life, is it incredible that the souls of the just and the unjust should exist as wandering spirits, and assume new tabernacles of clay? Where are the deathless souls of the wicked, do you think? Do you imagine them as Dante saw them in his dream—each in his allotted sphere, suffering torments commensurate to his guilt? Is it not more credible that the evil spirit should cling to the scenes of its lawless pleasures, thirsting for revenge upon unforgiven foes, longing to resume the carnal life it loves, the life of sensual indulgence and unbridled sin? This conviction has shaped itself in my mind with irresistible force: and as truly as I believe in my own existence at this moment, I believe that Michael Dartnell, the Michael I knew, left this earth, and that the hellish spirit of my enemy entered into his lifeless clay. To you it may seem the idea of a madman; but I know I am not mad."

"You are sane now. But who can answer for your sanity if you brood upon this wild imagination? The conception is like the beginning of madness—an *idée fixe* of the worst kind. My dear Arden, there is no help for you, except in Christ. If you cannot carry your troubles, your perplexities, your despair, to the Friend and Comforter of man, you reject the only means of cure that I can imagine, in such a case as yours. Your wife's affection, your consciousness of a life well spent in the cause of humanity, these have failed to bring you peace. There is but one resource, one refuge."

"That refuge is only open to the believer. For me the gates are closed, and they are gates of adamant. Flesh cannot prevail against them."

"But spirit can. The light will break through the darkness by-and-by, perhaps. Go on with your good work, and try to forget this horrible hallucination."

"I have sought forgetfulness in strenuous work; I have striven to give every thought of my brain to others, to lose my own identity in the sufferings of others; but the paramount thought is there still. I may lose consciousness of myself, but I cannot lose consciousness of my inexorable enemy. Wherever I go, *he* goes with me. He comes between me and suffering mankind."

"My dear friend, I am deeply sorry for you; but my sorrow is worth nothing. God alone can help you," St. Just answered earnestly.

"Your sympathy is worth much. It has been a relief to talk to you. A lunatic notion, isn't it?" added Arden, laughing excitedly, with a sudden change of tone. "And, after all, perhaps only a horrible hallucination, as you call it—a question of nerves."

"I believe it is a question of mind rather than nerves —a mind in peril of shipwreck for want of the Divine Helper of men. To be without God in the world! Oh, my dear Arden, you, and men like you, who so lightly renounce the privileges of the Christian life, who think it enough to say, 'I cannot believe in miracles, and I can steer my own course without any guiding star,' those men must be prepared for the worst that can happen to man. The empty house is there, swept and garnished, ready for visitants from hell, wild delusions, phantasmal horrors, the diabolical inventions of a mind that has lost its grasp on reality."

"In plain words, you take me for a madman?"

"No, no; not that,—but I take you for a man whose reason is in danger, whose conscience is more sensitive than he thinks, and who is in supreme need of the Divine Healer. Arden, believe me, on my honour, you have my heartfelt sympathy. I want to be your friend. I am your friend. I would do anything—anything that a man could do for his best-loved brother, to bring you peace of mind and happiness."

"You cannot do that; but I am grateful for your sympathy, and I ought not to feel angry if you think I am mad. Indeed, I sometimes think I am myself."

"Will you hear my view of your position without being offended, and let me help you? I believe I could help you, if you would let me."

"I will hear your words as the speech of a friend, and nothing you can say shall offend me."

"I think you are at heart a Christian, and that the idea of having killed a fellow-creature in cold blood is as repugnant to you as it would be to me. I believe that since that act, however you may excuse it to yourself by the consideration that he fell in a fair fight, your mind has been weighed down by the sense of sin. I believe that the haunting presence that has made your life a burden has been the agony of remorse in a mind too fine to bear the stain of blood, the ever-present consciousness of a sin unatoned. I believe that for this suffering of yours there is only one possible cure, the reconciliation of the soul with God; and that until by some Divine interposition, by some spiritual process whose mode and manner I cannot foresee, faith has drawn your wandering steps to the foot of the Cross, and rent the veil that hides the Redeemer's face, and has shown you where to seek and where to find forgiveness of sin, and peace on earth, and hope in heaven—until then, my poor friend, remorse for an act which was at variance with your own life and character will pursue you with those mental horrors which you take for a diabolical influence."

They had passed from the east to the west, and had arrived at Oxford Circus.

"I thank you with all my heart for being in earnest with me!" Arden said, as they clasped hands, and parted.

III.

Walter Arden's confession made a turning-point in St. Just's life. His course of action changed from that hour. He had resolved to restrict his friendship with Rachel; he had foreseen peril to his soul in his growing regard for her; but after Arden's revelation, he told himself that his first duty in life was to safeguard the woman who had given him her friendship, and who might be in bitter need of a friend. He had no doubt in his own mind that Arden was a monomaniac, unsuspected by the wife who loved him, or by the society in which he lived. Such a delusion as that under which he suffered could only have been engendered in a mind on the verge of madness; and there could be no doubt that this man, who had Rachel's happiness and life in his power, was an incipient lunatic, capable at the present time of conducting the business of his life like a reasonable being, but liable at any hour to develop a dangerous form of lunacy.

The man who loved Rachel, who had withdrawn himself from a friendship that was becoming too close and too dear, now resolved to continue that friendship at any risk of his own unhappiness. He had no fear of peril for her. He had seen her single-minded devotion to her husband. He knew the purity of a nature in which affection reigned supreme, free from the passions that lead to the tragedy of life. He had no fear that she would ever hold him too dear; though she might come to lean upon him for help and counsel, and to turn to him in any time of difficulty. It was for him to watch for the coming of evil. It might be that Arden's hallucination was only a passing phase of a brain weakened by periods of fever in the past, and that the cloud might lift.

In his fervent prayers for Rachel's peace, he prayed in singleness of heart for her husband's cure. The blessings he asked for her were those which her own heart desired. He gave himself to her service, as her guardian and protector, without one selfish thought. His religious fervour had lifted him above the things that make the bliss or woe of wordlings. He could go on loving without one guilty hope. He could devote his life to the beloved, and ask no higher recompense than the knowledge that he had shielded her from dangers of which she knew not. To work for her without reward and without praise was all he asked from Fate.

He associated himself now more nearly with the little company of workers within the sound of Bow-bells, whose Bishop and leader was Father Romney. He interested himself in all Mrs. Bellingham's schemes, and in all Rachel's favourite pensioners—her old men, and women, and children, her factory girls, and working lads, her day-nurseries for infants, and night-schools for adults. There were few days on which the friends did not meet; and there were quiet evenings in every week which St. Just spent in Rachel's drawing-room, with husband and wife.

He had watched Arden during more than a year of close friendship, and had seen no sign of the thing which he feared. Whatever delusions the man suffered in the realms of thought, he was able to conduct the business of life with good sense and discretion. But from the home of the wedded lovers, from the home that had once been so happy, the spirit of gladness had fled. The gaiety of heart, the pleasure in trifles, the interest in all the details of domestic life, which make the felicity of home, were wanting in the dainty little house in Guelph Place. Rachel struggled long against the thought that her husband was no longer happy; the change had been so gradual, so vague, that she had hardly realised it. There was only the sense of something wanting, a light gone out, shadow where there had been sunshine. She took to watching her husband's face, waiting for the smile that was now so rare. She questioned him often and anxiously about his health, fearing some subtle disease, that might cloud over his life; but he laughed off her fears, and even consented to go with her to a famous physician, in order that she might be reassured.

In a few minutes of confidential talk, after he had seen his patient, the doctor told her that she had no cause for anxiety. Her husband had a splendid constitution, unimpaired by his sufferings at Klondyke, and the subsequent breakdown. As for the depression, which had made her anxious, that was a matter of temperament.

"Some men have not the *joie de vivre,* and are rather difficult subjects in consequence," concluded the doctor. "Mr. Arden wants rousing—mental occupation. You should make him go into Parliament."

"I would do anything," said Rachel, with tears in her eyes; and that ended the interview, which took place while her husband was putting on his overcoat and waiting for his carriage.

"I hope you are satisfied now, Rachel," he said, as they drove away from Harley Street.

"Relieved, but not satisfied, Walter, while I see you unhappy."

"My dearest, I am not unhappy. I should be an ungrateful wretch if I could be unhappy, with the sweetest wife in the world."

She tried to persuade herself that all was well. Her husband was no less devoted than in the cloudless beginning of their union. He sought no pleasures out of his own house. His clubs knew him no more; but too many hours of his home life were spent in the solitude of his library, a large room built out at the back of the small house, covering the oblong space sacred to sparrows, that had once called itself a garden. He sat here alone day after day, seemingly absorbed in study, and no longer working with his secretary at the business of philanthropy. The secretary now came to Rachel for instructions; and it was she who wrote or dictated the answers to the daily letters. Most of the business of charity now devolved upon her; and she gradually came to lean upon St. Just for advice and help in all cases where her husband had been her ally and helper. And thus the bond of friendship grew closer and stronger, until she wondered what her life had been like before this earnest and deeply religious thinker had been her daily companion, sharing all her thoughts of the better life, looking as she looked beyond the grave for the answer to all that is darkest and most inexplicable upon earth. A perfect sympathy reigned between them.

It was during this period that St. Just suffered the first great sorrow of his life, in the almost sudden death of his mother, which happened after an illness of less than a week. She was gone, the companion and friend, and the house in Portland Place, which had been so pleasant a home, became hateful to him. He used it henceforward only as an office, a place in which to receive his fellow-workers, or to give dinners or evening entertainments to the young men of his University Mission. The spacious old rooms served for philanthropic purposes; but he could live under that roof no more. He took rooms in Berkeley Street, and was so much nearer to Guelph Place and the friends to whom he looked for consolation in his bereavement. His mother had seen much of Rachel in the last two years, and had loved her, too unworldly to apprehend evil from the close friendship between St. Just and Walter Arden's wife. Her son was to her as a saint on earth, secure from the snares of human passion, living only to do good works, and think high thoughts.

It needed the voice of a worldling to suggest danger in a friendship which St. Just knew to be pure and free from guile. Lady Mary Selby's was the voice, uplifted in all candour and kindliness, but still the voice of the world, which sees only the surface of things, and measures every life and every character by the same conventional standard; the rule of the things that are done and the things that are not done.

Lady Mary and St. Just had met often in Guelph Place, and occasionally in the great world, and they were on very friendly terms; so he was not surprised when she drew him aside at an evening party in one of the great houses of London, the house of a leader in the political world.

"I have been dying for a quarter of an hour's quiet talk. Shall we go into the winter garden?" she asked. "There are very few people there now; everyone is drifting to the supper-room."

"By all means, if you will let me take you to supper afterwards."

"Of course I will. Do you suppose I mean to go home unfed? The Lincolnshire House suppers are feasts of many inventions. It is a liberal education in gastronomy to feed here."

They went into the spacious conservatory, where the rose-scented atmosphere was cooler than the rooms, and where only a few couples sat secluded in shadowy corners, breathing odours of orange-blossom, which might be either a forecast or a mockery, as those low murmurings of neighbouring lips meant the making or the breaking of marriage vows.

St. Just and Lady Mary found a solitary sofa out of earshot.

"I want to talk to you about my sister-in-law," Lady Mary said, with her unflinching air.

"I shall be charmed to hear you on so admirable a subject. Mrs. Arden is my ideal of all that is best in a woman."

"I know that. But perhaps you don't know that you are dragging your ideal into the mud."

"Lady Mary!"

"Oh, of course you are astonished. You had no idea

what was happening, any more than Rachel, who is a baby in the ways of the world. You thought you could be at her house day after day; that you could go about the East End with her; drive from west to east and east to west *tête-à-tête* in her brougham; haunt all the houses she visits, and rarely appear when she is not expected. You thought—you, who have your clubs and your men-friends, and who ought to know something of the world you live in—you absolutely thought that you could carry on in this way and not set people talking."

"The people who can imagine evil of my friendship for Mrs. Arden would scent corruption in a garden of roses, see stains on the new-fallen snow upon the mountains, remote and pure under the eye of God. We need not give such people a thought."

"Oh, but you need; you must think of them. I am not a mischief-maker, or a scandal-bearer, Lord St. Just. I have lived too long in society to be keen about scandals; I have heard too many of them. They are all pretty much alike, and they soon pall on a woman with a ha'porth of brains. But I must stand up for my brother. He has had troubles—mental troubles—which have marred his life; and of late he has chosen to keep aloof from Rachel, whom he idolises. I don't want him to know what I am telling you—I don't want to make bad blood between you and him. I know you are a man of honour, of high principle even, of religious convictions such as few men hold. You are not a man to persist in conduct which reflection must show you to be wrong."

"I have never harboured one thought which you and

all the world might not know—in relation to your sister-in-law."

"I can believe that. I believe that you are a good man, capable even of that rare sentiment, friendship for a young and beautiful woman. But you have been forgetting that the world won't allow a woman to have a friend, not even if she is middle-aged and ugly; much less if she is as attractive as my brother's wife. I have been hearing insinuations, little hints, seeing smiles and significant looks, for a long time. Oh, you don't know how malignant the women who have 'thrown their caps over the mill' can be about a woman whose virtues are a standing reproach to them. Rachel has never posed as a saint, but they all know that she is a saint, and they loathe the saintly character. She has taken a strong line as a philanthropist too. They sneer at her plain frocks, and call her the sham Quakeress. They hate and envy her for not being up to her eyes in debt to milliners and hairdressers, as they are. And so they jump at the first chance of throwing mud at her."

"It cannot affect her. She is as remote from the sphere of such women as if she were among the stars."

"You are mistaken, Lord St. Just. There is only one sphere, bounded on the east by Carlton House Terrace, and on the west by Rutland Gate. The saints and the sinners are all moving in the same circle; and the sinners are trying their hardest to drag the saints down to their own level."

"You have noticed one malicious woman's sneer, Lady Mary. You have been hurt and made angry, and you unconsciously exaggerate. I cannot believe that my friendship for your sister-in-law could provoke slander.

I honour and revere her. I would make any sacrifice of my own happiness rather than that the breath of slander should sully her name."

"Her name is sullied already. You are talked of as the Kindred Spirits, the Saints, the Heavenly Lovers. I have heard enough to be sure of the mischief you are doing, though they daren't talk openly before me. My brother is asleep—hears nothing, sees nothing. It is my duty to speak plainly. I can't help it if you are angry."

"I am angry with the hatefulness of human nature, not with you. As if her life—her pure and perfect life—and my life, which has been spent for others ever since I learnt to think—as if that were not enough to save her from the evil-speaking of women whose only instinct is self-indulgence, who exist only for sensuous and sensual pleasures, and shut their eyes and ears against the sufferings of humanity."

"They are all that, and I detest them. But they are the world; and Rachel will have to live among them, and be judged by them, till she joins some Sisterhood and shuts herself behind a convent gate."

"And this world of yours will not let her have a friend?"

"It will not! It never did, and never will believe in friendship between man and woman. Why, if Rachel were elderly and blind, living in another country, and writing gossiping letters to you, as Madame du Deffand wrote to Horace Walpole, people would shrug their shoulders and say there was more in the correspondence than met the eye, and that only a careful selection of her letters were fit for publication. A man can't be a woman's friend without being her enemy."

"Well, I will not be Rachel's enemy," he said, drawing a deep breath, as if he were offering up the sacrifice of a life.

He had never called her Rachel before. Lady Mary noted the slip.

"I am sure you will do all that is honourable and kind," she said, rising and giving him her hand.

He had risen impetuously at the beginning of their conversation, and had remained standing.

"I will try to do what is best for her."

"I have unbounded faith in you, Lord St. Just. And now will you take me to the supper-room? These agitating discussions make one awfully hungry."

He smiled, with white lips, wondering if he would ever want to eat again, and loathing the crowd he would have to face in the struggle for champagne and quails; the trivial crowd that he hated; the crowd that scrambled for plovers' eggs and iced asparagus and '84 champagne, while thousand of fellow-creatures within a few miles of them were wasting away for lack of wholesome food.

Lady Mary noted his pallor, and was merciful. She seized upon the first "nice boy" who ran against them in the crush—a young guardsman, beardless and beautiful.

"Have you just come away from the supper-room, Dick?" she asked.

"This instant; but I'll go back with pleasure, if I may take you. The duke's Veuve Pommery is tipple for kings."

"Then I'll release you," she said to St. Just. "I know you are tired, and want to go home."

"I think you will be in better hands with Mr. Quindon," he said. "Good night."

"By Jupiter! St. Just looks bad," exclaimed the youth, when he was gone. "A man oughtn't to go to dances with such a death-bed face. He's as ghastly as the statue in *Don Giovanni*. He ought to stick to the philanthropic caper—Bethnal Green and Bermondsey, don't you know."

St. Just did not go straight home on leaving Lincolnshire House. His own rooms were within five minutes' walk, and he felt that he wanted the freedom of the empty streets and the deserted park under the starlit June sky. There would be no room inside four walls for the tempest of his thoughts. He had to think of *her*; of what was best for *her*—best, not happiest; for he could scarcely doubt that his friendship had been of value to her in the last year, a source of consolation in her sorrow at her husband's estrangement. He had filled the empty place in her life; he had been to her as a brother, and not one word had ever been breathed by her lips or by his that could offend the husband to whom she had given herself in purity of heart. But there had been the intimacy of minds that think alike, of hearts moved by the same emotions of pity and love, the same religious fervour, the same self-surrender for the service of Christ.

She had talked to him even of her dead child, that sacred theme which she could not speak of without tears. She had told him of her hopes and visions of the future while that child was with her; how she had pictured his life—the Christian life, the life that was to be a light in the darkness of the helpless and unfortunate. She talked of her child in the after-life, and loved to dwell upon the blessedness of the saints with God, with an implicit faith in the unseen.

"I do wrong to grieve for my son, knowing that I shall go to him in the new life," she said.

They had been in such perfect sympathy, a friendship so exalted, so free from guile. And this pure affection, held in check on his part with such undeviating self-control, had not escaped malignant remark. And then, awakened by that revelation of the world's malevolence, there came the thought of possible peril, peril to two souls now white and stainless, but which one impassioned moment, one lapse of self-mastery, might taint with at least the suggestion of sin. So far, he had never transgressed, never passed the limits of a friendship such as obtained among the brothers and sisters of the Early Church, when Christians heard the near echo of the Master's voice, and thought and talked of their Lord as of One who was with them yesterday. But could he be sure of himself to the end? Could he see her day after day in a growing intimacy, upon which her own purity of heart placed no restrictions, and trust himself never to betray the secret of a sinful love, a love that was an offence against her purity, however he might control all outward signs of the fire that burnt within?

"The worldling's voice is the voice of wisdom," he thought, slowly pacing to and fro in the summer darkness. "I have been playing with fire. How could I ever forgive myself if I let her guess my secret—if I startled that exquisite innocence which fears no evil with the revelation of a passionate love? It has been a lovely dream; but it is over. Neither her good name nor her peace of mind shall suffer by my wrong-doing."

For the three following days St. Just was absorbed in business details. He spent most of his time in Portland Place, where he had appointments with the men with whom he worked, his equals, or his subordinates, enthusiasts like himself, his friends and his disciples, and his paid helpers. He contrived to see them all, and to go into the particulars of every good work to which he had put his hand. He pledged his income to the uttermost in his contributions to the financial support of these home missions, which in the far-off golden age were to make the wilderness of pauper life in London blossom as the rose; and which had already reclaimed many pestilential swamps, and exterminated many poisonous weeds.

His friends were distressed at the idea of having to carry on their work without their leader.

"You are the moving spirit of exerything, St. Just," said one of his Oxford chums; "the only one of us who won't see failure, and whose pluck has never failed when the whole business seemed a hopeless muddle. I suppose it's some blessed alarmist in Harley Street who is sending you away. The modern doctor's favourite fad is the idea that an Englishman can't live in England?"

"No; I haven't asked the doctors. I know that I am not in good health, without their opinion. I have bought a two-hundred-ton yacht. She is at Marseilles, where I shall join her next week, and start on a vagabond voyage."

"Shall you go far?"

"Who knows? I said a vagabond voyage. If I don't find the Mediterranean good enough, I shall slip through the Suez and steer my course to the South Seas."

"Poor fellow!" his friends said, as they left his house.

"Lungs, of course," said one. "I shall be at Charing Cross on Saturday night, for a farewell hand-shake. Who knows if we shall ever see him again?"

"I shouldn't like to bet even money on his return," said another. "He looks awfully ill."

"The old story of the sword and the scabbard. This one is a fiery sword in an ivory scabbard. Knowing the work he has done since he left Oxford, I wonder he is alive!"

IV.

RACHEL was surprised at not having seen St. Just during those three days, for within the last half-year a day had rarely passed without their meeting, either in some scene of her daily work, at Mrs. Bellingham's house, or in her own drawing-room. She missed him sadly before the third day of his absence came to an end. Since her husband's isolation, she had come to depend upon St. Just's judgment on all doubtful questions, most of all as to the manner in which the innumerable appeals to her benevolence should be answered. St. Just was a shrewd judge of human nature, and rarely failed in his diagnosis. The professional begging-letter writer had a poor chance with him; and he was a shrewd judge of the worthiness or unworthiness of the amateur who has but lately begun to depend upon a facile pen and a penny stamp for increased income.

Rachel was sitting in the lamplight after dinner, with a pile of unanswered letters before her, on the third evening of St. Just's absence, when the servant announced him.

"I am so glad you have come," she said, going to meet him with outstretched hand. "I have been wanting your advice about so many of these letters—such piteous letters—from impostors perhaps—but they make one's heart ache all the same."

"The more heartrending the letter, the more need of verification. Indeed, Mrs. Arden, in your place I should be adamant to all letter-writers, and give all your help to those you know, face to face, in their own homes—whose characters, surroundings, necessities, you know at first hand. Even your resources have their limits. If you give all to those you know, you may forgive yourself for refusing those you don't know. Whatever their sphere, they too must have their helpers. There are good Samaritans upon every road nowadays."

"I know you are right; but these letters torture one, all the same."

"Oh, there must always be that kind of torture for sensitive minds, while the differences of fortune are as they are. There is the torture of seeing an overworked horse in a cart, the thought of the inequality in the fortunes of horses—the underfed cab-horse in the pelting rain, crawling along the streets at midnight, and the sleek carriage-horses dozing in their warm stable. You will have to harden your heart, my dear Mrs. Arden, to make up your mind that even all you do is but as a drop of sweetness in a sea of bitter waters."

Rachel looked at him wonderingly. There was something in his tone that was new to her—an indefinable difference.

"What have you been doing in the last three days?" she asked. "You are looking pale and overtired."

"I have been working very hard. I have been setting my house in order."

"But I thought your house was always in order.

Everyone says you are such a wonderful man of business."

"I have been setting my house in order before leaving England. The fact is, I find myself out of health; I want change of scene and atmosphere. It is a want all workers feel at some time in their lives; and I am going to give myself rest before I break down."

"That is very wise of you," she answered gravely; and the look of sorrow in her face sent a thrill through his overstrained nerves. "I shall miss you dreadfully in all our work—and—and in so many ways; but I am glad you are taking the first warning. Do you mean to be away long?"

"Till I am cured," he answered, with a faint, sad smile.

She would never know the malady which had need of cure, or how slow the healing process was likely to be.

"And are you going far?"

He told her how he had bought a friend's steam-yacht, a nearly new boat, by one of the best builders on the Clyde.

"Won't it be too hot in the Mediterranean in summer?"

"Oh, I can bask; I shall have rest, which I suppose will be all I want. And in October or November I shall make for the South Seas."

"Like Stevenson?"

"Stevenson's book has inspired me with a longing for the islands he loved."

"Perhaps you will be like him, and settle there for life."

"No, no; I don't contemplate such a possibility. I should always be thinking of what could be done in fifty years of Europe. A man would need the genius and the imagination of a Stevenson to find happiness in that primitive life."

"But in any case you will be away for years—for many years, perhaps."

"No, no; I hope my cure will not be so slow. A year or two should be enough. Two years would be a long exile from friends—like you!"

Her voice had been faintly tremulous, but his was steady. He had nerved himself for this farewell interview as a man nerves himself for a surgical operation; and in this case there could be no anæsthetic, he must needs feel all the pain, and all the peril of self-betrayal.

"You say that you are out of health," Rachel said, after a pause. "I hope there is nothing serious the matter—nothing that need make your friends anxious about you."

"Oh no, there is nothing serious. I am not ordered away by the doctors. My going is a precautionary step."

"I am glad of that. I shall miss you sadly. You have been so kind, and I have come to rely on your help so much—since—since my husband has taken less interest in my work."

"His interest may be revived, if you tell him you have need of his help. You must try to win him back into the old paths."

"Oh, if I only could! He began by being so warmly

interested, so helpful for all those poor people; but now he has ceased to care for them. I know he is unhappy, but I can find no reason for his trouble. He has a worried, haunted look, that grieves me more than I can say, and I can do nothing to brighten his life. I know nothing of the shadow that darkens it. Something—something I cannot understand—has come between us and made us almost strangers; and, now you are going away, I shall feel utterly alone."

Her voice faltered in her struggle not to give way to tears. Her sorrow, her appeal to his friendship, shook St. Just's resolution.

"Rachel, Rachel, cannot you understand, cannot you read my heart—the heart that aches for love of you? It is my love that is parting us—my hopeless love, the love of years. It was easy to call love friendship. Love has been sweet under that name; and you know that I have never offended, never said one word that you ought not to hear, never for one moment forgotten that you are Walter Arden's wife."

"No, no, no. You have always been my friend, my trusted friend. Why do you spoil our friendship now? I have honoured and looked up to you."

"I did not mean to tell you. I meant to carry my secret to my grave, and that you should never know all you have been to me; the one love of my life, loved from the hour of our first meeting, worshipped with every throb of my heart from that hour to this. But the words have been said, and at least you know that I am not leaving you for a light reason, that I am not false to the dear friendship you have given me. It is for your dignity, for my honour, that I go. I have been told that our friendship has provoked comment, that if it continued your name would suffer; and your good name is dearer to me than my own happiness. And now I have put a barrier between us."

"Yes, you have put a lifelong barrier between us," she said, with a profound sigh. "I am very sorry. I was so happy in your friendship; and now you have made friendship impossible. All things that I care for seem to fall away from me. I won't say that I have lost my husband's love—but I know that he is changed to me. A cloud has come between us; there is a mystery in his life that I cannot fathom. I should be utterly lonely if it were not for those poor castaways who depend upon me, and who love me a little, I think."

"They love you much," St. Just cried passionately. "How can they help loving you? To them you represent all that is purest and best in human love, the Christ-like love which forgives sin and believes in the regeneration of sinners. You enter their dark haunts like living sunlight; you lift them out of the slough of despond. Oh, be sure you have your guerdon of human love. Never believe the people who tell you the poor are ungrateful or unloving. Good-bye, Rachel. Forget this confession of mine, if you can. Think of me only as your friend, and as a man in whom honour is stronger than passion. Write to me when I am far away. I shall write to you sometimes, to tell you where my wanderings have brought me. Write and tell me of your own life, and all things that have to do with your happiness."

"Yes, I will write to you," she answered simply. "I shall forget every foolish word that you have spoken this night. I shall think of you when you are far away as I have known you in the last two years—my kind friend and counsellor. Good-bye."

She gave him her hand, looking at him with the clear and earnest gaze he knew so well. He had seen that look in her eyes when she had pleaded with some sinner whose fall she deplored—a look so mournful, yet so full of a divine compassion.

He bent his lips over the gentle hand, as he might have kissed the hand of a saint, and left her without a word.

"And now this world holds nothing for me but duty," he thought, as he left her. "The two women I loved are gone from me; one in death; one in lifelong severance. I have done with love for the individual, and must live for the species."

A strange grey life began for Rachel on the morning after St. Just's farewell. She felt as if all interest, all colour, had gone out of her life. She fought against her dejection, and went about her old work with untiring patience; but the mind within was dull and inert. She let her old women talk to her of their woes and grievances, and was kind and gentle with them; but it would have gone ill with her had she been called on to repeat their pitiful stories. It was a relief when one of them exclaimed—

"You ain't brought his lordship this arternoon. I do like to hear him talk the Gospel—he do make it all come out clear and strong, like as if it was in the morning paper; while in most sermons as I hear the preacher seems to beat about the bush, so as I can't follow him.

I can allus follow his lordship; and, to be sure, I ought to, when he was that kind and paid my rent for a year in advance, so as I sha'n't have to worrit myself all winter."

"He is very fond of you, Biddy. But you won't see him for a long time; he has gone on a sea-voyage for his health."

"Poor dear gentleman! He always looked a bit peaky—but so kind, and so generous. Then I suppose he'll be gone six months or so?"

"Longer than that, I think. But I shall take care of you, Biddy."

"And so you always have, mum. My life hasn't been the same since the day your pretty face came in at that door. Lor, I remember it as if it was yesterday. You was wearing a sweet hat, with forget-me-nots in it, and as it might be a bow of fine white lace. And I thinks here's another of them fine ladies come to nag about religion, and why don't I go to the week-day services, and the Wednesday and Friday evenings in Lent. But I soon found the difference. You didn't come to preach to me, but to try and make me a bit more comfortable."

"And when you were more comfortable you liked coming to the Lent sermons," said Rachel.

"Yes, mum. After a good cup of tea and a bloater, and with a bit of fire to come home to, I don't mind an evening service. They may sing a hanthem, and make the sermon as long as they like, when I'm feeling comfortable inside, and with a warm cape to my back such as you gave me. But I hope, now his lordship has gone away, Mr. Arden will come among us with you again, as he used to do when you and him was keeping company. He's as kind a gentleman as ever lived, and never one to worry folks about religion. I don't know as ever he mentioned the Gospel in my hearing."

"He will come back to his old friends by-and-by, I hope, Biddy. He has been depressed and out of spirits of late."

"Well, tell him, with my respects, that he ought to try Roupell's 'Mensanerincorperersaner.' It's a long word to pronounce, but it's rare stuff for the spirits. Thirty drops to be took on a lump of sugar, and warranted not poisonous if you was to drink the bottleful."

This was not the first time Rachel had heard lamentations at her husband's absenting himself from the dark places where his presence had brought comfort.

Father Romney had urged her to use her influence with him, and to persuade him to take up the work he had begun so well.

"I have seen so many instances of men who begin with tremendous fervour, and cool off and drop away, after working at white heat for a year or two, that I ought never to be surprised by a deserter," he said; "but I thought your husband was of a stronger fibre than most of my young disciples, and that his fire would not have burnt out in a few years. I thought he would not take his hand from the plough till he had come to the end of life's furrow, and the hand dropped in death. Mr. Arden's defection has disappointed me more than I can say."

Rachel could only reply with the same excuse she had made to old Biddy—depressed spirits, languid health. She assured him that her husband's heart was unchanged, his compassion for the unfortunate as intense as it had been in the beginning of his philanthropic work. He knew that she was doing all that could be done, and filling his place while he was unable to take his share of the burden.

Father Romney saw that she was unhappy, and did not press the point.

From Walter Arden, Guelph Place, St. James's, London, to Douglas Campbell, The Hut, Leith, Tasmania.

MY DEAR DOUGLAS,

Your kind, unanswered letter lies before me, and I can only say that it is very good of you to concern yourself about the fate of a wretched being who has not vital force enough to write a letter to the only man in whom he can confide the obscure trouble of mind that makes life a burden.

The dates of your letters tell me that it is nearly three years since I wrote to you. When that last letter was written all was well with me. I was happy in the love of the most lovable of women, an angel of charity and compassion, in whose company I had learnt that the happiest life a man can lead is the life that conduces to the happiness of others. The philanthropic work which I began for love of Rachel had grown as soul-satisfying to me as it is to her. The loss of our child in the dawn of infancy had been a heavy blow to us both; but I think that both of us had found consolation in brightening the lot of other children; and I know that Rachel took comfort from her unquestioning faith in the vague promises of reunion offered by the Gospel and the Church.

During those serene and exquisite years, if I had not forgotten the horrors of the past, I had at least been able to keep dark memories far away from me. I had indeed taught myself to believe that all I had suffered from the haunting presence of an evil spirit, the wicked mind of a dead man, disembodied and endowed with malignant power to harass and torment the living, was a delusion of my own troubled brain—a delusion engendered by long brooding over Manville's tragic death, a state of mind verging on melancholia.

As in our first meeting Rachel's presence had exorcised the fiend, so in the earlier years of our married life I felt myself so far removed from that baleful influence that I came to think the evil had been subjective from first to last—a morbid action of the mind, a phase of mental weakness, which happiness had cured. Rarely in those peaceful years did I recall the words that had once recurred in every hour of lonely brooding, and had flashed across my brain often and often in the busiest and the gayest scenes.

"When you are luckiest, when you are happiest, when woman's love is sweet and life is fair, I shall be near you. There is no path you tread where I may not cross your steps; there is no hour you live that shall be safe from me."

Hideous words, if they could take substance and shape; but commonsense would have brushed them aside as an impotent menace of one who could play the braggart even in the moment of death. I was weak enough to brood upon the ghastly idea till I came to think that his wild threat foreshadowed God's revenge for murder.

Hallucination or reality, I can recall the actual moment in which that evil presence re-entered my life. It was in one of the most brilliant assemblies of the London season, a gathering of wit and power, wealth and prestige, a galaxy of lovely women. I had watched my wife shining like a star of purer light in that firmament of beauty, conspicuous for her simple dress, and for an exquisite modesty which has ever been her highest charm. I was proud of her, happy in her love, a man without a care.

I left the dancing-room, and strolled into a long gallery, in which there were only a few couples, seated in the embrasures of the windows, or loitering in front of a picture or a statue. I stood before a picture of Watts's, at once a triumph of realism and of imagination—Milton's Satan, the incarnate image of evil, the angel in the instant of his fall. And as I gazed, the old horror fell over me like a pall. Again I had that overpowering sense of an impalpable presence, a spirit of evil close at my side, wordless whispers hissing in my ear, a creature not of earth, yet with power to torment mankind.

I turned sharply round, almost expecting to find myself confronted by a visible form, a fiend as terrible as the painted devil I had been looking at; and then I laughed at myself, remembering how my days and nights had been haunted by that impalpable presence which had been as real to my senses as flesh and blood.

From that hour the loathsome companion has been with me. For a long time I fought resolutely against the invisible demon. I gave myself up to the service of my fellow-creatures. I tried by strenuous, unremitting work to escape from the inexorable companion. I struggled to maintain an outward show of happiness, contrived even to deceive a devoted wife; but the continued effort was beyond human power, and I broke down miserably at last, and have had the agony of seeing Rachel's mute distress at a change in me that has made us almost strangers. I have isolated myself in my own house, the home that was once so full of charm, so dear, and so tranquil. Nothing can help me. I have had to abandon the philanthropic work which had become the business of my life. I can no longer go about among the poor, or consult with my fellow-workers, pursued by the demoniac influence which makes life hateful. I dare not trust myself in society of any kind; lest by some uncontrollable impulse I should reveal the horror that haunts me, and so brand myself as a madman, and end my wretched existence in a lunatic asylum. Solitude is my only refuge; and I must live out my life in silent misery.

To one man only, except yourself, have I lifted the curtain from my mind; and in him I perceived at once a doubt of my sanity. The border-line between reason and unreason is so narrow; and the very people who accept the Gospel miracles in unquestioning faith will question the sanity of a man who believes in ghosts. Liberty is too precious, even in my despairing state of mind, to be hazarded; so I must keep myself aloof, and confide in none but you—my faithful friend of the old undergraduate life. My wife is perfect in her gentleness and forbearance. She has never reproached me for my churlish preference of solitude to her dear company; but

I know she grieves over our estrangement, and her sorrow weighs me to the dust. Alas, to have won such a prize, the very pearl of womanhood, and to seem cold and indifferent. But if I were to open my heart to her, and describe my mental tortures, I should but make her life miserable, and risk being suspected of madness, even by her.

You see, therefore, my dear friend, that for such suffering as mine there is faint hope of cure.

Yours in profound dejection,

WALTER ARDEN.

V.

It was the beginning of November, and Lord St. Just had been absent from England five months. His disappearance from society had quieted Lady Mary Selby's fears, but it had not silenced the voice of slander. The people who want to think the worst of their fellow-creatures—especially of their particularly fortunate fellow-creatures—opined that the disease must have been virulent, or so drastic a remedy would hardly have been required.

"I suppose he was afraid the husband would make a row," said Lady Lammerton, whose well-trained spouse fetched and carried for her as meekly as Rawdon Crawley during his wife's affair with General Tufto.

"They do sometimes cut up rough, even in this enlightened age," said her friend; "but with the advance of civilisation the *ménage à trois* will, no doubt, be recognised by the marriage law. It is absurd for the divorce court to condemn a combination that society in general approves."

"And which helps to hold society together," remarked a third. "Half the houses in Mayfair would be to let if friendship were but a name."

"A name at the foot of a cheque," said another; "that's where friendship comes in."

Rachel rarely appeared in society now that her husband could no longer be persuaded to accompany her. The evening parties in Guelph Place had dwindled to a little knot of old friends and fellow-workers, of whom Mrs. Bellingham and Father Romney were the chief. They were to be found in Rachel's drawing-room almost every Thursday, both moved by sympathy with the wife whose existence seemed so solitary in her husband's house.

Mrs. Bellingham had tried to fathom the cause of Arden's altered way of life. She had broken boldly in upon his seclusion. She had questioned him, and remonstrated with him.

"I should never have wished Rachel to marry you if I could have thought you would make yourself almost a stranger to her, burying yourself alive among these wretched books."

Mrs. Bellingham indicated the choicest spirits of past and present with an abhorrent sweep of her hand. No woman better loved literature; but what are books when weighed against the living, loving, suffering heart of a neglected wife?

"I declare, Walter, that if I could have foreseen your conduct, I would not have said one word in your favour, when that dear girl was fretting herself to death about you—wanting you to be happy—and afraid to link her life with a heathen."

"My dear friend, you are giving yourself needless anxiety. There is nothing very remarkable in my secluded way of life; and Rachel has never complained. From my boyhood I have been something of a student; and for many years of my life I only lived to read."

"Then you ought never to have married. Rachel chose you because you were—or seemed to be—a kindred spirit, as unwavering as she herself is in the endeavour to make this wretched world better. And all at once, without reason, you take your hand from the plough."

"The hand may have lost its power to guide the plough."

"You mean that your health has broken down?"

"I mean that my capacity for work has failed. I come back to my quiet life in this room as the only life that suits me."

Mrs. Bellingham was not easily answered. She returned to the charge several times; but her most searching questions failed to bring her any nearer the mystery of Arden's conduct. He set a watch upon himself, with that ever-present fear of being taken for a madman, which was a part of his trouble. His guarded replies perplexed and baffled the questioner.

Rachel could not refuse to dine in Carlton House Terrace occasionally, though it was painful to her to appear there time after time without her husband, since his absence was a cause of offence to her father and mother. Mrs. Lorimer feared that her daughter's love-match had ended in failure; and Mr. Lorimer frankly confessed his disappointment in his son-in-law.

"Idlers and *dilettanti* are a kind of people I detest," he told his daughter, in one of his impetuous moods. "Life is too short, and there are too many things to be set straight in this world for any man to sit in a library and pose over the dreams and fancies of the dead past.

Life is too short for anything but living work; and for a man of your husband's age to turn his back upon active life is as bad as for a soldier to hang up his sword in the midst of a war."

Lady Mary Selby's was the only other house in which Rachel was to be met this winter. Here her husband's absence created no surprise. Semi-detached couples were rather the rule than the exception in Lady Mary's set; and if husband and wife were dining in Grosvenor Square on the same evening, it was odds they were at different numbers; or if Grosvenor Square were probable for the lady, one of the smaller streets between that place and Piccadilly would be a more likely draw for her better half. Those smaller streets, with their furnished houses, and temporary stars, had attractions known only to the few.

It was at Lady Mary's dinner-table that Rachel heard an alarming account of Lord St. Just. Mrs. Kelvin was there, the handsome Mrs. Kelvin, who had played for high stakes in the matrimonial game, and had seen her name bracketed with most of the great matches of the last seven seasons, and was still a widow; still frightfully in debt, still not a day older in face or manner, still avid for amusement of all kinds, and still hoping to see strawberry-leaves on her notepaper.

"Have you heard from your friend St. Just lately, Mrs. Arden?" she asked across the dinner-table, in a party of eight, which included a comedian, and his wife, retired from business; a French journalist of the most refined type; a successful novelist of the gentler sex, young enough to be called a girl by her relations and friends, and old enough to be told by women of seven-

and-twenty that they had gloated over her first book when they were "small."

It was one of those cosy little parties which Lady Mary loved, where, if anyone said an ill-natured thing, all the table could hear it; a party at which there were no millionaires, nobody who knew anything about company-promotion, or the last boom, or the approaching slump, in the city. It was the kind of party which Mr. Selby endured with a stoic indifference, holding all dinners worthless which did not further his financial interests. He was perfectly amiable, however, always gratified to sit opposite his wife and her diamonds, and to hear her say the fine things whose drift he took no pains to follow. For him she was the cleverest, as well as the handsomest, woman in the world—or in London, which was his world.

Rachel's dark blue eyes met Mrs. Kelvin's insistent gaze with an untroubled look.

"It is some time since I heard from him," she said quietly. "He was at Corfu with his yacht."

"And wrote in good spirits about his health?"

"He wrote of his travels only. He seemed interested and amused. I hope you have not heard any bad news of him?"

Mrs. Kelvin shrugged her shoulders, and looked right and left with a delicate air of distress. She was a mistress of the art of gesture and expression, and made as much play with a swan-like throat and dazzling shoulders as the immortal Becky. Mr. Bayning, the comedian, watched her with an amused smile, thinking how much good acting that was meant for mankind was being wasted on the few. Mrs. Bayning observed her with a merry twinkle in her bright grey eyes, as a good subject for drawing-room mimicry.

"I shall give them Mrs. Kelvin at the Rochforts to-morrow night," she thought.

"I am dreadfully sorry; I thought of course you would know," faltered Mrs. Kelvin, after her graceful byplay. "I wouldn't have spoken of him for the world, if I had known that you——"

"You mean that he is ill—that something bad has happened," Rachel said anxiously. "Pray tell me all you have heard."

"Oh, it may not be all true. It was from a boy I know in the Italian Legation. Did you know that St. Just was at Naples all through the outbreak of cholera in September?"

"He told me in his last letter that he was going to Naples; but he wrote before the cholera outbreak, and I hoped he would not go."

"Having the whole of the Mediterranean to choose from," said Miss Porter, the novelist. "But with an enthusiast like Lord St. Just, the cholera would act as a magnet."

"Well, he followed the king's example; went about among the people, into their loathsome dens, the most insanitary quarters of the city, into their hospitals. The young secretary almost wept when he told me about him," pursued Mrs. Kelvin.

Rachel was very pale, but perfectly calm.

"He has been among such people before," she said quietly. "It would be no new experience. What happened? Was he stricken with cholera?"

"No; he seems to have escaped the epidemic; but

his health broke down utterly. Hemorrhage of the lungs, I believe. He left Naples on his yacht, a doomed man, Donato told me; if not a dying man, as some people thought."

"How long is that ago?"

"Not very long—about a month, perhaps. Donato was at Naples when the yacht sailed for Palermo, just before he came to England."

"Will you ask Signor Donato to call upon me? I shall be at home to-morrow evening from nine o'clock, if that would suit him."

"I know he will be charmed. I'll write to him before I sleep," said Mrs. Kelvin, with eager sympathy.

She was greatly disappointed by the tranquillity with which Rachel had received her tidings, hazarded as a sudden blow that would bring about something in the way of a scene. Lord St. Just had been one of the numerous bachelors whom she had contemplated as a possible husband. A philanthropist, and by no means a millionaire; but still rich enough to pay her debts out of income, without being absolutely crippled. Not a great catch, but it would have been "a position, an establishment, don't you know?" And Mrs. Kelvin was pining for an establishment. She would have married a man who made lucifer matches, or sold tea, for vast wealth. She would have married St. Just for sheer respectability, and would have renounced her dream of strawberry-leaves.

But what could be hoped of a man who spent the best part of his days going about the East End with a beautiful young married woman for his companion; dining with her, walking with her, spending most of his evenings in her house?

Mrs. Kelvin's voice had led the chorus of slander. She had made mock of what she called the "saintly friendship." She had made mock of Rachel and her ways.

"Does she go about the East End in a short frock and a little cloak, with a basket of butter and honey, like Red Riding Hood?" she asked; "and does St. Just carry a cotton umbrella to shelter her from the rain?"

"And to protect her from all the other wolves."

"He being Lupus the First."

To Rachel's influence Mrs. Kelvin attributed the painful truth that she, like a play that has to be withdrawn after the third week, had failed to attract. She had done all that a clever woman, who had always prided herself upon the "straightness" of her conduct, could do to win a husband. She had thrown herself in St. Just's way on every opportunity, had offered him her shoulders and eyes, her arms, which were a strong point, and even her instep, in the Bond Street shoe which she hoped he would pay for post-matrimonially. She had affected an interest in his philanthropic work, had gushed and sparkled, and expended an amount of fascination-power which might have brought down an emperor; and she had left St. Just cold. Only to the counter influence of a married woman—the very worst kind of rival—could she attribute this frosty temperament.

"Sin must be irresistible for a saint," she thought, "from the force of contrast."

She gave up the chase some time before St. Just dropped out of London life; but she was a good hater, and she kept Mrs. Arden's name written large in her black books.

"I am sorry for St. Just," said Lady Mary, who had been talking to the Frenchman in his native tongue; "but don't let us be lugubrious, or Monsieur Reynaud will think we are victims of *le spleen*. You will put down this dismal talk to the month, monsieur," she added, turning to the journalist; "but I assure you *nous avons changé tout cela*, and what with the big shoots in Norfolk, and the skating at Prince's, November has become almost the pleasantest month of the year."

"Moi je le trouve, assurément pour ce soir," said her neighbour, with an air of being enchanted.

Mrs. Kelvin, having launched her thunderbolt with poor effect, tried to *accaparer* the journalist, who sat on her left, and made him almost blush by asking his opinion of the last audacity in French fiction—if that can be called fiction which invents nothing, imagines nothing, and begins and ends in the vivisection of vice.

Monsieur Reynaud confessed himself ashamed of his countrymen.

"I can pardon the aberrations of a man like Zola, who always writes with a purpose, and has the human race for his province; but these boudoir triflers, these miniature painters of vice in a *crêpe de chine peignoir,* and bestiality in varnished boots, they are only less revolting than they are *ennuyeux*."

"But their style," pleaded Mrs. Kelvin. "One can forgive so much for the sake of that exquisite French."

"English ladies are very forgiving, madame. The books that have most success here are rarely seen in a

French *intérieur.* Monsieur may read them, perhaps, in his *fumoir.* If madame reads them, *elle ne le dit pas.*"

"And you think the modern Englishwoman, with her classical and scientific education, and her broader views, is rather—shocking? *Hein?*"

"Oh, madame, I would not venture to criticise so exquisite a product of nature as the modern Englishwoman—such as I have the happiness to behold at this table," answered the Parisian, concentrating the adoration of a lifetime in a look, which Mrs. Kelvin's shoulders deprecated with a modest shrug.

The Italian secretary called on Rachel the following evening, before the arrival of her usual visitors, and from him she heard the story of St. Just's life during the month of September.

Signor Donato spoke of him with a warmth of feeling that touched Rachel.

"If there were many Englishmen like him, we should call your island the Isle of Saints," he said. "Like our noble king, he showed himself without fear of the pestilence which had made Naples a desert. Everybody who was free to leave the place had fled, as if the city were on fire. The priests, the doctors, the sisters of charity—all those who live for others and hold their own lives of small account—they alone remained. St. Just was perhaps the only Englishman in Naples during that dreadful month. He gave himself and his fortune to the blessed work. He comforted the dying, and fed the widows and children. Even the priests confessed that he was a saint, and forgave him for not being a Papist."

"I am not surprised," said Rachel. "He would not

6*

miss such an opportunity of doing his Master's work. But I hope it will not cost him his life."

"I hope not; but I am afraid he was in a very bad way when he left Naples. I was at Sorrento at the time, and I went on board his yacht to bid him good-bye. He had an English doctor with him, who told me in confidence that he had not much hope of his patient's living through the winter. His pluck might keep him alive, perhaps; but his lungs were seriously damaged."

"I am very sorry. He was my most valued friend, after my husband; the man to whom I looked for help and guidance," said Rachel, speaking of that cherished friendship in the past tense. "He was going to Palermo, Mrs. Kelvin said, when you saw him."

"Yes; he was to winter at Palermo, if the climate seemed to suit him. His doctor was to remain with him."

Mrs. Bellingham was announced, and other visitors followed. Arden always put in an appearance at some time on his wife's evenings, talked for a few minutes to two or three of her visitors, and quietly slipped away before people had been able to observe him closely. He looked worried, and even ill. So much was visible to the most casual observer. Mr. and Mrs. Lorimer, who often dropped in for an hour on a Thursday evening, were both disturbed by the change in him, but did not say too much to their daughter, for fear of making her unhappy; while Rachel on her part was careful to hide all her apprehensions and sorrows from her father and mother.

She wrote to St. Just on the morning after her interview with Donato. She reproached him for not having told her about his work in Naples, and for letting her hear of his illness from a woman she disliked, and among frivolous surroundings. She wrote hopefully of his future, urging him to do all that medical science could suggest for the restoration of his health. It was at a time when the Transvaal had become popular as a sanatorium for lung complaints, and she begged him, if Sicily failed, to try the great Karòo, of course always with the approval of medical authority. She wrote earnestly and urgently; but with the calm affection of a sister.

St. Just replied by return of post.

"Forgive me for having kept you in the dark as to my work in Naples," he wrote, after thanking her for her letter. "I did not want to trouble a friend with needless fears on my account, and I took care that no one in England should know my whereabouts. The cholera left me unscathed; though I spent the best part of my life among the sick and dying. As for the break-down in my health, that I believe would have come in any case. I have suffered more after a chill caught on board my yacht, on a voyage of pleasure, than I suffered from the fatigues and risks of my life in the slums and hospitals of Naples. With regard to your suggestion about South Africa, I confess that I should be very loath to go so far in quest of health; or if I went as far, I should infinitely prefer some station in the Himalayas. The idea of India has always fascinated me. It is to me as a dream-country; and I think if I found myself there, I should fancy myself escaped from the dull realities of earth into the land of dreams. My doctor has talked of the great Karoo, which it is a kind of fashion to believe in just now; but when I read of the dust-storms on those arid heights, I think myself happy to be lying here, surrounded by the blue waters of this exquisite bay.

"I am glad also to know that I am within easy reach of England and the friends I left there; for though I am content to live on the Mediterranean, I want to die at home. It is this desire that has fought against my plan of visiting the South Seas, and laying a flower on Louis Stevenson's grave. You know how I admire his books, and love the writer's beautiful nature. I think the South Sea Islands, to many of those who care for literature, and have not the geographical mind, mainly mean Stevenson's last home."

VI.

THE winter was over. April had filled the London streets with flowers, the yellow gold of spring—daffodils, jonquils, mimosa; the yellow flowers flamed in the yellow sunshine; and here and there, even in the East End streets, where Rachel Arden was an almost daily visitor, the glory of a window-garden bore witness of a good housewife and a decent home. Sometimes it was the master of the brick packing-case, with its four rooms and washhouse, who tended the window-garden; and these gardens were generally of a superior and more ambitious order; for the man's stronger and longer arms could do more in the use of nails, and wire, and string, and in training plants; and where there were great effects made with wistaria trained over a wall, or a hardy rose surrounding a window, or a curtain of scarlet-runners climbing upon string, one might be sure that the bread-winner had a taste for gardening, and did not spend all his evenings in a public-house.

Rachel's winter had passed in a quiet monotony of work. The trivial task, the daily round, had been enough for content. Arden had appeared in the old scenes now and then to please his wife; but he had tried in vain to interest himself in her work, or in the people for whom she toiled. The one haunting impression—the invisible presence—made a wall between him and the living world. He moved among this eager, striving multitude like a man in a dream. Father Romney could make nothing of him.

St. Just had written to Rachel several times between November and April, but his letters had told her very little about himself. He had put off her anxious questions about his health with vague replies. His doctor thought Palermo suited him. His yacht was a source of unfailing amusement.

"We potter about along the coast sometimes when the weather is favourable—a voyage of two or three days; or we lie at anchor and bask in the sun. I think of the East End and the people there, and think what a wonder and delight an hour of such sunshine would be to them in midwinter. And then I think that some day there may rise the white walls and red roof of a vast sanatorium on this lovely island; or at Capri, perhaps—the Capri of Tiberius. A world which has grown so much better, in its care for want and suffering, within my own short life, will go on improving, until, without any such universal confiscation as the socialist dreams of, the distribution of wealth will come about naturally, from the open hand of benevolence."

This letter had reached Rachel early in March; and it was late in April when she was surprised by seeing a long letter from St. Just among the letters which her husband had opened at the breakfast-table.

"I see you have heard from Lord St. Just," she said anxiously. "Is he still at Palermo?"

"No; he writes from Marseilles. He is on his way home," Arden answered gravely.

"I am glad of that."

"You will be sorry when you hear that he is seriously ill."

"Is that so? Then, indeed, I am sorry. I knew he was in bad health; but he said very little about himself in his letters, and I hoped for the best. Does he write very despondently?"

"You had better read his letter. It is a strange letter, Rachel, and it makes a strange appeal to you and me. Of course, I knew how close your friendship was—that you were to him the world's one woman, in the way of friendship—but I was never jealous."

"You never had cause," she answered, looking at him with a grave tenderness that had something of reproach. "I was grateful to St. Just for his sympathy and advice, when you lost interest in the things I love, and ceased to give me your help."

"I understand, Rachel. I was not complaining. My faith in your goodness and purity has never wavered. The life I have led during the last two years has been a life of unutterable misery; but distrust of you has had no part in my suffering. If I have isolated myself from you, and seemed cold to your mission of mercy, the cause of my desertion lies far away from my domestic life. You made this life heaven; but another influence has made it hell. And I cannot tell you the dark secret—I dare not—lest you should think——"

He stopped suddenly, with a look of apprehension, as if he had said too much, and then, after a pause, went on in a quieter voice—

"I told St. Just something about myself—more, perhaps, than I should have confided to any man. I believe he thought me mad; and he had good reason."

"No, no, no!" exclaimed Rachel. "You must not imagine such a thing."

"Other people would think as he thought, if I were to lift the veil from my life. That is why I mope alone, and keep myself aloof even from you—from you whom I love as dearly as in our first hour of wedded life."

"You should not keep aloof, Walter. It is cruel of you not to trust me, not to let me share your trouble of mind, whatever it is."

"Mental trouble knows no division, Rachel. I can tell you nothing—nothing. I say again, I dare not! But I want you to believe in my sanity to the last. Whatever may happen, remember that I am not mad."

"My dear husband, I have never doubted—and, please God, I shall never doubt—your sanity. But I should be so much happier if you would let me share your life, as I did in the dear days when we were all the world to each other. Let us leave London, and go to some lovely spot in Switzerland, or the Tyrol, where we can live quietly, far away from the world. If you must mope alone, let me share your solitude. I am only a part of yourself. I will not question you, or intrude upon your dark hours. But I want to be your companion again; I want you to know that I sympathise and suffer with you."

"My dearest and best! Alas, alas! to think that you were worthy of a better fate, and that a better man loved you, and might have made you happy, if I had cut my throat two years ago."

"Walter, how can you be so cruel?"

"Read St. Just's letter. A dying man has privileges. Read his letter, and decide upon the answer."

He gave her the letter, bent down to kiss her as she sat at the breakfast-table, with her head leaning on her hand, and then went quietly from the room, before her tears came, and she broke down altogether.

She had promised not to think him mad—not mad! But if he were perfectly sane, as she strove to believe, what was this mental trouble which he dared not tell her, and which had made an end of his happiness and hers? What was this influence which had made life hell? The change in him was palpable enough; but what of the impalpable, the unknown cause? What could that be but some morbid affection of the mind, some disease of the imagination, which physicians call madness?

It was long before she was able to control her troubled thoughts, and to fix her attention upon St. Just's letter.

Terminus Hotel, Marseilles.

My dear Arden,

You will, perhaps, be surprised that this letter should be addressed to you, instead of to your wife, to whom I have written from time to time during my wanderings in search of sunshine and calm seas; but I have a request to make which must be made in the first instance to you. I want you to bring her to me in my Cornish home, that I may bid farewell to the friend who has been more to me than anyone in this world since my mother died. I want to see her for the last time in the home of my childhood, the place I have loved better than any other spot on earth; as I have cherished her friendship more than that of any other friend.

It is a selfish desire, perhaps; and I ought rather to halt in London, on my last earthly journey, and say good-bye to you and your wife in your own house. But doomed men have a certain privilege of self-indulgence, and all the world is kind to them. I know you will be kind; and even more surely can I count on her kindness.

My days are numbered. When I leave Marseilles to-night with my doctor, I shall be carried to my bed in the train, carried from the train to the boat to-morrow evening, carried from station to station, like a dead thing, till I lie down to rest in the room where my father died, amidst the voices of the sea and the winds, blowing across the moorland where I was reared. I have made my doctor tell me the worst about myself, in spite of the professional anxiety to maintain hope even where the end is certain. He does not promise me many days after my arrival in Cornwall, if I live through the journey. He wanted to take me to some sheltered spot in Auvergne, or to Aix in Savoy, rather than to let me risk so long a pilgrimage. But my heart is set upon dying at home among the old familiar faces of servants and tenants, and to lie asleep in the shadow of the church tower that was my landmark in my rides and rambles, when I was a boy.

Will you bring your wife to Trevelyan, my dear Arden, and let me see the face that has been my dream of womanly kindness and pity, when my eyes are growing dim? I know that *she* will not refuse to visit my death-bed; for her Divine compassion would gratify the dying wish of the vilest sinner among Romney's flock. If you consent, I would beg you to start soon after you receive this letter, as I ought to be at Trevelyan within ten or twelve hours of its delivery; and who knows how long I may be found there?

Ever faithfully yours,

St. Just.

CHAPTER VII.

DARKNESS had closed over moor and sea, when the carriage that had brought Mr. and Mrs. Arden from the station drove along the avenue of beech and oak that wound uphill to Trevelyan Manor House; and through the open window the travellers could feel the salt breath of the sea, and hear the distant roar of the waves rolling into the caverns and hollows of that wild north coast. The house stood on a ridge of hill within a mile of the sea—a stone house, built when the last of the Tudors was nearing her end, and added to in the time of Charles the First; a house with a priest's hole, and a family ghost, which, being a purely domestic invention, hatched in the servants' hall, and developed between the butler's pantry and the housekeeper's room, had suffered many changes of circumstance and character — nay, even changes of sex; sometimes described as an infirm old man in a brown Georgian suit, anon vouched for by eye-witnesses as a lovely young woman in ruff and farthingale.

Rachel's eyes searched the rolling stretch of turf, and the wind-driven oaks. A young moon looked out fitfully from a sky darkened by ragged clouds, and all seemed chill and dreary in the uncertain light.

A curtain of gloom falls over a house whose master

lies dying; an influence subtle as a supernatural presence; and this house of Trevelyan had the gloom of past ages—the dark centuries when religious persecution and civil war made a hiding-place as necessary for hunted human creatures as a hole in the earth for the hunted fox. All that well-trained servants could do to prepare comfort and cheerfulness for the visitors had been done; and the architectural beauty of the hall and corridors, the carved ceilings and tapestried walls, appealed to Walter Arden's sense of the beautiful, and his love of the past. But the gloom was there all the same, in spite of blazing wood-fires, and many candles in old silver candelabra, and a dinner-table brightened by the deep purple and gold of old Worcester china, and the pale roses of spring, grown under glass.

The grey-haired housekeeper, in rustling black silk, was waiting in the hall when the travellers alighted; and it was to her Rachel turned, pale and expectant, with tremulous lips—

"Is Lord St. Just here?"

"Yes, ma'am; his lordship arrived three hours ago, by the eleven o'clock train from Waterloo. He is sitting up in his room; and he would like to see you and Mr. Arden before he goes to bed."

"Is he worse for the long journey?"

"Oh, ma'am, he is very, very bad. I'm afraid he will soon start on a longer journey; but the Lord's word will be a lantern unto his feet and a light unto his path. He has been a saint on earth, and he will soon be among the saints in heaven," the old woman said, with streaming eyes.

"Take me to his room, please, Mrs. Roper."

"You have heard my name, ma'am? His lordship has spoken of me?"

"Often and often. You were a part of his childhood."

"I loved him dearly, ma'am; but that's no merit. We all love him. Only I was his nurse, you see; and it was because he was so fond of me that I got promoted to be housekeeper. He didn't want me to leave the family, or to drop into a pensioner; and, as her ladyship's housekeeper was leaving on account of ill-health, I was given her place, though I had no experience in the management of a large establishment. There never was a sweeter child—or a nobler boy—or a better man. Though I'm a Bible Christian myself, and don't hold with his lordship's Church, I can reverence one who has shown himself a true disciple of Christ."

The length of the corridor gave an opportunity for the old servant's garrulous tongue, and Rachel was touched by the genuine affection indicated by the broken voice and uncontrollable tears.

The door of St. Just's room opened as they drew near. Lightly as their steps sounded on the thick carpet, he had heard the footfall for which he had been listening and longing. He had found Arden's telegram in the hall when he arrived—"We are starting by the afternoon train"—and he had counted the minutes till the first possible moment at which they could arrive. And from that moment his impatience had been at fever height.

The hectic flush upon the sunken cheeks, and the eager look in the too brilliant eyes, startled Rachel. Could those be dying eyes that gazed at her with an intense vitality which she had never seen in them before? Could the flame of life burn so fiercely on the verge of extinction?

Speech failed him in his agitation. He pointed to the vacant chair at his side with a radiant smile; and then she heard a faintly whispered, "This is kind."

He was half lying in a large armchair, a hospital nurse standing beside him, and his valet in the background. The room was larger than modern bedrooms. The low ceiling, supported by black oak beams, and the dark tapestry, gave an impression of unspeakable gloom to a mind overshadowed by impending sorrow.

The candles on the high mantelpiece gave less light than the logs burning on the hearth; and in the alternations of leaping flame and dull red glow Rachel had not seen the doctor till he came out of the shadows at the end of the room.

"Nurse and I will leave you with Lord St. Just for five or ten minutes, Mrs. Arden," he said quietly; "but you must not let him talk much, please."

The nurse showed her the restorative which might be given if there were signs of fainting. *Eau de Cologne,* smelling-salts, everything was ready on the table by his chair, with the little pile of books that had been his comforters in the long hours of weakness and decay.

"It was very good of Arden to bring you," St. Just said, when they were alone. "Can you forgive me for summoning you to this last dismal scene? Yes, I know you will forgive; you have often looked upon sickness and death; you have comforted other death-beds."

"Dear friend, how can you think I should hesitate to

come to you—or my husband," she said, interrupting him, shocked at the change in his voice, which had a dull hoarse sound. "If we had known you were so ill, and alone, we would have gone to Sicily to help in bringing you home. We are both of us glad to be with you. Walter has always admired and esteemed you. He is your friend as much as I am."

"Alas! that cannot be, Rachel; he and I are too far apart in our understanding of life. I may call you Rachel now, mayn't I? If I sinned in loving you too dearly, the sin belongs to the past; it is gone with my life. I am standing on the threshold, face to face with my Creator. All earthly dreams are past, and my sins are washed clean in the blood of my Saviour. Those long days and nights on the yacht, lying supine, too weak even to read, gave time for repentance."

"You had so little to repent of, you who gave your life for others."

"I gave them my labour and my thoughts. But the soldier in the rank-and-file does more when he dies to save a comrade. Will you be with me to-morrow morning, Rachel, when the priest who christened me comes to give me my last communion? Will you kneel among my faithful old servants?"

"Yes, yes; but you must not talk any more, St. Just."

"Not to-night; I have to live till to-morrow. But when the celebration is over I must open my heart to you and to your husband. I have much to say to you. You must not stop me then, Rachel. The thoughts in a dying man's mind are worth more than a few hours of his life. And now go, and dine, and rest after your journey."

"Good night," she said gently, bending down to kiss the wasted hand lying upon the arm of his chair; such a pure and passionless kiss as women give to the dying.

She did not plague him with any of the death-bed commonplaces—that he would weather the storm, that he might surprise his doctors, that there was hope still of long years to come. She accepted the inevitable, and bowed her head before the stroke of doom, with the meek submission of one for whom death did not mean the end.

Arden would have visited the invalid that night, but the doctor forbade any more talk or excitement for his patient.

"I believe he will be the better for your coming," the doctor said; "and he may get some sleep, perhaps, to-night, now his wish has been gratified. He wanted so much to see you and Mrs. Arden. He has talked to me again and again of her work among the poor, and of their love for her."

"It is easy to win their love," Rachel said. "They have so few to claim it, outside their own poor homes."

"And they don't get much of it inside, I reckon, if one allows for all those gentlemen whom Miss Trotwood called Poker husbands—the men who come home drunk and murder their wives in a casual way; or the men with irritable tempers, who come home sober and find a drunken wife and no dinner. I always feel rather sorry for those fellows," concluded Dr. Walsh, with a meditative air. "I had a cook once that I should have liked to murder—deliberately.

Rachel left her husband and the doctor to dine *tête-à-tête,* and refreshed herself with tea and toast in Lady St. Just's morning-room, which adjoined the bedroom that had been prepared for her. The housekeeper brought the tea-tray with her own hands, and waited on Rachel, trying to make her take something more substantial than the little bit of dry toast, which she ate only in order to satisfy the old woman.

"Indeed, ma'am, you ought to take something better than that scrap of toast—a new laid egg, now. These were laid this morning, and my brahmas are famous for their eggs.

"No, thank you, Mrs. Roper; I have no appetite. My husband made me eat something at Salisbury."

"But you'd miss your luncheon, leaving home, ma'am."

"Please don't trouble about me. I want you to tell me about his lordship—his doctors—his nurses—all that is being done for him."

Mrs. Roper asked nothing better than a talking licence. She accepted Rachel's invitation to be seated with ceremonious reluctance, but there was no ceremony in her use of her tongue. She sat with the visitor for an hour, talking of St. Just all the time—his ghastly appearance that afternoon when they carried him into the house; the impression made upon the doctor from Bude, who had been summoned to consult with his lordship's private doctor, who had travelled with him nearly a year, and watched him day and night from the beginning of his illness, and understood his case better than anyone else could, Mrs. Roper opined, though, of course, it was only right to have her ladyship's doctor from Bude—at least, not living in Bude, but in his own house and grounds in the neighbourhood, a gentleman who had known his lordship from a baby, and knew the St. Just constitution.

"It's in her ladyship's family," concluded the housekeeper. "All the Challoners have weak chests. They look strong and fine and handsome, and they're careless with themselves, feeling strong and active, and then in the prime of life they go off unexpected, after a short illness. But oh, ma'am, if there was ever anybody ready for heaven, it's my young master, and it seems almost a cruelty in those that love him to begrudge his going there."

The roaring of the wind and the waves had been in Rachel's ears all through a sleepless night, a melancholy, monotonous voice, that sounded like the voice of death —the calling of the sea.

The priest and his two attendant choir-boys had a stormy walk over the moor from Trevelyan village, confronting wind and rain, with their faces towards the Atlantic, and a tempest coming up from the waste of waters beyond the Land's End. The morning was dark, the sky covered with hurrying clouds, and the distant roar of the breakers mingled with the solemn words of the Communion Service, words broken now and then by the sound of stifled sobs among the men- and maid-servants, who knelt with bowed heads to participate for the last time, as they believed, in the ceremony which they had so often attended side by side with their master in the village church. Never had grey-haired butler and middle-aged footmen thought to kneel beside their master's death-bed. They were all sons of the soil, as much a part of the country where they had been born and bred as the largest landowner in Cornwall. They came of a race that had lived from generation to generation in the same parish, or in the same cottage, till the cob walls crumbled under the heavy slate-roof, or a beneficent landlord substituted stone for cob, and sash windows and flat roof and modern ugliness for picturesque discomfort.

For these the early death of a beloved master meant the break-up of their own lives. Good places were to be found, no doubt, for good service; but where could they be as well off and happy as they had been at Trevelyan? It was not leaving a "place." It was leaving home.

All was over; the Rector and his attendants had gone, comfortably sheltered from rain and wind in the late Lady St. Just's roomy landau. Rachel and the day-nurse were alone with the patient, while the doctor breakfasted belowstairs.

He had slept fairly well, the nurse told Rachel; and his temperature and pulse were both a shade better.

"He was restless till you came, ma'am, and that sent up the temperature."

"Will you send for your husband?" St. Just asked, when Rachel had taken the nurse's place at his bedside, while she took her breakfast in the adjoining room, within call. "I want to pour out my heart to him, and to you."

"He will be here directly, I think. He meant to come when——"

"When all signs of a Christian death-bed had vanished? I understand."

There was a discreet knock at the door, and Arden entered the room with hushed footsteps, and came to the bedside, where he bent down to lay his hand upon the spectral hand on the bed, in silent greeting. He was almost as pale as St. Just; and he was slow to put his sympathy into words.

"Will you leave us for a little while, Rachel. I want to speak to Arden alone."

She rose without a word, and moved towards the door, then stopped and said imploringly—

"Remember what the doctor said. You are not to talk much."

"Yesterday! I was obedient yesterday. I am free to-day."

The hoarse voice, the effect in speaking, agonised her; but she dared not oppose him. Excitement, distress of mind, might be worse than that effort of speech. She left the room in silence.

"Arden, it was kind of you to grant my request—pure charity—Christian charity. For I think you must have read between the lines—you must have known that I loved your wife—loved her, and fought the good fight, against love, against sin. I was her friend, her true and honest friend, for years; and when I felt the fight might be a losing battle, I fled from the face I loved, from the voice that was my music—the voice that was my music! Ah, how that line has haunted me."

"Yes, I understood your letter. And I know that you are a good man. I have not believed implicitly in all the professing Christians I have met; but I believe in you, and I believe in my wife. Nothing could ever make me doubt her. She did not know you loved her. You kept that secret to yourself?"

"Till the last hour—the hour in which I wished her good-bye, when I was leaving England, meaning never to return. In that unhappy hour I spoke words which I would have died to recall—words that made our life-long parting inevitable. I hope you know that I should not have asked to look on her dear face again if I had not known that my hours were numbered."

"I believe that with all my heart, St. Just."

"Enough of myself. I want to talk to you of your own life—the life that may be long, and that ought to be so deeply blessed. I want to talk to you of her and her happiness. Do you know why I courted her society, spent half my life with her, knowing that I loved her too well for my peace? It was because I saw how you neglected her; and because, after your confession that night, I feared for your reason. I wanted to be near her, a friend and protector, against the peril of a husband's insanity."

"I knew you thought me mad."

"No, not mad when you opened your mind to me; yet what might not be feared from a mind in which hallucination had taken the place of reality? But, as time went on, I saw no fresh cause for alarm. You were a most unhappy man, but your brain was strong enough to keep its balance, under conditions that in most men would have ended in lunacy. But think what it was for me, worshipping her beauty and her sweetness, to see such a flower neglected; to see a marriage, that all who knew you had admired as an idyllic love-match, drifting into hopeless estrangement, a husband in sullen isolation, a wife broken-hearted. After those years of severance she is unchanged. She loves you still. You have but to take her to your heart again."

"And to make her miserable; to let her share the horror of my haunted life; to let her see me in the hour when that spirit of evil holds my soul in thrall; to let her see me as I am for the greater part of my life, a man accursed. What could she think me but a madman? And then would come the horror I have been dreading for the last two years. A loving wife's anxiety for an afflicted husband—physicians called in—interviews with the patient—searching questions—the thin end of the wedge—the secret of my suffering extorted from me—and then the bland advice for self-control—and the certificate—and the asylum. I confided in you, St. Just, which was a mistake. I won't make that mistake again."

"Walter Arden," said St. Just, raising himself in his bed with a sudden energy, "if you believed in God, you would not believe in this devil. Men who love Christ, who live by the light of His word, are incapable of fantastic dreams like yours."

"Yet what if I am incapable of believing in God, or loving Christ, except as a Jewish philosopher of incomparable wisdom and gentleness?"

"Yet you believe in the invisible, the impalpable presence of a supernatural being. You do not shut your mind against the unseen world. You believe that the evil spirit of the man you killed—justly, as you think—has power to haunt your life, and even to enter the form of a dead man whom you loved—to live again, a devil's nature in a human form. You believe in the reality of that which reason should tell you to be a wild delusion of your own troubled brain, and you withhold your belief from the Creator of the universe, and the Saviour of mankind."

"I am as Nature made me. In the propensities and instincts that make up this being of mine, the instinct of faith in God is wanting."

"But not the instinct of superstition. Oh, my dear friend, what can I say to you, how can I convince you that in one refuge only can your troubled spirit find peace? I tell you, Arden, that in this brief life of ours, on this infinitesimal spot in illimitable space, we are surrounded with the unseen, and we cannot escape from its influence. The world invisible is round us and about us, in our childish dreams, our childish gropings after the mysterious and unknowable, the something near us that is not ourselves; and if we reject the messengers from heaven, we become the prey of the spirits from hell. God has given us minds that aspire, thoughts that break through the prison-house of clay. Somehow, by some half-conscious process, the spirit of man escapes the limitations of flesh, to find the peace of God, or the terrors of Satan. God or the devil! Man must choose under which master he will live and die."

"Why must there be a master? Why should not man be free—free as Huxley was; as Darwin was; believing only in the things that he can see and measure and test and compare; the things whose absolute reality he knows and understands? Those men lived out their lives without the necessity of a God, or the fear of a devil."

"Yes, there must always be exceptions, men of the scientific mind, men of vast intellectual force, who have the power to concentrate their thoughts upon the actual world, who know that they are labouring for a great cause—the cause of truth about material things. Such men can be satisfied without thought of the hereafter. Their work is the work of to-day; their discoveries, their achievements, their triumphs, are circumscribed by earthly limits. The world of sense, of fossils and dry bones, of insect and animal life, is their dominion. The scientific mind asks nothing better."

His voice was hoarse, and he breathed heavily; but the flushed cheek and brilliant eye, the energy of tone and manner, were full of vitality. It was difficult to think of him as a man whose life might not outlast the day. Difficult, agonising, to think that this ardent, beneficent spirit must soon be cold in death.

Arden was deeply moved.

"I wish to God I were like you, St. Just. But some men see the heavens opening, and the company of saints, where others see only the trackless wilderness of infinite space, the barren wastes of mindless matter—an illimitable universe, with no room for a personal God. I would give half the life that lies before me to have faith, simple and strong as yours, to help me through the other half."

"It will come to you. I believe with all my soul that the light will come; if you will give your mind and heart in perfect trustfulness to the wife who loves you. She will be your guide, Arden, strong in her childlike simplicity. A child shall lead you. Let me lie down to rest, with the assurance that you will be again to her as you were in the first years of your married life. Let no morbid fancy of an overwrought brain come between you and your guardian angel."

"My guardian angel!" echoed Arden. "That is what I thought her when we first met, and when the cloud of horror was lifted from me—the indescribable horror which no words can convey to the mind of another, but which is more real than the sternest realities of life are to me."

"Lean upon Rachel," said St. Just, laying his hand on Arden's with an affectionate pressure. "She will lead you to peace. And now I have said my last word—and last words are remembered when the speaker is no more. Good-bye."

They clasped hands, and Arden bent over the wasted hand with clouded eyes, and went quietly from the room as Dr. Walsh came in, bringing the Bude doctor, his senior by a quarter of a century.

There had been a question between the two men over-night as to the advisability of sending for a London specialist; and both had agreed that it would be useless. The end had long been inevitable. St. Just, always of a delicate frame and constitution, had shown wonderful vitality, but it was only the power of mind over matter. The mischief had progressed beyond hope of cure. Walsh was young, and a disciple of the newest school, full of intelligence, and warmly attached to St. Just, who had offered to take him on his yachting tour, with a liberal salary, at a time when the young man's constitution was in danger of breaking down altogether from overwork as a general practitioner in one of the poorest neighbourhoods in London. He had left the medical schools eager for experience, and not caring for income, beyond the absolute needs of existence; and he had been on foot early and late, working with heart and brain, in a practice that hardly brought him the rent of his surgery.

"The late Lady St. Just's people were a family of weak chests," the Bude doctor said. "I am not surprised at St. Just's break-up. But it's a great loss for this neighbourhood, for he was a model landlord. And it's a greater loss for the philanthropic world."

"He was the friend of the poor," answered Walsh. "He would wish for no higher title."

They both said he "was." They spoke and thought of him in the past.

"And title and estates go to a distant cousin?" interrogated Walsh.

"Yes, a small squire near Launceston, a fine sportsman. We shall have a pack of hounds here perhaps in a year or two. The kennels are on the other side of the park, where St. Just's grandfather built them eighty years ago. I've heard my grandfather talk of him."

"But you have a pack of hounds near Bude, haven't you?"

"Yes; but if we had a private pack at Trevelyan, we could hunt five days a week."

This conversation had taken place on the previous evening, after it had been agreed that the science of medicine could do no more for the present master of Trevelyan. In a few hours, more or less, the new master would be coming hotfoot to claim his own, the cheery hunting-squire, whose modest means hardly allowed of a second horse, and who had cast many a longing look at the spacious stables—room enough for twenty—and the kennels that had not echoed the voices of hounds for half a century. Only within the last six months, when the report of St. Just's bad health had appeared from time to time in the gossip column of the London papers, had the Launceston squire contemplated the future ownership of those admirable stables, and the rapture of improving the empty kennels on modern principles. The good man knew not yet how near his ownership might be. It was no man's business to inform him of his kinsman's return; and there was so little in common between the two men that no one had thought of suggesting the squire's presence in the sick-room. He had been asked to Trevelyan for a day's shooting now and then, when St. Just was at home, and had been allowed to shoot the covers as often as he chose when St. Just was away; but no familiarity could have made the men companions.

Arden found Rachel pacing the terrace on the south side of the house, careless of wind and rain. He went to her and drew her hand gently through his arm, and walked by her side in silence. Simple as the act was, it seemed to her like the breaking down of a barrier of ice that had gradually risen between husband and wife. She looked up at him wonderingly, and met his gaze of melancholy tenderness, ineffable love shadowed by ineffable pain.

"You have been a long time with St. Just," she said.

"Not long in minutes; but we have talked of things that fill a lifetime. He has been talking of you, Rachel, telling me to love you; as if I had ever ceased to do that, as if I had ever loved woman as I love you. He urged me to confide even my darkest thoughts to you—as I once confided them to him——"

"And you will trust me, Walter? If you only knew how miserable I have been in these wretched years of our estrangement—never estrangement on my side; but on yours the cruellest desertion. I was a deserted wife in our own house, husband and wife sitting face to face day after day, yet miles apart."

"Well, there shall be no more estrangement. If you can live with me and share my burden, I will not creep into my hole and hide my misery in darkness. I will hide myself from all the world except you. But you don't know the shadow you are bringing upon your life, if you are to be my companion. You don't know!"

"However darkly the shadow may fall, I would rather live in it than live as we have been living—you and I, Walter! You and I who were once in such perfect sympathy, who once seemed to have but one heart and mind, except in our thoughts of the world to come. Oh, Walter, if you could look there in your hour of trouble, you would surely find comfort. Morbid imaginings, fancied evils, cannot live in the light of heaven."

"Morbid imaginings! They are the realities."

"And if you cannot yet find the light—if the blessedness of belief in a Divine Friend and Saviour is denied you, dear husband, you have but to return to the little world of suffering humanity, where there are such real miseries, so many ill-used wives, and fatherless children, and sickly families, toiling from morning till night for such pitiful wages, so many heartbroken mothers grieving over the degradation of their daughters, or the wickedness of their sons. When I think of all that patient suffering, I cannot fathom the mind of a man who can turn his back upon it, having once seen and known it, as you have."

"You think I gave up without a struggle, that I wearied of the work you loved. You wrong me there, Rachel. I thought once, as you think now, that a man might arm himself against all the powers of hell by unflagging labour in the cause of humanity—that the human must vanquish the devilish. I thought that; and I wrestled with my enemy. But evil was stronger than good. Oh, for mercy's sake, don't drive me into explanations; don't force me to talk of myself! Shelter me with your love if you can. Save me from despair, from the peril of madness. I will be as a child in your hands; I will do whatever you bid me, go where you tell me to go; but don't question me."

"I will do nothing that can give you pain, Walter."

Dr. Walsh met them at the end of the terrace.

"Lord St. Just would like to see Mrs. Arden, if she would be kind enough to stay with him for a little while," he said; and then, in a lower voice, to Arden, "I think he wishes to bid her good-bye."

"I will go this instant," Rachel said, walking quickly towards the house.

"Is it really good-bye?" Arden asked, when he and the doctor were alone. "Have you given up hope?"

"Yes. We are near the end; but he is calm and happy. It is the death-bed of a saint."

"He was so full of life and energy half an hour ago, when he talked to me."

"The light that comes before the final darkness. He is without pain. His mental power is undiminished; but I doubt if he will live through the night."

"Does he know?"

"Yes. He made me tell him the truth. All that can prolong his life will be done till the last moment. He has two admirable nurses; and I shall be at hand all day and all night, if he live till night."

"Rachel," said St. Just, when she had seated herself by his bedside, Nurse Marian having withdrawn to a seat by an open window at the other end of the room, "I have done with most earthly things, but not with your friendship. I like to see you by my bed, though I see your face dimly through a pale grey mist. I like to hear your voice."

"Shall I read to you? It would tire you less than talking."

"No; sing to me, Rachel; sing one of the hymns we both love—the hymns I have heard you sing at St. Saviour's. Ah, if you could have known then how your voice thrilled me; how for me it was the only voice in that mass of people, singing in tune and out of tune, with their poor cockney accent, their heart-whole piety, so pathetic in its yearning for the Unseen. Your voice rose up from the multitude like a seraph's—so clear, so pure, so tender! Sing to me, Rachel."

"If my poor voice can soothe you."

"It will lift me up to heaven."

She rose and moved to a prie-Dieu chair at the foot of the bed, and knelt with clasped hands and upward gaze, as of one who sees something far away. She sang several hymns, making a long pause after each, while she prayed silently with bowed head. She knew the hymns he loved best; for she had heard him read them and talk of them to schoolchildren, to old men and women, to the sick and the dying. She sang—

"The King of love my Shepherd is,
Whose goodness faileth never;
I nothing lack if I am His
And He is mine for ever."

And then, in a low voice, attuned to that sad environment, she sang, "Lead, kindly Light," "Rock of Ages," 'Art thou weary?" And last of all—

"Abide with me; fast falls the eventide;
The darkness deepens; Lord, with me abide;
When other helpers fail, and comforts flee,
Help of the helpless, Oh abide with me."

Nurse Marian was kneeling by the distant window. The doctor had come into the room silently, and after looking at his patient, he too had knelt with bowed head. Sung under such conditions, those hymns were prayers.

A thrush was singing in the rainy shrubbery under the window; but his song was not more pure and true than Rachel's voice—steady and unfaltering, save when, at some too pathetic suggestion in the verse, there came the sound of tears.

"Rachel!"—the voice that called her had grown fainter than before.

She rose from her knees, and went to the bedside.

"Dear friend, I bless you for this happy hour. It was for such an hour as this I came from Sicily—for this, and to talk to your husband as I have talked to-day. He is the lost sheep of the Lord, Rachel. You must bring him home. Oh, my dear, you can do it, for he loves you, and love must conquer."

"I will try," she murmured brokenly.

"And now bid me the last good-bye. I have done with all things dear, till I recover my lost treasures in heaven. Shall we ever meet again? Shall we meet and remember, in the world of emancipated souls—spirits freed from the dominion of flesh? He whom we trust held out that blessed hope to the penitent sinner. To-morrow—the to-morrow of long years—we may be together in Paradise."

His hand was in hers as she stood beside the bed, his eyes looking up at her with unspeakable love.

She bent over him, and kissed the cold brow.

"Good-bye, St. Just," she said softly. "Your friendship has been very dear and precious to me. I shall never forget you—never cease to love your memory."

He lifted her hand to his lips, and kissed it passionately.

"Good-bye, earth," he said, and turned his face to the wall.

She kept back her tears till she was in the corridor outside, where Walsh followed her.

"I don't want to leave him," she said. "I would stay with him to the last if it were best."

"It is best for him to be alone now. He will fall into a dreamy state most likely, and pass away in his sleep. The nurse and I will keep watch."

All through the long spring day there was a silence in the spacious old house, a dumbness that seemed like the herald of death. The servants moved about the house no more than was absolutely necessary, and walked with hushed footsteps. They spent the intervals of their service in their own rooms, reading their Bibles, and breathing many a prayer for a beloved master. Every flutter of a bird's wings as it flew past an open window, every rustle of the boughs in the rising wind, seemed to have a melancholy significance, and to those simple minds whispered of the saintly soul passing from the dull grey things of earth to the rainbow light of the celestial city. The old butler and the old housekeeper sat with their open Bibles on their knees, and talked of the days that were gone—of St. Just's father, and grandfather, of his childhood, and boyhood. The head laundry-maid came to the housekeeper's room with reddened eyelids and pale cheeks. She had been under-nurse, and loved to talk of the childish illnesses through which she had helped Mrs. Roper to bring the young master. The Bible-reading and the rambling talk alternated in Mrs. Roper's room all the afternoon. There was no one but the servants in the lower part of the house; and the footmen had nothing to do but attend to the fires in the empty sitting-rooms, and shut the shutters and draw the curtains at nightfall.

At any moment they might hear that all was over. "All" in this case meaning that serviceable, unselfish life, whose years of reason had been spent in good works. At any moment the stable-messenger might be bidden to saddle his pony and carry the tidings to Trevelyan village;

and then the church bell would toll thirty times with slow and solemn sound across the darkness; and homestead and cottage would know that the landlord and master was dead. Inquirers had been coming to the lodge gates all day long—squire and parson, yeoman and cottager, from all the country round; but none had come up to the house to disturb the solemn silence around a vanishing life. The woman at the lodge had the doctor's bulletin, from hour to hour, and the inquirers left sorrowfully, being told that the case was hopeless.

Arden left the house after his interview with Rachel, and wandered over the moorland to the coast, choosing his path at random, and walking with his face seaward till he found himself standing on that rugged headland "where the great vision of the guarded mount looks toward Namancos and Bayona's hold."

He felt his burden lightened after that earnest talk with his wife, his guardian angel, as he loved to call her; but he knew not how long the tranquil mood would last, or when his haunting misery might come back upon him.

The wild beauty of hill and valley, and the granite coast that girdled them, the majesty of rocks that rose like the ramparts of a giant city, solitary and strange as a dream-picture in Christian's journey, helped to distract his mind from his intangible enemy. There was relief in having escaped from the densely peopled scenes of everyday life, to feel alone with Nature. He breathed the purer air; he gazed upon the wide expanse of sea and sky, with a new sense of liberty.

"I have hugged my ghost. I have shut myself in a prison-house with my spectral foe," he thought. "From henceforward I will fly from him. I will fling myself upon Nature's breast. I will worship mountains and rivers, sun and stars. I will cast away the consciousness of this petty stunted individuality, and lose the sense of horror in the sense of infinite beauty."

It was nearly ten o'clock when he went back to Trevelyan. Rachel was walking in the avenue, wrapped in a cloak, her hair blown about by the wind, her face pale with fear.

"Oh, Walter, what a scare you have given me!" she exclaimed, hurrying to meet him. "I was afraid some accident had happened. I thought of the most dreadful things. The stablemen have gone to look for you, and to make inquiries in the village."

"Because I was an hour or so late for dinner? My dear wife, that I should seem to neglect you, after our talk this morning! I wandered farther than I meant to go, lured on by the grandeur of the scenery—those stupendous cliffs, and the stormy sea, Tintagel, with its grim walls and romantic legends. I have been steeping myself in the wild beauty of this coast, finer than I had ever imagined it. It was dusk when I found myself in a fishing-village under the cliff, and found that I had a long way to walk home. How pale you look! Has the end come?"

"No, he is living still; but he lies half asleep. He opens his eyes sometimes and looks at the watchers, but gives no sign of recognition. Dr. Walsh thinks that consciousness has gone, never to return. Never to return here. I can but think of him as if he were now among the blessed souls in heaven."

"Ah, that is the mystery. Even your creed is vague

and wavering upon that question. In a paradise of dreamless sleep, or before the throne of God? You have no promise or assurance."

"'In my Father's house are many mansions,'" murmured Rachel.

"Vague, all vague! The children of Israel—God's chosen people—had no promise of the after-life. They were groping in the dark, and never thought that when they did well or ill they were choosing between eternal felicity and eternal pain."

"Christ brought us the promise. We can trust Him."

"Well, St. Just's life on earth was the ideal life—St. Paul's ideal—to spend and to be spent for others. He can face the great mystery without fear of the issue. Come what may, he has his reward—rest from toil, or joy unspeakable in the world we know not. Have you been with him lately?"

"I was with him for an hour this morning; and then he said good-bye, and I went away to hide my tears. Dr. Walsh thought it best that he should be alone after that. I have been sitting in my room all day. Nurse Marian has come to me from time to time and told me about him. She is a good nurse; but not so sympathetic as Nurse Ethel."

They went into the house together, and the old butler, who had been on the watch for them, ushered them into the dining-room, where all things were in readiness for the long-deferred dinner.

Rachel urged her husband to eat, having discovered that he had taken nothing all day; but she did not tell him that her only refreshment had been the tea that Nurse Marian had persuaded her to take at five o'clock.

The dinner was a mere pretence of a meal, in spite of the butler's tender ministrations. Who could eat in a house towards whose door the fatal footstep was approaching? Husband and wife sat in silence, listening for that other step on the old oak staircase, the step of the doctor coming to tell them of the end.

VIII.

The thin-spun thread held out longer than Dr. Walsh expected. Midnight struck from the big clock in the stable-yard, and St. Just still lived. He lived; but the end seemed very near—the inevitable end.

"He is sinking fast," Walsh whispered to the night-nurse, who had just taken her place at the bedside. "He will sleep till the last, most likely. I shall go and lie down in my clothes, for an hour or two. Be sure you call me if there is any change."

The nurse sat in the large armchair, watching the slumbering form, the wasted hand lying waxen white on the crimson silk coverlet. She watched the dying man with reverent gaze, knowing what manner of life he had led—a soldier of Christ, disbanded in the thick of the battle, but leaving his record of work well done, having borne such witness as few men bear to the faith that was in him—the implicit childlike faith which had been a lantern to light his steps, and a lamp shining in the distance, far away, at the end of the earthly vista, to beckon and guide him home.

Nurse Ethel was a religious woman, a member of that sect which has taken so strong a hold in the West of England—the Bible Christians. For her the solution of all life's enigmas was to be found in Holy Writ. She went to her Bible for comfort and guidance, in every sorrow and in every difficulty. And now, sitting in the silent room, in the dim light of the night-lamp, she thought of the Shunammite woman's son, and the Prophet of Israel, who gave the boy living to his mother's arms, the boy who had been dead.

Dr. Walsh had told her that there was no hope—none; but he looked at all things from his own narrow standpoint of the hospital and the dissecting-room. He spoke as a man in whom faith was utterly wanting. Alas! for the simple faith of old, the faith that made the Shunammite mother invoke the Prophet's power, albeit her child was dead. Here death had not yet come; but a good man lay sick, and in case so desperate that mortal hand could not prolong his life by a single hour. But God's hand could. There was no need of the Prophet of Israel, gifted with supernatural power. There was no need of any human intervener. The hand of Omnipotence, the invisible hand that kills and makes alive, need but to be stretched out over that dying head, and death would flee away, and life would come back to the friend of the sorrowing and the poor.

Nurse Ethel sank upon her knees beside the bed, bowed her face upon the coverlet, and prayed with the fervour of those who know not written prayer, the wild outpouring of an enthusiastic piety, belief that knew no bounds, an imagination that soared to the throne of God, and aspired even in this life to a familiar communing with Christ and His saints.

"My Redeemer and my Saviour, Saviour of Mankind, canst Thou suffer the death of this good man? Oh, loving Jesus, Thou who carest for the poor, look down and save Thy disciple and servant."

She lost herself in an ecstasy of prayer; lost count of time, lost consciousness of outer things—even of that motionless figure on the bed—in the fervour of supplications which she thought must needs be answered. She had been taught the efficacy of prayer, taught to believe in a Divine Friend whose ear was always open to the cry of the poor; and it was for them, for the poor and the forsaken, that she was pleading.

A window at the end of the room had been kept open to give air to the patient, and the wind had been rising since midnight. It was a freezing blast that startled Nurse Ethel from her ecstasy, and made her suddenly conscious of the wild shriek of the storm, shrill and loud, with a something human in its note; like the cry of a giant in agony.

She started to her feet, and bent over the bed to look and listen. The blanched face, the utter stillness, thrilled her with a sudden awe. She held her cheek above the lips of the patient. No breath touched it. She laid her ear above his heart; and there was no sound. "Oh, God, hast Thou no mercy?" While she had prayed, lifting her soul to heaven, full of faith and hope, the life she pleaded for had fled. God had refused to hear. Jesus had made no intercession. What power could she hope to exercise, she who had lived the life of common mortals, she who was not as the Man of God, the anchorite, the earthly saint, whose life had been sacrifice and obedience? Why should *her* prayers be answered; unselfish as they were, supplicating for the life of one whose face she had seen for the first time only yesterday?

The enthusiast remembered that she was a nurse on duty, and crept across the corridor to awaken the doctor. The light tap on the door roused that light sleeper, and Walsh answered her summons instantly, in shirt-sleeves and slippered feet.

"Well?" he asked, as he followed the nurse to St. Just's room.

"He is gone, sir."

"He went off quietly, as I expected?"

"He passed away in his sleep, without a struggle, without a groan."

Walsh bent over the bed for a minute in silence.

"You are mistaken, nurse," he said. "Lord St. Just is not dead."

"Oh, sir, there was not a breath from his lips, his hand was like marble."

Walsh plucked off the handkerchief which she had folded round the shrunken face.

"There is warmth and life in the hand now, and the pulse is stronger than it was this morning."

"Oh, God, I thank thee!" cried Nurse Ethel, bursting into tears.

"I had been praying for him, Dr. Walsh; praying that a good man's life might be spared," she said presently.

"Well, we shall see if your prayers are to be answered by your patient's recovery. I'm afraid that's out of the question. I have seen miraculous cures, Nurse Ethel, but I don't expect to see my poor friend rise from this bed."

He took his seat by the bed, surprised and interested, but not hopeful.

The stormy wind roared in the old Tudor chimneys all night; but when morning came the April sunshine and the soft April air filled Rachel's room with the glory of spring; that something of unspeakable loveliness that brings the glad sense of life even to desolate hearts; a momentary feeling, perhaps, followed by the bitter cry, "Oh, how can *I* be glad?"

Rachel leant out of her open window, breathing the freshness of the dawn, the scent of pale monthly roses growing round the casement—the first roses of the year—and of a bed of violets in the border below. She had spent the night in sleeplessness and prayer, while Arden slept heavily, worn out by the day's toil. She had crept along the corridor several times in those long, slow hours, to listen outside St. Just's door. All had been still; and she thought that silence meant death. She wept for him as for the dead; not the dead as the materialist counts his lost ones, dead for ever and for ever; but as the friend who has gone before, from the finite to the infinite, from the transient to the eternal. She was sorry with the sorrow that can find instant comfort in hope.

Nurse Ethel came to her at six o'clock, as she had promised overnight, tearful and agitated, but smiling through her tears.

"Oh, Mrs. Arden, I am so happy! He has lived through the night. He rallied at two o'clock, after I thought he was dead. Oh, I shall never forget that marble hand, those breathless lips! I had been praying

God to save him, asking Jesus to plead for that precious life. And I thought he was gone; and then came the sudden rally. Dr. Walsh is as much surprised as I was. His pulse is ever so much better this morning, and the temperature not quite so high. He has taken milk and brandy greedily—as if he wanted to live. Oh, dear Mrs. Arden, doesn't it seem as if our prayers had been heard?" added the enthusiast, with dilated eyes, and clasped hands.

"Yes, nurse, we know that our prayers are heard, even when the blessing we pray for is withheld. The Divine wisdom hears and judges. But can this change really mean recovery? Does Dr. Walsh think——"

"Oh, he won't speak out, Mrs. Arden; they never do. They treat us poor nurses like the dirt under their feet—very polite, some of them. 'Good morning, nurse,' and all that; but no confidence, and always thinking what we do is wrong, if it isn't to the very letter of their orders. No, we mustn't think for ourselves; though we are there to judge, and they are miles away. Dr. Walsh says he's astonished, and that's all he'll vouchsafe to *me*. He'll speak plainer to you and Mr. Arden, no doubt."

"Has St. Just awakened and spoken to you?"

"No; he lies asleep. He was half asleep even when I gave him the milk and the meat jelly. Oh, I feel sure he will recover. He may not live to be old, poor dear, with his weak chest, but he will get over this illness."

"It is very good of you to have felt so deeply for him."

"Oh, Mrs. Arden, that's my disposition. When I take to a patient, I do take to him; and I'd go through fire and water, or sit up six nights running, and not have three hours off in the day. And after what you told me about his lordship's goodness to the poor, giving up all his life to help others, I felt as if I was attending upon a saint. And I never prayed, never in my life, no not even for my own grandfather—for, after all, *his* death was a happy release—as I prayed last night. My spirit seemed lifted up to heaven. It was as if I was kneeling on the threshold of the golden gates."

"Well, nurse, we will not cease to pray, with thankful hearts; and now go and give yourself a few hours' good sleep."

"I'm going to bed, for Dr. Walsh says I *must;* but I'm much too excited and happy to sleep. Nurse Marian is as cool as a cucumber. She don't take to her cases as I do, and she hasn't sat under Mr. Cobbledick."

"Is that the vicar of your church at Launceston?"

"Oh dear, no, Mrs. Arden; none of your vicars for me! I was born and bred a Bible Christian. Mr. Cobbledick is minister at our chapel, an apostle, if ever there was one, and a first-class tailor by trade."

Arden had slept late, after his long tramp in the wind and rain; he had slept the sleep of exhaustion, and woke refreshed, and feeling himself a new man. He thought of his wife with unspeakable affection. She loved him still, in spite of his neglect. It was sweet to know that. He had let her see something of his trouble, of that darkened mind which made the sun a burden. His mind was more tranquil than it had been for a long time. That profound and dreamless sleep had soothed his nerves. He went out onto the terrace, and rejoiced in the morning freshness, the glory of flowers and foliage, blooming with the luxuriance of summer, in that mild climate, sheltered by the pine-clad hills that rose between the gardens and the sea.

He wondered if the closing scene had been acted during the night-silence; and suddenly, while he was thinking of St. Just, the man who had been to him once as a friend and counsellor, there came upon him the memory of that other friend, the humble friend of his Alaskan journey, his companion in labour and in rest after toil, the bold, strong spirit he had admired and loved. There came back to him the memory of that long tramp by the ice-bound river, when he and Stormont had been told that the end was near; and then there came into his mind, with lurid reality, the horror that had followed the miraculous recovery of a fast-ebbing life.

He turned at the end of the walk, and saw Rachel coming towards him, her white gown radiant in the morning sunshine, and a smile upon her lips.

"I have some good news for you," she said. "I have just seen Dr. Walsh. He is wonder-struck at the change in his patient. He says St. Just may weather the storm. Those were his very words; and he declares it will be a most remarkable case."

Arden looked at her with wild eyes, the look of a man who thinks he sees a ghost.

"Dear Walter, surely you are glad?" she exlaimed, scared by that strange look.

"Glad! No; I can't believe it. The man was dying —Walsh told me there was not a ray of hope. The doctor from Bude said the same. They had given him over. When did the change begin?"

"At two o'clock this morning. There was no one with him but Nurse Ethel. She had been watching him as he slept, and she thought that he was dead, and then the turn came——"

"She thought that he was dead? She had fallen asleep herself, perhaps?"

"No; she had been praying for him."

"Praying when she should have been watching. I must see Walsh immediately."

"He is waiting for us to go in to breakfast. But, Walter, are you not glad of this improvement? You speak so strangely. Surely you must wish that good man's life to be spared."

"That good man's life—yes. If *he* could be spared!"

He went hurriedly to the house, Rachel following him, surprised and pained by his manner. What could it mean, that look of horror, when she told him of the happy change? Could it be that he wanted St. Just to die? He had said that he was not jealous, had assured her of his perfect confidence; but this strange reception of her news alarmed her. Was it possible that he had secretly resented her friendship for St. Just, and that he had looked forward to his death as the removal of a rival in his wife's affection? Could it be that her husband, the man in whose nobility of mind she had believed, was capable of doing her this great wrong, capable of desiring a good man's death?

They sat down to breakfast with the young doctor, who took his coffee and grilled chicken and ham with a professional calm, while neither Arden nor his wife was able to eat. The meal passed almost in silence, and as they rose from the table, Arden asked Walsh to give him a few minutes' talk in the library.

"I am anxious to know your opinion about your patient's chance of recovery," he said.

"Then you had better wait till Dr. Dever has seen him, and we have talked over the symptoms, and then you can have our joint opinion," replied Walsh, who was standing by an open window looking down the drive. "There's his cart!"

The wheels sounded from far off in the crisp morning air.

"Very well, I'll wait," answered Arden.

"In the meantime, to relieve your anxiety, I may tell you that in my opinion there's an even chance of St. Just's recovery."

"And you are surprised?"

"As much surprised as a doctor ever ought to be, knowing as much as he ought to know of the mystery of human life, and the immeasurable power of certain constitutions to fight with disease and death."

Arden paced the terrace from end to end, while the two doctors were with their patient, blind to the beauty of the sunlit park and the far-off sea, showing through a gap in the hills. He spent nearly half an hour tramping to and fro, pausing in front of the open hall-door now and then, to watch and listen for any movement in the house; and at last when the time seemed endless, he heard the two doctors coming downstairs, conversing cheerfully about the weather and the young wheat, with that air of indifference which tortures a sick man's friends. They went into the library together; and Arden flung himself into one of the Glastonbury chairs in the porch, to wait a summons from Walsh. He waited a little more than ten minutes—minutes of intolerable length—before the young man came out to him.

Dr. Dever was walking up and down the library, a tall man, well set-up, with a fine open-air look, and a keen professional expression, very much the sportsman, but not the less the doctor.

"Well, doctor, your colleague waited for your opinion before he would give me a plain answer. What do you think of this case?"

"Only that it is the most wonderful case I have seen in the last ten years."

"A kind of miracle?"

"As near a miracle as one can expect to meet with in our day. I gave your friend over when I first put my stethoscope to his chest on Wednesday evening. I would have laid fifty to one against his recovery—and there he is, fighting for life, with a will-power I have rarely seen."

"And you, Walsh, do you call this almost a miracle?"

"It makes me more inclined to believe in the Resurrection."

"Oh, Dr. Walsh, we do not bring science to bear on the Gospels," remonstrated Dever.

"The man was sinking fast at midnight; and at ten minutes past three his pulse was stronger than it had been eighteen hours before. It was the arrest of death rather than the return of life. The case is remarkable; but as I—as Dr. Dever and I think, it is the case of an intense vitality acting upon a fragile frame, the conquest of will over matter."

"Undoubtedly," said Dever.

"It sets one's mind wondering what this will-power is that can overrule the conditions of flesh. It certainly is a force outside the scope of medical diagnosis. From my personal knowledge of St. Just, after living with him nearly a year, I thought he would have slipped out of life without a struggle. Never could I have anticipated this fierce fight for existence in such a man."

"And can he go on living?"

"Yes; if he can get over this attack, he may live for years, with care. Post-mortem research has shown that the active mischief may be arrested, and the wounded lung may scar over; and although the injured organ can never regain the functions of the healthy organ, the man may live; if he will be satisfied with a restricted existence, a life regulated by medical control. For the sake of the poor of London, I hope that St. Just may survive this crisis for many years, or even to be an old man."

"Then, after all our talk of miracles, this case comes within ordinary conditions, within the limits of the possible?"

Walsh smiled at the question, and wondered at the questioner's agitated manner of asking it.

"Within the limits of the possible—yes. I suppose we all use the word miraculous in a modern sense. But it is by no means an ordinary case."

Dr. Dever was looking out of the window, a little

bored by this interrogation from a layman. Surely it was enough for Mr. Arden to be told that his friend had a chance of recovery.

"I must be getting on the road again," he said; "I have to drive ten miles to my next patient. Good day, Walsh. I shall look in at the same time to-morrow. Good day, Mr. Arden."

Walsh went with him to his dogcart, in which he had put a young horse that he was breaking in for next winter's hunting, and which was employing his superfluous energy on the gravel drive.

"Nice-looking young 'un, ain't he?" Dr. Dever asked cheerily. "Rather too good for leather! But it makes 'em handy, and gives 'em a taste of the hills. He'll feel it a game to carry me over our country, after having the cart behind him;" and with a jovial wave of his doe-skin glove, Dr. Dever took leave of his brother practitioner.

"Country *versus* town," thought Robert Walsh, sniffing the fresh morning air, and watching the smart dogcart trundling down the avenue behind the eager young horse. And then he thought of the fœtid alleys, the insanitary tenement houses in which his medical experience had lain; the sickness, and hunger, and dirt; the misery he had been powerless to help, and for which the only panacea was the hospital or the workhouse.

Town *versus* country; and the strength and intelligence of the land is all drifting to the town! He remembered a London workhouse under the smoke-darkened sky, hemmed round with bricks and mortar, and he thought of the Union at Stratton, which they had passed on their way from the station; a grey stone house in a garden, with windows that all looked to the sea or the wooded hills; a building that he had taken for the home of some prosperous squire, till St. Just enlightened him.

IX.

From Walter Arden to Douglas Campbell.

Klosterberg, Switzerland,
June 15th, 189-.

MY DEAR DOUGLAS,

Strange things have happened since I received your comforting answer to my last letter, and again I find myself dominated by the same hideous idea that made my life by the Klondyke river a time to look back upon with horror: again I find myself in the power of a spirit from hell, recreated in the human semblance of an earthly saint. I think I must have told you in previous letters of our intimate acquaintance with St. Just, the well-known philanthropist, a man of strong religious bias and saintly character, who, during the time of my miserable isolation, became my wife's helper and counsellor in her mission of charity. Unfortunately for the poor of London, he broke down under the strain of incessant work, and after nearly a year's absence in Southern Italy, came back to his Cornish birthplace in a dying state, given over by every doctor who had seen him.

He came home to die; and he summoned Rachel and me to his death-bed. No pang of jealousy had ever disturbed my mind. I knew my wife's purity of soul, and I knew St. Just's fine nature, lifted above the things of earth by a profound belief in the Unseen, an absolute submission to the law of an unknown God. I admired and revered that perfect faith which Fate or character had denied to me. I had never been jealous of his influence, or doubted his honour; but in that letter from a dying man I read the secret of a despairing love; and I felt that I had wronged both St. Just and my wife by the desertion which had given him the privilege of too close a friendship. I submitted that dying appeal to Rachel; and, at her desire, we started for Cornwall without an hour's delay. We found our friend apparently at the last extremity, but with his mind as luminous as in his best day, and his spirits exalted by the piety of the Christian enthusiast, for whom, in old Sir Thomas Browne's happy phrase, "Death is the Lucina of Life."

He had his resident doctor—a young man who had been with him on his yacht for nearly a year—and two hospital nurses, in close attendance upon him; and these three people assured me, each unprompted by the other, that the case was hopeless, and the end only a question of hours. An experienced general practitioner from the neighbourhood, who had attended St. Just from his childhood, was of the same opinion. Not one of these persons entertained the faintest hope, or expressed the slightest uncertainty. The case had passed beyond the chance of any change for the better.

I saw St. Just on the morning after our arrival, when he had received the last sacrament, and had, as it were, closed the book of religious observances. He talked to me of my mental trouble, which I had confided to him in an hour of supreme depression, and of the influence of that trouble on my wife. He spoke of Rachel with a pathetic earnestness, urging me to confide in her, and to look to her for the lifting of the shadow from my life; to look to her as my guide to that peace of mind which passeth all understanding. When I had clasped his feeble hand, and bent in silence over the emaciated form, I left him with the conviction that we had parted for ever. His words had affected me deeply, and they had inspired me with a faint hope that by Rachel's aid I might escape from the self-torments of the past. I went straight to her, and in that solemn hour, with death hovering near, as I believed, I bared my mind to her as I had never done before, yet keeping the secret of my misery. It was enough to tell her of a mind tortured to the verge of madness, and to throw myself upon her pitying love for help and consolation. I am thankful to say that from that hour she has been my friend and comforter, and that our union has become again as perfect as in those cloudless years when I thought my spectral foe was banished for ever.

You will remember the history of Michael Dartnell's illness in our hut by the Klondyke river, and of a return to life so sudden, so swift, so altogether strange as to touch the border-line of the miraculous; a restoration to life that was followed by a total change in the character of the man, so that the creature who rose up from Michael's sick-bed, wearing his form and substance, had no quality or characteristic of the creature who lay there at the point of death. It may be that such a transformation in the nature of a man who has gone so near the final dissolution is not unknown to experience, that, in a malady which brings the subject so close to actual extinction, there may arise some subtle change in the brain of the man, the original intelligence fading into blankness, and a new mind being born in its place—new instincts, animal instincts, the vilest side of human nature, where previously the brain had held only generous impulses and noble desires. I have never heard of such a case; but it seems to me not impossible—the case of a mind new-born, and born for evil instead of for good.

But in that last tragic experience of the Klondyke Rapids there had flashed upon me the horrible idea that in this loathsome being I beheld, not my old friend, but a new incarnation of the man I killed, and whose blood-bespattered lips had menaced me with an undying hate —a hate that should survive the clay I saw before me—inexorable, unextinguishable. I had known the fulfilment of that hideous threat in the haunting invisible presence that had made this gracious, beautiful earth a hell; and it was but natural that I should recognise a new form of that horror in the murderer who stood over me on the waters of the Klondyke. Hallucination, perhaps; but to me reality. Only to you, Douglas, dare I write freely of these things, by reason of your dabblings in occult science, and your willingness to consider, if not to accept, every form of the supernatural, whether it bring us "airs from heaven or blasts from hell."

You will bear with me then when I tell you of my instant feeling of horror when on the morning after my farewell conversation with St. Just I was told that he had taken a most unexpected turn for the better, rallying in a manner which his doctor called little short of the miraculous. The night-nurse, a somewhat hysterical young woman, had actually thought him dead. She told me afterwards, with dilated eyes, how she had held her cheek above his livid lips, and had not felt the faintest breath; how she had touched his lifeless hand; before she went to awaken the doctor, who was resting in a room close by, and to tell him that the momently expected end had come.

History repeats itself, no doubt, in medical experience as in public events; but this close resemblance to the case in the log-hut filled me with a horror which I could not overcome, and which it was difficult to hide from Rachel.

In vain I struggled against the hideous suggestion: in vain I told myself that I was harbouring a delusion that might end in madness. I could not believe that the man lying in the room upstairs, unconscious, but with a vitality that was a marvel to those who watched him, eating, drinking, sleeping, with an animal enjoyment of sensual comfort, was the man with whom I had parted, after those earnest and pathetic words which had gone home to my heart.

The nurse Ethel, whose excitable temperament was kept in a fever by the surprises and perplexities of the case, came to Rachel from time to time with her account of the sick man. She is one of those irrepressible people whose communicativeness is not easily checked; and in those hours when life trembled in the balance and death hovered near, Rachel had, no doubt, encouraged her to talk. As the days went on, all that she told us of St.

Just in the awakening of consciousness filled me with horror. She wept as she described his altered bearing—an impatience that amounted to brutality, rough gestures, violent language. She wept as she told us how sweet and Christian a gentleman he had seemed to her during the earlier part of her attendance. She admitted that illness often made a startling change in the disposition of a patient. The best of husbands would be fretful and unkind to a devoted wife; mothers, sisters, nurses even, would be snubbed and treated with rudeness. But the alteration in St. Just was more startling, more perplexing, than any deterioration of character that had come within her experience. The fierce light in his eyes when he was angered by having his medicine pressed upon him, the roughness with which he pushed away the hand that held the glass, were so unlike his former gentleness. Every detail of his conduct surprised and scared her.

"He is not the same man, Mrs. Arden," she exclaimed, in conclusion.

He had been conscious for twenty-four hours, and he had not asked to see my wife or me; and on hearing from the resident doctor that he might now be considered out of danger, and in a fair way to such partial recovery as a man in his condition would hope for—a patching up of the damaged lungs which might carry on the life for some time—I persuaded Rachel to go back to London with me. We had done what we had been asked to do. We had gratified the wish of a man who thought himself dying; and now the man had been restored to life, and there could be no reason for our presence in his house. If, as I had reason to believe, his attachment to Rachel had been something deeper than friendship, a despairing love kept nobly in check, there was every reason why their paths in life should henceforward lie wide apart. For myself, tortured by the hideous suspicion of a supernatural substitution of a spirit of evil for a spirit of good, every hour that I spent at Trevelyan was a time of horror. I breathed more freely as St. Just's horses carried us to the station; and the thought of our cosy London house was no longer painful to me. The invisible presence no longer hung over me like a cloud. The spirit from hell had now its habitation in mortal flesh, and was no longer a disembodied malignity haunting and overshadowing my life. I had to do now with a man, and not with a ghost.

To write these words is to admit that the horrible idea, which even you may look upon as the delusion of a disorganised intellect, had by the time I left Trevelyan become an absolute belief. It was so. I left the Cornish manor-house with the conviction that the man who was master there was no longer the beneficent and holy-minded St. Just, but the re-incarnation of the heartless profligate, whose vicious career my sword had cut short

To be once more with Rachel, free from the loathsome presence, was bliss unspeakable. I sunned myself in the atmosphere of her love. We went about among the old scenes and the old faces together, as in the days when we were lovers, whose love had not yet found a voice. It was my delight to go back into the old paths, to talk with the old acquaintances, who welcomed my return with enthusiasm. I was reproached for my desertion: I was praised for coming back to them. My heart went out to these humble friends with warm affection. They were so human; and there was unspeakable comfort in this humanity, for me who had been existing in that frozen region of mysterious influences that lies beyond the limit of human feeling and human knowledge.

Nothing in that darker London where Father Romney's mission lay seemed to me common or unclean. My fellow-man, however low he had sunk in the vices of the abject poor, seemed to me as an angel of light compared with that unseen enemy from an unknown world. At his worst he was a creature of feelings like my own; and I could appeal to him as man to man. Never had I worked more earnestly, or with better results, than I worked last May, from the beginning till the end of the month.

It was late in May that I met Dr. Walsh, the young medical man who had been with Lord St. Just on his yacht, and had helped to bring him from Palermo to his house in Cornwall, when he was supposed to be at the point of death. We ran against each other in the Commercial Road; and I found that Walsh was now living in that neighbourhood, where he had been practising when Lord St. Just found him in broken health, and carried him off for a sea-voyage.

I asked him when he left Cornwall. I could not bring myself to make any inquiry about his patient.

He told me that he had been in London a fortnight; and then he continued in words that I shall try to render faithfully—words to which I listened with acute interest.

"You see, Mr. Arden, there are some things worse than dirt and squalor, worse even than suffering, before which a man stands helpless, a witness of miseries he has no power to lessen. I thought my experience in this neighbourhood was about the worst that life had to offer me; but I have had a worse experience in Cornwall since you left Trevelyan. I have seen a man whom I loved and honoured, a man whose beautiful nature had been my wonder and delight, as much my wonder and delight after nearly a year's closest intimacy, the life of every day spent in each other's company, as it was in the first days of our acquaintance. I have seen that man's character changed in every attribute, that spiritual nature degraded to a debased animalism, that lovely temper changed to fierce impatience of the faintest contradiction, and become savage and overbearing beyond endurance; yet the man capable on occasion of simulating every charm of manner and bearing with which a profligate can beguile a woman's simplicity or impose upon his fellow-man."

I asked him if in his medical experience he had ever known such a change following upon such an illness as St. Just's.

"Not such a change," he replied. "But I have known a man become a lunatic after a severe attack of influenza; and I suspect that this change in St. Just is an indication of obscure brain-disease, which might ultimately take the form of acute mania. It would be a very interesting case to watch, for a man who had not loved the original St. Just; but it was too painful for me. I couldn't stick it any longer. I left Trevelyan as if I had had the devil behind me."

I asked him if St. Just meant to remain long in Cornwall. Walsh thought not. He had expressed contempt and hatred for the place. He who had been the most abstemious of men had taken to drinking heavily, to the amazement and distress of the old butler, who had even ventured on a mild remonstrance, which brought upon him a burst of fury from his master.

"I never saw a man so cowed or so bewildered," Walsh told me. "He complained to me afterwards, with tears in his poor old eyes, that it was the first time his lordship had ever spoken to him in anger. 'And I don't think I deserved it,' said the old man, 'for I spoke for his lordship's good, seeing he was only just beginning to get his strength back again.' It was not the last time he was to experience the rough side of his master's tongue," Walsh added, "for the slightest shortcoming in the service brought a storm of abuse on the old servants; and yet I never saw better servants or more careful service. Dr. Dever told me that the household had been trained by Lady St. Just, who was a woman of remarkable capacity in small as well as in great things. To hear these old servants abused got upon my nerves, and I let St. Just see what I thought of him; and so, gradually, our friendship cooled, and I took myself off."

I asked him if he thought St. Just would live long. His answer was in the negative. Wonderful as the recovery had been, he did not think his patient could last long. The frame was fragile, and the constitution enfeebled by a life of anxious endeavour in the Sisyphus labours of a reformer, rolling stones uphill and having them roll back upon him, accomplishing the preliminary steps in some good cause, only to find himself baffled by the lukewarm spirit of those for whom he worked. Walsh did not believe the wasted frame and injured lungs could hold out many years.

"It is a case in which an intense vitality has conquered death," he said. "St. Just has been kept alive by the force of an indomitable will; and his hold upon life, I take it, henceforth will be the hold of the mind rather than the flesh. His vehemence, his impatience, his eagerness for sensual pleasures, such as wine and food, warmth and sleep, indicate an intense vitality, and a predominant self-love."

Walsh had heard nothing of his patient since he left Trevelyan; but he opined that St. Just would not remain in Cornwall an hour after he felt himself strong enough to travel. He had talked of his London house, questioning Walsh about it in a curious way, as if he had forgotten what it was like. He had spoken of other things relating to his past life in the same vague way; and Walsh thought that his memory had suffered in the illness which had wrought such an extraordinary deterioration of character.

"The contradictions and perplexities of the case are more startling than anything that has come within my experience," Walsh said, in conclusion, "and whenever I can get a leisure evening, I shall write a detailed description of the illness and recovery for the *Lancet*, of course withholding the patient's name, in the hope that it may produce accounts of other cases of a similar nature."

Some days after my chance meeting with the doctor, I saw a paragraph in a morning paper to the effect that Lord St. Just, who had made a complete recovery from his serious illness of the winter and spring, had arrived at his house in Portland Place for the season.

Rachel read the announcement as we sat at breakfast.

"For the season!" she exclaimed, laughing. "How unlike St. Just that sounds! I don't think he knew when the season began or ended."

I told her that if they were to meet, she would find the St. Just of to-day very unlike the friend she had known in the past, but that I hoped she would never see his face again. And then I repeated Walsh's account of his patient, to which she listened with sorrowful surprise.

She was silent and grave for some time afterwards, and then she reminded me of the morning when I heard of St. Just's wonderful recovery, and the strangeness of my manner on that occasion.

"You had a look of absolute horror," she said, "as if something dreadful had happened. Could you have had any foreboding of this change in his nature? Had you ever known such a case in your past life?"

I admitted that I had known a restoration to life as seemingly miraculous, followed by a hideous transformation in the nature of the man who recovered; and that I had been filled with an uncontrollable horror when I heard of circumstances which seemed absolutely to repeat that past history. And now that Walsh's experience had realised my fear, I implored my wife never again to think of St. Just as a friend, or even to allow him to cross her threshold as a guest.

She answered with the sweet submission with which she had always yielded to any wish of mine.

"Of course I shall do as you tell me, Walter; and now I have your help and advice in all our work, I don't want any other helper. But all the same, I believe this dreadful change in St. Just to be only a passing phase, a deterioration that has to do with weak health, and not with character. He will go back to his philanthropic work, and the old tenderness of heart will return. I cannot believe that so good a man could become debased and unworthy."

I had spoken only just in time. The weather that day was too bad for our East End peregrinations, and I spent the afternoon at my club, where I had been so long a stranger, and where I now found myself, as it were, among a generation "who knew not Joseph," so completely had I dropped out of the old easy-going intimacies of billiard and card-rooms. When I went home at tea-time, I found St. Just's cards in the hall. He had called twice, the butler told me, and had been very pressing in his inquiries as to when Mrs. Arden was to be found at home.

This decided me upon a step which I had been considering all day; and over the tea-table, set in front of a window in my wife's pretty drawing-room, I reminded her of our conversation some months ago, when she had offered to go with me to some romantic spot, remote from the world, where we might live happily together in a tranquil solitude. She had not forgotten. She was ready to go with me anywhere, near or far; although she would be sorry to leave the neighbourhood of her father and mother, who liked so much to have her near them, and often in their house.

I should add that since our reunion, and my happier frame of mind, we had been frequent visitors in Carlton House Terrace; and I had been received with the utmost kindness by Mr. and Mrs. Lorimer, who refrained from all allusions to my past isolation, my churlish refusal of their hospitality.

And now I felt that London would be intolerable. I could not live in peace in the city that held St. Just. It would be hopeless to try to keep him at a distance. The indomitable will which I had known on the shores of the Yukon river, the brute force that had flourished in the Miner's City, would again be set in opposition to me and my happiness, this time under a smoother outward garb, with perhaps even some semblance of refinement. And this time the point of attack would not be myself, but the wife I adored, the lovely and innocent woman whose pure mind could not conceive the wickedness of a spirit from hell.

From hell! Laugh at me, the unbeliever, to whom all the hierarchy of heaven has seemed as mythic as the Homeric gods! I have learnt to believe in a hell; a bottomless pit peopled with evil spirits; a hell from which the children of darkness are sent out to war against the children of light. I have advanced so far from the barren waste of materialism. I have learnt to believe in devils.

My sweet wife assented without a murmur to an indefinite period of separation from her kith and kin, and from the work which she loves only a little less than she loves father and mother. It was decided that we would go first to Klosterberg, a village above the Lake of Thun, which I had discovered in my Swiss rambles, a quiet little place, four thousand feet above the sea, a place of wooded hills, and winding paths, and a luxury of wild-flowers; and it is from this delicious retreat, which is happily known to very few people at this present time, that I am writing to you.

We have found a *châlet* on the slope of a wooded hill above the village; a humble wooden house, with wide covered balconies on each side, and a *façade* decorated with pious adages, a garden running over with common English flowers, which here have larger and more luxuriant blossoms, and a more brilliant colouring, than in England. We have our man and maid, old and tried servants both, and three stalwart Swiss maidens in short skirts and velvet bodices, adorned with massive silver chains. We wander in the woods, or sit in picturesque spots with the books we love best, and in the tranquil afternoons sit in our garden, and dream our day-dreams to the music of the cow-bells in the pastures, that slope from our hedge, at an acute angle, down to the shore of the lake. We have adopted a St. Bernard puppy, which Rachel adores; and she has found something to do in visiting the peasants, and in ministering to their children, most especially to the poor half-witted creatures who are too common in this part of the world; and I think I may say that we are perfectly happy. But how long this elysian bliss may last I know not. For me there must ever be a shadow and a fear, while that spirit of evil walks the earth, in palpable or impalpable form.

X.

"St. Just has chucked the East End," was the careless comment of the clubs, after the well-known philanthropist had been seen about London in those resorts of pleasure where he had been a stranger hitherto.

The men of his own age, men about town, the idle and the dissipated, who had looked upon the philanthropist as a creature of another world, a prig, perhaps a hypocrite, and most certainly a person whose acquaintance they did not desire, were surprised and amused by the change which had reduced him to their own level, a haunter of the music-hall and the night-club, a worshipper of venal beauty, a patron of prize-fights, a determined backer of his fancy on the racecourse, winning or losing with an equal imperturbability.

"At this rate he will soon run through his money," said a man who had watched his aspect under heavy losses.

"Oh, he wins much oftener than he loses," said another. "St. Just has a long head, and knows how to make a safe book."

"There's no more desperate rake than a reformed saint," said a third speaker. "When I meet St. Just on the prowl in the wickedest streets of London, after two o'clock in the morning, and remember him on the platform at a temperance lecture, or as a leading light in rescue work, I find myself echoing Macbeth's question—

> "'Can such things be, and overcome us like a summer cloud,
> Without our special wonder?'"

"My dear fellow, there are very few things that can't be, in this enlightened century; and the stranger the thing is the more likely to be true."

To the London world in general St. Just's new mode of life was a matter of slightest importance; but to the little world of philanthropic London his defection was a heavy blow. His old friends left the big house in Portland Place, surprised and wounded, after being told that he meant to cut his connection with the numerous charitable organisations of which he had been the generous and honoured leader. Seldom in the history of philanthropic endeavour had there been so sad a falling away. His manner and his words had an insolence that forbade argument; and men who had admired and loved him left his house in sorrow and in anger, shaking the dust off their feet, and meaning never again to cross his threshold, while a Jewish missionary, white-haired and patriarchal, spat upon the renegade's doorstep, in solemn abjuration. He had talked of his past work with a brutal levity, telling them that he was sick of the poor and all their ways; a rabble of ungrateful curs, who would drain a man's last drop of blood like vampires, and leave his carcase to rot on a dunghill.

"You have been very near the gates of death, St. Just," said an elderly Rector, from the east of London, an indefatigable labourer in a troublesome vineyard, where the vines for the most part brought forth wild grapes, very sour and bitter to the taste. "You have been through the valley of the shadow; and upon most Christians such an experience has a softening influence. A year ago, when you bade us good-bye in this house, we left you in sorrow, few of us hoping ever to see your face again. And now I tell you frankly that I would rather that had been our last parting in this world, than that I should hear you talk as you have talked to-day."

If Lord St. Just's altered character made but a slight impression upon the men among whom his new existence was spent, it created a considerable sensation among the women whose society he cultivated. He was unpopular in masculine circles; for his splendours and arrogant bearing were accounted "bad form;" and he took no trouble to make friends among his own sex. He was a fine card-player, but he played with a ferocious intensity which made him disliked either as a partner or an opponent; and men who owned race-horses soon began to think of him as a bringer of bad luck, since on several occasions the favourite had gone down before some rank outsider upon which St. Just was afterwards discovered to have piled his money. Men rather avoided him; but upon the women of that class which lives only for amusement, St. Just exercised a potent influence. The mothers of fair daughters looked doubtfully upon him; since at his rate of living the St. Just property could not hold out many years, and he could not therefore be considered a good *parti;* but the daughters listened with a too indulgent ear to his insidious flatterings; and the semi-detached wives, who could regulate their existence according to their own fancy, cultivated his society with a reckless indifference to character or morals, trifling with his attentions; as the moth glances across the flame, confident in the strength of his wings, to escape the destroying fire.

Lady Mary Selby was conspicuous among that particular set in which St. Just shone as a star. She was one of the women who had taken him up; and she made him the ornament of those small dinners for which she was celebrated, dinners at which the women all belonged to her own esoteric circle, and at which the men came from all the four winds—literary, musical, painters, sculptors, architects, actors, journalists, inventors, speculators; the notorieties of the passing hour, forgotten next year. These were charmed to meet St. Just, whom they regarded as an interesting study, a modern D'Orsay, whose foppery was spiced with the insolence of an age of free thought in art and morals; and as none of these transient acquaintance presumed to be in love with Lady Mary, St. Just had the field to himself.

Mrs. Kelvin contrived to be at most of these merry little parties, going so far even as to ask her friend to ask her, if there were too long an interval between the invitations.

"Your dinners are adorable; and you have such a power of attracting the right people," she said. "Don't forget me, Mary, when you have anyone extra nice."

Two years ago Mrs. Kelvin had given up St. Just in despair. She was now more hopeful. The shoulders and arms and swan-like throat evidently made an impression; the flashing glances of fine eyes were no longer ineffectual fires. She felt that there might have been a chance of a baron's coronet on her writing-paper, if Mary Selby had not been in the way; handsome, daring, and not wanting the man for a husband, which might make all the difference in her value to the man himself.

Lady Mary had avoided even the faintest approach to flirtation, since the scene in the Parisian restaurant. People who had talked about her in the past had left off talking, or agreed to praise her for her goodness in putting up with such a husband as Selby; not giving her credit for really liking the man as a friend and comrade, if not with a romantic attachment. Selby worshipped his handsome wife, and made her the confidante of all his financial schemes, associating her with every success; and she had gradually become keenly interested in the operations by which money was doubled or quadrupled on the stock-exchanges of Europe. Her subtle brain delighted even in the risks, the touch-and-go of a financier's career, being assured that Selby would never hazard the house that sheltered her, or the income that maintained her comfort. He had resources with which he could afford to gamble, a capital so far beyond the needs even of a fine lady, that it seemed justifiable to run big hazards in order to achieve big results. He laid all his plans before his wife. He had the highest opinion of her judgment, and a superstitious belief in her luck. Theirs was an ideal union, as compared with the marriages of most of their neighbours.

Mary had always prided herself upon keeping "straight," and never till she met Konstantin Manville had her honour been in peril. That peril had left her mind and conscience seared and branded; as of one who had passed through the fiery furnace of sin, and about whom the smell of fire still hung. She remembered the man with horror, yet remembered a fascination that had made him irresistible; and she remembered with a deeper horror that period after his death, in which she had been perpetually haunted by his image, a shadow that made solitude unbearable.

She pretended at first to ridicule the change in St. Just; but by degrees the man began to exercise a subtle influence which made his society almost a necessity to her. He gave new colour to her life, and made old things seem hateful. She could not even pretend to be interested in her husband's financial operations. She turned a cold eye upon his pass-book, which she had been wont to accept as the most attractive form of literature. Gain or loss, thousands or hundreds of thousands, on the right hand or the left, no longer concerned her. She told Selby that figures made her head ache; and he shut the book submissively, with spirits dashed by her coldness, having thought to astonish her by the evidence of a *coup* on the mineral market.

Alas, for Mary Selby! She had entered upon a new phase of her existence, in which she cared no more for loss or gain, or for any of the common things of this work-a-day world. What was the influence that subjugated her? Was it love or fear? It seemed to her sometimes that there was more of repulsion than of attraction in the sensations which St. Just's presence evoked. She feared his coming; yet life was dull and motiveless in his absence. There were moments when the sound of his voice, a flashing glance from the grey eyes, a word, a gesture, recalled days that were gone, an infatuation that she remembered with shame, for which she had wept remorseful tears, and whispered penitential prayers, on her knees in one of those dim churches she loved, where the muffled bass of the organ and the faint odours of incense seemed to belong to a better world. She had repented of that unholy dream. She knew that she had sinned in thought, and that she had been on the brink of hell. She recalled Manville's poisonous words in the box at the Paris opera-house, when they two sat alone in the shadow of the velvet curtain, when he held her hand for the last time, and breathed his passionate prayer in her ear, while the harsh brasses in the orchestra, the clang of cymbals, and beat of drums, rang loud in the pandemonium below. That low whisper was heard above all the uproar of voices, and dancing feet, and cornet and trombone. She knew that she had been on the edge of the pit that night, the Tophet to which fallen women go down, lost to their place and name. Only her brother's interposition had saved her. From the supper-room to the Vienna express, *en route* for Petersburg, would have been the next stage in her life-journey. She knew that her resolution had begun to waver, that a will-power stronger than her own was gaining the mastery.

She remembered her vision of him as they found him two days afterwards, lying alone under the open sky, in a shabby outskirt of the great city, in his blood-stained shirt. His image had haunted her with a maddening persistence for a year after that dreadful doom. She had not dared to be alone, had scarcely dared to look round, even in the midst of a brilliant assembly;

lest she should see the man himself, the dead man alive, with the mysterious life of ghosts, pointing to the mortal wound, killed because of her folly.

And now, after years of peace, something of that old feeling had come back. Mind and senses again were subjugated. She was no longer Mary Selby, the woman of the world, the kindly, generous, honest wife of an honest man. She knew that she was at heart a wanton. She was glad of her husband's absence. She listened for a footstep. She counted the hours of St. Just's absence. She was under a spell. Was it love or fear? She knew that a thrill of fear stirred her heart at his approach; that the sound of his voice subjugated her, as lions are subdued by the lion-tamer. She had made up her mind to keep to that straight line which she had drawn for her future life, when she resigned herself to the humdrum of a loveless marriage. She had asked herself which was best, wealth or love? a life of ease with all the things she wanted, or a brief dream of bliss—a honeymoon and an awakening? She had seen such marriages among her bosom friends—a year of infatuation, and then grumblings and lamentings about the general behaviour of "that man." And she had taken Selby for her mate deliberately, meaning to use him well, to play the game of married life fairly, with no hidden card, no stealthy revoke.

She was happy—happy in that existence of fashionable humdrum, content to move in the same circle, monotonous as a steam merry-go-round in a country fair—when Manville came across her path. He impressed her at once. Here was someone at last who did not belong to the world of humdrum. He was unconventional to the verge of brutality. His eyes had flashes of lurid light, his deep-toned voice had accents that were strange to her. His strangeness captivated her fancy. She admired him at first as she might have admired a wild beast in the Zoological Gardens, a something handsome and terrible that was not of her world. Then when he became too attentive, following in her footsteps wherever she went, laying traps in order to have her alone with him, in the brief snatches of *tête-à-tête* that are possible in the modish merry-go-round, she found herself growing afraid of him. He had the air of a man who knew not failure—the successful man, the born master of men, still stronger in his mastery of women. She recoiled from him. Her womanly instincts told her that he was dangerous. She was cold, even uncivil, to him, and kept him at bay; but she could not make up her mind to break with him altogether. His influence over her was like witchcraft. She shuddered at the thought of his power; and in her inmost soul she knew that he belonged to the sons of darkness; yet only death was strong enough to break the spell.

And now, as her acquaintance with St. Just grew closer, the memory of that one romantic episode in her life, the passion, the danger, the guilt of it all, came back upon her with vivid power. Again she saw the vision of the blood-bespattered form, lying abandoned in the desolate waste. She knew not how or why those old feelings—the sense of subjugation, the thrill of love and fear—should have again blotted out the common things of life, and made the beaten round odious. Money-getting, money-spending, jewels, fine clothes, a better house, a better *chef*, better horses, better dogs, than her legion of dearest friends had! These things had satisfied her in the last five years; and now, as it were in a moment, as with the stroke of Harlequin's bat, how trivial, how futile, how detestable, the vulgar commonplace existence had become! She felt a wild longing to escape from it all. Alone, if it were possible; to escape from the lover, and the Golgotha he had made of her life. She was not a vicious woman. She could not even imagine herself yielding to the tempter. But she was wretched; and her days and nights were shadowed by a nameless terror. It was as if she felt herself on the slope that leads to hell, and felt a hand dragging her down, a hand that was strong as iron, yet tender as passionate love, the irresistible hand of the tempter.

Archer Stormont and his pretty American wife had crossed from New York in the newest and largest liner, and were treating themselves to a London season. They had taken a first-floor flat in Mount Street, the best and most expensive that the Mayfair house-agents could find for them. Mrs. Stormont was not boastful about her wealth; but she saw no harm in mentioning that money was no object. "We want just the very best diggings you can find for us," she told the agent.

She met Lady Mary at the Lorimers two days after landing, and wanted to swear eternal friendship on the spot.

"My husband positively doats upon your brother," she said; "so I think you and I ought to be pals. I admire you more than anyone I've seen this side. Your frock is just perfect, and your figure is equal to it. But, of course, you know that. Don't suppose I'm pushing. I'm only open-hearted; and I must say what I think straight out. I've come to this side to enjoy myself, and make nice friends. Archer did uncommonly well in the North West—your brother the same, by-the-bye, and poppa's operations in grain have just trebled Archer's capital; so you see expense don't stop us in anything. I mean to give London an eye-opener before I go back."

Mary asked what kind of eye-opener.

"Well, I guess it will take the shape of a dance; but I'm bothered how to lift it out of the commonplace. Your London balls are done so well nowadays, that it is difficult to imagine how one could beat the record. I want to strike out a line—something quite new and a bit eccentric. But how is it to be done? The *café chantant* is played out; or I'd have got some singers over from Paris—some of the risky ones. I believe I shall be driven to make it a water-party."

"A water-party and a dance! That seems a difficult combination."

"Not for anyone that has the inventive faculty and the dollars. I've got both, thank Providence."

Lady Mary was amused. Vanessa's delicate prettiness and frank vulgarity made a piquant mixture. She invited Mrs. Stormont to her next little dinner—a dinner of six—Mrs. Kelvin, Mr. and Mrs. Stormont, Lord St. Just, and Sir Frederick Marwood, a guardsman, who wrote verses of the most advanced character, and published them in a luxurious binding at his own expense. Mr. Selby was at Liége, acting like an octopus upon an embryo railway, which he meant first to strangle as a Belgian enterprise, and then to launch with an English company.

It was one of Lady Mary's most successful dinners. Never had Mrs. Kelvin's shoulders been more dazzling, her Parisian diamonds more brilliant, or her speech more daring. Even the outspoken Vanessa was astonished at the startling propositions flashed across the table by the time the ices were being handed.

"I didn't mind the company," she told Archer, afterwards, "but I believe I was as red as a peony when I had to look at the servants."

They adjourned *en masse* from the dinner-table to the smoking-room, built at the back of the house, over an unornamental space that had once been called a garden; a room with a movable roof, which was raised on a night like this, letting in the cool air, with glimpses of stars in a purple sky. The room was furnished with an Oriental luxury of divans and pillows, covered with gold inwrought brocade, rich and ancient fabrics, plundered from the vestiaries of old Italian churches, the copes of Renaissance bishops.

The three women smoked their cigarettes lightly and delicately, with an airy indifference to the charm of tobacco that made smoking coquetry, and not vice.

Vanessa, who was primitively egotistical as a child of seven, could talk hardly of anything but her coming party.

"I don't want it to be passed over in the paper with three lines—'Mrs. Stormont's party was a great success,' or something mawkish of that kind. I do want my party to stand alone. I've been thinking of a water-party."

"Admirable!" exclaimed Sir Frederick. "A water-party would be new. Eighteenth-century to the fortieth power—suggestive of Sir Plume and Belinda."

"Never heard of the lady. Is she one of your professional beauties?" asked Vanessa.

"Alas!" sighed Sir Frederick, "Belinda belongs to the

past. She has gone up aloft among the constellations, after her stolen ringlet. I congratulate you on your idea, Mrs. Stormont. A water-party in this tropical weather would be of all things the most delicious. But you must not waste your July, and eighty in the shade, on long invitations. A week at most can be hazarded. Send out your cards the instant they are ready. St. Just and I will put it about that your party will eclipse everything ever seen; and people will throw over their engagements to go to it. And then you need not start till midnight; and people can come on to you after other things."

"Yes, that's about the size of it," replied Vanessa, elated, having found a man who understood her. "Will you help me through with it, Sir Frederick? I'll do just whatever you tell me. Money no object."

"If money were an object, dear Mrs. Stormont, it would be futile to attempt anything of the kind. But if Mr. Stormont approve, I shall be charmed to run the thing for you."

"Archer! He never disapproves. He knows when it comes to entertaining the swells he's got to take a back seat."

Stormont had been telling Mrs. Kelvin Chicago anecdotes, racy of the soil, and received with silvery laughter; although the lady's attention had often wandered to the conservatory beyond the curtained archway at the end of the room. It was not a large conservatory, space in Grosvenor Square being a difficult problem for the architect; but it was large enough to contain a few fine palms, a screen of Maréchal Niel and Niphetos roses, with a bank of choice carnations in front of them; it was also large enough to hold two luxurious armchairs, in which

Lady Mary and St. Just were seated, the lady's white brocade train and the point of a jewelled shoe just visible between the Oriental curtains, and the sound of lowered voices faintly audible to one keen listener.

"It's the old, old story," thought Mrs. Kelvin. "What kind of chance can any marriageable woman have while the married ones are such abominable flirts?"

The raciest American stories left her cold.

"Let us hear what Sir Frederick is saying about Mrs. Stormont's party," she said, whereupon the conversation became a quartette; but there was not a word more about the party.

"It is to be a surprise," Sir Frederick said, "and nobody except Mrs. Stormont and me is to know anything about it."

"Isn't it lovely?" exclaimed Vanessa; "a kind of gunpowder plot."

Engravers were expeditious, and Mrs. Stormont's cards were sent out on the following evening.

"Mrs. Stormont requests the pleasure of Lady Blank's company at a river-party on Tuesday, July 13th. Boats will leave Hammersmith pier at midnight. Carriages to be ordered at 4.30 a.m. at Vauxhall Station, L.S.W.R."

XI.

THE elements were kind to Vanessa. The night of her party was blest with a purple sky, in which the stars looked nearer and brighter than their wont, and a sultry stillness which seemed almost tropical. Airy gowns and feathered cloaks were scarcely stirred by the soft warm air, as Vanessa's guests alighted from the line of carriages on the bridge, a line that extended all the length of the road as far back as the old parish church, where the deep-toned clock was striking the first hour of morning before the last carriage had deposited its occupants on the bridge, and the last of the ten electric launches had moved from the pier.

One o'clock, and even Hammersmith—with silvered roofs and glorified chimneys, under the moon that rode triumphant in a dark blue sky, the moon in her fullest, maturest beauty—had a picturesque semi-Dutch appearance, as wharf and warehouse lay fast asleep.

The Thames, under that enchanting light, rippled and danced like a river of molten gold; and the shore, the poor suburban shore that was once only a line of willows against a background of cornfields—even the shore of villadom had a vague charm when seen betwixt purple sky and golden river.

The midnight assembly was a success. It had allowed people to go to other parties, to prime themselves for pleasure. Everybody had dined somewhere. Most of the young people had come away from dances they had just looked at—a valse, an ice, and good-bye.

"Going on to Mrs. Stormont's." "A long drive!" "Ridiculous, ain't it?" "Haven't the least idea what's going to happen." "An American surprise party, don't you know." "Rich?" "Oh, stupendously." "Sure to do us well."

And now on the ten launches, each holding thirty people, the ripple of animated talk was louder than the ripple of the moonlit water. A smaller launch carrying an orchestra headed the procession, and the music floated back loud or low, as distance varied—gay operatic music, bridal marches, famous waltzes, familiar serenades, melodies that all the world loves, from *Lohengrin, Faust, Rigoletto, Don Giovanni,* the music that thrills with old memories and vanished loves. And there were intervals when reeds and brasses were mute, and a trio of strings played some old song that once filled all the air—"Good-bye, Sweetheart," "Come into the Garden, Maud."

One old lady in a cloak, brilliant with peacock plumage, wept quietly in her corner when that last song was played, wept to think that Sims Reeves was dead, and that she was no longer young.

Everybody agreed that it was an enchanting party. People were curious; but no one cared much whither the boats were going. It was enough to exist in that delicious atmosphere, sitting by the girl one loved, perhaps, or the man one wanted to marry, with ices and tea and coffee in abundance, and all manner of possibilities, between dark and daylight. Alas! dawn would come too soon, and carriages at half-past four. Brentford clock chimed the third quarter after one, as the boats passed the fair lawns of Syon House, a sheet of white light, and then plunged into the dark shadow of the trees on the island below Isleworth ferry, which looked like a home for ghosts.

"I'm sure ghosts live there," said Vanessa; "the ghost of Pope, perhaps."

"Pope has an island more convenient to his grave."

"The Eel Pie, where there's an inn, and people drink beer," cried Vanessa, disgusted. "No, he would much rather haunt a desert island like that."

"Too many rats," said her companion.

Vanessa was on the last of the launches. She knew her duties too well to leave the pier till the last of her guests had embarked. She would like to have been on all the boats, flitting from group to group, the moving spirit of the scene; but she knew that her time was coming.

Lady Mary Selby and Lord St. Just were in the leading launch, sitting in a shadowy corner side by side, and talking in undertones. They had been among the earliest arrivals at Hammersmith, driving down together in the lady's neat little brougham, balanced lightly on C-springs. They had dined together, and alone. St. Just had supplicated for a *tête-à-tête* dinner.

"Are we never to be together, always to be performing before an audience? Can I never look into your eyes, or hold your hand a moment longer than your troop of casual friends? Mary, we *must* be together to-night."

The must—impassioned, imperious, which would have seemed unpardonable from any other lips—conquered.

"We shall set people talking," she said.

"What do we care for people? I count all the world rabble when I have the one adorable woman sitting opposite me. Let us dine *tête-à-tête* for once in our lives. Shall it be in your house, or at the Savoy?"

"At the Savoy, if it must be. Just a table in a window in the room where all the people dine."

But when the evening came, St. Just conducted his guest to a small room facing the river, a room that had been made into a bower of roses. The windows were open, and the newly risen moon was looking in upon them, a shining disk, orange-red, out of the vague purple of the night.

"This isn't fair, St. Just," Mary said angrily. "I told you we were to dine in the public room. Nobody could have said anything malicious about that; but this is just the kind of thing to set them talking."

"The roses, or the moon, or what? Do you think that would have been a *tête-à-tête,* Mary, with people jabbering at the next table? Do you suppose I wanted to dine with you, hemmed round with curious eyes and deafening chatter? One of your *parties carrées* in Grosvenor Square would have been better than that. I wanted to have you to myself—my companion, my friend, soul of my soul, heart of my heart—just for one delicious hour before we go on to Mrs. Stormont's party."

He called her Mary unreproved. The hour of quibbling about trifles had gone by. She looked him full in the face, her eyes flashing. She stood as it were on guard, with her sword drawn, a woman of high courage. He could not doubt that, though he watched her with a fond smile, as if she had been a pretty child playing some childish part.

"*Va pour le dîner à deux,* if it must be," she said, throwing off her long white satin cloak, fringed from collar to hem with ostrich plumage.

Her gown was softest chiffon, gauze, lace; an artistic mingling of delicatest fabrics, white as snow, with no gaudy glitter of gold or spangles, no suggestion of tawdriness. The only touch of colour was the ruby necklace which showed blood-red against the marble whiteness of her neck, and the ruby brooches on her corsage. Never had she looked lovelier, in spite of the thirty-five years recorded against her by Debrett.

She was conscious of her beauty and her splendour; eyes and complexion as incomparable as her jewels, a queen in stature, a figure built for grace and dignity. For this hour she felt mistress of the situation; and she treated St. Just with a certain hauteur even in the midst of their confidential talk. She was full of gaiety; ridiculed her friends, talked of private and public people, and would suffer no lapse into sentiment. Nothing could be more correct than her attitude through that hour in the rose-scented room, and on the balcony, where they took their coffee, looking out over the moonlit river, or to the brazen-faced clock, and the beacon light shining above the great grey palace where the everlasting problem of "how not to do it" was in process of solution.

No word that could offend matronly modesty was spoken during that *tête-à-tête* dinner, nor in the carriage as it rolled swiftly through the lighted streets, and along the suburban road, spinning on noiseless wheels past omnibus and van, waggon and cab. But later, when they two were sitting in the shadow, lulled by the ripple of the stream, words were spoken, such fatal and pernicious words as have been breathed into the ear of woman from the dim beginning of time, when this world's first woman heard and trembled at the voice of the serpent; always the same words, the same impassioned prayer, the same perfidious promise of a life of bliss, the same reckless vow of unalterable love.

Mary Selby listened—silent, unreproving, yet unyielding. No, not for worlds would she be false to her husband. Not for worlds would she suffer the lot of divorced wives, and women who have lost caste. She would dismiss St. Just out of her life to-morrow. She would never of her own free will see his face after to-night.

But this night, while the moon shone, and the river flowed,—that delicious river whose suburban shores needed only the veil of shadow and the fitful purple light to make them lovely—what did it matter if wild words were spoken, and if she listened, without too harsh a protest against the guilt of it all?

"What midsummer madness this is, St. Just. You know that I am not the kind of woman to endure disgrace," she said, in a low voice, trying to speak lightly, with her head turned from him, while she watched the shore that seemed gliding away as she looked at it, gliding from her sight into the unknown darkness, and carrying her past existence with it.

All her married life, the gaudy pleasures—the luxury of money-spending, of caprices gratified on the instant, the villa at Cannes, the boat on the Nile, the cottage at Newmarket, the ceaseless round of banal pleasures—faded from her memory, like the vague shapes in a half-forgotten dream. Family, husband, caste, the world—all had become as nothing. Life was narrowed to a point; and time meant only these moments while she sat in shadow, with a hand holding hers, and a lowered voice breathing the seducer's impassioned prayer.

He wanted her to go back to London with him. He could get a carriage at Richmond. His yacht was at Greenhithe, fitted and manned for a long cruise. He had made all things ready for the voyage which was to carry them to an Eden of their own. Or they would be ocean wanderers, if she so willed it, remote from the common earth, flitting from one delicious spot to another, as her caprice dictated. Disgrace, the shame of looking into familiar faces and seeing estrangement there, need never come near her. They would live in a world of their own—emancipated spirits, roving far and ever farther from all that was petty and dry-as-dust in every-day life. She let him rave. The low deep tones of the perfect voice lulled her like the distant music of Schubert's serenade, the languid sweetness of the violins, singing the melody, the organ notes of the 'cello accompanying, like the ground-swell of a summer sea.

She let him rave. What did it matter? To-night she was in fairyland, like the lady in *Comus;* there was no reality in this sense of peril. To-morrow, if there were no notice of Selby's immediate return, she would start by the night mail for Liége. She would swoop down upon the good honest husband, and give him a delightful surprise; as she had done more than once in the past, when she had wearied of London and liberty. She really liked the good man better than any of her friends. He was her best "pal," after all; and if art and literature were outside his comprehension, and his pass-book was the only volume he ever opened, he read the newspapers diligently, and could always talk about things. And then he admired her with a quiet dog-like worship which was more flattering than all the airy nothings of "haw-haw" guardsmen and society poets, the men who gave themselves airs upon the strength of "a rivulet of print meandering through a meadow of margin." Selby was at least better than any of these.

A blaze of light in the distance awoke a chorus of exclamations. The boats had passed under Richmond Bridge, where Mrs. Stormont's boat shot past the others and went to the front. They had passed Buccleuch House, with its river-kissed lawn, and the big hotel crowning the wooded hill. They were in a lonely reach of the river, no one knew exactly where, no one cared to know; and there in front of them they beheld a fairy palace, chains of coloured lights hanging all along the shore, a landing-stage with the same rainbow brightness of hanging lamps, and a lawn surrounded by a lamplit arcade, while in the background a vast marquee aped the form and substance of an Oriental palace, every line, domes and minarets, doors and windows, edged with rainbow light from electric globes that shone like the jewels in Aladdin's cave. And from this fairy palace there came more music, this time the unmistakable music of a military band, playing the gavotte from the *Gondoliers,* so gay, so light, so sparkling, carrying a sense of unreasoning joy even to jaded hearts. Praises were loud and enthusiastic as Vanessa stood on the landing-stage to receive her party.

"So glad you like it all," she said gaily. "The idea was mine; but the carrying out is all Sir Frederick Marwood's. I'm not going to be mean and deny it."

Sir Frederick hovered near her, and accepted everybody's compliments; and then, the cool night air having prepared the modern unashamed appetite for something more substantial than the ices and cool drinks served on the boats, the magic word of supper floated in the atmosphere; and there was a rapid and simultaneous movement towards the fairy palace.

"Supper's ready," Vanessa told her friends, adding the hospitable assurance that they need have no fear of the quails or the champagne giving out. "And there's a fine floor for those that hanker after the light fantastic," she said, "and I mean to have a twirl round myself before daylight, if anybody will ask me."

Meanwhile Sir Frederick and Stormont had gone about, telling the men that there would be a special train at Twickenham station, to start punctually at four o'clock, and carriages ready to take people to the station at a quarter to four.

"You can't have carriages enough for everybody," said one of the men.

"We sha'n't leave a mortal behind, unless he wants to stop. There'll be room for everyone in our sixty breaks and landaus."

"Sixty! That's a large order."

"Oh, we didn't want to be in the position of the ancient Nabob, who had to order 'more curricles' for his guests. It might not be easy to raise extra conveyances at four o'clock in the morning."

The grounds were spacious, and thickly wooded; and all beyond that brilliant nucleus of coloured light lay in shadow under the sinking moon, a place in which it was easy for those unfamiliar with the scene by daylight to lose themselves. Only here and there a lamp had been hung on the dark trunk of a tree, to mark a footpath, or the parting of the ways; and this glow-worm glimmer served to intensify the darkness, and gave a mystic air as of an enchanted forest. There were not many wanderers; for the attractions of the supper-tent and the ballroom prevailed over the romance of the shadowy grounds, or the footpath on the edge of the river. Dancing was going on furiously in the spacious marquee, for a cotillon was in full swing, led by Sir Frederick and Vanessa, both alike possessed with an untiring ardour, and the waltzing power of phantom dancers in a German legend. Rumour had described the presents as unparalleled even among millionaire hostesses; and the moment when a beribboned cart drawn by a snow-white donkey brought these treasures into the ballroom was a thrilling episode in this midsummer night's dream.

Lady Mary was not in the cotillon; but this fact was not surprising, as she rarely danced. A waltz once in a way, with a favourite partner, just to show her dearest friends that she waltzed more exquisitely than the best of them, sufficed her. To be eager for dances, to give her hand freely to the first comer, she considered unbefitting the dignity of her five-and-thirty years, the royal repose of her manner. To waltz with Lady Mary Selby was an honour which golden youth knew how to appreciate.

She had been seen with St. Just in the supper-tent, but only for a few minutes. She would take nothing but a sandwich, and a glass of champagne in a tumbler of seltzer. Her friends watched her, criticised her gown and her rubies, and noted that she was very pale, save for a hectic flush that came and went upon her cheek. They noted also that St. Just never left her; and, in the shorthand vocabulary of our time, told each other that "M. was giving herself away."

The atmosphere of the tent stifled her; the crowd, the odours of hot soups and coffee and chocolate from the buffet, where lamps were burning under copper heaters—all was oppressive. She was glad to escape into the coolness outside.

"Let us go and watch the cotillon," she said. "It is going to be something tremendous—with all sorts of absurdities."

"No, no; you have seen hundreds of cotillons. Let

us watch the dying moon upon the river." He drew her hand through his arm, and led her away from the gaudy light, into an avenue of old trees, tall beeches that were ancient when Horace Walpole was busy with his toy castle in his beloved "County of Twicks;" when Lady Suffolk was building herself a dower house hard by; when Twickenham and Richmond were secluded villages, the favoured homes of the learned and the *élite*. All was changed since those days; but to-night all seemed unchanged in the glimmer of a sinking moon and the first faint lilac of dawn.

A narrow backwater wound among the trees; it was scarcely more than a ditch, but there was water enough to reflect the fading stars and that faint daffodil glimmer of the coming dawn, through an opening in the leafy roof. It was a place of silence and seclusion, a narrow path following the edge of the water, a low, irregular bank, broken here and there where cattle had trampled the ground, going down to drink. It was a spot for lovers, perhaps, since it was remote and unfrequented, a winding track under leafy shade, where with the first faint promise of dawn there came the low sweet chorus of awakening birds, that sound which of all others suggests the birth of a new day. But it was hardly a spot to charm a solitary straggler; yet here was Mrs. Kelvin, wrapped in a black satin cloak, the hood drawn over her head and covering her face, with just space for gleaming eyes to look out, peering round, piercing the shadows under the trees, glancing this way and that, eager, alert, expectant. So shrouded there was little fear of her being observed by anyone else who might be sauntering along the narrow track; but she was particularly careful to avoid the possibility. Stealthy of foot, creeping from tree to tree, not upon the path itself, but on the rank dry grass beside it, moving slowly, so as to avoid the rustling of silken skirts or of the long rank grass, she stole through the shadows, following the stream to the river in the ghostly dawn, a phantom, a ghoul, an evil spirit.

Was it a rendezvous or an espial?

CHAPTER XII.

Walter Arden was destined to suffer a rude awakening from the halcyon days of tranquillity and content which had followed his reunion with his wife. He had been supremely happy, and had almost forgotten the sufferings of the past. He had knelt in the little Lutheran church with Rachel, and had heard the message of peace, not as the believer hears, but touched by the wisdom of the Divine words, the beauty of the Divine life, sympathising with his wife in her implicit faith, her unquestioning acceptance of the miraculous element in a life which to him had never been more than a tradition and an example.

He was happy, and his mind was at rest; and in his musings on this happy change he recalled one of the strange features of Chaldean magic; the belief that the soul which had been held in bondage by an evil spirit could, after the expulsion of the demon, only be made secure from future harm by becoming the tabernacle of a good spirit. Possession could only be cured by possession. The counter influence was needed for safety.

"Rachel is my good spirit," he thought. "The mind that gentle spirit rules ought to be invincible against demoniac power. To live with her, to live for her, shall be my religion; and who knows, some day I may come to think as she thinks, and may learn to trust in the unknown good, as I have learnt to fear the unknown evil."

They had left the mountain village above the Lake of Thun, and had travelled by easy stages, in extra post carriages, stopping at any halting-place that took their fancy, from Thun to the Engadine, where they had spent the first fortnight of July, not at Pontresina, or St. Moritz, or Maloja, but at the smaller hotels in less frequented places, where there were none of the attractions which the average tourist demands: no tennis tournaments or hotel dances, no band, no amateur theatricals or *tableaux vivants.* They spent some days at Samaden, taking long walks in the neighbourhood, perfectly happy in each other's company; and from Samaden they made a leisurely journey to Damezzo, a village near the Italian frontier, a valley embowered in chestnut woods, and with a narrow river rushing between steep banks crowned with sedges, through meadows sprinkled with purple crocuses, and merry with the fairy music of innumerable grass-hoppers.

Here Arden meant to make a halt till September, when he wanted to take Rachel to that Italian lake-land which she had never seen, and where he had been a lonely and miserable wanderer in the unhappy time before he met her. To be in those lovely scenes with her, to be able to take pleasure in their romantic beauty, and to be soothed by their tranquil atmosphere, would be ineffable bliss.

The hotel at Damezzo was of modest proportions, and there were few visitors at this time, while the season was still too warm for going on to Italy. They had a suite of rooms looking towards the river, with a wide view of distant hills, and in the foreground a picturesque one-arched bridge that spanned a waterfall. They had a garden, and a spacious summer-house trellised with roses, where they read and wrote and rested through the heat of the day, and where they took their breakfast and tea; and for their morning and evening rambles they had mountain roads, through immeasurable chestnut woods, roads leading up to white-walled villages that seemed hanging in the sky.

It was from this haven of rest that Arden was called away by news that came upon him like a thunderclap.

He opened a London daily paper, sitting among the roses in the golden evening light, in an atmosphere of supreme peace, silent, save for the rush of the waterfall and the thin shrill chorus of the grasshoppers in the meadows below. He was alone, his wife having gone upon a mission of charity to a bedridden old woman in a lonely homestead, where the peasant farmer and his kine lived in friendly propinquity. He was alone when the thunderbolt fell.

"MURDER OF LADY MARY SELBY.

"Society has experienced a terrible shock in the tragic fate of a lady who was eminently popular in a wide circle, and whose beauty and talent made her a conspicuous figure among the many lovely and clever women of the day. As a hostess, Lady Mary Selby was incomparable. She had made her house a focus for beauty, wit, and art, which recalled the choicer gatherings in the houses of Lady Waldegrave and Lady Molesworth. Gifted with singular tact, and with a charm of manner that was more potent even than her commanding beauty, Lady Mary was a centre of attraction in every circle; and, being endowed with a fine physique and inexhaustible vivacity, she took a leading position in all fashionable gaieties, whether in the London season, in Egypt, or on the Riviera. Happily married to a man of vast wealth, her fine and original taste never suffered restraint for lack of means; and society was to be congratulated upon the union of so much charm and talent with such ample fortune. With Lady Mary the power to achieve went along with the genius that could invent; and the world of fashion was on tip-toe at the beginning of a London season, to discover what new and striking form of entertainment would be given at her palatial house in Grosvenor Square.

"The hand of an undiscovered assassin has cut short that brilliant career, and Mr. Selby, Lady Mary's brother, Lord Wildernsea, and a large circle of relations and friends, are mourning for the unhappy fate of an amiable and gifted woman, while the police are endeavouring to solve the mystery of her cruel death. A detailed description of the brilliant *fête* given by a Chicago belle and millionaire, at which Lady Mary Selby was a prominent figure, appeared in our issue of Wednesday; and a report of the coroner's inquest upon the unhappy lady will be found in another part of this paper."

Arden's eye had rushed over the prolix article, transfixed by the hideous fact embodied in the journalist's florid paragraphs. Death! Murder! The two most horrible words in the language—the second infinitely more terrible than the first. He turned the paper with trembling hands, looking for the report of the inquest. It occupied two columns of closely printed matter; and the name of one of the witnesses deepened the horror in Arden's mind as he read the ghastly details.

The first witness to be examined was a boatman, who discovered the body of the murdered woman in the backwater in the grounds of Montpelier House, Twickenham. His attention had been attracted by the appearance of some white object lying in the narrow inlet at a little distance from the river bank, too far off for him to see what it was as he rowed past, but near enough to excite his curiosity, and induce him to pull his boat ashore and go to the spot, where he found the body of a lady dressed in white, lying in about a foot of water. She wore a white cloak trimmed with feathers. She had no necklace, but there were jewels on the bosom of her gown. Seeing that there was no doubt as to her being dead, he had gone at once in search of a policeman. The time when he made this discovery was between six and seven o'clock on the morning of Wednesday.

The evidence of the police-constable followed. He described the appearance of the corpse, and the marks upon the throat, which clearly pointed to strangulation. Death by drowning under the conditions would have been impossible, unless anyone had fallen face downward into the water, or had fallen there in a fainting state and so been suffocated. The lady's face was hardly covered by the water.

Dr. Stedman, a local medical man, confirmed the constable's view. He declared that the signs of strangulation were unmistakable. The throat, which was cruelly bruised, showed the grip of a powerful hand, the finger-marks being clearly defined. When asked if he could form any opinion as to the character of the hand that had made this imprint, he replied that he did not think it was the hand of a man employed in rough labour. The distinct lines of the bruises gave the shape of the fingers, and indicated a long slender hand, rather than a broad and coarse one. Asked if he believed there had been a struggle, the doctor replied yes: that the hair of the deceased was dishevelled, her left arm showed the imprint of a hand that had grasped it violently, and her dress, which was of a very delicate fabric, was a good deal torn. He had gone over the ground with the constable. There was a spot some ten or twelve yards from the water, where the grass was trampled, and where they discovered the marks of a lady's high-heeled shoes. He believed that the murder had occurred at this spot; and that the body had been carried from there to the ditch where it was found. In reply to the coroner's question, he said that there were no indications of the body having been dragged over the grass. The murderer must have been a powerful man, the deceased lady being considerably above the common height.

The coroner reminded the witness that he had described the marks upon the throat as indicating a delicate rather than a powerful hand.

"I said they were the marks of slender fingers," answered the doctor; "but there is a sinewy nervous strength which is no less powerful than weight and bulk. The grip upon the throat of the deceased must have been the grip of a hand with muscles of steel."

Mrs. Stormont, who was painfully agitated, gave evidence as to the last time she had seen Lady Mary Selby on the evening of her *fête*. It was in the supper-tent, where the deceased was standing near the buffet, talking to Lord St. Just. They were only taking some light refreshment, and she did not see them sit down at one of the little tables, which were mostly crowded at this time. She did not observe them leaving the tent. She was there herself only a few minutes; as she had her duties as hostess in the marquee where the dancing was going on. She looked for Lady Mary at the station before the starting of the train, but was not surprised at failing to discover her, among nearly three hundred people. Lord St. Just helped her in her search on the platform, and in the waiting-rooms. He had lost sight of Lady Mary some time before the carriages left for the station.

St. Just, who had volunteered his evidence, stated that he and Lady Mary had walked round the grounds together; and that at her request he had taken her back to the marquee, where she left him to look at the end of the cotillon. He did not go into the marquee, and afterwards, when the prizes had been distributed, there was considerable confusion; as there was very little time left for the drive to the station, and people were rushing to the carriages, and looking for each other in a distracted way.

The coroner asked if St. Just could remember the precise time at which he had seen Lady Mary enter the marquee.

Yes, he had looked at his watch immediately after leaving her. It was five-and-twenty minutes past three, and the carriages were to leave for the station at a quarter to four. The cotillon must have lasted nearly twenty minutes after this. He was walking up and down the lawn in front of the marquee, waiting to escort Lady Mary to the station; but in the rush of people, who poured out of the tent *en masse*, after the cotillon, he failed to discover her, and he accompanied Mrs. Stormont to her carriage, and took his seat beside her, when they drove away.

"You felt no uneasiness about the missing lady?"

"No; I had no suspicion that she was missing, although I failed in finding her. I had only time to walk along the line of carriages, into which people were hurrying, afraid of being left behind. Although I could not see Lady Mary, I thought that she must be in one of the crowded vehicles. There was only time for a hasty search. The same thing occurred at the station."

"When you were walking in the grounds with the deceased, did you see any suspicious character lurking about?"

"No; we met no one who did not belong to Mrs. Stormont's party."

"Did you notice what jewels the deceased was wearing?"

"Nobody could fail to notice Lady Mary's ruby necklace, and the jewels on her corsage."

"Were these jewels exposed to view while she was walking with you?"

"She was wearing a cloak all the time; but the night was sultry, and she had thrown her cloak open at the throat, so that her necklace might have been seen by anyone who passed us."

"Did you meet many of Mrs. Stormont's guests?"

"An occasional couple only, sauntering under the trees, as we were."

"Did your walk extend to the spot where the body was found?"

"No; we walked in that direction, but not so far. I never saw the place till this morning, when I went to look at it with the police."

"Can you account for Lady Mary Selby having gone back to that lonely part of the grounds, after she left the dancing-tent?"

"I imagine that she may have loitered at the last, and then may have become confused and agitated on finding herself left behind, and so may have taken a wrong turn."

"That would seem unlikely, while a crowd of people were all hurrying in one direction," said the coroner.

"The crowd was not all going in one direction. Ladies were running about confusedly, asking the way to the gate where the carriages were waiting."

"But it was broad daylight at four o'clock."

"It was daylight; but there was a good deal of confusion notwithstanding."

"There must be someone who saw the deceased in the dancing-tent, if she stayed there twenty minutes," said the coroner.

"No doubt she must have been seen by a good many people."

No further questions were asked of Lord St. Just. Lady Mary's French maid was the next witness, who had been brought there only to state what jewels her mistress was wearing on the evening of Mrs. Stormont's *fête*. She described the ruby and diamond necklace, which she had been told had cost thirteen thousand pounds, and a number of ruby and diamond brooches, also of considerable value.

The inquest was adjourned, to give time for further evidence to be obtained.

CHAPTER XIII.

Arden arrived in London two days after the inquest at Twickenham, and went straight to his brother's house in Hertford Street, where he found Lord Wildernsea and his wife and daughters in a state of unspeakable consternation. The elder of the two girls had made her *début* this season, and had still a goodly number of balls and parties on her list. The society papers had enthroned her among the beauties; and her mother expected her to make a great marriage. Perhaps the aspect in which Lady Mary's dreadful fate most strikingly presented itself to the Wildernsea household was as a thing that ought not to have occurred in a respectable family; a sensational kind of calamity that people would never leave off talking about; and which would prove a hotbed for scandalous details, for imputations and insinuations running underground in endless ramifications, like a pernicious weed under a grass lawn, spreading over the whole of the unhappy lady's married life.

"I knew how reckless Mary was, and how very near the wind she sailed sometimes," Wildernsea said to his brother, after the first few words of unalloyed grief had been spoken, "but I never thought such a horror as this would come upon her."

"I hope you don't think my poor sister was to blame

for being murdered—that this hideous tragedy was her fault," Arden said indignantly.

"Her fault, poor soul! No no, of course not! Still, don't you know, if she hadn't gone to that odious party —a flashy, vulgar American thing—my wife had a card, and the girl wanted to go, but I wouldn't hear of it—if Mary had kept herself aloof, as she ought to have done, she would have been alive and happy. I never saw her looking handsomer than two or three nights before, at the opera. And to go to a nobody's party, in a mob of silly people, roaming about a strange place in the dead of the night! What could come of it but harm? That poor devil Selby is broken-hearted. I never saw a fellow so crushed. And as for myself, I sha'n't enter one of my clubs this season. I can't stand being pitied, and stared at, and whispered about. Notoriety of any kind is poison to me—and such notoriety as this is more than I can stand. I don't believe there has been anything as horrible since Lord Ferrers was hanged for shooting his steward."

The younger brother looked at him with unmitigated scorn. Her ways were not his ways, but Walter Arden had loved his sister; and it enraged him to hear her miserable fate considered from the society point of view. Wildernsea was walking about the room in a distracted way, unconscious of that contemptuous glance. He was not altogether heartless; he had given his murdered sister two days and nights of profound grief; but then had come the reaction, and the idea of the catastrophe as it affected his own family. To his mind there was unspeakable disgrace in the tragedy. He had always supposed that murders of this kind were peculiar to the

East End slums, the dark places of the great city; or, at any rate, to the lower middle classes. The murder of Lord William Russell by his valet, and an agrarian murder or two in Ireland, were all the crimes of this nature that he could recall among people of importance; and those had been respectable murders, leaving no trail of slander behind them.

"Poor Honoria!" he muttered, as he paced the room. "It is hard lines for her."

"Honoria?" questioned Arden.

"Yes, her first season; and she has been tremendously admired. The young Duke of Lincolnshire has been very marked in his attentions, her mother tells me; waltzed with her no end, and always sitting out together. And now this business will upset everything. I shall take them all to Wildernsea to-morrow. It will spoil Honoria's season; but there's no use staying in town, now we're in deep mourning. I can run up for the day, if I'm wanted."

"Do you know who murdered your sister?" Arden asked suddenly.

"Know? Why, of course not! Nobody knows. But I hope the police will find the wretch. Some miserable tramp, I suppose, who was prowling about the place on the look-out for business, and met her alone, blazing with jewels, and strangled her for the sake of the plunder. The police are hunting for him, and hope to trace him through the jewellery. Selby wanted to offer a thousand pounds reward; but the Chief recommended him to keep quiet, and leave everything to the Criminal Investigation Department. Twickenham is within the London radius, so the affair rests with Scotland Yard."

"Is that the theory? A casual member of the criminal classes—who met her alone, and in a solitary part of the grounds? Is that your idea?"

"What else can I think, after St. Just's evidence? She must have taken a wrong turn, when the crowd were hurrying to the gates, and lost her way."

"Is that like Mary? She was not the kind of woman to lose her head, and take a wrong path in broad daylight. Was not! Oh, God, that we must speak of her in the past! I don't believe in your theory. I don't believe that Scotland Yard will find the murderer, starting with the idea that he is a member of the criminal classes, who will try to dispose of the jewels."

"Have you a theory of your own?"

"I have; but I shall keep it locked in my own mind, for the present."

"I don't think anybody's theories can be of much use. We must look to Scotland Yard for the solution of the mystery—if you can call it a mystery, when the motive of the crime was so obvious. Poor Mary! We had drifted apart since her marriage. My wife couldn't stand the kind of people Mary cultivated—actors, and newspaper men, and painters, and such-like. But I was very fond of her. The funeral is arranged for to-morrow, at two o'clock, at Kensal Green. But there will be a service at St. Aldate's, her favourite church, at twelve. You will be there, of course?"

"Yes, I shall be there. Good-bye."

Arden went from his brother's house to Grosvenor Square, to the house of death, where the spacious splendour of hall and staircase was wrapped in gloom; and where the atmosphere was laden with the sickly subtle perfume of gardenias and tube-roses. He found Mr. Selby in the library, a room which had always been devoted to his particular use, where he received business visitors, and where he had elaborated those financial schemes which had built up his fortune. The room was at the back of the house, lighted by one wide window, which commanded only the dead wall of the smoking-room, across a space of ten feet, a gloomy outlook to a room furnished with dark oak, and lined with those time-honoured works which every gentleman's library should contain, and which very few gentlemen who buy a library *en bloc* are in the habit of reading.

No need to draw the blinds down here. The window was wide open, and in the sunless light Selby sat staring at the opposite wall, haggard, livid, with eyes that had shed passionate tears, in the night silence, and were dim, and pale, and tired, and hopeless, beyond all eyes that Arden had ever looked upon. The daily papers were on the table, folded as the servant had placed them. The lid of the massive silver inkstand had not been lifted. All the usual signs of occupation were absent. The man was sitting there, motionless, listless, inert, a mechanism whose springs were broken.

On the table in front of him, Arden noticed an open sandal-wood box, the contents covered with jewellers' wool. He did not rise to receive his brother-in-law, or give any indication of surprise at his appearance. He held out his hand without a word, and it was deadly cold in Arden's grasp.

"I am profoundly sorry for you, Selby. There are troubles too dreadful to be expressed in words—and this is one."

"I loved her, Arden. God knows how dearly. I had nothing else in the world. You've heard how I began life—an office-boy, motherless, with a drunken father, kicked out-of-doors before I was thirteen, to sink or swim. I had never loved anybody till I met Mary. I had nothing but her—her and money; and I only cared for money because she liked to spend it. There is nothing left, now she is gone."

Arden seated himself in silence. Yes, this was a pure and perfect love. He had always respected Selby for his straightforward, purposeful life, for his unwavering affection for the woman he had chosen for his helpmeet, his willingness to take the lower place, to submit his own inclinations to his wife's pleasure.

Selby sat silent, with his hand shading his eyes, for a few minutes, while the ticking of the tall eight-day clock seemed to grow more insistent with every moment it checked off; and Arden found himself looking automatically at the long rows of books in their rich and sober bindings of dull red and dark brown, olive and black—Gibbon, Hume, Grote, Froude, Macaulay, Dickens. Their names meant nothing to him in this hour of agonising thoughts; but he looked at them all the same.

"She was brought home last night," Selby said, in a low voice, "and the coffin was nailed down this morning. They were in a hurry to hide her face—her beautiful face—the only face I loved. You don't know what desolation means, Arden. No man can know, who hasn't lost all—as I have. My life is broken off short. If I live to be eighty, there will be no meaning in my existence. It will be just dragging on a load of misery, like a galley-slave toiling in irons. I hope I shall die before the year is out."

"Time brings consolations," Arden said gently. "Your wealth is a great power. You will find a beneficent use for it."

"Build a hospital in memory of my wife? God knows I wouldn't stint the cost; but that's soon done. And after——"

"Time will bring you something else; some new tie, perhaps, in the far-off years."

"Another wife, do you mean? A strange woman to take Mary's place. No, no, no; no strange woman shall ever take her place or name. If I were fool enough, in some weak moment, to think I cared for another woman; and were to marry her and bring her home to this house, I should hate her. I should hate her all the days of my life, and hate myself for having thought I could care for her. No, Arden, my life, as a man, is finished. I may go on, perhaps, as a money-making machine; but for the rest, Amen."

There was a silence, and Arden saw slow tears stealing down the haggard face, under the shading hand, and then the low dull voice went on—

"She is lying in her own room, the large front room on the second floor. The view from the windows used to look green and countryfied in summer-time. She made her rooms so beautiful. She had such perfect taste. Every piece of furniture, the colouring of the walls, the draperies, everything, was her own choice. The upholsterers and people said that her taste was faultless. She never made a mistake."

He had said no word as to the manner of her

death. Arden wondered at this. There was a touch of egotism, perhaps, here. It seemed as if the one thought in his mind was of his own loss—the beautiful thing that had been his, and that Fate had snatched from him.

"Have there been no discoveries?" Arden asked at last, "no clue to the murderer?"

"Discoveries? Yes; there is this," Selby answered, with his hand on the sandal-wood box. "It came this morning, addressed to me. Her necklace—the only necklace she wore that night."

"The necklace which was supposed to have tempted the murderer! I knew, I knew, that it was no common criminal who killed her. Who sent it to you? Where did it come from?"

"I don't know. The parcel was insured and posted at Charing Cross. There was no name—no word in the box; nothing but her necklace—her favourite necklace. God! what a happy man I was the day I clasped it round her neck. It was the anniversary of our wedding. I had pulled off something rather big in Russia; and I wanted to give her the best that money could buy. And all last night I was walking about this room like a madman, thinking that my gift had been the cause of her death."

Arden took the box from his hand, and examined it carefully. The address was written in a stiff upright hand, like a schoolboy's—a feigned hand, no doubt; but every stroke was broad and strong. There were no signs of weakness.

Was it the murderer who had sent the necklace? No; he could not believe that. If the crime had been done for plunder, the necklace would have been broken up within an hour, and the loose stones disposed of before the murder was known. There were dealers in London who would not ask too many questions, and who had a ready market for gems of exceptional value. The rubies would have been sent out of the country before the transaction could be investigated. No; the return of the jewels was not the act of a panic-stricken thief, afraid to hold the booty for which he had stained his soul with blood. If the murderer was the man Arden thought, nothing seemed less likely than that he should restore the necklace, nothing less likely than that he should have taken it from his victim's neck.

He went up to the chamber of death with Selby, and looked at the coffin, heaped with white flowers, wreaths and crosses, hearts and lyres; the tribute of many of those trivial friends who in their trivial way had loved the dead woman for her graciousness, for her hospitality, for her liberal view of other women's false steps and escapades, for her readiness to interest herself in other people's loves and sorrows. She was *simpatica.* Everyone had repeated the phrase. Poor Mary was *simpatica;* and her house was delightful. So the wreaths of white lilies and Niphetos roses were not such empty tributes to state and position as they sometimes are.

The room was lovely—white walls, white curtains, white bed, all the furniture of white enamelled wood, only relieved by the pale pink roses on the chintz and the pale green of the carpet sprinkled with rosebuds. A few choice Bartolozzi rustic subjects in oval frames, a stand of delicately bound books, were the only ornaments. A spacious simplicity was the dominant note.

Arden marked every detail, as he stood beside the coffin, with the same automatic observation that he had given to the books in the room below.

Selby looked at the room with admiring tenderness. His own bedchamber was on the same floor, furnished with a Spartan severity. This room had always been to him as a temple, sacred and beloved.

"My Mary—my beautiful Mary!" he sobbed, with clasped hands pressed upon the coffin, heedless of the havoc those heavy hands made among the fragile blossoms.

A shower of white petals rained upon the carpet. He fell on his knees, and laid his haggard face against the side of the coffin.

"Good-bye, Arden," he said; "don't wait for me. You can find your way downstairs, like a good fellow. I shall stay here a little longer. God help me! It is our last day together."

"I shall come to you to-morrow, in the afternoon," said Arden, gently.

"Yes, to-morrow—after the funeral. Come back to this desolate house with me, and see how empty it is without her."

Arden left him on his knees, among the shattered flowers, with his head bowed, and his tears hidden behind the strong hands. There had been nothing said of the manner of his wife's death—no speculations about the murderer. The one paramount fact that she was gone from him absorbed all the thinking power in Selby's mind.

Arden's next visit was to Portland Place. Though he shrank with horror from an encounter with St. Just, the time had come when he must see this man face to face, must try to penetrate the mystery of his existence, find the devil under the mask of humanity.

He was baffled at the outset. Lord St. Just had left London that morning, the servant told him. Questioned closely, the man gave scanty information. He believed that his lordship had gone to Paris, but could not say whether he was going beyond Paris, or how long he was to be away from London. He had taken no one but his Hungarian valet with him. The butler did not know at what hotel his lordship stayed in Paris. He was a new servant, and had no knowledge of his master's habits.

Arden left Portland Place, doubtful as to his next step. His most urgent desire was to return to Rachel immediately after the funeral. He had hated leaving her far away, and among strangers; and though no place could seem safer than that quiet valley amidst the chestnut woods, and though she had two trustworthy servants to protect her, he was not the less uneasy at being separated from her. Otherwise, his course would have been to go straight to Paris, with the detective he had employed in the past, to follow the movements of St. Just. But whatever his duty to the dead, his duty to the living was paramount. He meant to start for Damezzo by the night train for Basle, on the following evening.

On returning to Guelph Place, he was told that a lady had called during his absence. She had not given the servant her name, but she had inquired when his master was likely to be at home, and had left a note, and would call again at three o'clock.

The note was from Mrs. Kelvin.

I write this in case you should be out when I call, in which case I shall return later. Pray do not refuse to see me, dear Mr. Arden. I have something of dire importance to tell you, something which comes neare you and yours than it does to me.

Yours in great distress of mind,

ISABEL KELVIN.

Mrs. Kelvin? Yes, he remembered meeting her at his sister's house. She was one of Mary's friends, a woman of whom he had never approved as his sister's intimate companion; an embodiment of all that is shallow, and frivolous, and unprincipled, in the world of pleasure; a woman who lived only to dress expensively and be admired, and gad from party to party, and talk slightingly of everybody she knew; a beautiful viper, he thought, a creature without soul or conscience, always ready to bite the hand that fed it. She had something to tell him—something terrible—something about his murdered sister. He shuddered at the thought of a revelation from those malicious lips, remembering the cynical airy phrases which had blown away a friend's character, to spice an after-luncheon cigarette. But he could not refuse to hear what she had to tell him. "Something of dire importance."

He walked up and down his library, the only room that he had allowed to be opened, waiting for his visitor, with a heavy heart, and a mind distraught by shapeless morbid fancies, the old trouble coming back upon him, too disturbed to open one of the books piled on the tables, the surplus volumes for which there was no shelf-room, and which were stacked on every available piece of furniture, the accumulations of the last year.

A telegram from Rachel, delivered an hour before, told him that all was well with her. She had promised to telegraph to him every morning, and to write to him every day. He would thus be kept in touch with her during his enforced absence, which he measured anxiously by moments. Since he had heard of St. Just's departure for the Continent, it seemed to him as if the devil were at large, a foul fiend, whose existence menaced Rachel.

She would think of him as the man by whose sick-bed she had knelt in prayer and pious meditation. She could never picture him as Arden knew him, the deathless spirit of evil, passing from phase to phase of human life.

Mrs. Kelvin was announced, and he was surprised to see, not the futile being he remembered of old, not the airy, fluttering creature, tricked out in the last caprice of fashionable extravagance, but a woman, an actual woman, pale, emotional, with frightened eyes and a trembling breathlessness, as of a woman near the fainting-point.

"It is very good of you to see me," she faltered, sinking into the chair he drew forward for her. "I have something terrible to tell you—about your sister."

"If it is anything that reflects upon my sister's character, I must beg you to refrain," he said. "I could not consent to believe it; and I should be sorry to express my anger too strongly to a woman."

"No, no; it is nothing against Mary. I should be the last to breathe one word against her. She was my friend, I was very fond of her. We have had many light-hearted hours together—our butterfly pleasures. Oh, it is agonising to think how that happy life ended. No, no; I have not a thought that wrongs your sister. She was always straight. I want to tell you something horrible—something unbelievable—about her murderer."

"Her murderer! St. Just?"

"What, you know? You *know* that he killed her?"

"I have never doubted it since I read the story of her death."

"How strange! And you could believe it? You could believe anything so horrible of a man who a year ago was counted the very pattern of the Christian life, a saint on earth? You could believe that such a man could suddenly become a murderer?"

"I had reason to believe as much. But how do you come to know his guilt? Is it an instinct, a guess, on your part?"

"No, no; it is not a guess. I was there—close by. I saw the cruel, cruel murder. I saw my poor friend in the clutch of a human fiend, a maniac—for he must be mad. Nothing but madness could account for such a deed."

"You saw the murder; and you did not give evidence against him! You let the murderer escape! He has left the country; and may never be brought to justice. Where was your love for my sister when you let her murderer escape the gallows?"

"Oh, I know how vile it was in me. But he had been my friend. It would be dreadful to doom him to a murderer's death. And then, for my own sake, I could not bear to come forward and confess that I was there, creeping about among the trees, a listener, a spy.

It seemed so contemptible. And I know what lawyers are. I should have been questioned and badgered, and made to commit myself. Why was I there? What was I doing? What was my motive? I should be held up to ridicule and contempt, as a jealous woman, a spy, a listener."

"And, after the inquest, your conscience upbraided you?"

"Yes, I hated myself for having been so cowardly; and I made up my mind that I would come forward at the adjourned inquest, whatever it cost me."

"I'm afraid your repentance has come too late. If St. Just is the man I believe him to be, he will escape all human retribution. And now tell me—tell me every detail of that dreadful night—everything that came within your knowledge."

"That is what I want to do, Mr. Arden. I want to get this load off my mind—this load of misery. I will tell you—everything. I won't spare myself, however you may despise me."

"I shall not despise you. I respect the feeling that has brought you here to-day; and I believe what you tell me—that you really loved my sister."

"Indeed, that is true. She was my favourite friend. She was always kind, always generous. She has helped me often with money when I have been stranded. I was never afraid to go to her in a difficulty. I felt as much at home in her house as in my own. Well, I must begin at the beginning, and must confess that St. Just had an extraordinary influence over my mind. I had always admired him, even when he was a saint, and when people were inclined to laugh at what they called his philanthropic fads; but this summer, after he had broken away from his old life, and had made himself notorious by his dissipated habits, his influence over me became an infatuation. I cannot describe his power over women. Whatever the charm may be, it escapes analysis: but I have seen it as strong upon other women as it was upon me. And I saw your sister yielding to that power in a way that made me tremble for her—even for her, who had been so thoroughly able to hold her own against every danger."

She stopped short, in her hurried and half-breathless speech, sniffed at a bottle of smelling-salts; then, with a burning blush, went on.

"I wanted to marry him, you see. I am always hard up, and I am awfully tired of knocking about the world alone; and though he is not rich, it would have been a decent match for me. I wanted him to care for me, and to offer to marry me. I think he admired me a little, when we met this season. He hung about me at parties, and seemed to like to talk to me. Women have a kind of instinct, don't you know, that tells them they are admired. I thought the rest would follow, and that I should have someone to care for me and pay my debts, and give me an assured position. And then, all at once, I saw that it was hopeless. Your sister had captivated him. He cared for no one else. He devoted himself to her, and followed her about in a way that meant mischief. I think he tried to compromise her, to blight her character, before he asked her to throw everything to the winds for his sake. People began to talk about her infatuation. But, after all, I knew how strong she was; that she could go to the brink of the precipice and not fall over; and so I didn't give up hope. She would lead him on, and then laugh in his face; and when he was piqued and angry, I thought perhaps my chance might come. I could soothe his wounded vanity. I could let him see that I worshipped him; and so I might snatch the prize. Horrid, isn't it, Mr. Arden? But that's what women come to, when they struggle to keep afloat in an expensive set without the means. I often wish I had the strength of mind to chuck it all, and hide myself in a Buckinghamshire village, and teach in the Sunday school."

"For God's sake, come to the vital point," Arden entreated. "The murder! What did you see or hear that night? What do you know of my sister's death?"

"I saw them leave the supper-tent, and saunter away into the darkness under the trees. I followed them, watching and listening. I wanted to hear how far things had gone—whether Mary would be staunch. I knew she loved him. But which would be stronger—love or pride? I followed them to the edge of the narrow backwater. It was moonlight in places, and then dark under the trees. I followed close enough to hear their talk. They were too much absorbed in each other to hear me creeping near them. He was imploring her to go away with him, to lead a wandering life with him, and laugh the world to scorn; and when she was resolute in her refusal—when she declared again and again that nothing would induce her to disgrace her name and break her husband's heart—he began to be angry. He told her that she had led him on, fooled him to the top of his bent, had treated him as no woman would dare to treat a man if she did not mean to belong to him. He told her that she belonged to him already, by an unspoken concession, by a tacit surrender. There was no one of that night's mob who did not believe her to be his mistress; and to prate to him of her good name, and her husband's honour, after she had listened to him as she had listened to-night, after she had let him read the secret of her heart, was childish folly. And then, as she answered him indignantly, he grew even more insulting; he grasped her arm violently—they were standing in an opening of the trees with the moonlight on them—and he told her that she was his by their mutual love, and that he would not give her up. She should not leave that place alive, if she did not promise to belong to him, from that hour, in spite of the world."

Again she paused, breathless, her eyes dilated as memory set the scene before her, so recent, so vivid in its reality.

Arden was pacing the room, speechless, his clenched hands before his eyes, dry and burning, and in an agony of rage too fierce for tears.

"She was frightened when he seized her arm; she broke away from him with a scream, and rushed through the trees, past where I was hiding. I was going to her, forgetful of myself, only wanting to help her; but he was too quick for me. He rushed after her, and caught her in his arms. I saw his face in the moonlight—the face of a fiend, murderous, diabolical. His left arm was round her waist, and I saw him throw the beautiful frightened face, the beautiful head and neck, back across his arm, while his right hand grasped her throat. I heard her choking cry, the horrible death-agony; and then I saw him lift her on his shoulder, and carry her towards the backwater. I was paralysed with horror, and I fell on the ground under the trees, not fainting, but utterly helpless. I could not move. I don't know how long it was, but it was daylight when I crept away. I don't know how he left the place. I never saw him after that moment till an hour after, when he was among the crowd at the station—talking, laughing, with Mrs. Stormont."

"Did you go back to the water to look at his victim?"

"No; I was afraid. I dared not see her face again—the face I had seen in her death-agony—the wild eyes, the writhing lips. I did not know where he had taken her. I dared not go to look for her. I felt powerless to do anything, except creep back to the other people and get home, anyhow. I had to pass over the spot where he killed her—the hateful spot—an open space between two great beeches, and as I went stumbling along, my foot struck against something; and I looked down and saw Mary's ruby necklace lying in the trampled grass."

"Then it was you who sent it to Selby?"

"Yes; it was I. I wanted him to know that the murderer was no common thief. I picked up the necklace, and put it round my neck, under my cloak; and then I ran to the gates, losing my way ever so many times in my confusion I was half demented, and hardly knew where I was going, or even who I was. I caught myself wondering about the place, and the time, and the meaning of everything. I must have looked like a madwoman; but nobody noticed me in the *sauve qui peut* at the gates; and I got into a brake with a crowd of chattering girls, who sat on each other's laps, and talked of the cotillon, and I scrambled into a saloon carriage with them, and sat in a corner, and pretended to be asleep, and so got to Vauxhall, where my brougham was waiting for me."

"Well, you must appear at the adjourned inquest, and describe the murder as you saw it. No one will ask you how you came to be at that spot. You have only to relate what you saw and heard, and can swear to. But you must not wait for the inquest. You must come with me at once to Scotland Yard, and make your deposition to the Chief of the Criminal Investigation Department, so that their machinery for the pursuit of an absconding felon may be put in motion."

He rang the bell, and gave his order.

"A hansom at the door immediately."

The shrill whistle rang through Guelph Place, and was heard in St. James's Street. Mrs. Kelvin offered no objection.

"It is a horrible thing to have to do," she said, "but it is for Mary's sake."

They were not more than half an hour in the Chief's spacious room, where the narration of St. Just's crime was received with a businesslike air by an imperturbable official. A murder, more or less, could not agitate the mind that had to carry the burden of metropolitan crime within a radius of fifteen miles from his office. The Chief was, as it were, a Mezzofanti, or a Bunsen, in the criminal tongues. He had the grammar of every species of criminality at his finger's end. He was grave, and profoundly attentive, taking rapid notes of every particular; but he was not astonished. That Lord St. Just should have done this murder seemed to strike him as no more curious than if a shoeless tramp off the high-road had been accused of the crime.

"It looks like a case of homicidal mania," he said; and that was his only comment.

He had watched Mrs. Kelvin closely as she told her story, which she made brief and direct on this occasion, nerving herself to the effort. He wanted to make sure that it was not a case of hysteria, the fabrication of a neurotic brain.

From Scotland Yard Arden went to Grosvenor Square, after having taken Mrs. Kelvin to her house in Half Moon Street. She was worn out by the emotions of the last two hours, and sat silent and speechless in the hansom as they drove through the crowded streets between Whitehall and Mayfair.

The house was small, a *façade,* two windows broad, with pink geraniums from basement to garrets, and a white door. It was a house like a *bonbonnière,* that gave an impression of charm and prettiness, which the visitor carried in with him, and transferred to his hostess. There was no discordant note in the gamut of beauty, between the pavement outside and the perfectly dressed woman sitting by an artistic hearth.

To-day Mrs. Kelvin was out of tune with this futile prettiness, and did not look as if she belonged to the house. Indeed, she stared about her vaguely when the hansom stopped, and Arden alighted to hand her out, as if she hardly knew that she lived there.

"I thank you for having carried this thing through," he said, as he parted with her. "Be assured that there was nothing else to be done."

"And my evidence will hang St. Just," she said, looking at him with agonised eyes. "If you knew how I admired him—what dreams I have had about him!"

"But they were deluding dreams. You know now that the man is a monster. You will forget him, I hope, when all is over. And as for his fate, I think you need have little fear. I don't believe his crime will ever be brought to justice."

The door had been opened, and they were speaking in lowered accents, while the highly respectable butler waited in the hall.

The hardest part of Arden's work remained to be done. He had to tell Selby the story of his wife's death, a story in which, however he might soften details and throw a gloss over cruel facts, the adoring husband must needs discover that his wife had dallied with the tempter, had suffered herself to be courted and pursued; only making a stand against the destroyer when her folly had brought about a crisis that meant life or death—at least, the death of character and honour, the ruin of a woman's soul. That in this case it should have meant murder was an abnormal development of a normal situation.

Walter Arden spoke as a man who loved the dead woman, and pitied her devoted husband. If these ghastly details of the tragedy could have been kept from Selby's knowledge, he would have been silent; but for Selby to hear the story at the inquest, from Mrs. Kelvin's lips, unprepared for such a revelation, would be a harder blow.

Arden tried to excuse his sister. Her folly had been the common indiscretion of women of her class. She had allowed a man to pursue her, meaning only to trifle with him, flattered by attentions that had neither value nor significance for her. She had not reckoned with the fierce passions of a profligate—a homicidal maniac, perhaps; for the crime, as witnessed by Mrs. Kelvin, seemed the crime of a madman. She had not understood.

Selby caught at every excuse that spared his idol.

"No, no; she did not understand," he sobbed. "How should she understand her danger? She was accustomed to be admired, to have the best men in London society hanging round her, worshipping her. We used to talk of her conquests. I used to chaff her about her victims. It was a favourite joke with us. She knew what perfect confidence I had in her. I knew her character—such pride; such fearlessness. Women of that stamp never go wrong. How should she reckon with a profligate and a madman, like this devil? Oh, God, that I may see him swing! They must let me see him. I have the right, whatever their law may be. I shall never believe he has paid the penalty, unless I see him fall through the drop."

From Douglas Campbell, Tasmania, to Walter Arden, London.

My dear Arden,

Your last letter interested me profoundly, as indeed all your letters have done, and however beyond the limits of human thought your idea of the entrance of an evil spirit into the tabernacle of a pure departed soul may be, it does not pass beyond my conception of the things that may be. I have never acknowledged that the manifestation of the powers of good and evil ended with the Apostolic age; and that after Peter and Paul had passed from earth there were to be no more miraculous healing of the blind and the lame, no more raising of the dead, no more angelic visitants, before whose coming prison walls fell, and iron fetters were loosened, no more visions, no more opening of the heavens, as they opened before Saul of Tarsus, transforming the pitiless persecutor into the ardent disciple. There are those who see life in its material, and those who see it in its spiritual, aspect. To me nothing is incredible; for I believe in the spirit-world. I walk as one who moves among the unseen. The transmigration of souls is no more wonderful than the communication of thought from the mind of the dead to the mind of the living; and you know that *this* is with me a fixed article of faith. I therefore recognise no impossibility in the lifeless clay of a good man becoming the tenement of an evil spirit. I confess to a deep-seated belief in a universe ruled by conflicting powers, a ceaseless battle between good and evil, a beneficent God, a malignant devil. I know this is not the modern view. We have eliminated incarnate iniquity from our namby-pamby latter-day creed; and by banishing the devil we have made it easier to do without God. Yet in the experience of every man's life there is the sense of an abiding Beneficence, towards which his hands stretch out in the hour of despair, when the deep waters of sorrow are closing over his head; and of an omnipresent power of evil luring him, dragging him into the depths of sin, working against his peace, turning the innocent joys of life to dust and ashes, making the good things that he has loved hateful. I am ready to believe that in your sufferings of the past years you have been the sport of the enemy of man; but on the other hand I am constrained to consider your state of mind from a commonsense standpoint; and so considered, I see in you the victim of a horrible hallucination, the morbid growth of a highly nervous temperament, and the not unnatural development of thought, in a mind unsustained by the belief in something higher and nobler than itself.

In plain words, my dear Arden, I believe that the materialist, in shutting his mind against the idea of God, is in danger of opening his mind to the idea of Satan. It is the old parable of the empty house and the seven devils. So large a part of man's existence is imagination and thought, that he cannot be satisfied without a belief in the supernatural, the something stronger, or the something better than himself; and if imagination has no dream of heaven, and thought is fettered to the sordid realities of earth, what can the end be but despair? If God is not a necessary fact in the universe, the idea of God is a necessary element in the mind of man. I do not despair of you. Dark as your horizon has been, and obstinate as your rejection of the faith in the world beyond, the faith that upheld me in the hour when Death struck my promised bride, and when the light went out of my life for ever, I believe that peace may yet be yours, if you, who have been so ready to believe in the children of darkness, will open your heart and mind to the children of light; that invisible legion of angels who encompass and protect the righteous upon earth. From those ministering spirits to the Omnipotent Ruler of the universe is a natural and easy transition. Years ago, in our heated discussions, you declared yourself an absolute materialist. You scoffed at all things unthinkable or unknowable. A terrible experience has shown you the diabolical side of the unknowable. God grant that your future experience may show you the divine and the infinitely good.

You will say this is a sermon instead of a letter, but I know you will forgive the preacher.

Yours always,

DOUGLAS CAMPBELL.

Campbell's letter was delivered in Guelph Place on the morning of the funeral, and was hastily read and laid aside for consideration later. The previous evening had brought Arden a letter from James Walsh, the East End doctor, which he read with eager interest, even at a time when all his thoughts were centred on the tragedy of his sister's death.

Maple Row, Commercial Road,
July 16th, 189-.

DEAR MR. ARDEN,

When we met after my return from Trevelyan, I told you that I meant to send an account of Lord St. Just's case to the *Lancet*. I carried out this intention, and wrote a detailed description of the strange experience, taking care to give no clue to my patient's identity, and therefore withholding my own name from the foot of the letter.

Well, my communication attracted more attention than I had anticipated, and gave rise to a discussion which lasted some time, other examples being cited that bore more or less resemblance to my case; but there was only one of these in which I saw a startling correspondence in the manifestations of the patient's altered nature; and seeing that this account was contributed by a very old doctor, whom I had known as an occasional visitor during my hospital practice, I was induced to call upon him, in the hope of obtaining further details.

Dr. Maldon, who for about forty years was head physician at one of the great city hospitals, has lived the greater part of his life in the heart of commercial London. While almost all his brother practitioners have pitched their tents in Harley Street and Cavendish Square, or places of corresponding gentility, old Dr. Maldon has been content to live in an early Georgian court, buried among banking-houses and mercantile offices, a silent solitude amidst the throbbing pulses of the great city. He is known to be a rich man—rich enough to gratify his taste in a West End house, and a country seat, if he so willed; but he has the adhesive temperament, the love of old things long used and familiar; and I could see by the way he walked round his sombre panelled sitting-room, with its ponderous early Victorian furniture, its cockatoo cage, and wicker dog-kennel, where a plethoric fawn-coloured pug lay perdu, that in this city abode of his were garnered all the things he cares for.

I told him who I was, and reminded him of our meetings in the hospital, when I had been proud to follow him in his round of the wards, and to listen to his words of wisdom, as he stood beside the beds. He remembered me, and was quite ready to talk of the strange case which he had written about, when he found that I was the writer of the first letter.

He said that of course all he was going to tell me

would be told in confidence, and he would therefore withhold no particulars. The experience had come upon him as a very young man, when he was assistant to a general practitioner in the Midlands, in a hunting-country. During his principal's absence he was called in to attend a young man, who was lying at the chief hotel in the town, after a bad accident in the hunting-field. His horse had turned a somersault over a stiff timber fence; and the rider had been pitched upon his head. It was a bad case of concussion of the brain, with other injuries. Valet and grooms were in despair. Their master was the best and kindest of men. If he had been their own flesh and blood they could not have been fonder of him. There were friends of the young man staying at the hotel, who gave him as good a character, and showed the keenest interest in his welfare.

It was a very bad case, and the patient went very near the gates of death. The hunting-season was over before he began to recover, and the convalescence was very slow; but from the hour of restored consciousness the character of the man, as demonstrated in every word and every act, appeared the very opposite of the character described by his friends and servants. The kind and generous master, the sweet-tempered, unselfish friend, had become a selfish and savage tyrant, subject to paroxysms of blind unreasoning fury that touched the border-line of madness. The valet was an elderly man, and had been servant to his master's father; so the young doctor ventured to question him as to the family history. Had there ever been madness in the family? Yes, the man admitted, there had been a terrible case among his master's remote ancestry, more than a hundred years ago, a case of madness and homicide, the murder of a mad-house doctor, in the days when lunatics were treated with infernal cruelty. This unhappy man, the patient's great-grandfather, had been one of the early followers of the Wesleys, a fanatic in religion, and notorious in his own county for leading the life of an anchorite, and spending his fortune upon works of charity, his manner of going about among the labouring classes of the district, mostly miners, becoming more and more eccentric, until his eccentricities culminated in unmistakable indications of insanity.

Dr. Maldon never met his patient again after he saw him drive away from the hotel in a post-chaise, with his valet and head groom in attendance, on the first stage of his long cross-country journey to the West of England.

The mention of the West of England startled me. I asked if the man's home was in Cornwall. The reply was more startling, for it told me that the man was our man's grandfather, the ninth Lord St. Just; and his after-history was no less tragical than the transformation of the man you and I loved. Dr. Waldon's patient survived his accident only three years, married, became the father of a son and heir, and six months after his boy's birth drowned himself in a lake in the grounds of his Highland shooting-box. Dr. Maldon heard later from a member of the family that there could be no doubt of this Lord St. Just's madness; though the devoted care of his wife, a remarkably clever woman, had kept the secret of his infirmity, at the cost of great suffering to herself.

Now, in Dr. Maldon's view of the case, the strain of

madness latent in the St. Just family had reappeared in his patient, as a consequence of a serious injury to the brain. My own view of what I call *our* case corresponds with his view. I believe that during St. Just's illness some subtle change took place in his brain; and that the man whose conduct and instincts so perplexed us was, to all intents and purposes, a madman. I await with profound anxiety the future development of his character, so changed from all I remember of benevolence and noble feeling.

Believe me, with apologies for the length of this letter,

Ever faithfully yours,

RICHARD WALSH.

Madness! Atavism! The strain of insanity in the blood of his race! Could the change in the man he had known be so plausibly, so reasonably, accounted for? Arden brooded over the doctor's letter during the night journey to Basle, sleepless among slumbering fellow-passengers. The few hours of the summer night seemed intolerably slow, and a long day's journey was to follow before he could reach his young wife in the quiet valley, an hour's drive from Chiavenna.

Lucerne, the St. Gothard, Como, the lake, the railway again; and then extra post to his destination. As he thought of the different stages of his journey it seemed endless. Such a pleasant holiday trip for the mind at ease—a luxurious progress through scenes of surpassing beauty—eating, drinking, reading, talking, while that lovely panorama of mountain and torrent, village and vineyard, river and garden and meadow, slowly unfolds itself, and Switzerland melts into Italy; but for the mind racked with fear, what slow torture!

St. Just was at large, a homicidal madman, relentless, a devil of insane fury. After Mrs. Kelvin's account of the murder, could Arden doubt that the man was mad? A murder so cruel, so motiveless, could have its beginning only in the brain of insanity. St. Just was at large; St. Just who, in his better nature, had been Rachel's secret adorer. The fear that he had gone, not to Paris, as his servant affirmed, but in pursuit of Rachel, filled Arden's mind with unspeakable horror. It was an idle fear, perhaps—one of his morbid imaginings—but it was a fear that made the night and day one long agony.

XIV.

THE solitary days had passed slowly, but peacefully, for Rachel in the quiet valley, where the glory of the surrounding hills, the deep peace of the chestnut woods, the long level pastures sprinkled with pale purple crocuses, alive with the fairy music of unseen grasshoppers, the river creeping lazily between verdant banks, and reflecting the cloudless blue, the sense of summer in the air, all made for contentment and joy. Rachel was peculiarly sensitive to the influence of natural beauty; and though her mind dwelt much upon the tragedy of Mary Selby's death, she could but feel the Divine gift of life, in a world where there was so much of varied and romantic loveliness. Her reunion with her husband had brought an abiding peace into her life. Sympathy, confidence, the perfect bond between man and wife, had been made good as in the early days of their marriage. She thought of him in his trouble with profound tenderness, and longed for his return, but without anxiety; for post and telegraph had kept them in touch with each other in the few days of their severance; and to-night she was to welcome him back to a place which seemed like home, so deep was the charm of its tranquil beauty, and the sense that she had been happy there.

She had made friends of the children and the

women; and was almost as much in sympathy with them as if they had been her old pensioners of East-End London. She had sat in their little gardens, and heard the story of their simple lives, their hard work, and many deprivations—a life as laborious as the life of the London poor, but with less of struggle and uncertainty. The children admired and adored the beautiful stranger, who talked to them in her slow careful Italian, and who took such pains to understand their patois; they hung about her footsteps as she walked by the river, and brought her flowers, which were really the gifts of love, not the offering of the cadging child greedy for the stranger's pence. Her money gifts were to the house-mothers, or the old women, never to the children, for whom she had cakes and fruit sometimes in the trellised arbour where she spent the hottest hours of the day. She liked to see the bright olive faces, and the dark eyes, peering in at the leafy door, smiling and beaming at her, eager for her notice. She would take the smallest children on her lap, and let them touch her laces, and her hair, with inquisitive little fingers; and as she looked at the dark heads crowding round her chair, she would select the boy whose age came nearest to the years of her son, had he lived. He was never forgotten, never long absent from her mind, and often—very often—present in her dreams. She had dreamt lately that he was given back to her. She had held him in her arms, with a sense of overwhelming joy. The dream haunted her, and was with her in all her solitary hours. Every night on her knees she read the story of the Christ-Child's coming, of the gladness on earth and in heaven; and that Divine Image went with all her thoughts of the child she had lost, and the child she had seen in her dreams.

The hour of her husband's return was approaching. She had postponed dinner till his arrival, though she did not expect him till nearly ten o'clock. It was past nine, and she was walking in the garden, with her young St. Bernard frolicking round her, in the cool evening air. The clock of the neighbouring church had not long struck the first quarter, when she heard traveller wheels on the road from the frontier, and rejoiced wonderingly at this early arrival. She did not pause to question whether the carriage could be bringing her husband. Impulsive in her glad surprise, she ran to the gate to meet the traveller. She stood beside the drive, a few paces from the open gates, an ethereal figure, in her white gown, with bare head. Her dog growled angrily when the carriage stopped, and a man sprang out and stood in front of her with outstretched hands. It was not her husband.

The moonlight flashed upon a pale, resolute face.

"Lord St. Just!" she cried, startled and scared at the unexpected appearance.

The St. Bernard made a whining noise that was almost a howl, and slunk into the shrubbery.

Rachel shrank away from those outstretched hands with a sudden sense of loathing, as if some unclean animal had approached her. And then there flashed upon her all that her husband had said of the change in St. Just's nature, and it seemed, as she looked at him, paralysed by an inexplicable fear, that this was not the man she had known, the friend she had trusted, the saint by whose bed she had knelt in an hour that had been a sacred memory, even after the peril of death was past; an hour on the threshold of the grave, hallowed by the most solemn rites of the Church she loved.

"You look frightened, Mrs. Arden," he said. "Is it such a very startling thing to see me in Switzerland?"

"I am expecting my husband—I thought he was coming, when I heard your carriage. But he is not really due for another quarter of an hour."

"You are expecting him from England? From Chiavenna?"

"Yes. He was to be at Chiavenna at eight o'clock."

"I travelled by the same train. I am sorry I have some bad news for you," St. Just said slowly, after a few moments' silence.

The measured words and compassionate tone scared her, and instantly suggested calamity.

"There has been an accident. He is hurt—dangerously hurt!" she exclaimed, panic-stricken.

"No, no. Pray be calm. There has been an accident. Not on the railway. He has been hurt, but not dangerously. I have come to take you to him."

"You are very good. I will go this instant. Where is he?"

"At a village a few miles off. He was driving in an open carriage; his horses bolted at the bridge near the frontier, and he was thrown out. He fell against one of those granite posts that guard the road. There are contusions, a broken collar-bone, severe injuries—but nothing dangerous to life. It was a wonderful escape. If he had fallen over the edge of the road, he must have been killed. Will you go to the inn where he is lying?

My carriage will take you. I changed horses at the frontier."

"Yes; I will go this instant. It was kind of you to come for me. I had better bring my maid, and Walter's servant. They can be useful."

"No, no; time is too precious. He had not recovered consciousness when I left him; and the doctor thought it important that he should see a familiar face when he comes to himself. Your people can follow."

"Yes, they can follow in another carriage. I will give orders. What is the name of the place?"

"It is the village nearest the Custom House. There is only one inn. There can be no mistake."

"You say he has a doctor with him?"

"Yes, an Italian—an intelligent little man, who seemed quite equal to the occasion."

"And he told you there was no danger?"

"None, that he could foresee, with proper care."

Rachel ran to the house, and to her room, where she summoned her faithful handmaid, and gave the necessary instructions. Valet and maid were to follow, directly a carriage could be got for them. She put on a hat and cloak, and hurried back to the gate where St. Just was waiting for her. He had not entered the house during her brief absence. The driver was in his seat, ready to start.

The carriage was a closed landau, from which it was not easy to see the road in the varying lights and shadows. The moon was waning, that moon which had looked upon the murder of Mary Selby. For some way the road was familiar to Rachel. They crossed the bridge over the torrent, passed two or three white houses, where lights were glowing in the windows, then drove rapidly downhill, to the road along which Rachel passed and repassed in her daily walks. She knew every yard of the way they were going, up to this point, but she saw very little of the passing scene. The glass on her side of the carriage was drawn up, and St. Just's figure hid the open window on his side.

Her whole mind was absorbed in questioning him about her husband—the kind of inn to which he had been taken, the attendance and accommodation, the distance from the scene of the accident, the manner in which he had been carried. Every detail was vital. She had no faith in the Italian doctor's knowledge or skill. A village doctor! She would telephone from the frontier to St. Moritz, for the English doctor she knew there. They had been driving for half an hour before she began to think of the road on which they were travelling, so keen had been her anxiety about her husband's condition. And then suddenly it occurred to her that, although the horses were going at a good pace, they seemed always going uphill.

"Are we on the right road?" she asked, in an agitated voice. "I thought it was all downhill to Chiavenna."

"No; the road varies. There is a stiffish hill on this side of the frontier."

The horses were going slowly now, and they were obviously going uphill. Rachel was bewildered, doubtful, and perplexed; for it seemed to her, on reflection, that they had been travelling upward the whole way, though her troubled mind had failed to note the fact before.

She put down the window hurriedly and looked out.

They were in a street of white houses, on the ridge of a hill; an old gateway, a big church, looked ghostly in the wan light of the moon. It might have been a phantom city, a place of dreams. She looked up at the church, with its high tower and cupola, the classic archway.

"Why, this is Locco!" she cried; "the village on the top of the hill. What does it mean, Lord St. Just? Why have you deceived me? Is my husband here?"

"Yes, he is here."

"But why—why so far off the main road. No, no; it can't be true. It is a trick of some kind. Where is he?"

The carriage turned a sharp corner in the narrow street, passed under the archway, and pulled up in an open space in front of a large house, a palace once, now an inn.

A man opened the door as the carriage stopped. Lights were burning in the hall—spacious, gloomy; a place of faded splendours and dense shadows, a low ceiling, with carved cornice and heavy cross-beams. A wide stone staircase, with ponderous balusters of dark Sienna marble, faced the doorway. An elderly chambermaid was in attendance. Travellers were evidently expected, albeit the hour was late.

Rachel questioned the man in Italian.

"The gentleman who had been thrown out of a carriage, was he in that house?"

"The fellow understands nothing but his own patois," said St. Just, hurriedly. "Come, come, Mrs. Arden, don't waste time, now you are here."

She followed him up the shallow marble steps, almost mechanically, the chambermaid going in front, carrying a pair of tall candles in copper candlesticks. The unaccountable repulsion she had felt on St. Just's appearance in the garden was stronger now. In doubt, and in a vague horror, she followed him, not in fear. She who had never shrunk from danger in the East End slums, who had sat in the house of crime, knelt by the bed of the dying convict, knew not fear. But a sense of aversion, an instinctive recoil from the man who had once been her trusted friend, chilled her with a sickening dread. She looked about her with wide eyes, as she followed St. Just up four flights of the broad staircase, to the second floor—the noble floor, as it had once been called—and into a large sitting-room, where the two candles, which the chambermaid placed on a centre table, served only to indicate the gloomy spaciousness, the tapestried walls, tarnished gilding, and sombre colouring.

"Where is my husband?" she cried, hurrying across the room, to a door opposite the one by which they had entered.

She tried the door in front of her, and found it locked; then turned and saw St. Just standing before the entrance door, and heard the key turn as he locked it.

"A thousand miles away; in London, so far as I know," he answered, smiling at her.

"What do you mean? Is it a trick, then? He was right. You are changed—utterly changed. You who were so good, so honourable."

"A man may grow tired of being good, as you call it. Goodness earns such poor wages. All the best things in this world are for the not good; the wicked, perhaps, you would call them; the men who desire gladness, and beauty, and the joy of life."

"Why did you bring me here? Is my husband safe—unhurt? Have you told me nothing but lies?"

"I have spread a net for a glorious bird, that could be caught no other way. It was a stale device, my love, but the only one that would serve. And you are here, you are my companion, in this lonely mountain inn, empty of people, except the inn servants, who take us for man and wife. My queen, my goddess, you belong to me now, and for ever—this world's paltry for ever. You are mine to the end of this mortal life, my life or yours."

She saw the light in his eyes, the light of madness as she thought. Two spots of hectic red flamed on his hollow cheeks, but his lips were ashen. Nothing but a maddened brain could account for the devilry of his conduct. She braced her nerves to meet the danger.

"Open that door," she said, looking at him with resolute eyes, an indomitable spirit shining out of her pale face, every line rigid, her head held high, a noble fearlessness in her attitude as she confronted him. "Unlock that door, this instant. Do you think I am afraid of you?"

"Afraid? No, no, Rachel. You know your power, the power of your Divine beauty. I am master of the situation; but I am your slave, ready to crawl at your feet, to let you set your foot upon my neck. Hard words from those sweet lips will fall like roses. You cannot treat me so ill that I shall love you less. Do with me what you will; only stay with me, only give me love for love."

In that moment, seeing the fierce passion in his face, her courage failed all at once, and she realised her helplessness, caught in the toils, a bird in the snare of the fowler, a pure woman for the first time face to face with impurity, the passion of the Satyr for the nymph.

She shrank from him with such aversion as she had never felt for human kind. The light in his eyes was devilish; the lurid patches on his cheeks suggested the fires of hell. She had faced madness before to-night, and had not feared; but now she knew that she was facing something worse than madness. She felt as if she were standing amidst the roar of waters, with the rising tide encircling her, great waves leaping up to overwhelm her, and storm-winds shrieking round her, drowning her call for help. She gave one wild cry, looked about her in her desperation, saw that one of the long casement windows was ajar, and moved towards it as St. Just approached her, facing him with widely opened eyes.

He came towards her quietly, with a smile upon his pale lips.

"Your master, my beloved, and yet your slave," he said, holding out his arms, and then stopped suddenly and reeled against a chair, as she rushed to the window, flung it open, and vanished from his sight.

Still leaning over the chair, struggling for breath, he heard the muffled sound of something falling in the garden below, and knew that she had thrown herself from the balcony. He felt a torrent of blood welling up in his throat and choking him, as he staggered to the open window, and on to the light iron balcony, and, looking down through the darkness, he saw the white figure lying in the long grass by the side of a stone fountain, fifteen feet below.

The house was built on the steep slope of the hill, and the garden at the back was not more than fifteen feet below the rooms on the second floor.

He had scarcely strength to drag himself back into the room, and to the bell, and then he sank into one of the mammoth sixteenth-century chairs, and let his head fall back against the tapestried cushion.

Rage, disappointment, humiliation, had been in his mind as he saw his prey escape him; but now there was but one passion left in him, the fierce love of life. He knew that he was dying. This bright red stream which was pouring from his lips was life—life ebbing momently—the life he loved, the life in which he had triumphed over weaker lives, had always felt himself the stronger in every contest of human force. It was going from him: and when again should he taste the joy of living—how win his way back to the earth he loved? The machine was broken.

Someone knocked at the door. He could not open it. Or, if he could, what could mortal aid do for him? The machine was broken. He knew that this was the end.

He heard people trying to open the door, then voices, then someone came to the other door, and tried it, the door he had locked that afternoon when he had engaged the rooms, and made his survey of the bower he had chosen for his caged bird. He had heard of this mountain village from the Italian courier whom he had employed to discover Arden's whereabouts in Switzerland, and report his movements; a man of many languages, and no prejudices. And from this retreat he meant to convey his captive to Genoa—a willing captive, he hoped—and thence to far-off seas, beyond the reach of social laws, or a husband's revenge; far off to loveliest lands under torrid skies, and that semi-savage life for which he had longed with a fervid desire, while hemmed round with the restraints of modern civilisation; the life of the savage and the brute, for whom to exist means to enjoy, whose vision of life knows neither past nor future.

XV.

THE white walls of Locco were shining in the morning sun, and the church bells were ringing for mass, when Arden alighted in front of the old-world palace that was now an inn. He looked a spectral figure in the vivid light, his haggard face grey with anguish. He had been driving to and fro since ten o'clock on the previous night, when he arrived at Damezzo, where he was received as if he had been a ghost, and was told of the supposed accident, and of his wife's hurried departure for an inn near the frontier, with Lord St. Just. Man and maid had followed half an hour later, by their mistress's order.

Frantic with anxiety, Arden started in pursuit, as soon as fresh horses could be got for him; but it was a wild pursuit, since he had no clue to the way St. Just's carriage had gone. The innkeeper declared it had taken the Chiavenna road; but Arden had met only one carriage, which might have been the one containing his servants. He had not noticed the occupants, as it drove past him in the doubtful light.

He went to the station at Chiavenna, after having made inquiries for newly arrived travellers, at two hotels. There was a train that left after midnight, and he waited till that was gone; since it was possible that

St. Just might have tricked a distracted wife into going farther than he had urged her at first. With that story of her husband's danger, he might take her where he chose. In her agitation and distress she might scarcely know where she was being taken. The midnight train left; but there was no sign of the travellers he was watching for. He started on the way back, after changing horses, but it was a slower and longer journey, and he was tortured by the knowledge of his helplessness. What next could he do, and what next, and what next? His wife was in the power of a murderer; fiend, or madman, he knew not which. A homicidal lunatic, the victim of hereditary mania; or the reincarnation of the wickedest human being he had ever known. Whichever view he chose to take of the man St. Just, the knowledge that his wife was in that man's power was equally appalling.

There were no tidings of his wife at Damezzo. The two servants had come back, after their ineffectual search for the inn near the frontier, where they had been told their master would be found. The false information, and their mistress's hurried departure with St. Just, had awakened suspicion; and the valet had spent the early morning hours going about the neighbourhood, in the hope of getting on the track of the carriage that had spirited away his master's wife. There was the possibility of error rather than villainy; but while the woman inclined to think there had been a mistake in the direction that her mistress had given her, the man believed the worst, and devoted himself with unflagging energy to the search for information.

The people of Damezzo were early risers, whose day

began soon after the sun appeared above the edge of the eastern hills, a golden light behind the dark line of fir-trees, the white homesteads, and cattle-sheds. From one of this industrious race the valet heard of an empty landau that had been seen returning from Locco at day-break; and the description of the carriage, with a grey and a brown horse, tallied with that in which the man had seen his mistress leave the hotel. The valet now thought it possible that there had been a mistake on his mistress's part as to the place of the accident; and that his master was lying at Locco.

He went back to the hotel, and met Arden in the hall; so that last possibility of honest dealing on St. Just's part was at an end. He told his master what he had heard; and a quarter of an hour later Arden was on his way to Locco behind another pair of horses.

At the inn at Locco all was confusion and terror. The unknown traveller of yesterday, a great gentleman who had engaged the whole of the noble floor for him-self and his lady, was quite dead; and the lady, the beautiful young wife, was lying unconscious, and in peril of death, having fallen, the good God alone knew where-fore, from the balcony of the saloon.

"By the merciful interpositon of our blessed Lady, the fall had not been fatal," the innkeeper said piously. "The sweet young English lady was still living."

"Was the signor a relation—perhaps the honourable lady's brother?" suggested the chambermaid.

"I am her husband."

"Heavens! And the gentleman who brought her here, and who spoke of her as his wife——"

"Was an unspeakable villain. Is it true that he is dead?"

"True as the sky above us. He had not been in this house ten minutes; the saloon bell rang violently—we have no electric bells here; it is a loud bell that can be heard all over the house—we rushed to answer it, for it had the sound of danger. We found both doors locked—the door on the landing, and the door in the bedroom where he now lies. All the rooms on the noble floor have doors of communication. We heard strange sounds within—sounds of choking—deep groans; and we broke open the door. He was lying in the armchair. His head had fallen across the arm, his hands were grasping the woodwork convulsively, as in the last struggle; the blood was bubbling from his lips, but slower and slower. His eyes were wide open—glassy, horrible. Ah, signor, it will be long before we forget that sight. All has been done that was needful. I have taken care of that. I sent for the mayor last night. The signor had a letter-case in his pocket, stuffed with bank-notes, which has been put in a sealed envelope. Everything has been done in proper order. They will bury him this night, in our little cemetery, unless you have the body removed before the evening."

"Let him lie where his last crime brought him. He is lucky to have escaped a worse fate. And now take me to my wife."

"La signora is in the room at the other end of the noble floor," said the landlord, and led the way to a spacious chamber, which looked like a state bedroom in the castle of Otranto, a panelled room, of a sombre magnificence, and with a castellated ebony and alabaster bedstead of the sixteenth century, huge as the bed of Ware, gloomy as a mausoleum.

And the figure that lay on it, lightly covered with a silken counterpane, looked so fragile, the white face so still and lifeless, that Arden's heart sank with a sudden despair. If this was not death, it was too like death; and he gazed at those marble features in an agony of fear. Would those eyelids ever again unveil the lovely eyes, those pallid lips ever smile again? Speechless, motionless, she lay there, like a broken lily.

They had found her lying on the grass by the fountain. She had fallen upon her right arm, which was broken, the woman who was nursing her told Arden. They feared there might be fracture of the skull, but the doctor from Damezzo had not yet come, though a messenger had been sent at daybreak. He was absent, at a distant village, where he had gone to a bad case overnight.

Arden asked for another messenger, and sent him with a letter to the landlord of the Damezzo hotel, begging him to telephone to St. Moritz, for the English doctor, and an English nurse, if one could be found there. He went down to the hall, put his letter into the messenger's hand, with full instructions. He was to insist upon seeing the hotel-keeper without an instant's delay, on a matter of life and death; he was to wait at Damezzo for the answer on the telephone; and he was to take a telegram to the post-office, a telegram which Arden had written, informing the Cornish squire of St. Just's sudden death, and the interment arranged for that evening in the cemetery at Locco. Another telegram was to be sent to the Chief at Scotland Yard, to convey the same information. Arden watched the young man pass under the archway, with rapid steps, a slim, long-legged youth, who would be likely to get over the ground quickly, having been promised a generous reward. The innkeeper said he would make the downhill journey, by cross cuts across the woods, as fast as a horse could do it; and there being no horse available, Arden had to be content with his assurance.

He went back to the room where Rachel was lying, and sat by the bed, motionless, silent, scarcely seeming to breathe, a statue of despair.

A fractured skull; reason perhaps fled for ever. Would she live—if her life were spared—a mindless image; not the Rachel he had loved, but a beautiful ghost, the semblance of that sweet companion, that bright intelligence?

The messenger brought back the reply from St. Moritz. The doctor would start immediately, and bring a nurse with him. Arden calculated that he might arrive in three hours; three hours of waiting, perhaps of peril. The Damezzo doctor had not been heard of, and, had he appeared, Arden would have hesitated about allowing him to touch the patient. The nurse had applied cold lotions to the broken arm. She seemed a capable person; but she had not ventured to examine the patient's head, and it was only the stains of blood on the pillow that had suggested fracture.

The day wore on; the slow weary hours of suspense crawled by; till the time when the doctor might be expected. Every sound of wheels in the stony street now became an agitating fact. Happily, such sounds were not frequent in this torrid month, when the tourist season had not yet begun at Locco. At last there came the sound of quick, light wheels; and a carriage drew up below. He had come, the bringer of hope, or the bringer of woe. He had come, to pronounce sentence of doom, or give promise of healing. Arden rose, pale as death, and offered the doctor a shaking hand, and murmured a word of welcome to the nurse whom he brought with him, a young Englishwoman, in a neat grey uniform.

"You are good to come so quickly. My wife fell off the balcony last night. She has been lying senseless ever since. Her arm is broken; and this good woman thinks there may be injury to the skull. No one has dared to look. We waited for you."

He spoke with effort, in short sentences, breathlessly.

"When did the accident happen?"

"Between ten and eleven o'clock last night."

"Over eighteen hours! That's long!"

The doctor went to the bedside, and helped the nurse to raise the prostrate form, and then, with skilled touches, examined the head under the soft brown hair.

These are the moments that age a man—the moments that after-years of happiness cannot blot from the memory.

The doctor looked up, after a slow and careful examination.

"There is no injury to the bone. It is a bad case of concussion. And now we will look at the arm."

That was a more difficult business. Arm and collar-bone were broken, and there were broken ribs. Arden stood with his face to the open window, with his hands clenched, and his heart beating furiously, waiting for the verdict.

"Is it—is it likely to be fatal?" he asked, when the doctor came to him.

"It need not be fatal—if all go well; but she has been badly hurt. I can't conceal from you that it is a serious case. I don't think the arm will give much trouble. The broken ribs are the worst. There is always fear of lung trouble; and I don't like the long spell of unconsciousness. You have got a good nurse by a fluke. Nurse Mabel had just finished with a case at Pontresina. She would have been on her way back to England to-morrow."

"It was lucky. The person here seems capable. She can help Nurse Mabel, I suppose?"

"Oh yes, we'll make her useful."

"Shall you set the broken arm at once?"

"I think not. I shall wait for some recovery of consciousness. She is almost pulseless. I should be afraid to do anything in her present condition."

"Can you stop with her?"

"I'll stop to-night; but I must go back to St. Moritz early to-morrow morning."

"And after that?"

"I'll come back to-morrow night. And now you had better go and walk about a little. You can be no good here; and I don't want another patient. I shall have my hands full by-and-by with your wife."

He spoke with a friendly roughness, which was more cheering than the usual professional manner. Arden had made his acquaintance on the golf-links at Samaden, and had consulted him about some trivial matter, so they were on friendly terms; and now it was evident the doctor's sympathies were awakened by the piteous condition of his patient, whom he had admired in perfect health and beauty less than a month ago.

Arden did not mean to go farther than the garden. He had been shown the spot where Rachel had been found by the hotel servants, who had been so distracted by the catastrophe of St. Just's sudden death that they remained for some time in ignorance of her fate. The grass still bore the impress of the form that had lain there, and he found stains of blood and a broken comb that had fallen from her hair. He fled from the horror of the spot, and went through the little street, with slow, dejected steps, and along the hillside road, till he came to a tiny cemetery, a place of black wood crosses and neglected graves, where flower and weed grew at random, a lonely graveyard, girdled by a low stone wall.

A man was digging a grave near the gate. Arden stood and watched him with melancholy eyes. Another grave might have to be dug there, a grave which for him would mean the end of all things. Was she to be taken from him, this sweet woman whom he had loved with all his power of loving; albeit to-day he felt as if he had never loved her well enough, never given her the absolute unqualified adoration which her exquisite nature deserved? Never before had he known fear for her well-being. Sickness had never tried her; not even when her child was born, or when her child died. Neither joy nor sorrow had broken that perfect health with which Nature had gifted her.

He asked the grave-digger for whom he was working.

"For the foreigner who died at the inn last night: a rich nobleman. He is to be buried at eight o'clock. His friends will take the coffin up again in a week or two perhaps, and carry his excellence back to his own country. This is a poor place for a rich nobleman."

"Where the tree falls, there let it lie," said Arden. "If I were to die in this quiet place, I would rather rest here than be carted over half Europe."

"Ah, but the signor is not going to die, though he looks ill. But I may have another grave to dig to-morrow; for the foreign excellency's wife threw herself out of window in a passion of grief, when she saw her husband dying, and they tell me she can't live long."

Arden went back to the inn. He had asked for a room next that where his wife was lying. He found his servant there, unpacking and arranging things, while Rachel's maid had established herself in the sick-room. There was a door between the two rooms; but the doctor forbade his seeing his wife again that evening. There had been some faint return of consciousness; but there were also indications of fever, and the patient must be kept perfectly quiet. Fever was now what they had to fear. He could have the satisfaction of knowing that he was near her, and could have frequent tidings of her condition; and his friendly doctor told him that the best thing he could do was to eat a light supper, and try to get a good night's rest.

"You think I can rest while her life hangs in the balance?"

"It'll be hard, perhaps, but you ought to do it, for her sake. We are going to pull her through; and when she begins to mend, it won't do for her to see the spectre of despair at her bedside. You will have to be cheerful, when she gets better."

"When she gets better! Tell me that the danger is past, and I will be as merry as a grig."

"Not if you've let yourself run down, and are looking like an anæmic ghost. Come, I want some food myself; and I shall insist on your eating a cutlet. They profess to be able to give us soup and cutlets at nine o'clock—after the gentleman at the end of the passage has been taken to his last home. Do you know anything about him, by-the-bye?"

"I know a good deal about him; but I'd rather not talk of him to-night, if you'll excuse me. I may tell you more some day, perhaps."

"Are you going to the funeral?"

"No."

"I have established Mrs. Arden's maid as night nurse. The Locco woman will wait upon the sick-room, and help the nurses on occasion. I feel sure we shall do very well."

"And you will come every day?"

"Every night, while the case is urgent. It'll mean my living on the road. But God grant the worst trouble may soon be over, and we shall get into smooth water. I rely upon you for helping me by keeping very quiet."

"And I am not even to see her?"

"Not till I give you leave."

And now came the dark passage through the valley of the Shadow of Death; that long agony of suspense, when the life of the creature we love trembles in the balance, and each new sun may rise upon a day of despair. In Arden's case the time was long; the alternations of hope and fear were frequent. The slow hours crawled by—unrest by day, and fear by night. There were many days and nights in which he was not allowed to see his wife, when her frail hold upon existence would be jeopardised by the slightest agitation, and when the doctor's best hope was to keep her in a state of semi-consciousness, all emotions, all knowledge of the life around her, held in suspense.

"It is hard lines for you," he said kindly; "but you will have your reward by-and-by, if we pull her through."

If! That was the terrible word which hung upon Arden's soul like a leaden weight. If! It was in his mind day after day, as he paced the little garden behind the hotel, miserably restless, yet not daring to go farther from the house, roaming up and down, and in and out, by the old yew hedges, the scarlet and orange salvias, tall and bright, like flowers of fire and flame; the roses and carnations, jessamine, and myrtle, all the beauty of that summery land, which his weary eyes looked at unseeing.

There came one terrible sundown, when the fever was at its height, and when the life hung by a thread so fine that the doctor was constrained to speak words of warning.

"I don't like the look of things, Arden. I am afraid——"

"You are afraid that she will die?"

"It is very serious."

"Let me see her, then—don't keep me from her. Don't let her die without my seeing her. Man alive, if you knew how I love her!"

"You can come in and look at her. It will make no difference to her, poor soul. She will not know you. You can come into the room—softly, in your slippers—and keep in the shadow. Don't let her see you."

Arden crept, shoeless, into the shadowy room, where only one feeble light was burning on the dressing-table. Rachel was lying with wide-open eyes, looking straight before her, and talking rapidly, in a low troubled voice. Who could tell what strange visions were moving before those fever-bright eyes? They were blind to earthly things, and she did not see her husband, as he stood a little way from the bed, gazing at her.

He stood so for some time, motionless, till the doctor touched him on the shoulder, and gently drew him from the room.

"You see, my dear fellow, you can do no good here. You must be patient. We are in God's hand."

Arden remembered a line of Browning's—"We are in God's hand to-night."

Browning believed in God. The strong, staunch, manly confidence in something higher and nobler than humanity rings out clear and loud in that noble verse. It rings as true at the beginning as at the end of the poet's earthly pilgrimage. It was his message to mankind, and it knew no wavering when he passed through the valley of the shadow, and the wife he idolised was taken from him.

Arden went out of the house into the moonlit garden. It was the first week in October, and the hotel was empty again, as it had been in July. The horror of seeing strange faces, and hearing careless, happy voices, was no longer to be suffered. There had been only a few people, for he had retained the whole of the principal floor, including that locked bedchamber where the dead man had lain, and which he had never entered. All visitors were gone now, and the mountain air blew keen over the long grass in the quaint old garden. He went from the garden to the street. The great church rose up before him, tower and cupola silver white against the dark blue sky. The door was open. He had but to lift the curtain and go in. All was dark and cold, save for the sacred lamp hanging before the altar, and a feeble taper burning here and there in a side chapel.

He had sat in churches to please his wife, had knelt and listened to the prayers, not in a mocking spirit, not as a hypocrite, but pitying himself for his unbelief, for his having missed that which gave gladness and consolation to other people. But to-night he crept into the vast empty church, into the gloom and silence, crushed and broken, feeling his utter helplessness in the hand of Omnipotence. To-night he wanted God; and if belief could grow in an hour, and if a man who had rejected Christ from his youth upward could change in an instant, and supplicate and adore, and stretch out his hands across the darkness, to touch the hem of the miracle-working garment, and win healing for the creature he loved—if that were possible, there was no depth of self-humiliation, no surrender of intellectual pride, from which he would recoil. He would have made himself a monk of the most fanatical order in Christendom, would have devoted all his future life to automatic prayers and superstitious penances, only to keep his beloved back from the grave; only to know, even while parted from her by the tyranny of his order, that she lived; and that in some distant day their hands might meet across the convent bars, and he might see and hear her, were it but for a few moments.

So far as he could see in the dim light, the church was empty. He knelt in front of the high altar, under the dark-red lamp. He bowed his head on the broad marble railing, grovelling before the Power that he could only half acknowledge.

He pressed his burning forehead on the old marble, worn by many a weary brow, by the forehead of sinner and saint, in the centuries that were gone, since the piety of the rich built a cathedral for this small flock, dwelling among the hills, remote from the traffic of life. The silence and the dim light seemed to him like the quiet gloom of the grave. How glad he would be to be dead; if she were doomed to die. Kneeling there in his despair, he debated within himself the manner of his death; for he did not mean to go on living after she was gone.

There was the river, the swift, deep river in the valley below, by which they had walked in the clear morning light, and in the golden hour before sunset. A river of rest, he thought, picturing the bright blue stream, the grey-green sward purpled with crocuses. Where could he find an easier close to a hateful life? But he wanted her to live, and bless him with her love. He wanted life with her, life that is so sweet where love is; so bitter and barren where love is not.

Involuntarily there came from the agonised heart man's despairing cry to God.

"What am I, Oh Thou unknown Omnipotence, that I should question Thy power to punish, to annihilate, or to save? I am a worm, and no man. I tremble while I doubt. I have known the powers of hell; oh, give me to learn the dominion of heaven. Give me back my wife, my peace of mind; lift this shroud of horror from my soul.

"I am humbled to the dust. I cannot pray, but I

can suffer and submit. Oh, let my sufferings count as prayers; accept the sacrifice of my troubled mind. Oh unknown Power, inscrutable, unthinkable, Thou who hast neither habitation, nor name, but who livest in the instinct of mankind. Thou whom the believer adores, and whom the sceptic longs for, without whose promise of immortality our life is but a mockery of man's capacity to live; enter into my barren mind, Oh unknown Power, and bend my spirit to Thy will. Let me be as the lowest of Thy worshippers, as the savage who has heard of Thee with fear and trembling, who offers himself to Thee in unquestioning faith. I have been made to tremble before unseen malignity; oh, let me feel the might of unseen Beneficence."

XVI.

From Walter Arden to Douglas Campbell.

Grove Park, near Bargrave, Herts,
Midsummer Day, 190-.

MY DEAR DOUGLAS,

This delicious summer day is my wife's birthday, and I think I could not choose a better date on which to write to my dear old friend, after an interval of more than half a year. You will receive this letter, with its odour of fresh-gathered roses, by your winter hearth, piled with the spoil of your neighbouring forest; and, had I the pen of an impressionist, I might make you envious with a vivid picture of the garden I look out upon through the wide Tudor window, an old-world garden of level paths, box borders, clipped yews, and long arcades, curtained with climbing roses. No doubt, were I to take so much pains, you would reply that everything floral thrives in Tasmania as it can never thrive in England; and that my roses would make a sorry show beside your pelargoniums, your myrtles, and orange-trees, flourishing in the open air. I hope you will tire of your perfect climate, and your superior floriculture, some day, and give Rachel and me the happiness of welcoming you to this dear old English manor-house, which we love quite as well as if the sons of the soil who dwelt here from generation to generation—till the end of last century—had been our ancestors.

In your last letter you reproached me for not having given you fuller details of my life during the last three happy years; since the passing of that inexplicable trouble upon which I was able to expatiate to you, with the assurance of your compassion and your patience. I wrote to you then as to the one friend in whom I dared to confide; for I knew that no experience of the Unseen was without interest for you.

But since I have come out of that dark cloud—out of that mystery which I am content to leave for ever unexplained—the course of my life has been smooth and uneventful, and offers little to record; except the fulfilment of almost every wish, and a happiness far beyond my deserts, and even beyond my fondest hopes. I have restrained myself in writing of these things, lest I should lapse into twaddle; but since you ask for details, you shall have the history of the Arden settlement, in the leafy glades and upland commons of the prettiest part of Hertfordshire.

I have just one hour of leisure in which to write, before I start with Rachel, for a picnic in the adjacent wood, which is to honour the anniversary; a quiet luncheon for Mr. and Mrs. Lorimer, my wife, and me; to be followed by a picnic tea, at which all our workpeople and their families are to assemble, for which reason our two factories are to stop work two hours earlier than usual. How I wish you could be among us, Douglas, to see all those cheerful faces, all that happiness so cheaply purchased. Happiness that lasts for a day, you might answer; but believe me, when you give your guinea for a day's pleasure for old or young, of the class whose pleasures are so rare, you buy something more than the day's outing, the plenteous meal, and the boisterous games. You buy happy memories that linger through the monotonous months, and lighten toil, memories that are fresh perhaps when the circling year brings its new festival, and the van-wheels are rolling once again on the white summer road, and the children singing—most discordantly, alas!—in their joy.

Our two modest factories—the toy-making and the jam-making—have thriven wonderfully; and the profit-sharing system, which some economists condemn, has been thoroughly successful in our small communities. Our men and women, and even the children, take a pride in the organisation with whose prosperity they prosper; and they all talk of "our factory" with a proud sense of ownership.

Sitting in this grave old oak-panelled room, with the sunlit flower-garden in front of my window, and my heart full of the tranquil happiness of a life that realises all my ideals, I look back, across the last happy years, to the year of Mary Selby's tragic death, and the long agony of my wife's terrible illness, the illness which lasted, from that hideous night in July, till the birth of our boy in the following February; and I wonder that after such darkness should come such light. It was not till her son was born that the mother's peril was past. He came to us as the child of promise, bringing healing and peace. Her mind came out of the cloud which had darkened it through those dismal months; her physical health was gradually restored; and before the end of the year she was yearning for the renewal of her work in the slums of East-end London.

It was then that I framed the scheme that has succeeded beyond my hopes. I told my wife that, with my consent, she should never revisit those dark places, never hazard her life, and the life of her child, among those fever-haunted dens, those loathsome tenement houses which cry aloud to heaven against the wretches who own them, and batten on the needs of abject poverty. She should still work for the poor, still move among her fellow-creatures as a ministering angel; but her poor should live in pure air, and their paths should be paths of pleasantness. The mountain should be brought to Mahomet.

And then I unfolded my plans, and told her how I was negotiating for an estate of nearly a thousand acres in the prettiest part of Hertfordshire, less than three miles from a market town and railway-station, with an old Tudor manor-house, and gardens and park, embosomed in lovely woods. On an outlying field I proposed to build two small factories—one for jam-making, from fruit grown on our own land; the other for toy-making, which was an idea of my own, as I wanted to see whether small English fingers were not as capable as small German fingers. For this purpose I meant to bring over half a dozen toy-makers, men and women, from Nuremburg, to teach our children their art.

My plans were approved by my dear wife; and I lost no time in realising them. Both our factories have been in full swing for two years, and are doing good business. Our men and women work in the fruit-gardens and in the jam-making; while almost all the work in the toy-factory is done by children from twelve years old, half-timers, whose mornings are spent in our schools. We have built a model village for our work-people, and we have given them a communal dairy and poultry farm of two hundred acres, where all work in turn, for the benefit of all. We have a cricket and foot-ball ground, and a shooting-range equal to the best in the county. We have a club and library, and my gener-ous father-in-law has built us a church, severely Gothic, of small size, but capable of extension should the need arise in days to come. Our curate-in-charge, who came to us from the East End, is a man of broad views, and warm sympathy.

You may imagine my wife's delight in superintending the building of our cottages, healthful homes for the families we have brought from that foul ant-heap in East London, to these wide commons and woods. We were careful in our choice of people for our new settle-ment, knowing that there were many among our old friends in whom the love of cities was stronger than the desire for health and cleanliness; and these we had to leave in their miserable environment. There were more by hundreds than we could accommodate who yearned for fresh air and decent homes, and who came eagerly, with their rejoicing children, as to a land of milk and honey; and I think I may say without boasting that our village has been to these a veritable Canaan. If you could see how the pinched gutter-snipe face of our nine and ten year old boys has filled out and reddened in the sun, how the wan cheeks of the mothers have grown plump and rosy, and how self-respect and the love of fresh air and clean water have increased with every month of rural life, you would think as I do, that the solution of that great problem—the housing of the London poor—could best be found in the transplantation of the factories round which the poor have to live. The country is wide enough for all, and the ugliness of a chimney here and there need not spoil the face of it; while to bring the people back to the wide village street, the woods and fields, the green lanes, white with flowering hawthorns, and commons, golden with gorse and broom, is to bring them from misery to comfort.

I could write at much greater length of all that Rachel has done for the welfare of our people, and of the love they bear her; but I hope the day is not far distant when you will see with your eyes and hear with your ears what can be done by those who love their fellow-creatures, and who have means which enable them to realise their dreams of benevolence.

I must add that Mr. and Mrs. Lorimer are large helpers in all our schemes; and they are both completely satisfied with their daughter's life and surroundings. We have the house in Guelph Place still. So much of that first home was a gift from Rachel's father that it would have been churlish for us to abandon it; and as our country home is little more than an hour's journey from the West End, we are able to see a good deal of the dear people in Carlton House Terrace; without deserting those other people who look to us for so much, for evening lectures, and concerts, for out-of-door sketching-classes, for mothers' meetings, for Saturday payments to their clubs and societies; for all that makes for thrift, improvement, and recreation; and for all that strengthens the bond between rich and poor.

I must add that our toy-making has been particularly successful, and that some of our guttersnipes have developed a remarkable inventiveness and adroitness in their work; and furthermore that a wholesale house near Liverpool Street has within the last half-year bought our goods as largely as the German toys in which they dealt exclusively, before we came into the field.

So much for temporal things, and the interests which involve the happiness of so many outside the narrow circle of our home. What shall I say of spiritual things, to you from whom I have withheld none of the dark secrets of my mind in the mysterious sufferings of past years? What shall I say of myself, now that my cup of content is full; now that I have nothing left to desire, except that to-morrow may be as to-day, and that the dear wife in whom I find the supreme good, and for whom I live, may bear me company to the end of my journey; lovely in age as in youth, with the spiritual light that shines through corporal beauty, and makes it divine? What shall I say? I dare not call myself a believer, for the consummate mind that governs the universe, and the after-life of man, are still inexplicable, unimaginable problems, for which I can find no answer in the Book that Rachel accepts as the clue to all mysteries. But I am no longer a materialist. I have been brought to acknowledge the something more than the machine of bone and flesh, evolved through countless ages from lowliest beginnings, perfected protoplasm. I have felt and suffered the influence of an unseen Enemy; and in that crisis of my life when I stood in danger of losing all that made life dear, my heart seemed lightened by the influence of an unseen Friend. And from that hour of peril until now I have seemed to live in the warm radiance of that Influence, an unknown Beneficence, mysterious, indefinable. In that vague Presence, in the perfect beauty of my wife's nature, and in the many fine impulses and generous feelings which I discover among the humble and meek ones of this earth, I find the surest pledge of the life immortal; for these things are not of flesh, but of spirit, and I tell myself that spirit cannot die.

THE END.

PRINTING OFFICE OF THE PUBLISHER.

TAUCHNITZ EDITION.

June 1, 1903.

Contents:

Collection of British and American Authors.

Besides this complete list of the Tauchnitz Edition, a *larger and more fully-detailed catalogue* of the Tauchnitz publications—containing much important and useful information in regard to authors and their works, and specially arranged for ready reference—is to be had *gratis* of all booksellers *on application.*

Collection
of
British and American Authors.

3658 Volumes. 384 British, 47 American Authors.

3331 Volumes by British, 327 Volumes by American Authors.

— Price 1 M. 60 Pf. or 2 Fr. per Volume. —

Each volume is published with Continental Copyright by special agreement with the author or his representative, but may on no account be taken into England or any British Colony. Nor may the works of American authors be introduced into the U. S. of America.

Latest Volumes:

Park Lane. By PERCY WHITE. 2 vols.-3657/58.

A new satirical "Society" novel by the author of "Mr. Bailey-Martin" and "The West End." The characters include a successful company promoter and a beautiful lady's-maid who marries a peer.

The Untilled Field. By GEORGE MOORE. 1 vol.-3656.

A collection of more or less correlative sketches of Irish peasant life, drawn by a genuine artist. Mr. Moore dexterously handles many of the vital Irish problems of the day.

The Pit. By FRANK NORRIS. 2 vols.-3654/55.

This novel is the second part of the author's projected trilogy "The Epic of the Wheat," and the successor of "The Octopus." "The Pit" treats of the distribution of the wheat and the reckless speculation indulged in on the Chicago exchange.

The Striking Hours. By EDEN PHILLPOTTS. 1 vol.-3653.

The author is a master not only of the Devonian dialect, but also of the art of putting it into a readable and intelligible form. The volume contains fourteen stories—gay, grave and tragic.

The Hosts of the Lord. By FLORA ANNIE STEEL. 2 vols.-3651/52.

Mrs. Steel is one of the best writers on India and Indian life. The present work has already met with a tremendous reception.

The Splendid Idle Forties. By GERTRUDE ATHERTON. 1 v.-3650.

A collection of tales of old California. The charm of the *Señoritas* loses nothing in Mrs. Atherton's hands.

Pearl-Maiden. By H. RIDER HAGGARD. 2 vols.-3648/49.

A historical novel of the fall of Jerusalem, and of Rome in the days of Nero and Vespasian. Mr. Haggard shows that he can thrill his readers with scenes from other countries than South Africa.

The Eternal Woman. By DOROTHEA GERARD. 1 vol.-3647.

A study of the world-old power of sex. The heroine, who takes Becky Sharp as her model, ends by falling in love with the man she sets out in cold blood to captivate.

A Londoner's Log-Book. By GEORGE W. E. RUSSELL. 1 vol.-3646.

Mr. Russell, the author of "Collections and Recollections," paints his supposed surroundings and neighbours with a light and humorous touch that makes cheerful, pleasant reading. The seventeen short and chatty articles are full of good things.

A Humble Lover. By M. BETHAM-EDWARDS. 1 vol.-3645.

Another tale of the East-Anglian country. The authoress is equally at home with the people and their dialect.

Lady Rose's Daughter. By MRS. H. WARD. 2 v.-3643/44.

Mrs. Ward's new work is a thoroughly enjoyable novel on society people of our own day. The absence of asceticism and mysticism in the characters of her hero and heroine by no means detracts from their interest.

The Little White Bird. By J. M. BARRIE. 1 vol.-3642.

Mr. Barrie is always at his best when writing of children. We seem to see in the elderly soldier whose diary the book is supposed to be, a portrait of Mr. Barrie himself in the rôle of father.

The Seats of the Mighty. By GILBERT PARKER. 2 vols.-3640/41.

A thrilling historical romance of the days of the siege and fall of Quebec. The author shows some skill in the portrayal of historical scenes and characters.

Lord Leonard the Luckless. By W. E. NORRIS. 1 vol.-3639.

A modern English story—though the reader is incidentally taken to Paris. Mr. Norris succeeds in enlisting one's sympathy for his rather excentric hero from the start.

Donna Diana. By RICHARD BAGOT. 2 vols.-3637/38.

Another Roman drama by the author of "A Roman Mystery" and "Casting of Nets." Mr. Bagot understands how to point his moral without sacrificing the interest of his story thereto.

The Reflections of Ambrosine. By ELINOR GLYN, author of "The Visits of Elizabeth." 1 vol.-3636.

Mrs. Glyn's new heroine is an aristocrat of very ancient family and the bluest blood, and well bears comparison with her predecessor.

The Leopard's Spots. By THOMAS DIXON, JR. 2 vols.-3634/35.

A novel based on the negro question by a new American author. The horrors attendant on the sudden emancipation of the slaves in the South are vividly portrayed in the first volume.

Moth and Rust, etc. By MARY CHOLMONDELEY. 1 vol.-3633.

The volume contains a short Parisian story, most gruesome in its nature, and two other longer ones, which will add to the authoress' already great reputation.

The House under the Sea. By MAX PEMBERTON. 1 vol.-3632.

A tale of adventure and of a lonely island. The book teems with exciting and even awful situations.

The Four Feathers. By A. E. W. MASON. 2 vols.-3630/31.

A well conceived romance finely written. The author evokes both admiration for his heroine and sympathy for his hero, while the description of the prisoners' life among the Mahdists is both thrilling and true to fact.

Donovan Pasha, and Some People of Egypt. By GILBERT PARKER. 1 vol.-3629.

Egypt again. The volume leaves us with a deep sense of the difficulties which beset the path of the European advisers to the Khedive.

The Lady of the Barge, etc. By W. W. JACOBS. 1 vol.-3628.

The type of character which this favourite humourist has chosen for his own particular study does not pall, but one or two stories in the volume show him to be also a master of the gruesome.

A Bayard from Bengal. By F. ANSTEY. With eight Illustrations by BERNARD PARTRIDGE. 1 vol.-3627.

This volume is pure and undiluted fun throughout. No better description can be given of its contents than a glance at its title and its numerous and marvellous illustrations.

Lavinia. By RHODA BROUGHTON. 1 vol.-3626.

Miss Broughton has added one more to her long list of pleasant romances. The story is thoroughly readable throughout. A healthy volume equally suited to one's own library or the drawing-room table.

The Lord Protector. By S. LEVETT-YEATS. 1 vol.-3625.

As the title itself explains, a historical novel of Cromwell's time. The great commander is cleverly drawn in picturesque surroundings, and the usual heart-stirring episodes of love and steel are not wanting.

Cecilia. By F. MARION CRAWFORD. 2 vols.-3623/24.

Mr. Crawford takes us again to Italy. Certain theories, such as that of the transmigration of souls, lend local colour and a spice of mystery to a pretty and well told romance.

*

Felix. By ROBERT HICHENS. 2 vols. - 3621/22.

In Mr. Hichens' new tale we dig beneath the veneer of society and the outer surface of things. The women morphinomaniacs of the London and Paris of our day are realistically analysed.

The Highway of Fate. By ROSA NOUCHETTE CAREY. 2 vols. - 3619/20.

A modern book for girls. The characters are natural and sympathetic; there is the right amount of marrying and giving in marriage, and the story does not flag.

The Sea Lady. By H. G. WELLS. 1 vol. - 3618.

A tragi-humorous tale of a visit paid by a mermaid to the haunts and habitations of mere earthly men. Mr. Wells' genius for making the impossible seem possible has never been better exemplified.

The Credit of the County. By W. E. NORRIS. 1 v. - 3617.

Mr. Norris does not need to search among Dukes and Duchesses to find interesting actors for his stories, nor does he take us far afield. A good story of English people in the England of to-day.

Fuel of Fire. By ELLEN THORNEYCROFT FOWLER. 1 v. - 3616.

The authoress has produced a work which well repays the care and trouble evidently spent upon it. Her characters are commonplace yet full of interest, while the story itself is full of incident and yet nowhere open to the charge of sensation.

Just So Stories for Little Children. By RUDYARD KIPLING. Illustrated by the Author. 1 vol. - 3615.

Delightful children's stories of prehistoric men and beasts. It is however doubtful whether the children or the parents will read them with the more pleasure.

The Intrusions of Peggy. By ANTHONY HOPE. 2 vols. - 3613/14.

There are no Princesses or hairbreadth adventures in this book. Mr. Hope treats us to a tale of modern English society, but the two heroines—Peggy and the other—are none the less delightful and out of the usual groove.

In Kings' Byways. By STANLEY J. WEYMAN. 1 v. - 3612.

Mr. Weyman has given us in this volume some capital descriptions of interesting incidents of old Court life in France. His stories are full of life and form excellent historical studies.

Paul Kelver. By JEROME K. JEROME. 2 vols. - 3610/11.

The author's humour is as predominant as ever, though the story is of ordinary people in ordinary times, and Mr. Jerome has proved his capability of writing a serious book and dealing in pathos of no mean order.

Wind and Wave. By FIONA MACLEOD. 1 vol. - 3609.

A collection of tales and episodes of old Gaelic and Celto-Scandinavian life and mythology, specially selected by the authoress for the Tauchnitz Edition.

Stronger than Love. By the late MRS. ALEXANDER. 2 vols. - 3607/8.

A pleasant and readable story of modern English life and society. The hand of the authoress had not lost its cunning, and her characters are as sympathetic as of yore.

East of Paris. By M. BETHAM-EDWARDS. 1 vol. - 3606.

Sketches in the Gâtinais, Bourbonnais and Champagne. M. Betham-Edwards has studied her France well. The descriptions are always true to life, and bring the scenes she depicts vividly before the mind's eye.

Complete List
of the
Collection of British and American Authors.

Published with Continental Copyright by special agreement with the authors. Vide p. 1.

— Price 1 M. 60 Pf. or 2 Fr. per Volume. —

Rev. W. Adams, † 1848.
Sacred Allegories 1 v.

Grace Aguilar, † 1847.
Home Influence 2 v. — The Mother's Recompense 2 v.

Hamilton Aïdé.
Rita 1 v. — Carr of Carrlyon 2 v. — The Marstons 2 v. — In that State of Life 1 v. — Morals and Mysteries 1 v. — Penruddocke 2 v. — "A nine Days' Wonder" 1 v. — Poet and Peer 2 v. — Introduced to Society 1 v.

W. Harrison Ainsworth, † 1882.
Windsor Castle 1 v. — Saint James's 1 v. — Jack Sheppard (with Portrait) 1 v. — The Lancashire Witches 2 v. — The Star-Chamber 2 v. — The Flitch of Bacon 1 v. — The Spendthrift 1 v. — Mervyn Clitheroe 2 v. — Ovingdean Grange 1 v. — The Constable of the Tower 1 v. — The Lord Mayor of London 2 v. — Cardinal Pole 2 v. — John Law 2 v. — The Spanish Match 2 v. — The Constable de Bourbon 2 v. — Old Court 2 v. — Myddleton Pomfret 2 v. — The South-Sea Bubble 2 v. — Hilary St. Ives 2 v. — Talbot Harland 1 v. — Tower Hill 1 v. — Boscobel 2 v. — The Good Old Times 2 v. — Merry England 2 v. — The Goldsmith's Wife 2 v. — Preston Fight 2 v. — Chetwynd Calverley 2 v. — The Leaguer of Lathom 2 v. — The Fall of Somerset 2 v. — Beatrice Tyldesley 2 v. — Beau Nash 2 v. — Stanley Brereton 2 v.

Louisa M. Alcott (Am.), † 1888.
Little Women 2 v. — Little Men 1 v. — An Old-Fashioned Girl 1 v. — Jo's Boys 1 v.

Thomas Bailey Aldrich (Am.).
Marjorie Daw and other Tales 1 v. — The Stillwater Tragedy 1 v.

Mrs. Alexander (Hector), † 1902.
A Second Life 3 v. — By Woman's Wit 1 v. — Mona's Choice 2 v. — A Life Interest 2 v. — A Crooked Path 2 v. — Blind Fate 2 v. — A Woman's Heart 2 v. — For His Sake 2 v. — The Snare of the Fowler 2 v. — Found Wanting 2 v. — A Ward in Chancery 1 v. — A Choice of Evils 2 v. — A Fight with Fate 2 v. — A Winning Hazard 1 v. — A Golden Autumn 1 v. — Mrs. Crichton's Creditor 1 v. — Barbara, Lady's Maid and Peeress 1 v. — The Cost of Her Pride 2 v. — Brown, V.C. 1 v. — Through Fire to Fortune 1 v. — A Missing Hero 1 v. — The Yellow Fiend 1 v. — Stronger than Love 2 v.

Alice, Grand-Duchess of Hesse, † 1878.
Letters to Her Majesty the Queen (with Portrait). With a Memoir by H. R. H. Princess Christian 2 v.

Lizzie Alldridge.
By Love and Law 2 v. — The World she awoke in 2 v.

Grant Allen, † 1899.
The Woman who did 1 v.

Author of "All for Greed" (Baroness de Bury).
All for Greed 1 v. — Love the Avenger 2 v.

F. Anstey (Guthrie).
The Giant's Robe 2 v. — A Fallen Idol 1 v. — The Pariah 3 v. — The Talking Horse and other Tales 1 v. — Voces Populi *(First and Second Series)* 1 v. — The Brass Bottle 1 v. — A Bayard from Bengal 1 v.

Mrs. Argles, *vide* Mrs. Hungerford.

Author of "The Aristocrats," *vide* Gertrude Atherton.

Sir Edwin Arnold.
The Light of Asia (with Portrait) 1 v.

Matthew Arnold, † 1888.
Essays in Criticism 2 v. — Essays in Criticism *(Second Series)* 1 v.

Gertrude Atherton (Am.).

American Wives and English Husbands 1 v. — The Californians 1 v. — Patience Sparhawk and her Times 2 v. — Senator North 2 v. — The Doomswoman 1 v. — The Aristocrats 1 v. — The Splendid Idle Forties 1 v.

Jane Austen, † 1817.

Sense and Sensibility 1 v. — Mansfield Park 1 v. — Pride and Prejudice 1 v. — Northanger Abbey, and Persuasion 1 v. — Emma 1 v.

Author of "Autobiography of Lutfullah," *vide* E. B. Eastwick.

Richard Bagot.

A Roman Mystery 2 v. — Casting of Nets 2 v. — The Just and the Unjust 2 v. — Donna Diana 2 v.

S. Baring-Gould.

Mehalah 1 v. — John Herring 2 v. — Court Royal 2 v.

Lady Barker (Lady Broome).

Station Life in New Zealand 1 v. — Station Amusements in New Zealand 1 v. — A Year's Housekeeping in South Africa 1 v. — Letters to Guy, and A Distant Shore—Rodrigues 1 v.

Frank Barrett.

The Smuggler's Secret 1 v. — Out of the Jaws of Death 2 v.

J. M. Barrie.

Sentimental Tommy 2 v. — Margaret Ogilvy 1 v. — Tommy and Grizel 2 v. — The Little White Bird 1 v.

Author of "Miss Bayle's Romance," *vide* W. Fraser Rae.

Rev. Robert H. Baynes.

Lyra Anglicana, Hymns and Sacred Songs 1 v.

Lord Beaconsfield, *vide* Disraeli.

Averil Beaumont (Mrs. Hunt).

Thornicroft's Model 2 v.

Currer Bell (Charlotte Brontë—Mrs. Nicholls), † 1855.

Jane Eyre 2 v. — Shirley 2 v. — Villette 2 v. — The Professor 1 v.

Ellis & Acton Bell (Emily, † 1848, and Anne, † 1849, Brontë).

Wuthering Heights, and Agnes Grey 2 v.

Edward Bellamy (Am.), † 1898.

Looking Backward 1 v.

Frank Lee Benedict (Am.).

St. Simon's Niece 2 v.

Arnold Bennett.

The Grand Babylon Hotel 1 v.

E. F. Benson.

Dodo 1 v. — The Rubicon 1 v. — Scarlet and Hyssop 1 v.

Sir Walter Besant, † 1901.

The Revolt of Man 1 v. — Dorothy Forster 2 v. — Children of Gibeon 2 v. — The World went very well then 2 v. — Katharine Regina 1 v. — Herr Paulus 2 v. — The Inner House 1 v. — The Bell of St. Paul's 2 v. — For Faith and Freedom 2 v. — Armorel of Lyonesse 2 v. — Verbena Camellia Stephanotis, etc. 1 v. — Beyond the Dreams of Avarice 2 v. — The Master Craftsman 2 v. — A Fountain Sealed 1 v. — The Orange Girl 2 v. — The Fourth Generation 1 v. — The Lady of Lynn 2 v.

Sir Walter Besant, † 1901, & James Rice, † 1882.

The Golden Butterfly 2 v. — Ready-Money Mortiboy 2 v. — By Celia's Arbour 2 v.

M. Betham-Edwards.

The Sylvestres 1 v. — Felicia 2 v. — Brother Gabriel 2 v. — Forestalled 1 v. — Exchange no Robbery, and other Novelettes 1 v. — Disarmed 1 v. — Doctor Jacob 1 v. — Pearla 1 v. — Next of Kin Wanted 1 v. — The Parting of the Ways 1 v. — For One and the World 1 v. — The Romance of a French Parsonage 1 v. — France of To-day 1 v. — Two Aunts and a Nephew 1 v. — A Dream of Millions 1 v. — The Curb of Honour 1 v. — France of To-day (*Second Series*) 1 v. — A Romance of Dijon 1 v. — The Dream-Charlotte 1 v. — A Storm-Rent Sky 1 v. — Reminiscences 1 v. — The Lord of the Harvest 1 v. — Anglo-French Reminiscences, 1875—1899 1 v. — A Suffolk Courtship 1 v. — Mock Beggars' Hall 1 v. — East of Paris 1 v. — A Humble Lover 1 v.

Ambrose Bierce (Am.).

In the Midst of Life 1 v.

Mabel C. Birchenough.

Potsherds 1 v.

E. Bisland, *v.* Rhoda Broughton.

Prince Bismarck, *vide* Butler. *Vide* also Wilhelm Görlach (Collection of German Authors, p. 29); *vide* also Whitman.

William Black, † 1898.

A Daughter of Heth 2 v. — In Silk Attire 2 v. — The Strange Adventures of a Phaeton 2 v. — A Princess of Thule 2 v. — Kilmeny 1 v. — The Maid of Killeena, and other Stories 1 v. — Three Feathers 2 v. — Lady Silverdale's Sweetheart, and other Stories 1 v. — Madcap Violet 2 v. — Green Pastures and Piccadilly 2 v. — Macleod of Dare 2 v. — White Wings 2 v. — Sunrise 2 v. — The Beautiful Wretch 1 v. — Mr. Pisistratus Brown, M.P., in the Highlands; The Four Macnicols; The Pupil of Aurelius 1 v. — Shandon Bells (with Portrait) 2 v. — Judith Shakespeare 2 v. — The Wise Women of Inverness, etc. 1 v. — White Heather 2 v. — Sabina Zembra 2 v. — The Strange Adventures of a House-Boat 2 v. — In Far Lochaber 2 v. — The New Prince Fortunatus 2 v. — Stand Fast, Craig-Royston! 2 v. — Donald Ross of Heimra 2 v. — The Magic Ink, and other Tales 1 v. — Wolfenberg 2 v. — The Handsome Humes 2 v. — Highland Cousins 2 v. — Briseis 2 v. — Wild Eelin 2 v.

Author of "The Black-Box Murder."

The Black-Box Murder 1 v.

Richard Doddridge Blackmore, † 1900.

Alice Lorraine 2 v. — Mary Anerley 3 v. — Christowell 2 v. — Tommy Upmore 2 v. — Perlycross 2 v.

"Blackwood."

Tales from "Blackwood" *(First Series)* 1 v. — Tales from "Blackwood" *(Second Series)* 1 v.

Isa Blagden, † 1873.

The Woman I loved, and the Woman who loved me; A Tuscan Wedding 1 v.

Countess of Blessington (Marguerite Gardiner), † 1849.

Meredith 1 v. — Strathern 2 v. — Memoirs of a Femme de Chambre 1 v. — Marmaduke Herbert 2 v. — Country Quarters (with Portrait) 2 v.

Baroness Bloomfield.

Reminiscences of Court and Diplomatic Life (with the Portrait of Her Majesty the Queen) 2 v.

Rolf Boldrewood.

Robbery under Arms 2 v. — Nevermore 2 v.

Miss Braddon (Mrs. Maxwell).

Lady Audley's Secret 2 v. — Aurora Floyd 2 v. — Eleanor's Victory 2 v. — John Marchmont's Legacy 2 v. — Henry Dunbar 2 v. — The Doctor's Wife 2 v. — Only a Clod 2 v. — Sir Jasper's Tenant 2 v. — The Lady's Mile 2 v. — Rupert Godwin 2 v. — Dead-Sea Fruit 2 v. — Run to Earth 2 v. — Fenton's Quest 2 v. — The Lovels of Arden 2 v. — Strangers and Pilgrims 2 v. — Lucius Davoren 3 v. — Taken at the Flood 3 v. — Lost for Love 2 v. — A Strange World 2 v. — Hostages to Fortune 2 v. — Dead Men's Shoes 2 v. — Joshua Haggard's Daughter 2 v. — Weavers and Weft 1 v. — In Great Waters, and other Tales 1 v. — An Open Verdict 3 v. — Vixen 3 v. — The Cloven Foot 3 v. — The Story of Barbara 2 v. — Just as I am 2 v. — Asphodel 3 v. — Mount Royal 2 v. — The Golden Calf 2 v. — Flower and Weed 1 v. — Phantom Fortune 3 v. — Under the Red Flag 1 v. — Ishmael 3 v. — Wyllard's Weird 3 v. — One Thing Needful 2 v. — Cut by the County 1 v. — Like and Unlike 2 v. — The Fatal Three 2 v. — The Day will come 2 v. — One Life, One Love 2 v. — Gerard 2 v. — The Venetians 2 v. — All along the River 2 v. — Thou art the Man 2 v. — The Christmas Hirelings, etc. 1 v. — Sons of Fire 2 v. — London Pride 2 v. — Rough Justice 2 v. — In High Places 2 v. — His Darling Sin 1 v. — The Infidel 2 v.

Lady Brassey, † 1887.

A Voyage in the "Sunbeam" 2 v. — Sunshine and Storm in the East 2 v. — In the Trades, the Tropics and the Roaring Forties 2 v.

Author of "The Bread-Winners" (Am.).

The Bread-Winners 1 v.

Bret Harte, *vide* Harte.

Rev. William Brock, † 1875.

Sir Henry Havelock, K. C. B. 1 v.

Charlotte Brontë, *vide* Currer Bell.

Emily & Anne Brontë, *vide* Ellis & Acton Bell.

Shirley Brooks, † 1874.

The Silver Cord 3 v. — Sooner or Later 3 v.

Lady Broome, *vide* Lady Barker.

Rhoda Broughton.

Cometh up as a Flower 1 v. — Not wisely, but too well 2 v. — Red as a Rose is She 2 v. — Tales for Christmas Eve 1 v. — Nancy 2 v. — Joan 2 v. — Second Thoughts 2 v. — Belinda 2 v. — Doctor Cupid 2 v. — Alas! 2 v. — Mrs. Bligh 1 v. — A Beginner 1 v. — Scylla or Charybdis? 1 v. — Dear Faustina 1 v. — The Game and the Candle 1 v. — Foes in Law 1 v. — Lavinia 1 v.

Rhoda Broughton & Elizabeth Bisland.

A Widower Indeed 1 v.

John Brown, † 1882.

Rab and his Friends, and other Papers 1 v.

Elizabeth Barrett Browning, † 1861.

A Selection from her Poetry (with Portrait) 1 v. — Aurora Leigh 1 v.

Robert Browning, † 1889.

Poetical Works (with Portrait) 4 v.

Frank T. Bullen.

The Cruise of the "Cachalot" 2 v.

Edward Bulwer, Lord Lytton, † 1873.

Pelham (with Portrait) 1 v. — Eugene Aram 1 v. — Paul Clifford 1 v. — Zanoni 1 v. — The Last Days of Pompeii 1 v. — The Disowned 1 v. — Ernest Maltravers 1 v. — Alice 1 v. — Eva, and The Pilgrims of the Rhine 1 v. — Devereux 1 v. — Godolphin and Falkland 1 v. — Rienzi 1 v. — Night and Morning 1 v. — The Last of the Barons 2 v. — Athens 2 v. — The Poems and Ballads of Schiller 1 v. — Lucretia 2 v. — Harold 2 v. — King Arthur 2 v. — The New Timon, and St. Stephen's 1 v. — The Caxtons 2 v. — My Novel 4 v. — What will he do with it? 4 v. — Dramatic Works 2 v. — A Strange Story 2 v. — Caxtoniana 2 v. — The Lost Tales of Miletus 1 v. — Miscellaneous Prose Works 4 v. — Odes and Epodes of Horace 2 v. — Kenelm Chillingly 4 v. — The Coming Race 1 v. — The Parisians 4 v. — Pausanias, the Spartan 1 v.

Henry Lytton Bulwer (Lord Dalling), † 1872.

Historical Characters 2 v. — The Life of Viscount Palmerston 3 v.

John Bunyan, † 1688.

The Pilgrim's Progress 1 v.

Author of "Buried Alone" (Charles Wood).

Buried Alone 1 v.

Mrs. Frances Hodgson Burnett (Am.).

Through one Administration 2 v. — Little Lord Fauntleroy 1 v. — Sara Crewe, and Editha's Burglar 1 v. — The Pretty Sister of José 1 v. — A Lady of Quality 2 v. — His Grace of Osmonde 2 v.

Miss Burney (Madame D'Arblay), † 1840.

Evelina 1 v.

Robert Burns, † 1796.

Poetical Works (with Portrait) 1 v.

Richard F. Burton, † 1890.

A Pilgrimage to Mecca and Medina 3 v.

Baroness de Bury, *vide* "All for Greed."

A. J. Butler.

Bismarck. His Reflections and Reminiscences. Translated from the great German edition, under the supervision of A. J. Butler. With two Portraits. 3 v.

Mrs. B. H. Buxton, † 1881.

Jennie of "The Prince's," 2 v. — Won! 2 v. — Great Grenfell Gardens 2 v. — Nell—on and off the Stage 2 v. — From the Wings 2 v.

Lord Byron, † 1824.

Poetical Works (with Portrait) 5 v.

Mrs. Mannington Caffyn, (Iota).

A Yellow Aster 1 v. — Children of Circumstance 2 v. — Anne Mauleverer 2 v.

Hall Caine.

The Bondman 2 v. — The Manxman 2 v. — The Christian 2 v. — The Eternal City 3 v.

Verney Lovett Cameron.

Across Africa 2 v.

Mrs. Campbell Praed, *vide* Praed.

Rosa Nouchette Carey.

Not Like other Girls 2 v. — "But Men must Work" 1 v. — Sir Godfrey's Granddaughters 2 v. — The Old, Old Story 2 v. — Herb of Grace 2 v. — The Highway of Fate 2 v.

Thomas Carlyle, † 1881.
The French Revolution 3 v. — Frederick the Great 13 v. — Oliver Cromwell's Letters and Speeches 4 v. — The Life of Schiller 1 v.

Alaric Carr.
Treherne's Temptation 2 v.

Egerton Castle.
Consequences 2 v. — "La Bella," and Others 1 v.

Mrs. Elizabeth Rundle Charles, † 1896, *vide* Author of "Chronicles of the Schönberg-Cotta Family."

Maria Louisa Charlesworth, † 1880.
Oliver of the Mill 1 v.

Mary Cholmondeley.
Diana Tempest 2 v. — Red Pottage 2 v. — Moth and Rust 1 v.

Princess Christian, *vide* Alice, Grand Duchess of Hesse.

Author of "Chronicles of the Schönberg-Cotta Family" (Mrs. E. Rundle Charles), † 1896.
Chronicles of the Schönberg-Cotta Family 2 v. — The Draytons and the Davenants 2 v. — On Both Sides of the Sea 2 v. — Winifred Bertram 1 v. — Diary of Mrs. Kitty Trevylyan 1 v. — The Victory of the Vanquished 1 v. — The Cottage by the Cathedral and other Parables 1 v. — Against the Stream 2 v. — The Bertram Family 2 v. — Conquering and to Conquer 1 v. — Lapsed, but not Lost 1 v.

Alfred Clark.
The Finding of Lot's Wife 1 v.

Samuel L. Clemens, *vide* Twain.

Mrs. W. K. Clifford.
Love-Letters of a Worldly Woman 1 v. — Aunt Anne 2 v. — The Last Touches, and other Stories 1 v. — Mrs. Keith's Crime 1 v. — A Wild Proxy 1 v. — A Flash of Summer 1 v. — A Woman Alone 1 v. — Woodside Farm 1 v.

Mrs. Caroline Clive, † 1873, *vide* Author of "Paul Ferroll."

Frances Power Cobbe.
Re-Echoes 1 v.

C. R. Coleridge.
An English Squire 2 v.

M. E. Coleridge.
The King with two Faces 2 v.

Samuel Taylor Coleridge, † 1834.
Poems 1 v.

Charles Allston Collins, † 1873.
A Cruise upon Wheels 2 v.

Mortimer Collins, † 1876.
Sweet and Twenty 2 v. — A Fight with Fortune 2 v.

Wilkie Collins, † 1889.
After Dark 1 v. — Hide and Seek 2 v. — A Plot in Private Life, etc. 1 v. — The Woman in White 2 v. — Basil 1 v. — No Name 3 v. — The Dead Secret, and other Tales 2 v. — Antonina 2 v. — Armadale 3 v. — The Moonstone 2 v. — Man and Wife 3 v. — Poor Miss Finch 2 v. — Miss or Mrs.? 1 v. — The New Magdalen 2 v. — The Frozen Deep 1 v. — The Law and the Lady 2 v. — The Two Destinies 1 v. — My Lady's Money, and Percy and the Prophet 1 v. — The Haunted Hotel 1 v. — The Fallen Leaves 2 v. — Jezebel's Daughter 2 v. — The Black Robe 2 v. — Heart and Science 2 v. — "I say No," 2 v. — The Evil Genius 2 v. — The Guilty River, and The Ghost's Touch 1 v. — The Legacy of Cain 2 v. — Blind Love 2 v.

Author of "Cometh up as a Flower," *vide* Rhoda Broughton.

Joseph Conrad.
An Outcast of the Islands 2 v. — Tales of Unrest 1 v.

Hugh Conway (F. J. Fargus), † 1885.
Called Back 1 v. — Bound Together 2 v. — Dark Days 1 v. — A Family Affair 2 v. — Living or Dead 2 v.

James Fenimore Cooper (Am.), † 1851.
The Spy (with Portrait) 1 v. — The Two Admirals 1 v. — The Jack O'Lantern 1 v.

Mrs. Cooper, *vide* Katharine Saunders.

Marie Corelli.
Vendetta! 2 v. — Thelma 2 v. — A Romance of Two Worlds 2 v. — "Ardath"

3 v. — Wormwood. A Drama of Paris 2 v. — The Hired Baby, with other Stories and Social Sketches 1 v. — Barabbas; A Dream of the World's Tragedy 2 v. — The Sorrows of Satan 2 v. — The Mighty Atom 1 v. — The Murder of Delicia 1 v. — Ziska 1 v. — Boy. A Sketch. 2 v. — The Master-Christian 2 v. — "Temporal Power" 2 v.

Mrs. Everard Cotes.

Those Delightful Americans 1 v.

Author of "The County."

The County 1 v.

George Lillie Craik, † 1866.

A Manual of English Literature and of the History of the English Language 2 v.

Mrs. Craik (Miss Dinah M. Mulock), † 1887.

John Halifax, Gentleman 2 v. — The Head of the Family 2 v. — A Life for a Life 2 v. — A Woman's Thoughts about Women 1 v. — Agatha's Husband 1 v. — Romantic Tales 1 v. — Domestic Stories 1 v. — Mistress and Maid 1 v. — The Ogilvies 1 v. — Lord Erlistoun 1 v. — Christian's Mistake 1 v. — Bread upon the Waters 1 v. — A Noble Life 1 v. — Olive 2 v. — Two Marriages 1 v. — Studies from Life 1 v. — Poems 1 v. — The Woman's Kingdom 2 v. — The Unkind Word, and other Stories 2 v. — A Brave Lady 2 v. — Hannah 2 v. — Fair France 1 v. — My Mother and I 1 v. — The Little Lame Prince 1 v. — Sermons out of Church 1 v. — The Laurel-Bush; Two little Tinkers 1 v. — A Legacy 2 v. — Young Mrs. Jardine 2 v. — His Little Mother, and other Tales and Sketches 1 v. — Plain Speaking 1 v. — Miss Tommy 1 v. — King Arthur 1 v.

Georgiana M. Craik (Mrs. May).

Lost and Won 1 v. — Faith Unwin's Ordeal 1 v. — Leslie Tyrrell 1 v. — Winifred's Wooing, etc. 1 v. — Mildred 1 v. — Esther Hill's Secret 2 v. — Hero Trevelyan 1 v. — Without Kith or Kin 2 v. — Only a Butterfly 1 v. — Sylvia's Choice; Theresa 2 v. — Anne Warwick 1 v. — Dorcas 2 v. — Two Women 2 v.

Georgiana M. Craik & M. C. Stirling.

Two Tales of Married Life (Hard to Bear, by Miss Craik; A True Man, by M. C. Stirling) 2 v.

Mrs. Augustus Craven, *vide* Lady Fullerton.

F. Marion Crawford (Am.).

Mr. Isaacs 1 v. — Doctor Claudius 1 v. — To Leeward 1 v. — A Roman Singer 1 v. — An American Politician 1 v. — Zoroaster 1 v. — A Tale of a Lonely Parish 2 v. — Saracinesca 2 v. — Marzio's Crucifix 1 v. — Paul Patoff 2 v. — With the Immortals 1 v. — Greifenstein 2 v. — Sant' Ilario 2 v. — A Cigarette-Maker's Romance 1 v. — Khaled 1 v. — The Witch of Prague 2 v. — The Three Fates 2 v. — Don Orsino 2 v. — The Children of the King 1 v. — Pietro Ghisleri 2 v. — Marion Darche 1 v. — Katharine Lauderdale 2 v. — The Ralstons 2 v. — Casa Braccio 2 v. — Adam Johnstone's Son 1 v. — Taquisara 2 v. — A Rose of Yesterday 1 v. — Corleone 2 v. — Via Crucis 2 v. — In the Palace of the King 2 v. — Marietta, a Maid of Venice 2 v. — Cecilia 2 v.

S. R. Crockett.

The Raiders 2 v. — Cleg Kelly 2 v. — The Grey Man 2 v. — Love Idylls 1 v. — The Dark o' the Moon 2 v.

J. W. Cross, *vide* George Eliot's Life.

Mrs. Pender Cudlip, *vide* A. Thomas.

Miss Cummins (Am.), † 1866.

The Lamplighter 1 v. — Mabel Vaughan 1 v. — El Fureidîs 1 v. — Haunted Hearts 1 v.

Paul Cushing.

The Blacksmith of Voe 2 v.

"Daily News."

War Correspondence, 1877, by Archibald Forbes and others 3 v.

Author of "Dark."

Dark 1 v.

Richard Harding Davis (Am.).

Gallegher, etc. 1 v. — Van Bibber and Others 1 v.

Daniel De Foe, † 1731.

Robinson Crusoe 1 v.

Margaret Deland (Am.).

John Ward, Preacher 1 v.

Author of "Democracy" (Am.).

Democracy 1 v.

Author of "Demos," *vide* George Gissing.

Author of "Diary and Notes," *vide* Author of "Horace Templeton."

Charles Dickens, † 1870.

The Pickwick Club (with Portrait) 2 v. — American Notes 1 v. — Oliver Twist 1 v. — Nicholas Nickleby 2 v. — Sketches 1 v. — Martin Chuzzlewit 2 v. — A Christmas Carol; The Chimes; The Cricket on the Hearth 1 v. — Master Humphrey's Clock (Old Curiosity Shop; Barnaby Rudge, etc.) 3 v. — Pictures from Italy 1 v. — Dombey and Son 3 v. — David Copperfield 3 v. — Bleak House 4 v. — A Child's History of England (2 v. 8° M. 2,70.) — Hard Times 1 v. — Little Dorrit (with Illustrations) 4 v. — The Battle of Life; The Haunted Man 1 v. — A Tale of two Cities 2 v. — Hunted Down; The Uncommercial Traveller 1 v. — Great Expectations 2 v. — Christmas Stories, etc. 1 v. — Our Mutual Friend (with Illustrations) 4 v. — Somebody's Luggage; Mrs. Lirriper's Lodgings; Mrs. Lirriper's Legacy 1 v. — Doctor Marigold's Prescriptions; Mugby Junction 1 v. — The Mystery of Edwin Drood (with Illustrations) 2 v. — The Mudfog Papers, 1 v. — The Letters of Charles Dickens, ed. by his Sister-in-law and his eldest Daughter 4 v. — *Vide* also Household Words, Novels and Tales, and John Forster.

Charles Dickens & Wilkie Collins.

No Thoroughfare; The Late Miss Hollingford 1 v.

Benjamin Disraeli, Lord Beaconsfield, † 1881.

Coningsby 1 v. — Sybil 1 v. — Contarini Fleming (with Portrait) 1 v. — Alroy 1 v. — Tancred 2 v. — Venetia 2 v. — Vivian Grey 2 v. — Henrietta Temple 1 v. — Lothair 2 v. — Endymion 2 v.

Ella Hepworth Dixon.

The Story of a Modern Woman 1 v.

W. Hepworth Dixon, † 1879.

Personal History of Lord Bacon 1 v. — The Holy Land 2 v. — New America 2 v. — Spiritual Wives 2 v. — Her Majesty's Tower 4 v. — Free Russia 2 v. — History of two Queens 6 v. — White Conquest 2 v. — Diana, Lady Lyle 2 v.

Thomas Dixon, Jr. (Am.).

The Leopard's Spots 2 v.

L. Dougall (Am.).

Beggars All 2 v.

Ménie Muriel Dowie.

A Girl in the Karpathians 1 v.

A. Conan Doyle.

The Sign of Four 1 v. — Micah Clarke 2 v. — The Captain of the Pole-Star, and other Tales 1 v. — The White Company 2 v. — A Study in Scarlet 1 v. — The Great Shadow, and Beyond the City 1 v. — The Adventures of Sherlock Holmes 2 v. — The Refugees 2 v. — The Firm of Girdlestone 2 v. — The Memoirs of Sherlock Holmes 2 v. — Round the Red Lamp 1 v. — The Stark Munro Letters 1 v. — The Exploits of Brigadier Gerard 1 v. — Rodney Stone 2 v. — Uncle Bernac 1 v. — The Tragedy of the Korosko 1 v. — A Duet 1 v. — The Green Flag 1 v. — The Great Boer War 2 v. — The War in South Africa 1 v. — The Hound of the Baskervilles 1 v.

Professor Henry Drummond, † 1897.

The Greatest Thing in the World; Pax Vobiscum; The Changed Life 1 v.

Dunton, *vide* Th. Watts-Dunton.

The Earl and the Doctor.

South Sea Bubbles 1 v.

The Earl of Dufferin.

Letters from High Latitudes 1 v.

Edward B. Eastwick, † 1883.

Autobiography of Lutfullah 1 v.

Maria Edgeworth, *vide* Series for the Young, p. 29.

Mrs. Annie Edwardes.

Archie Lovell 2 v. — Steven Lawrence, Yeoman 2 v. — Ought we to visit her? 2 v. — A Vagabond Heroine 1 v. — Leah: A Woman of Fashion 2 v. — A Blue-Stocking 1 v. — Jet: Her Face or Her Fortune? 1 v. — Vivian the Beauty 1 v. — A Ballroom Repentance 2 v. — A Girton Girl 2 v. — A Playwright's Daughter, and Bertie Griffiths 1 v. — Pearl-Powder 1 v. The Adventuress 1 v.

Amelia B. Edwards, † 1892.

Barbara's History 2 v. — Miss Carew 2 v. — Hand and Glove 1 v. — Half a Million of Money 2 v. — Debenham's Vow 2 v. — In the Days of my Youth 2 v. —

Untrodden Peaks and Unfrequented Valleys 1 v. — Monsieur Maurice 1 v. — A Night on the Borders of the Black Forest 1 v. — A Poetry-Book of Elder Poets 1 v. — A Thousand Miles up the Nile 2 v. — A Poetry-Book of Modern Poets 1 v. — Lord Brackenbury 2 v.

M. Betham-Edwards, *v.* Betham.

Edward Eggleston (Am.).

The Faith Doctor 2 v.

Barbara Elbon (Am.).

Bethesda 2 v.

George Eliot (Miss Evans — Mrs. Cross), † 1880.

Scenes of Clerical Life 2 v. — Adam Bede 2 v. — The Mill on the Floss 2 v. — Silas Marner 1 v. — Romola 2 v. — Felix Holt 2 v. — Daniel Deronda 4 v. — The Lifted Veil, and Brother Jacob 1 v. — Impressions of Theophrastus Such 1 v. — Essays and Leaves from a Note-Book 1 v. — George Eliot's Life, edited by her Husband, J. W. Cross 4 v.

Author of "Elizabeth and her German Garden."

Elizabeth and her German Garden 1 v. — The Solitary Summer 1 v. — The Benefactress 2 v.

Mrs. Frances Elliot, † 1898.

Diary of an Idle Woman in Italy 2 v. — Old Court Life in France 2 v. — The Italians 2 v. — The Diary of an Idle Woman in Sicily 1 v. — Pictures of Old Rome 1 v. — The Diary of an Idle Woman in Spain 2 v. — The Red Cardinal 1 v. — The Story of Sophia 1 v. — Diary of an Idle Woman in Constantinople 1 v. — Old Court Life in Spain 2 v. — Roman Gossip 1 v.

Author of "An Englishwoman's Love-Letters."

An Englishwoman's Love-Letters 1 v.

Henry Erroll.

An Ugly Duckling 1 v.

E. Rentoul Esler.

The Way they loved at Grimpat 1 v.

The Authors of "Essays and Reviews."

Essays and Reviews. By various Authors 1 v.

Author of "Estelle Russell."

Estelle Russell 2 v.

Elsa D'Esterre-Keeling.

Three Sisters 1 v. — A Laughing Philosopher 1 v. — The Professor's Wooing 1 v. — In Thoughtland and in Dreamland 1 v. — Orchardscroft 1 v. — Appassionata 1 v. — Old Maids and Young 2 v. — The Queen's Serf 1 v.

Author of "Euthanasia."

Euthanasia 1 v.

Juliana Horatia Ewing, † 1885.

Jackanapes; The Story of a Short Life; Daddy Darwin's Dovecot 1 v. — A Flat Iron for a Farthing 1 v. — The Brownies, and other Tales 1 v.

Author of "Expiated."

Expiated 2 v.

F. J. Fargus, *vide* Hugh Conway.

F. W. (Dean) Farrar.

Darkness and Dawn 3 v.

Authors of "The Fate of Fenella."

The Fate of Fenella, by 24 Authors 1 v.

Percy Fendall, *vide* F. C. Philips.

George Manville Fenn.

The Parson o' Dumford 2 v. — The Clerk of Portwick 2 v.

Henry Fielding, † 1754.

Tom Jones 2 v.

Five Centuries

of the English Language and Literature: John Wycliffe. — Geoffrey Chaucer. — Stephen Hawes. — Sir Thomas More. — Edmund Spenser. — Ben Jonson. — John Locke. — Thomas Gray (vol. 500, published 1860) 1 v.

George Fleming (Am.).

Kismet 1 v. — Andromeda 2 v.

Archibald Forbes, † 1900.

My Experiences of the War between France and Germany 2 v. — Soldiering and Scribbling 1 v. — Memories and Studies of War and Peace 2 v. — *Vide* also "Daily News," War Correspondence.

R. E. Forrest.

Eight Days 2 v.

Mrs. Forrester.

Viva 2 v. — Rhona 2 v. — Roy and Viola 2 v. — My Lord and My Lady 2 v. — I have Lived and Loved 2 v. — June 2 v. — Omnia Vanitas 1 v. — Although he was a Lord, and other Tales 1 v. — Corisande, and other Tales 1 v. — Once Again 2 v. — Of the World, Worldly 1 v. — Dearest 2 v. — The Light of other Days 1 v. — Too Late Repented 1 v.

John Forster, † 1876.

The Life of Charles Dickens (with Illustrations and Portraits) 6 v. — Life and Times of Oliver Goldsmith 2 v.

Jessie Fothergill.

The First Violin 2 v. — Probation 2 v. — Made or Marred, and "One of Three" 1 v. — Kith and Kin 2 v. — Peril 2 v. — Borderland 2 v.

Author of "Found Dead," *vide* James Payn.

Ellen Thorneycroft Fowler.

A Double Thread 2 v. — The Farringdons 2 v. — Fuel of Fire 1 v.

Caroline Fox, † 1871.

Memories of Old Friends from her Journals and Letters, edited by Horace N. Pym 2 v.

Author of "Frank Fairlegh" (F. E. Smedley), † 1864.

Frank Fairlegh 2 v.

M. E. Francis.

The Duenna of a Genius 1 v.

Harold Frederic (Am.), † 1898.

Illumination 2 v. — March Hares 1 v.

Edward A. Freeman, † 1892.

The Growth of the English Constitution 1 v. — Select Historical Essays 1 v. — Sketches from French Travel 1 v.

James Anthony Froude, † 1894.

Oceana 1 v. — The Spanish Story of the Armada, and other Essays 1 v.

Lady Georgiana Fullerton, † 1885.

Ellen Middleton 1 v. — Grantley Manor 2 v. — Lady Bird 2 v. — Too Strange not to be True 2 v. — Constance Sherwood 2 v. — A Stormy Life 2 v. — Mrs. Geralds' Niece 2 v. — The Notary's Daughter 1 v. — The Lilies of the Valley, and The House of Penarvan 1 v. — The Countess de Bonneval 1 v. — Rose Leblanc 1 v. — Seven Stories 1 v. — The Life of Luisa de Carvajal 1 v. — A Will and a Way, and The Handkerchief at the Window 2 v. — Eliane 2 v. (by Mrs. Augustus Craven, translated by Lady Fullerton). — Laurentia 1 v.

Marguerite Gardiner, *vide* Lady Blessington.

Mrs. Gaskell, † 1865.

Mary Barton 1 v. — Ruth 2 v. — North and South 1 v. — Lizzie Leigh, and other Tales 1 v. — The Life of Charlotte Brontë 2 v. — Lois the Witch, etc. 1 v. — Sylvia's Lovers 2 v. — A Dark Night's Work 1 v. — Wives and Daughters 3 v. — Cranford 1 v. — Cousin Phillis, and other Tales 1 v.

Author of "Geraldine Hawthorne," *vide* Author of "Miss Molly."

Dorothea Gerard (Madame Longard de Longgarde).

Lady Baby 2 v. — Recha 1 v. — Orthodox 1 v. — The Wrong Man 1 v. — A Spotless Reputation 1 v. — A Forgotten Sin 1 v. — One Year 1 v. — The Supreme Crime 1 v. — The Blood-Tax 1 v. — Holy Matrimony 1 v. — The Eternal Woman 1 v.

E. Gerard (Emily de Łaszowska).

A Secret Mission 1 v. — A Foreigner 2 v. — The Extermination of Love 2 v.

Agnes Giberne.

The Curate's Home 1 v.

George Gissing.

Demos. A Story of English Socialism 2 v. — New Grub Street 2 v.

Rt. Hon. W. E. Gladstone, † 1898.

Rome and the Newest Fashions in Religion 1 v. — Bulgarian Horrors, and Russia in Turkistan, with other Tracts 1 v. — The Hellenic Factor in the Eastern Problem, with other Tracts 1 v.

Elinor Glyn.

The Visits of Elizabeth 1 v. — The Reflections of Ambrosine 1 v.

Hal Godfrey (Charlotte O'Conor-Eccles).

The Rejuvenation of Miss Semaphore 1 v.

Oliver Goldsmith, † 1774.

Select Works (with Portrait) 1 v.

Edward J. Goodman.

Too Curious 1 v.

Julien Gordon (Am.).
A Diplomat's Diary 1 v.

Major-Gen. C. G. Gordon, † 1885.
His Journals at Kartoum. Introduction and Notes by A. E. Hake (with eighteen Illustrations) 2 v.

Mrs. Gore, † 1861.
Castles in the Air 1 v. — The Dean's Daughter 2 v. — Progress and Prejudice 2 v. — Mammon 2 v. — A Life's Lessons 2 v. — The Two Aristocracies 2 v. — Heckington 2 v.

Sarah Grand.
Our Manifold Nature 1 v. — Babs the Impossible 2 v.

Miss Grant.
Victor Lescar 2 v. — The Sun-Maid 2 v. — My Heart's in the Highlands 2 v. — Artiste 2 v. — Prince Hugo 2 v. — Cara Roma 2 v.

Maxwell Gray.
The Silence of Dean Maitland 2 v. — The Reproach of Annesley 2 v.

E. C. Grenville: Murray (Trois-Etoiles), † 1881.
The Member for Paris 2 v. — Young Brown 2 v. — The Boudoir Cabal 3 v. — French Pictures in English Chalk *(First Series)* 2 v. — The Russians of To-day 1 v. — French Pictures in English Chalk *(Second Series)* 2 v. — Strange Tales 1 v. — That Artful Vicar 2 v. — Six Months in the Ranks 1 v. — People I have met 1 v.

Ethel St. Clair Grimwood.
My Three Years in Manipur (with Portrait) 1 v.

W. A. Baillie Grohman.
Tyrol and the Tyrolese 1 v.

Archibald Clavering Gunter (Am.).
Mr. Barnes of New York 1 v.

F. Anstey Guthrie, *vide* Anstey.

Author of "Guy Livingstone" (George Alfred Laurence), † 1876.
Guy Livingstone 1 v. — Sword and Gown 1 v. — Barren Honour 1 v. — Border and Bastille 1 v. — Maurice Dering 1 v. — Sans Merci 2 v. — Breaking a Butterfly 2 v. — Anteros 2 v. — Hagarene 2 v.

John Habberton (Am.).
Helen's Babies & Other People's Children 1 v. — The Bowsham Puzzle 1 v. — One Tramp; Mrs. Mayburn's Twins 1 v.

H. Rider Haggard.
King Solomon's Mines 1 v. — She 2 v. — Jess 2 v. — Allan Quatermain 2 v. — The Witch's Head 2 v. — Maiwa's Revenge 1 v. — Mr. Meeson's Will 1 v. — Colonel Quaritch, V. C. 2 v. — Cleopatra 2 v. — Allan's Wife 1 v. — Beatrice 2 v. — Dawn 2 v. — Montezuma's Daughter 2 v. — The People of the Mist 2 v. — Joan Haste 2 v. — Heart of the World 2 v. — The Wizard 1 v. — Doctor Therne 1 v. — Swallow 2 v. — Black Heart and White Heart, and Elissa 1 v. — Lysbeth 2 v. — A Winter Pilgrimage 2 v. — Pearl-Maiden 2 v.

H. Rider Haggard & Andrew Lang.
The World's Desire 2 v.

A. E. Hake, *vide* Gen. Gordon.

Mrs. S. C. Hall, † 1881.
Can Wrong be Right? 1 v. — Marian 2 v.

Philip Gilbert Hamerton, † 1894.
Marmorne 1 v. — French and English 2 v.

Miss Iza Hardy, *vide* Author of "Not Easily Jealous."

Thomas Hardy.
The Hand of Ethelberta 2 v. — Far from the Madding Crowd 2 v. — The Return of the Native 2 v. — The Trumpet-Major 2 v. — A Laodicean 2 v. — Two on a Tower 2 v. — A Pair of Blue Eyes 2 v. — A Group of Noble Dames 1 v. — Tess of the D'Urbervilles 2 v. — Life's Little Ironies 1 v. — Jude the Obscure 2 v.

Beatrice Harraden.
Ships that pass in the Night 1 v. — In Varying Moods 1 v. — Hilda Strafford, and The Remittance Man 1 v. — The Fowler 2 v.

Agnes Harrison.
Martin's Vineyard 1 v.

Bret Harte (Am.), † 1902.
Prose and Poetry (Tales of the Argonauts: — The Luck of Roaring Camp; The Outcasts of Poker Flat, etc. — Spanish and American Legends; Condensed Novels; Civic and Character Sketches; Poems) 2 v. — Idyls of the Foothills 1 v. — Gabriel Conroy 2 v. — Two Men of Sandy Bar 1 v. — Thankful Blossom, and other Tales 1 v. — The Story of a Mine 1 v. — Drift from Two

Shores 1 v. — An Heiress of Red Dog, and other Sketches 1 v. — The Twins of Table Mountain, and other Tales 1 v. — Jeff Briggs's Love Story, and other Tales 1 v. — Flip, and other Stories 1 v. — On the Frontier 1 v. — By Shore and Sedge 1 v. — Maruja 1 v. — Snow-bound at Eagle's, and Devil's Ford 1 v. — The Crusade of the "Excelsior" 1 v. — A Millionaire of Rough-and-Ready, and other Tales 1 v. — Captain Jim's Friend, and the Argonauts of North Liberty 1 v. — Cressy 1 v. — The Heritage of Dedlow Marsh, and other Tales 1 v. — A Waif of the Plains 1 v. — A Ward of the Golden Gate 1 v. — A Sappho of Green Springs, and other Tales 1 v. — A First Family of Tasajara 1 v. — Colonel Starbottle's Client, and some other People 1 v. — Susy 1 v. — Sally Dows, etc. 1 v. — A Protégée of Jack Hamlin's, etc. 1 v. — The Bell-Ringer of Angel's, etc. 1 v. — Clarence 1 v. — In a Hollow of the Hills, and The Devotion of Enriquez 1 v. — The Ancestors of Peter Atherly, etc. 1 v. — Three Partners 1 v. — Tales of Trail and Town 1 v. — Stories in Light and Shadow 1 v. — Mr. Jack Hamlin's Mediation, and other Stories 1 v. — From Sand-Hill to Pine 1 v. — Under the Redwoods 1 v. — On the Old Trail 1 v.

Sir Henry Havelock, *vide* Rev. W. Brock.

Nathaniel Hawthorne (Am.), † 1864.

The Scarlet Letter 1 v. — Transformation (The Marble Faun) 2 v. — Passages from the English Note-Books of Nathaniel Hawthorne 2 v.

Mrs. Hector, *vide* Mrs. Alexander.

Author of "The Heir of Redclyffe," *vide* Charlotte M. Yonge.

Sir Arthur Helps, † 1875.

Friends in Council 2 v. — Ivan de Biron 2 v.

Mrs. Felicia Hemans, † 1835.

Select Poetical Works 1 v.

Maurice Hewlett.

The Forest Lovers 1 v. — Little Novels of Italy 1 v. — The Life and Death of Richard Yea-and-Nay 2 v. — New Canterbury Tales 1 v.

Robert Hichens.

Flames 2 v. — The Slave 2 v. — Felix 2 v.

Admiral Hobart Pasha, † 1886.

Sketches from my Life 1 v.

John Oliver Hobbes.

The Gods, Some Mortals and Lord Wickenham 1 v. — The Serious Wooing 1 v.

Mrs. Cashel Hoey.

A Golden Sorrow 2 v. — Out of Court 2 v.

Annie E. Holdsworth.

The Years that the Locust hath Eaten 1 v. — The Gods Arrive 1 v. — The Valley of the Great Shadow 1 v. — Great Lowlands 1 v.

Holme Lee, *vide* Harriet Parr.

Oliver Wendell Holmes (Am.), † 1894.

The Autocrat of the Breakfast-Table 1 v. — The Professor at the Breakfast-Table 1 v. — The Poet at the Breakfast-Table 1 v. — Over the Teacups 1 v.

Anthony Hope (Hawkins).

Mr. Witt's Widow 1 v. — A Change of Air 1 v. — Half a Hero 1 v. — The Indiscretion of the Duchess 1 v. — The God in the Car 1 v. — The Chronicles of Count Antonio 1 v. — Comedies of Courtship 1 v. — The Heart of Princess Osra 1 v. — Phroso 2 v. — Simon Dale 2 v. — Rupert of Hentzau 1 v. — The King's Mirror 2 v. — Quisanté 1 v. — Tristram of Blent 2 v. — The Intrusions of Peggy 2 v.

Tighe Hopkins.

An Idler in Old France 1 v. — The Man in the Iron Mask 1 v. — The Dungeons of Old Paris 1 v. — The Silent Gate 1 v.

Author of "Horace Templeton."

Diary and Notes 1 v.

Ernest William Hornung.

A Bride from the Bush 1 v. — Under Two Skies 1 v. — Tiny Luttrell 1 v. — The Boss of Taroomba 1 v. — My Lord Duke 1 v. — Young Blood 1 v. — Some Persons Unknown 1 v. — The Amateur Cracksman 1 v. — The Rogue's March 1 v. — The Belle of Toorak 1 v. — Peccavi 1 v. — The Black Mask 1 v. — The Shadow of the Rope 1 v.

"Household Words."

Conducted by Charles Dickens. 1851-56. 36 v. — Novels and Tales reprinted from Household Words by Charles Dickens. 1856-59. 11 v.

Mrs. Houstoun, *vide* "Recommended to Mercy."

Author of "How to be Happy though Married."

How to be Happy though Married 1 v.

Blanche Willis Howard (Am.), † 1899.

One Summer 1 v. — Aunt Serena 1 v. — Guenn 2 v. — Tony, the Maid, etc. 1 v. — The Open Door 2 v.

Blanche Willis Howard, † 1899, & William Sharp.

A Fellowe and His Wife 1 v.

William Dean Howells (Am.).

A Foregone Conclusion 1 v. — The Lady of the Aroostook 1 v. — A Modern Instance 2 v. — The Undiscovered Country 1 v. — Venetian Life (with Portrait) 1 v. — Italian Journeys 1 v. — A Chance Acquaintance 1 v. — Their Wedding Journey 1 v. — A Fearful Responsibility, and Tonelli's Marriage 1 v. — A Woman's Reason 2 v. — Dr. Breen's Practice 1 v. — The Rise of Silas Lapham 2 v. — A Pair of Patient Lovers 1 v.

Thomas Hughes, † 1898.

Tom Brown's School-Days 1 v.

Mrs. Hungerford (Mrs. Argles), † 1897.

Molly Bawn 2 v. — Mrs. Geoffrey 2 v. — Faith and Unfaith 2 v. — Portia 2 v. — Loÿs, Lord Berresford, and other Tales 1 v. — Her First Appearance, and other Tales 1 v. — Phyllis 2 v. — Rossmoyne 2 v. — Doris 2 v. — A Maiden all Forlorn, etc. 1 v. — A Passive Crime, and other Stories 1 v. — Green Pleasure and Grey Grief 2 v. — A Mental Struggle 2 v. — Her Week's Amusement, and Ugly Barrington 1 v. — Lady Branksmere 2 v. — Lady Valworth's Diamonds 1 v. — A Modern Circe 2 v. — Marvel 2 v. — The Hon. Mrs. Vereker 1 v. — Under-Currents 2 v. — In Durance Vile, etc. 1 v. — A Troublesome Girl, and other Stories 1 v. — A Life's Remorse 2 v. — A Born Coquette 2 v. — The Duchess 1 v. — Lady Verner's Flight 1 v. — A Conquering Heroine, and "When in Doubt" 1 v. — Nora Creina 2 v. — A Mad Prank, and other Stories 1 v. — The Hoyden 2 v. — The Red House Mystery 1 v. — An Unsatisfactory Lover 1 v. — Peter's Wife 2 v. — The Three Graces 1 v. — A Tug of War 1 v. — The Professor's Experiment 2 v. — A Point of Conscience 2 v. — A Lonely Girl 1 v. — Lovice 1 v. — The Coming of Chloe 1 v.

Mrs. Hunt, *vide* Averil Beaumont.

Violet Hunt.

The Human Interest 1 v.

Jean Ingelow, † 1897.

Off the Skelligs 3 v. — Poems 2 v. — Fated to be Free 2 v. — Sarah de Berenger 2 v. — Don John 2 v.

The Hon. Lady Inglis.

The Siege of Lucknow 1 v.

John H. Ingram, *vide* E. A. Poe.

Iota, *vide* Mrs. Mannington Caffyn.

Washington Irving (Am.), † 1859.

The Sketch Book (with Portrait) 1 v. — The Life of Mahomet 1 v. — Lives of the Successors of Mahomet 1 v. — Oliver Goldsmith 1 v. — Chronicles of Wolfert's Roost 1 v. — Life of George Washington 5 v.

Mrs. Helen Jackson (H. H.) (Am.), † 1885.

Ramona 2 v.

W. W. Jacobs.

Many Cargoes 1 v. — The Skipper's Wooing, and The Brown Man's Servant 1 v. — Sea Urchins 1 v. — A Master of Craft 1 v. — Light Freights 1 v. — At Sunwich Port 1 v. — The Lady of the Barge 1 v.

Charles T. C. James.

Holy Wedlock 1 v.

G. P. R. James, † 1860.

Morley Ernstein (with Portrait) 1 v. — Forest Days 1 v. — The False Heir 1 v. — Arabella Stuart 1 v. — Rose d'Albret 1 v. — Arrah Neil 1 v. — Agincourt 1 v. — The Smuggler 1 v. — The Step-Mother 2 v. — Beauchamp 1 v. — Heidelberg 1 v. — The Gipsy 1 v. — The Castle of Ehrenstein 1 v. — Darnley 1 v. — Russell 2 v. — The Convict 2 v. — Sir Theodore Broughton 2 v.

Henry James (Am.).

The American 2 v. — The Europeans 1 v. — Daisy Miller; An International Episode; Four Meetings 1 v. — Roderick Hudson 2 v. — The Madonna of the Future, etc. 1 v. — Eugene Pickering, etc. 1 v. — Confidence 1 v. — Washington Square, etc. 2 v. — The Portrait of a Lady 3 v. — Foreign Parts 1 v. — French Poets and Novelists 1 v. — The Siege of London; The Point of View; A Passionate Pilgrim 1 v. — Portraits of Places 1 v. — A Little Tour in France 1 v.

J. Cordy Jeaffreson.

A Book about Doctors 2 v. — A Woman in spite of Herself 2 v. — The Real Lord Byron 3 v.

Mrs. Charles Jenkin, † 1885.

"Who Breaks—Pays" 1 v. — Skirmishing 1 v. — Once and Again 2 v. — Two French Marriages 2 v. — Within an Ace 1 v. — Jupiter's Daughters 1 v.

Edward Jenkins.

Ginx's Baby, his Birth and other Misfortunes; Lord Bantam 2 v.

Author of "Jennie of 'The Prince's,'" *vide* B. H. Buxton.

Jerome K. Jerome.

The Idle Thoughts of an Idle Fellow 1 v. — Diary of a Pilgrimage, and Six Essays 1 v. — Novel Notes 1 v. — Sketches in Lavender, Blue and Green 1 v. — The Second Thoughts of an Idle Fellow 1 v. — Three Men on the Bummel 1 v. — Paul Kelver 2 v.

Douglas Jerrold, † 1857.

History of St. Giles and St. James 2 v. — Men of Character 2 v.

Author of "John Halifax, Gentleman," *vide* Mrs. Craik.

Johnny Ludlow, *vide* Mrs. Henry Wood.

Samuel Johnson, † 1784.

Lives of the English Poets 2 v.

Emily Jolly.

Colonel Dacre 2 v.

Author of "Joshua Davidson," *vide* Mrs. E. Lynn Linton.

Miss Julia Kavanagh, † 1877.

Nathalie 2 v. — Daisy Burns 2 v. — Grace Lee 2 v. — Rachel Gray 1 v. — Adèle 3 v. — A Summer and Winter in the Two Sicilies 2 v. — Seven Years, and other Tales 2 v. — French Women of Letters 1 v. — English Women of Letters 1 v. — Queen Mab 2 v. — Beatrice 2 v. — Sybil's Second Love 2 v. — Dora 2 v. — Silvia 2 v. — Bessie 2 v. — John Dorrien 3 v. — Two Lilies 2 v. — Forget-me-nots 2 v. — *Vide* also Series for the Young, p. 29.

Annie Keary, † 1879.

Oldbury 2 v. — Castle Daly 2 v.

D'Esterre-Keeling, *vide* Esterre.

Thomas a Kempis.

The Imitation of Christ. Translated from the Latin by W. Benham, B.D. 1 v.

Richard B. Kimball (Am.), †

Saint Leger 1 v. — Romance of Student Life Abroad 1 v. — Undercurrents 1 v. — Was he Successful? 1 v. — To-Day in New York 1 v.

Alexander William Kinglake, † 1891.

Eothen 1 v. — The Invasion of the Crimea 14 v.

Charles Kingsley, † 1875.

Yeast 1 v. — Westward ho! 2 v. — Two Years ago 2 v. — Hypatia 2 v. — Alton Locke 1 v. — Hereward the Wake 2 v. — At Last 2 v. — His Letters and Memories of his Life, edited by his Wife 2 v.

Henry Kingsley, † 1876.

Ravenshoe 2 v. — Austin Elliot 1 v. — Geoffry Hamlyn 2 v. — The Hillyars and the Burtons 2 v. — Leighton Court 1 v. — Valentin 1 v. — Oakshott Castle 1 v. — Reginald Hetherege 2 v. — The Grange Garden 2 v.

Albert Kinross.

An Opera and Lady Grasmere 1 v.

Rudyard Kipling.

Plain Tales from the Hills 1 v. — The Second Jungle Book 1 v. — The Seven Seas 1 v. — "Captains Courageous" 1 v. — The Day's Work 1 v. — A Fleet in Being 1 v. — Stalky & Co. 1 v. — From Sea to Sea 2 v. — The City of Dreadful Night 1 v. — Kim 1 v. — Just So Stories 1 v.

May Laffan.

Flitters, Tatters, and the Counsellor, etc. 1 v.

Charles Lamb, † 1834.

The Essays of Elia and Eliana 1 v.

Mary Langdon (Am.).

Ida May 1 v.

Author of "The Last of the Cavaliers" (Miss Piddington).

The Last of the Cavaliers 2 v. — The Gain of a Loss 2 v.

Mme de Laszowska, *vide* E. Gerard.

The Hon. Emily Lawless.

Hurrish 1 v.

George Alfred Laurence, *vide* Author of "Guy Livingstone."

"Leaves from the Journal of our Life in the Highlands," *vide* Victoria R. I.

Holme Lee, † 1900, *vide* Harriet Parr.

J. S. Le Fanu, † 1873.

Uncle Silas 2 v. — Guy Deverell 2 v.

Mark Lemon, † 1870.

Wait for the End 2 v. — Loved at Last 2 v. — Falkner Lyle 2 v. — Leyton Hall, and other Tales 2 v. — Golden Fetters 2 v.

Author of "The Letters of Her Mother to Elizabeth," *vide* W. R. H. Trowbridge.

Charles Lever, † 1872.

The O'Donoghue 1 v. — The Knight of Gwynne 3 v. — Arthur O'Leary 2 v. — Harry Lorrequer 2 v. — Charles O'Malley 3 v. — Tom Burke of "Ours" 3 v. — Jack Hinton 2 v. — The Daltons 4 v. — The Dodd Family Abroad 3 v. — The Martins of Cro' Martin 3 v. — The Fortunes of Glencore 2 v. — Roland Cashel 3 v. — Davenport Dunn 3 v. — Confessions of Con Cregan 2 v. — One of Them 2 v. — Maurice Tiernay 2 v. — Sir Jasper Carew 2 v. — Barrington 2 v. — A Day's Ride 2 v. — Luttrell of Arran 2 v. — Tony Butler 2 v. — Sir Brook Fossbrooke 2 v. — The Bramleighs of Bishop's Folly 2 v. — A Rent in a Cloud 1 v. — That Boy of Norcott's 1 v. — St. Patrick's Eve; Paul Gosslett's Confessions 1 v. — Lord Kilgobbin 2 v.

S. Levett-Yeats.

The Honour of Savelli 1 v. — The Chevalier d'Auriac 1 v. — The Traitor's Way 1 v. — The Lord Protector 1 v.

G. H. Lewes, † 1878.

Ranthorpe 1 v. — The Physiology of Common Life 2 v. — On Actors and the Art of Acting 1 v.

Mrs. E. Lynn Linton, † 1898.

The true History of Joshua Davidson 1 v. — Patricia Kemball 2 v. — The Atonement of Leam Dundas 2 v. — The World well Lost 2 v. — Under which Lord? 2 v. — With a Silken Thread, and other Stories 1 v. — Todhunters' at Loanin' Head, and other Stories 1 v. — "My Love!" 2 v. — The Girl of the Period, and other Social Essays 1 v. — Ione 2 v.

Laurence W. M. Lockhart, † 1882.

Mine is Thine 2 v.

Lord Augustus Loftus.

Diplomatic Reminiscences 1837-1862 (with Portrait) 2 v.

Mme de Longard, *vide* D. Gerard.

Henry Wadsworth Longfellow (Am.), † 1882.

Poetical Works (with Portrait) 3 v. — The Divine Comedy of Dante Alighieri 3 v. — The New-England Tragedies 1 v. — The Divine Tragedy 1 v. — Flower-de-Luce, and Three Books of Song 1 v. — The Masque of Pandora, and other Poems 1 v.

Margaret Lonsdale.

Sister Dora (with a Portrait of Sister Dora) 1 v.

Author of "A Lost Battle."

A Lost Battle 2 v.

Sir John Lubbock, Bart.

The Pleasures of Life 1 v. — The Beauties of Nature (with Illustrations) 1 v. — The Use of Life 1 v. — Scenery of Switzerland (with Illustrations) 2 v.

"Lutfullah," *vide* Eastwick.

Edna Lyall, † 1903.

We Two 2 v. — Donovan 2 v. — In the Golden Days 2 v. — Knight-Errant 2 v. — Won by Waiting 2 v. — Wayfaring Men 2 v. — Hope the Hermit 2 v. — Doreen 2 v. — In Spite of All 2 v. — The Hinderers 1 v.

Lord Lytton, *vide* E. Bulwer.

Robert Lord Lytton (Owen Meredith), † 1891.

Poems 2 v. — Fables in Song 2 v.

Maarten Maartens.

The Sin of Joost Avelingh 1 v. — An Old Maid's Love 2 v. — God's Fool 2 v. — The Greater Glory 2 v. — My Lady Nobody 2 v. — Her Memory 1 v. — Some Women I have known 1 v.

Thomas Babington, Lord Macaulay, † 1859.

History of England (with Portrait) 10 v. — Critical and Historical Essays 5 v. — Lays of Ancient Rome 1 v. — Speeches 2 v. — Biographical Essays 1 v. — William Pitt, Atterbury 1 v. — (See also Trevelyan).

Justin McCarthy.

The Waterdale Neighbours 2 v. — Dear Lady Disdain 2 v. — Miss Misanthrope 2 v. — A History of our own Times 5 v. — Donna Quixote 2 v. — A short History of our own Times 2 v. — A History of the Four Georges vols. 1 & 2. — A History of our own Times vols. 6 & 7 (supplemental). — A History of the Four Georges and of William IV. Vols. 3, 4 & 5 (supplemental).

George Mac Donald.

Alec Forbes of Howglen 2 v. — Annals of a Quiet Neighbourhood 2 v. — David Elginbrod 2 v. — The Vicar's Daughter 2 v. — Malcolm 2 v. — St. George and St. Michael 2 v. — The Marquis of Lossie 2 v. — Sir Gibbie 2 v. — Mary Marston 2 v. — The Gifts of the Child Christ, and other Tales 1 v. — The Princess and Curdie 1 v.

Mrs. Mackarness, † 1881.

Sunbeam Stories 1 v. — A Peerless Wife 2 v. — A Mingled Yarn 2 v.

Eric Mackay, † 1898.

Love Letters of a Violinist, and other Poems 1 v.

Charles McKnight (Am.).

Old Fort Duquesne 2 v.

Ian Maclaren.

Beside the Bonnie Brier Bush 1 v. — The Days of Auld Langsyne 1 v.

Fiona Macleod.

Wind and Wave 1 v.

Norman Macleod, † 1872.

The Old Lieutenant and his Son 1 v.

James Macpherson, † 1696, *vide* Ossian.

Mrs. Macquoid.

Patty 2 v. — Miriam's Marriage 2 v. — Pictures across the Channel 2 v. — Too Soon 1 v. — My Story 2 v. — Diane 2 v. — Beside the River 2 v. — A Faithful Lover 2 v.

Author of "Mademoiselle Mori" (Miss Roberts).

Mademoiselle Mori 2 v. — Denise 1 v. — Madame Fontenoy 1 v. — On the Edge of the Storm 1 v. — The Atelier du Lys 2 v. — In the Olden Time 2 v.

Lord Mahon, *vide* Stanhope.

E. S. Maine.

Scarscliff Rocks 2 v.

Sir Edward Malet, G.C.B., G.C.M.G.

Shifting Scenes 1 v.

Lucas Malet.

Colonel Enderby's Wife 2 v. — The History of Sir Richard Calmady 3 v.

The Earl of Malmesbury, G.C.B.

Memoirs of an Ex-Minister 3 v.

Mary E. Mann.

A Winter's Tale 1 v. — The Cedar Star 1 v.

Robert Blachford Mansfield.

The Log of the Water Lily 1 v.

Mark Twain, *vide* Twain.

Author of "Marmorne," *vide* P. G. Hamerton.

Capt. Marryat, † 1848.

Jacob Faithful (with Portrait) 1 v. — Percival Keene 1 v. — Peter Simple 1 v. — Japhet in Search of a Father 1 v. — Monsieur Violet 1 v. — The Settlers in Canada 1 v. — The Mission 1 v. — The Privateer's-Man 1 v. — The Children of the New-Forest 1 v. — Valerie 1 v. — Mr. Midshipman Easy 1 v. — The King's Own 1 v.

Florence Marryat, † 1899.

Love's Conflict 2 v. — For Ever and Ever 2 v. — The Confessions of Gerald Estcourt 2 v. — Nelly Brooke 2 v. — Véronique 2 v. — Petronel 2 v. — Her Lord and Master 2 v. — The Prey of the Gods 1 v. — Life and Letters of Captain Marryat 1 v. — Mad Dumaresq 2 v. —

No Intentions 2 v. — Fighting the Air 2 v. — A Star and a Heart; An Utter Impossibility 1 v. — The Poison of Asps, and other Stories 1 v. — A Lucky Disappointment, and other Stories 1 v. — "My own Child" 2 v. — Her Father's Name 2 v. — A Harvest of Wild Oats 2 v. — A Little Stepson 1 v. — Written in Fire 2 v. — Her World against a Lie 2 v. — A Broken Blossom 2 v. — The Root of all Evil 2 v. — The Fair-haired Alda 2 v. — With Cupid's Eyes 2 v. — My Sister the Actress 2 v. — Phyllida 2 v. — How they loved Him 2 v. — Facing the Footlights (with Portrait) 2 v. — A Moment of Madness, and other Stories 1 v. — The Ghost of Charlotte Cray, and other Stories 1 v. — Peeress and Player 2 v. — Under the Lilies and Roses 2 v. — The Heart of Jane Warner 2 v. — The Heir Presumptive 2 v. — The Master Passion 2 v. — Spiders of Society 2 v. — Driven to Bay 2 v. — A Daughter of the Tropics 2 v. — Gentleman and Courtier 2 v. — On Circumstantial Evidence 2 v. — Mount Eden. A Romance 2 v. — Blindfold 2 v. — A Scarlet Sin 1 v. — A Bankrupt Heart 2 v. — The Spirit World 1 v. — The Beautiful Soul 1 v. — At Heart a Rake 2 v. — The Strange Transfiguration of Hannah Stubbs 1 v. — The Dream that Stayed 2 v. — A Passing Madness 1 v. — The Blood of the Vampire 1 v. — A Soul on Fire 1 v. — Iris the Avenger 1 v.

Mrs. Anne Marsh (Caldwell), † 1874.

Ravenscliffe 2 v. — Emilia Wyndham 2 v. — Castle Avon 2 v. — Aubrey 2 v. — The Heiress of Haughton 2 v. — Evelyn Marston 2 v. — The Rose of Ashurst 2 v.

Mrs. Emma Marshall, † 1899.

Mrs. Mainwaring's Journal 1 v. — Benvenuta 1 v. — Lady Alice 1 v. — Dayspring 1 v. — Life's Aftermath 1 v. — In the East Country 1 v. — No. XIII; or, The Story of the Lost Vestal 1 v. — In Four Reigns 1 v. — On the Banks of the Ouse 1 v. — In the City of Flowers 1 v. — Alma 1 v. — Under Salisbury Spire 1 v. — The End Crowns All 1 v. — Winchester Meads 1 v. — Eventide Light 1 v. — Winifrede's Journal 1 v. — Bristol Bells 1 v. — In the Service of Rachel Lady Russell 1 v. — A Lily among Thorns 1 v. — Penshurst Castle 1 v. — Kensington Palace 1 v. — The White King's Daughter 1 v. — The Master of the Musicians 1 v. — An Escape from the Tower 1 v. — A Haunt of Ancient Peace 1 v. — Castle Meadow 1 v. — In the Choir of Westminster Abbey 1 v. — The Young Queen of Hearts 1 v. — Under the Dome of St. Paul's 1 v. — The Parson's Daughter 1 v.

A. E. W. Mason.

The Four Feathers 2 v.

Helen Mathers (Mrs. Henry Reeves).

"Cherry Ripe!" 2 v. — "Land o' the Leal" 1 v. — My Lady Green Sleeves 2 v. — As he comes up the Stair, etc. 1 v. — Sam's Sweetheart 2 v. — Eyre's Acquittal 2 v. — Found Out 1 v. — Murder or Manslaughter? 1 v. — The Fashion of this World (80 Pf.)—Blind Justice, and "Who, being dead, yet Speaketh" 1 v. — What the Glass Told, and A Study of a Woman 1 v. — Bam Wildfire 2 v. — Becky 2 v. — Cinders 1 v. — "Honey" 1 v.

Colonel Maurice.

The Balance of Military Power in Europe 1 v.

George du Maurier, † 1896.

Trilby 2 v. — The Martian 2 v.

Mrs. Maxwell, *vide* Miss Braddon.

Author of "Mehalah," *vide* Baring-Gould.

George J. Whyte Melville, † 1878.

Kate Coventry 1 v. — Holmby House 2 v. — Digby Grand 1 v. — Good for Nothing 2 v. — The Queen's Maries 2 v. — The Gladiators 2 v. — The Brookes of Bridlemere 2 v. — Cerise 2 v. — The Interpreter 2 v. — The White Rose 2 v. — M. or N. 1 v. — Contraband 1 v. — Sarchedon 2 v. — Uncle John 2 v. — Katerfelto 1 v. — Sister Louise 1 v. — Rosine 1 v. — Roys' Wife 2 v. — Black but Comely 2 v. — Riding Recollections 1 v.

Memorial Volumes, *vide* Five Centuries (vol. 500); The New Testament (vol. 1000); Henry Morley (vol. 2000).

George Meredith.

The Ordeal of Richard Feverel 2 v. — Beauchamp's Career 2 v. — The Tragic Comedians 1 v. — Lord Ormont and his Aminta 2 v. — The Amazing Marriage 2 v.

Owen Meredith, *vide* Robert Lord Lytton.

Leonard Merrick.

The Man who was good 1 v. — This Stage of Fools 1 v. — Cynthia 1 v. — One Man's View 1 v. — The Actor-Manager 1 v. — The Worldlings 1 v. — When Love flies out o' the Window 1 v.

Henry Seton Merriman.

Young Mistley 1 v. — Prisoners and Captives 2 v. — From One Generation to Another 1 v. — With Edged Tools 2 v. — The Sowers 2 v. — Flotsam 1 v. — In Kedar's Tents 1 v. — Roden's Corner 1 v. — The Isle of Unrest 1 v. — The Velvet Glove 1 v. — The Vultures 1 v.

H. S. Merriman & S. G. Tallentyre.

The Money-Spinner, etc. 1 v.

James Milne.

The Epistles of Atkins 1 v.

John Milton, † 1674.

Poetical Works 1 v.

Author of "Miss Molly."

Geraldine Hawthorne 1 v.

Author of "Molly Bawn," *vide* Mrs. Hungerford.

Florence Montgomery.

Misunderstood 1 v. — Thrown Together 2 v. — Thwarted 1 v. — Wild Mike 1 v. — Seaforth 2 v. — The Blue Veil 1 v. — Transformed 1 v. — The Fisherman's Daughter, etc. 1 v. — Colonel Norton 2 v. — Prejudged 1 v.

Frank Frankfort Moore.

"I Forbid the Banns" 2 v. — A Gray Eye or So 2 v. — One Fair Daughter 2 v. — They Call it Love 2 v. — The Jessamy Bride 1 v. — The Millionaires 1 v. — Nell Gwyn—Comedian 1 v. — A Damsel or Two 1 v.

George Moore.

Celibates 1 v. — Evelyn Innes 2 v. — Sister Teresa 2 v. — The Untilled Field 1 v.

Thomas Moore, † 1852.

Poetical Works (with Portrait) 5 v.

Lady Morgan, † 1859.

Memoirs 3 v.

Henry Morley, † 1894.

Of English Literature in the Reign of Victoria. With Facsimiles of the Signatures of Authors in the Tauchnitz Edition (v. 2000, published 1881) 1 v.

William Morris.

A Selection from his Poems. Edited with a Memoir by F. Hueffer 1 v.

Arthur Morrison.

Tales of Mean Streets 1 v. — A Child of the Jago 1 v. — To London Town 1 v. — Cunning Murrell 1 v. — The Hole in the Wall 1 v.

James Fullarton Muirhead.

The Land of Contrasts 1 v.

Miss Mulock, *vide* Mrs. Craik.

David Christie Murray.

Rainbow Gold 2 v.

Grenville: Murray, *vide* Grenville.

Author of "My Little Lady," *vide* E. Frances Poynter.

The New Testament.

The Authorised English Version, with Introduction and Various Readings from the three most celebrated Manuscripts of the Original Text, by Constantine Tischendorf (vol. 1000, published 1869) 1 v.

Mrs. C. J. Newby.

Common Sense 2 v.

Dr. J. H. Newman (Cardinal Newman), † 1890.

Callista 1 v.

Mrs. Nicholls, *vide* Currer Bell.

Author of "Nina Balatka," *vide* Anthony Trollope.

Author of "No Church" (F. Robinson).

No Church 2 v. — Owen:—a Waif 2 v.

Lady Augusta Noel.

From Generation to Generation 1 v. — Hithersea Mere 2 v.

Frank Norris (Am.), † 1902.

The Octopus 2 v. — The Pit 2 v.

W. E. Norris.

My Friend Jim 1 v. — A Bachelor's Blunder 2 v. — Major and Minor 2 v. — The Rogue 2 v. — Miss Shafto 2 v. — Mrs. Fenton 1 v. — Misadventure 2 v. — Saint Ann's 1 v. — A Victim of Good Luck 1 v. — The Dancer in Yellow 1 v. — Clarissa Furiosa 2 v. — Marietta's Marriage 2 v. — The Fight for the Crown

1 v.—The Widower 1 v.—Giles Ingilby 1 v. — The Flower of the Flock 1 v. — His Own Father 1 v. — The Credit of the County 1 v. — Lord Leonard the Luckless 1 v.

Hon. Mrs. Norton, † 1877.

Stuart of Dunleath 2 v. — Lost and Saved 2 v. — Old Sir Douglas 2 v.

Author of "Not Easily Jealous" (Miss Iza Hardy).

Not Easily Jealous 2 v.

"Novels and Tales," *vide* "Household Words."

Charlotte O'Conor-Eccles, *vide* Hal Godfrey.

Laurence Oliphant, † 1888.

Altiora Peto 2 v. — Masollam 2 v.

Mrs. Oliphant, † 1897.

The Last of the Mortimers 2 v. — Mrs. Margaret Maitland 1 v. — Agnes 2 v. — Madonna Mary 2 v. — The Minister's Wife 2 v. — The Rector and the Doctor's Family 1 v. — Salem Chapel 2 v. — The Perpetual Curate 2 v. — Miss Marjoribanks 2 v. — Ombra 2 v. — Memoir of Count de Montalembert 2 v. — May 2 v. — Innocent 2 v. — For Love and Life 2 v. — A Rose in June 1 v. — The Story of Valentine and his Brother 2 v. — Whiteladies 2 v. — The Curate in Charge 1 v. — Phœbe, Junior 2 v. — Mrs. Arthur 2 v. — Carità 2 v. — Young Musgrave 2 v. — The Primrose Path 2 v. — Within the Precincts 3 v. — The Greatest Heiress in England 2 v. — He that will not when he may 2 v. — Harry Joscelyn 2 v. — In Trust 2 v. — It was a Lover and his Lass 3 v. — The Ladies Lindores 3 v. — Hester 3 v. — The Wizard's Son 3 v. — A Country Gentleman and his Family 2 v. — Neighbours on the Green 1 v.—The Duke's Daughter 1 v. — The Fugitives 1 v. — Kirsteen 2 v. — Life of Laurence Oliphant and of Alice Oliphant, his Wife 2 v. — The Little Pilgrim in the Unseen 1 v. — The Heir Presumptive and the Heir Apparent 2 v. — The Sorceress 2 v. — Sir Robert's Fortune 2 v. — The Ways of Life 1 v. — Old Mr. Tredgold 2 v.

"One who has kept a Diary," *vide* George W. E. Russell.

Ossian.

The Poems of Ossian. Translated by James Macpherson 1 v.

Ouida.

Idalia 2 v. — Tricotrin 2 v. — Puck 2 v. — Chandos 2 v. — Strathmore 2 v. — Under two Flags 2 v. — Folle-Farine 2 v. — A Leaf in the Storm; A Dog of Flanders; A Branch of Lilac; A Provence Rose 1 v. — Cecil Castlemaine's Gage, and other Novelettes 1 v. — Madame la Marquise, and other Novelettes 1 v. — Pascarèl 2 v. — Held in Bondage 2 v. — Two little Wooden Shoes 1 v. — Signa (with Portrait) 3 v. — In a Winter City 1 v. — Ariadnê 2 v. — Friendship 2 v. — Moths 3 v. — Pipistrello, and other Stories 1 v. — A Village Commune 2 v. — In Maremma 3 v. — Bimbi 1 v. — Wanda 3 v. — Frescoes and other Stories 1 v. — Princess Napraxine 3 v. — Othmar 3 v. — A Rainy June (60 Pf.). Don Gesualdo (60 Pf.). — A House Party 1 v. — Guilderoy 2 v. — Syrlin 3 v. — Ruffino, and other Stories 1 v. — Santa Barbara, etc. 1 v. — Two Offenders 1 v. — The Silver Christ, etc. 1 v. — Toxin, and other Papers 1 v. — Le Selve, and Tonia 1 v. — The Massarenes 2 v. — An Altruist, and Four Essays 1 v. — La Strega, and other Stories 1 v. — The Waters of Edera 1 v. — Street Dust, and Other Stories 1 v. — Critical Studies 1 v.

Author of "The Outcasts," *vide* "Roy Tellet."

Sir Gilbert Parker.

The Battle of the Strong 2 v. — Donovan Pasha, and Some People of Egypt 1 v. — The Seats of the Mighty 2 v.

Harriet Parr (Holme Lee), † 1900.

Basil Godfrey's Caprice 2 v. — For Richer, for Poorer 2 v. — The Beautiful Miss Barrington 2 v. — Her Title of Honour 1 v. — Echoes of a Famous Year 1 v. — Katherine's Trial 1 v. — The Vicissitudes of Bessie Fairfax 2 v. — Ben Milner's Wooing 1 v. — Straightforward 2 v. — Mrs. Denys of Cote 2 v. — A Poor Squire 1 v.

Mrs. Parr.

Dorothy Fox 1 v. — The Prescotts of Pamphillon 2 v. — The Gosau Smithy, etc. 1 v. — Robin 2 v. — Loyalty George 2 v.

George Paston.

A Study in Prejudices 1 v. — A Fair Deceiver 1 v.

Mrs. Paul, *vide* Author of "Still Waters."

Author of "Paul Ferroll" (Mrs. Caroline Clive).

Paul Ferroll 1 v. — Year after Year

1 v. — Why Paul Ferroll killed his Wife 1 v.

James Payn, † 1898.

Found Dead 1 v. — Gwendoline's Harvest 1 v. — Like Father, like Son 2 v. — Not Wooed, but Won 2 v. — Cecil's Tryst 1 v. — A Woman's Vengeance 2 v. — Murphy's Master 1 v. — In the Heart of a Hill, and other Stories 1 v. — At Her Mercy 2 v. — The Best of Husbands 2 v. — Walter's Word 2 v. — Halves 2 v. — Fallen Fortunes 2 v. — What He cost Her 2 v. — By Proxy 2 v. — Less Black than we're Painted 2 v. — Under one Roof 2 v. — High Spirits 1 v. — High Spirits *(Second Series)* 1 v. — A Confidential Agent 2 v. — From Exile 2 v. — A Grape from a Thorn 2 v. — Some Private Views 1 v. — For Cash Only 2 v. — Kit: A Memory 2 v. — The Canon's Ward (with Portrait) 2 v. — Some Literary Recollections 1 v. — The Talk of the Town 1 v. — The Luck of the Darrells 2 v. — The Heir of the Ages 2 v. — Holiday Tasks 1 v. — Glow-Worm Tales *(First Series)* 1 v. — Glow-Worm Tales *(Second Series)* 1 v. — A Prince of the Blood 2 v. — The Mystery of Mirbridge 2 v. — The Burnt Million 2 v. — The Word and the Will 2 v. — Sunny Stories, and some Shady Ones 1 v. — A Modern Dick Whittington 2 v. — A Stumble on the Threshold 2 v. — A Trying Patient 1 v. — Gleams of Memory, and The Eavesdropper 1 v. — In Market Overt 1 v. — The Disappearance of George Driffell, and other Tales 1 v. — Another's Burden etc. 1 v. — The Backwater of Life, or Essays of a Literary Veteran 1 v.

Frances Mary Peard.

One Year 2 v. — The Rose-Garden 1 v. — Unawares 1 v. — Thorpe Regis 1 v. — A Winter Story 1 v. — A Madrigal, and other Stories 1 v. — Cartouche 1 v. — Mother Molly 1 v. — Schloss and Town 2 v. — Contradictions 2 v. — Near Neighbours 1 v. — Alicia Tennant 1 v. — Madame's Granddaughter 1 v. — Donna Teresa 1 v. — Number One and Number Two 1 v.

Max Pemberton.

The Impregnable City 1 v. — A Woman of Kronstadt 1 v. — The Phantom Army 1 v. — The Garden of Swords 1 v. — The Footsteps of a Throne 1 v. — Pro Patriâ 1 v. — The Giant's Gate 2 v. — I crown thee King 1 v. — The House under the Sea 1 v.

Bishop Thomas Percy, † 1811.

Reliques of Ancient English Poetry 3 v.

F. C. Philips.

As in a Looking Glass 1 v. — The Dean and his Daughter 1 v. — Lucy Smith 1 v. — A Lucky Young Woman 1 v. — Jack and Three Jills 1 v. — Little Mrs. Murray 1 v. — Young Mr. Ainslie's Courtship 1 v. — Social Vicissitudes 1 v. — Extenuating Circumstances, and A French Marriage 1 v. — More Social Vicissitudes 1 v. — Constance 2 v. — That Wicked Mad'moiselle, etc. 1 v. — A Doctor in Difficulties, etc. 1 v. — Black and White 1 v. — "One Never Knows" 2 v. — Of Course 1 v. — Miss Ormerod's Protégé 1 v. — My little Husband 1 v. — Mrs. Bouverie 1 v. — A Question of Colour, and other Stories 1 v. — A Devil in Nun's Veiling 1 v. — A Full Confession, and other Stories 1 v. — The Luckiest of Three 1 v. — Poor Little Bella 1 v. — Eliza Clarke, Governess, and Other Stories 1 v. — Marriage, etc. 1 v. — Schoolgirls of To-day, etc. 1 v.

F. C. Philips & Percy Fendall.

A Daughter's Sacrifice 1 v. — Margaret Byng 1 v.

F. C. Philips & C. J. Wills.

The Fatal Phryne 1 v. — The Scudamores 1 v. — A Maiden Fair to See 1 v. — Sybil Ross's Marriage 1 v.

Eden Phillpotts.

Lying Prophets 2 v. — The Human Boy 1 v. — Sons of the Morning 2 v. — The Good Red Earth 1 v. — The Striking Hours 1 v.

Miss Piddington, *vide* Author of "The Last of the Cavaliers."

Edgar Allan Poe (Am.), † 1849.

Poems and Essays, edited with a new Memoir by John H. Ingram 1 v. — Tales, edited by John H. Ingram 1 v.

Alexander Pope, † 1744.

Select Poetical Works (with Portrait) 1 v.

Miss E. Frances Poynter.

My Little Lady 2 v. — Ersilia 2 v. — Among the Hills 1 v. — Madame de Presnel 1 v.

Mrs. Campbell Praed.

Zéro 1 v. — Affinities 1 v. — The Head Station 2 v.

Mrs. E. Prentiss (Am.), † 1878.

Stepping Heavenward 1 v.

The Prince Consort, † 1861.

His Principal Speeches and Addresses (with Portrait) 1 v.

Richard Pryce.
Miss Maxwell's Affections 1 v. — The Quiet Mrs. Fleming 1 v. — Time and the Woman 1 v.

Hor. N. Pym, *vide* Caroline Fox.

Q (A. T. Quiller-Couch).
Noughts and Crosses 1 v. — I Saw Three Ships 1 v. — Dead Man's Rock 1 v. — Ia and other Tales 1 v. — The Ship of Stars 1 v.

H. M. the Queen, *vide* Victoria R. I.

W. Fraser Rae.
Westward by Rail 1 v. — Miss Bayle's Romance 2 v. — The Business of Travel 1 v.

C. E. Raimond (Miss Robins).
The Open Question 2 v.

Author of "The Rajah's Heir."
The Rajah's Heir 2 v.

Charles Reade, † 1884.
"It is never too late to mend" 2 v. — "Love me little, love me long" 1 v. — The Cloister and the Hearth 2 v. — Hard Cash 3 v. — Put Yourself in his Place 2 v. — A Terrible Temptation 2 v. — Peg Woffington 1 v. — Christie Johnstone 1 v. — A Simpleton 2 v. — The Wandering Heir 1 v. — A Woman-Hater 2 v. — Readiana 1 v. — Singleheart and Doubleface 1 v.

Author of "Recommended to Mercy" (Mrs. Houstoun).
"Recommended to Mercy" 2 v. — Zoe's "Brand" 2 v.

Mrs. Reeves, *vide* Helen Mathers.

Grace Rhys.
Mary Dominic 1 v. — The Wooing of Sheila 1 v.

James Rice, *vide* Walter Besant.

Alfred Bate Richards, † 1876.
So very Human 3 v.

S. Richardson, † 1761.
Clarissa Harlowe 4 v.

Mrs. Riddell (F. G. Trafford).
George Geith of Fen Court 2 v. — Maxwell Drewitt 2 v. — The Race for Wealth 2 v. — Far above Rubies 2 v. — The Earl's Promise 2 v. — Mortomley's Estate 2 v.

Mrs. Anne Thackeray Ritchie, *vide* Miss Thackeray.

Miss Roberts, *vide* Author of "Mademoiselle Mori."

Rev. Frederick W. Robertson, † 1853.
Sermons 4 v.

Miss Robins, *vide* Raimond.

F. Robinson, *vide* Author of "No Church."

Charles H. Ross.
The Pretty Widow 1 v. — A London Romance 2 v.

Martin Ross, *vide* Somerville.

Dante Gabriel Rossetti, † 1882.
Poems 1 v. — Ballads and Sonnets 1 v.

"Roy Tellet."
The Outcasts 1 v. — A Draught of Lethe 1 v. — Pastor and Prelate 2 v.

J. Ruffini, † 1881.
Lavinia 2 v. — Doctor Antonio 1 v. — Lorenzo Benoni 1 v. — Vincenzo 2 v. — A Quiet Nook in the Jura 1 v. — The Paragreens on a Visit to Paris 1 v. — Carlino, and other Stories 1 v.

W. Clark Russell.
A Sailor's Sweetheart 2 v. — The "Lady Maud" 2 v. — A Sea Queen 2 v.

George W. E. Russell.
Collections and Recollections. By One who has kept a Diary 2 v. — A Londoner's Log-Book 1 v.

George Augustus Sala, † 1895.
The Seven Sons of Mammon 2 v.

John Saunders.
Israel Mort, Overman 2 v. — The Shipowner's Daughter 2 v. — A Noble Wife 2 v.

Katherine Saunders (Mrs. Cooper).
Joan Merryweather, and other Tales 1 v. — Gideon's Rock, and other Tales 1 v. — The High Mills 2 v. — Sebastian 1 v.

Richard Henry Savage (Am.).
My Official Wife 1 v. — The Little Lady of Lagunitas (with Portrait) 2 v. — Prince Schamyl's Wooing 1 v. — The Masked Venus 2 v. — Delilah of Harlem 2 v. — The Anarchist 2 v. — A Daughter of Judas 1 v. — In the Old Chateau 1 v. — Miss Devereux of the Mariquita 2 v. — Checked Through 2 v. — A Modern Corsair 2 v. — In the Swim 2 v. — The White Lady of Khaminavatka 2 v. — In the House of His Friends 2 v. — The Mystery of a Shipyard 2 v.

Olive Schreiner.
Trooper Peter Halket of Mashonaland 1 v.

Sir Walter Scott, † 1832.
Waverley (with Portrait) 1 v. — The Antiquary 1 v. — Ivanhoe 1 v. — Kenilworth 1 v. — Quentin Durward 1 v. — Old Mortality 1 v. — Guy Mannering 1 v. — Rob Roy 1 v. — The Pirate 1 v. — The Fortunes of Nigel 1 v. — The Black Dwarf; A Legend of Montrose 1 v. — The Bride of Lammermoor 1 v. — The Heart of Mid-Lothian 2 v. — The Monastery 1 v. — The Abbot 1 v. — Peveril of the Peak 2 v. — Poetical Works 2 v. — Woodstock 1 v. — The Fair Maid of Perth 1 v. — Anne of Geierstein 1 v.

Prof. J. R. Seeley, M.A., † 1895.
Life and Times of Stein (with a Portrait of Stein) 4 v. — The Expansion of England 1 v. — Goethe 1 v.

Elizabeth Sewell.
Amy Herbert 2 v. — Ursula 2 v. — A Glimpse of the World 2 v. — The Journal of a Home Life 2 v. — After Life 2 v. — The Experience of Life 2 v.

William Shakespeare, † 1616.
Plays and Poems (with Portrait) *(Second Edition)* 7 v. — Doubtful Plays 1 v.

Shakespeare's Plays may also be had in 37 numbers, at ℳ 0,30. each number.

William Sharp, *v.* Miss Howard.

Percy Bysshe Shelley, † 1822.
A Selection from his Poems 1 v.

Nathan Sheppard (Am.), † 1888.
Shut up in Paris 1 v.

Richard Brinsley Sheridan, † 1816.
The Dramatic Works 1 v.

J. Henry Shorthouse.
John Inglesant 2 v. — Blanche, Lady Falaise 1 v.

Rudolf C. Slatin Pasha, C.B.
Fire and Sword in the Sudan (with two Maps in Colours) 3 v.

F. E. Smedley, *vide* Author of "Frank Fairlegh."

Tobias Smollett, † 1771.
Roderick Random 1 v. — Humphry Clinker 1 v. — Peregrine Pickle 2 v.

Author of "Society in London."
Society in London. By a Foreign Resident 1 v.

E. Œ. Somerville & Martin Ross.
Naboth's Vineyard 1 v.

Author of "The Spanish Brothers."
The Spanish Brothers 2 v.

Earl Stanhope (Lord Mahon), † 1875.
The History of England 7 v. — Reign of Queen Anne 2 v.

Flora Annie Steel.
The Hosts of the Lord 2 v.

G. W. Steevens, † 1900.
From Capetown to Ladysmith 1 v.

Laurence Sterne, † 1768.
Tristram Shandy 1 v. — A Sentimental Journey (with Portrait) 1 v.

Robert Louis Stevenson, † 1894.
Treasure Island 1 v. — Dr. Jekyll and Mr. Hyde, and An Inland Voyage 1 v. — Kidnapped 1 v. — The Black Arrow 1 v. — The Master of Ballantrae 1 v. — The Merry Men, etc. 1 v. — Across the Plains, etc. 1 v. — Island Nights' Entertainments 1 v. — Catriona 1 v. — Weir of Hermiston 1 v. — St. Ives 2 v. — In the South Seas 2 v.

Author of "Still Waters" (Mrs. Paul).
Still Waters 1 v. — Dorothy 1 v. — De Cressy 1 v. — Uncle Ralph 1 v. — Maiden Sisters 1 v. — Martha Brown 1 v. — Vanessa 1 v.

M. C. Stirling, *vide* G. M. Craik.

Frank R. Stockton (Am.).
The House of Martha 1 v.

Author of "The Story of a Penitent Soul."
The Story of a Penitent Soul 1 v.

Author of "The Story of Elizabeth," *vide* Miss Thackeray.

Mrs. Harriet Beecher Stowe (Am.), † 1896.
Uncle Tom's Cabin (with Portrait) 2 v. — A Key to Uncle Tom's Cabin 2 v. — Dred 2 v. — The Minister's Wooing 1 v. — Oldtown Folks 2 v.

Author of "Sunbeam Stories," *vide* Mrs. Mackarness.

Jonathan Swift (Dean Swift), † 1745.
Gulliver's Travels 1 v.

Algernon Charles Swinburne.
Atalanta in Calydon: and Lyrical Poems (edited, with an Introduction, by William Sharp) 1 v.

John Addington Symonds, † 1893.
Sketches in Italy 1 v. — New Italian Sketches 1 v.

S. G. Tallentyre, *v.* H. S. Merriman.

Tasma.
Uncle Piper of Piper's Hill 2 v.

Baroness Tautphoeus, † 1893.
Cyrilla 2 v. — The Initials 2 v. — Quits 2 v. — At Odds 2 v.

Col. Meadows Taylor, † 1876.
Tara; a Mahratta Tale 3 v.

Templeton, *vide* Author of "Horace Templeton."

Alfred (Lord) Tennyson, † 1892.
Poetical Works 8 v. — Queen Mary 1 v. — Harold 1 v. — Becket; The Cup; The Falcon 1 v. — Locksley Hall, sixty Years after; The Promise of May; Tiresias and other Poems 1 v. — A Memoir. By His Son (with Portrait) 4 v.

The New Testament, *vide* New.

William Makepeace Thackeray, † 1863.
Vanity Fair 3 v. — Pendennis 3 v. — Miscellanies 8 v. — Henry Esmond 2 v. — The English Humourists of the Eighteenth Century 1 v. — The Newcomes 4 v. — The Virginians 4 v. — The Four Georges; Lovel the Widower 1 v. — The Adventures of Philip 2 v. — Denis Duval 1 v. — Roundabout Papers 2 v. — Catherine 1 v. — The Irish Sketch Book 2 v. — The Paris Sketch Book (with Portrait) 2 v.

Miss Thackeray (Mrs. Ritchie).
The Story of Elizabeth 1 v. — The Village on the Cliff 1 v. — Old Kensington 2 v. — Bluebeard's Keys, and other Stories 1 v. — Five Old Friends 1 v. — Miss Angel 1 v. — Out of the World, and other Tales 1 v. — Fulham Lawn, and other Tales 1 v. — From an Island. A Story and some Essays 1 v. — Da Capo, and other Tales 1 v. — Madame de Sévigné; From a Stage Box; Miss Williamson's Divagations 1 v. — A Book of Sibyls 1 v. — Mrs. Dymond 2 v. — Chapters from some Memoirs 1 v.

Thomas a Kempis, *vide* Kempis.

A. Thomas (Mrs. Pender Cudlip).
Denis Donne 2 v. — On Guard 2 v. — Walter Goring 2 v. — Played Out 2 v. — Called to Account 2 v. — Only Herself 2 v. — A Narrow Escape 2 v.

James Thomson, † 1748.
Poetical Works (with Portrait) 1 v.

Author of "Thoth."
Thoth 1 v.

Author of "Tim."
Tim 1 v.

F. G. Trafford, *vide* Mrs. Riddell.

Right Hon. Sir George Otto Trevelyan.
The Life and Letters of Lord Macaulay (with Portrait) 4 v. — Selections from the Writings of Lord Macaulay 2 v. — The American Revolution (with a Map) 2 v.

Trois-Etoiles, *vide* Grenville: Murray.

Anthony Trollope, † 1882.
Doctor Thorne 2 v. — The Bertrams 2 v. — The Warden 1 v. — Barchester Towers 2 v. — Castle Richmond 2 v. — The West Indies 1 v. — Framley Parsonage 2 v. — North America 3 v. — Orley Farm 3 v. — Rachel Ray 2 v. — The Small House at Allington 3 v. — Can you forgive her? 3 v. — The Belton Estate 2 v. — Nina Balatka 1 v. — The Last Chronicle of Barset 3 v. — The Claverings 2 v. — Phineas Finn 3 v. — He knew he was right 3 v. — The Vicar of Bullhampton 2 v. — Sir Harry Hotspur of Humblethwaite 1 v. — Ralph the Heir 2 v. — The Golden Lion of Granpere 1 v. — Australia and New Zealand 3 v. — Lady Anna 2 v. — Harry Heathcote of Gangoil 1 v. — The Way we live now 4 v. — The Prime Minister 4 v. — The American Senator 3 v. — South Africa 2 v. — Is He Popenjoy? 3 v. — An Eye for an Eye 1 v. — John Caldigate 3 v. — Cousin Henry 1 v. — The Duke's Children 3 v. — Dr. Wortle's School 1 v. — Ayala's Angel 3 v. — The Fixed Period 1 v. — Marion Fay 2 v. — Kept in the Dark 1 v. — Frau Frohmann, and other Stories 1 v. — Alice Dugdale, and other Stories 1 v. — La Mère Bauche, and other Stories 1 v. — The Mistletoe Bough, and other Stories 1 v. — An Autobiography 1 v. — An Old Man's Love 1 v.

T. Adolphus Trollope, † 1892.
The Garstangs of Garstang Grange 2 v. — A Siren 2 v.

W. R. H. Trowbridge.
The Letters of Her Mother to Elizabeth 1 v. — A Girl of the Multitude 1 v.

Mark Twain (Samuel L. Clemens) (Am.).

The Adventures of Tom Sawyer 1 v. — The Innocents Abroad; or, The New Pilgrims' Progress 2 v. —A Tramp Abroad 2 v. — "Roughing it" 1 v. — The Innocents at Home 1 v. — The Prince and the Pauper 2 v. — The Stolen White Elephant, etc. 1 v. — Life on the Mississippi 2 v. — Sketches (with Portrait) 1 v. — Huckleberry Finn 2 v. — Selections from American Humour 1 v. — A Yankee at the Court of King Arthur 2 v. — The American Claimant 1 v. — The £ 1 000 000 Bank-Note and other new Stories 1 v. — Tom Sawyer Abroad 1 v. — Pudd'nhead Wilson 1 v. — Personal Recollections of Joan of Arc 2 v.—Tom Sawyer, Detective, and other Tales 1 v. — More Tramps Abroad 2 v. — The Man that corrupted Hadleyburg, etc. 2 v. — A Double-Barrelled Detective Story, etc. 1 v.

Author of "The Two Cosmos."

The Two Cosmos 1 v.

Author of "Venus and Cupid."

Venus and Cupid 1 v.

Author of "Vèra."

Vèra 1 v. — The Hôtel du Petit St. Jean 1 v. — Blue Roses 2 v. — Within Sound of the Sea 2 v. — The Maritime Alps and their Seaboard 2 v.—Ninette 1 v.

Victoria R. I.

Leaves from the Journal of our Life in the Highlands from 1848 to 1861 1 v. — More Leaves, etc. from 1862 to 1882 1 v.

Author of "Virginia."

Virginia 1 v.

Ernest Alfred Vizetelly.

With Zola in England 1 v.

L. B. Walford.

Mr. Smith 2 v. — Pauline 2 v. — Cousins 2 v. — Troublesome Daughters 2 v. — Leddy Marget 1 v.

D. Mackenzie Wallace.

Russia 3 v.

Lew. Wallace (Am.).

Ben-Hur 2 v.

Eliot Warburton, † 1852.

The Crescent and the Cross 2 v. — Darien 2 v.

Mrs. Humphry Ward.

Robert Elsmere 3 v. — David Grieve 3 v. — Miss Bretherton 1 v. — Marcella 3 v. Bessie Costrell 1 v. — Sir George Tressady 2 v. — Helbeck of Bannisdale 2 v. — Eleanor 2 v. — Lady Rose's Daughter 2 v.

Susan Warner, *vide* Wetherell.

Samuel Warren, † 1877.

Diary of a late Physician 2 v. — Ten Thousand a-Year 3 v. — Now and Then 1 v. — The Lily and the Bee 1 v.

Author of "The Waterdale Neighbours," *vide* Justin McCarthy.

Theodore Watts-Dunton.

Aylwin 2 v.

H. G. Wells.

The Stolen Bacillus, etc. 1 v. — The War of the Worlds 1 v. — The Invisible Man 1 v. — The Time Machine, and The Island of Doctor Moreau 1 v. — When the Sleeper Wakes 1 v. — Tales of Space and Time 1 v. — The Plattner Story, and Others 1 v. — Love and Mr. Lewisham 1 v. — The Wheels of Chance 1 v. — Anticipations 1 v. — The First Men in the Moon 1 v. — The Sea Lady 1 v.

Hugh Westbury.

Acte 2 v.

Elizabeth Wetherell (Susan Warner) (Am.), † 1885.

The wide, wide World 1 v. — Queechy 2 v. — The Hills of the Shatemuc 2 v. — Say and Seal 2 v. — The Old Helmet 2 v.

Stanley J. Weyman.

The House of the Wolf 1 v. —The Story of Francis Cludde 2 v. — A Gentleman of France 2 v. — The Man in Black 1 v. — Under the Red Robe 1 v. — My Lady Rotha 2 v. —From the Memoirs of a Minister of France 1 v. — The Red Cockade 2 v. — Shrewsbury 2 v. — The Castle Inn 2 v. — Sophia 2 v. — Count Hannibal 2 v. — In Kings' Byways 1 v.

Author of "A Whim, and its Consequences."

A Whim, and its Consequences 1 v.

Beatrice Whitby.

The Awakening of Mary Fenwick 2 v. — In the Suntime of her Youth 2 v.

Percy White.

Mr. Bailey-Martin 1 v. — The West End 2 v.— The New Christians 1 v.— Park Lane 2 v.

Walter White.

Holidays in Tyrol 1 v.

Richard Whiteing.

The Island; or, An Adventure of a Person of Quality 1 v. — No. 5 John Street 1 v. — The Life of Paris 1 v.

Sidney Whitman.

Imperial Germany 1 v. — The Realm of the Habsburgs 1 v. — Teuton Studies 1 v. — Reminiscences of the King of Roumania, edited by Sidney Whitman 1 v. — Conversations with Prince Bismarck, edited by Sidney Whitman 1 v. — Life of the Emperor Frederick 2 v.

George J. Whyte Melville, *vide* Melville.

Author of "Who Breaks—Pays," *vide* Mrs. Jenkin.

Kate Douglas Wiggin (Am.).

Timothy's Quest 1 v. — A Cathedral Courtship, and Penelope's English Experiences 1 v. — Penelope's Irish Experiences 1 v.

Mary E. Wilkins (Am.).

Pembroke 1 v. — Madelon 1 v. — Jerome 2 v.—Silence, and other Stories 1 v. — The Love of Parson Lord, etc. 1 v.

C. J. Wills, *vide* F. C. Philips.

Mrs. J. S. Winter.

Regimental Legends 1 v.

Charles Wood, *vide* Author of "Buried Alone."

H. F. Wood.

The Passenger from Scotland Yard 1 v.

Mrs. Henry Wood (Johnny Ludlow), † 1887.

East Lynne 3 v. — The Channings 2 v. — Mrs. Halliburton's Troubles 2 v. — Verner's Pride 3 v.—The Shadow of Ashlydyat 3 v. — Trevlyn Hold 2 v. — Lord Oakburn's Daughters 2 v. — Oswald Cray 2 v. — Mildred Arkell 2 v. — St. Martin's Eve 2 v. — Elster's Folly 2 v. — Lady Adelaide's Oath 2 v. — Orville College 1 v. — A Life's Secret 1 v. — The Red Court Farm 2 v. — Anne Hereford 2 v. — Roland Yorke 2 v. — George Canterbury's Will 2 v. — Bessy Rane 2 v. — Dene Hollow 2 v. — The Foggy Night at Offord; Martyn Ware's Temptation; The Night-Walk over the Mill Stream 1 v. — Within the Maze 2 v. — The Master of Greylands 2 v. — Johnny Ludlow 2 v. — Told in the Twilight 2 v. — Adam Grainger 1 v. — Edina 2 v. — Pomeroy Abbey 2 v. — Court Netherleigh 2 v. — (The following by Johnny Ludlow): Lost in the Post, and Other Tales 1 v.—A Tale of Sin, and Other Tales 1 v. — Anne, and Other Tales 1 v. — The Mystery of Jessy Page, and Other Tales 1 v. — Helen Whitney's Wedding, and Other Tales 1 v. — The Story of Dorothy Grape, and Other Tales 1 v.

Daniel Woodroffe.

Tangled Trinities 1 v.

Margaret L. Woods.

A Village Tragedy 1 v. — The Vagabonds 1 v. — Sons of the Sword 2 v.

William Wordsworth, † 1850.

Select Poetical Works 2 v.

Lascelles Wraxall, † 1865.

Wild Oats 1 v.

Edmund Yates, † 1894.

Land at Last 2 v.—Broken to Harness 2 v. — The Forlorn Hope 2 v. — Black Sheep 2 v. — The Rock Ahead 2 v. — Wrecked in Port 2 v. — Dr. Wainwright's Patient 2 v. — Nobody's Fortune 2 v. — Castaway 2 v. — A Waiting Race 2 v. — The yellow Flag 2 v. — The Impending Sword 2 v. — Two, by Tricks 1 v. — A Silent Witness 2 v. — Recollections and Experiences 2 v.

Yeats, *vide* Levett-Yeats.

Charlotte M. Yonge, † 1901.

The Heir of Redclyffe 2 v. — Heartsease 2 v. — The Daisy Chain 2 v. — Dynevor Terrace 2 v. — Hopes and Fears 2 v. — The Young Step-Mother 2 v. — The Trial 2 v. — The Clever Woman of the Family 2 v. — The Dove in the Eagle's Nest 2 v. — The Danvers Papers; The Prince and the Page 1 v. — The Chaplet of Pearls 2 v. — The two Guardians 1 v. — The Caged Lion 2 v. — The Pillars of the House 5 v. — Lady Hester 1 v. — My Young Alcides 2 v. — The three Brides 2 v. — Womankind 2 v. — Magnum Bonum 2 v. — Love and Life 1 v. — Unknown to History 2 v. — Stray Pearls (with Portrait) 2 v. — The Armourer's Prentices 2 v. — The two Sides of the Shield 2 v. — Nuttie's Father 2 v. — Beechcroft at Rockstone 2 v. — A Reputed Changeling 2 v. — Two Penniless Princesses 1 v. — That Stick 1 v. — Grisly Grisell 1 v. — The Long Vacation 2 v. — Modern Broods 1 v.

Author of "Young Mistley," *vide* Henry Seton Merriman.

I. Zangwill.

Dreamers of the Ghetto 2 v.

"Z. Z."

The World and a Man 2 v.

Series for the Young.

30 Volumes. Published with Continental Copyright on the same conditions as the Collection of English and American Authors. Vide p. 1.

— Price 1 M. 60 Pf. or 2 Fr. per Volume. —

Lady Barker (Lady Broome).
Stories About:— 1 v.

Maria Louisa Charlesworth, † 1880.
Ministering Children 1 v.

Mrs. Craik (Miss Mulock), † 1887.
Our Year 1 v. — Three Tales for Boys 1 v. — Three Tales for Girls 1 v.

Georgiana M. Craik (Mrs. May).
Cousin Trix, and her welcome Tales 1 v.

Maria Edgeworth, † 1849.
Moral Tales 1 v. — Popular Tales 2 v.

Bridget & Julia Kavanagh, † 1877.
The Pearl Fountain, and other Fairy-Tales 1 v.

Charles & Mary Lamb, † 1834 and 1847.
Tales from Shakspeare 1 v.

Captain Marryat, † 1848.
Masterman Ready 1 v.

Mrs. Emma Marshall, † 1899.
Rex and Regina 1 v.

Florence Montgomery.
The Town-Crier; to which is added: The Children with the Indian-Rubber Ball 1 v.

Author of "Ruth and her Friends."
Ruth and her Friends. A Story for Girls 1 v.

Mrs. Henry Wood, † 1887.
William Allair 1 v.

Charlotte M. Yonge.
Kenneth; or, the Rear-Guard of the Grand Army 1 v. — The Little Duke. Ben Sylvester's Word 1 v. — The Stokesley Secret 1 v. — Countess Kate 1 v. — A Book of Golden Deeds 2 v. — Friarswood Post-Office 1 v. — Henrietta's Wish 1 v. — Kings of England 1 v. — The Lances of Lynwood; the Pigeon Pie 1 v. — P's and Q's 1 v. — Aunt Charlotte's Stories of English History 1 v. — Bye-Words 1 v. — Lads and Lasses of Langley, etc. 1 v.

Collection of German Authors.

51 Volumes. Translations from the German, published with universal copyright. These volumes may be imported into any country.

— Price 1 M. 60 Pf. or 2 Fr. per Volume. —

Berthold Auerbach, † 1882.
On the Heights, *(Second Edition)* 3 v. — Brigitta 1 v. — Spinoza 2 v.

Georg Ebers, † 1898.
An Egyptian Princess 2 v. — Uarda 2 v. — Homo Sum 2 v. — The Sisters [Die Schwestern] 2 v. — Joshua 2 v. — Per Aspera 2 v.

De la Motte Fouqué, † 1843.
Undine, Sintram, etc. 1 v.

Ferdinand Freiligrath, † 1876.
Poems *(Second Edition)* 1 v.

Wilhelm Görlach.
Prince Bismarck (with Portrait) 1 v.

W. v. Goethe, † 1832.
Faust 1 v. — Wilhelm Meister's Apprenticeship 2 v.

Karl Gutzkow, † 1878.
Through Night to Light 1 v.

F. W. Hackländer, † 1877.
Behind the Counter [Handel und Wandel] 1 v.

Wilhelm Hauff, † 1827.
Three Tales 1 v.

Paul Heyse.
L'Arrabiata, etc. 1 v. — The Dead Lake, etc. 1 v. — Barbarossa, etc. 1 v.

Wilhelmine von Hillern.
The Vulture Maiden [die Geier-Wally] 1 v. — The Hour will come 2 v.

Salomon Kohn.
Gabriel 1 v.

G. E. Lessing, † 1781.
Nathan the Wise and Emilia Galotti 1 v.

Fanny Lewald, † 1889.
Stella 2 v.

E. Marlitt, † 1887.
The Princess of the Moor [das Haideprinzesschen] 2 v.

Maria Nathusius, † 1857.
Joachim v. Kamern, and Diary of a poor young Lady 1 v.

Fritz Reuter, † 1874.
In the Year '13 1 v. — An old Story of my farming Days [Ut mine Stromtid] 3 v.

J. P. Friedrich Richter (Jean Paul), † 1825.
Flower, Fruit and Thorn Pieces 2 v.

Victor von Scheffel, † 1886.
Ekkehard 2 v.

George Taylor.
Klytia 2 v.

Heinrich Zschokke, † 1848.
The Princess of Brunswick-Wolfenbüttel, etc. 1 v.

Students' Series for School, College, and Home.

Ausgaben
mit deutschen Anmerkungen und Special-Wörterbüchern.
Br. = Broschiert. Kart. = Kartoniert.

Edward Bulwer, Lord Lytton, † 1873.
The Lady of Lyons. Von Dr. *Fritz Bischoff*. Br. ℳ 0,50. Kart. ℳ 0,60.

Frances Hodgson Burnett (Am.).
Little Lord Fauntleroy. Von Dr. *Ernst Groth*. Br. ℳ 1,50. Kart. ℳ 1,60. — Anmerkungen und Wörterbuch. Br. ℳ 0,40.
Sara Crewe. Von *Bertha Connell*. Br. ℳ 0,50. Kart. ℳ 0,60. — Anmerkungen und Wörterbuch. Br. ℳ 0,40.

Thomas Carlyle, † 1881.
The Reign of Terror (French Revolution). Von Dr. *Ludwig Herrig*. Br. ℳ 1,00. Kart. ℳ 1,10.

Mrs. Craik (Miss Mulock), † 1887.
A Hero. A Tale for Boys. Von Dr. *Otto Dost*. Br. ℳ 0,80. Kart. ℳ 0,90.— Wörterbuch. Br. ℳ 0,40.

Charles Dickens, † 1870.
Sketches. First Series. Von Dr. *A. Hoppe*. Br. ℳ 1,20. Kart. ℳ 1,30.
Sketches. Second Series. Von Dr. *A. Hoppe*. Br. ℳ 1,40. Kart. ℳ 1,50.—Wörterbuch (First and Second Series). Br. ℳ 1,00.
A Christmas Carol in Prose. Being a Ghost Story of Christmas. Von Dr. *G. Tanger*. Br. ℳ 1,00. Kart. ℳ 1,10.

George Eliot (Miss Evans—Mrs. Cross), † 1880.
The Mill on the Floss. Von Dr. *H. Conrad*. Br. ℳ 1,70. Kart. ℳ 1,80.

Juliana Horatia Ewing, † 1885.
Jackanapes. Von *E. Roos*. Br. ℳ 0,50. Kart. ℳ 0,60. —Wörterbuch. Br. ℳ 0,20.
The Brownies; and The Land of Lost Toys. Von Dr. *A. Müller*. Br. ℳ 0,60. Kart. ℳ 0,70.—Wörterbuch Br. ℳ 0,30.
Timothy's Shoes; An Idyll of the Wood; Benjy in Beastland. Von *E. Roos*. Br. ℳ 0,70. Kart. ℳ 0,80. — Wörterbuch. Br. ℳ 0,30.

Benjamin Franklin (Am.), † 1790.
His Autobiography. Von Dr. *Karl Feyerabend*. I. Teil. Die Jugendjahre (1706—1730). Br. ℳ 1,00. Kart. ℳ 1,10.
II. Teil. Die Mannesjahre (1731 bis 1757). Mit einer Beigabe: The Way to Wealth. Von Dr. *Karl Feyerabend*. Br. ℳ 1,20. Kart. ℳ 1,30.

Edward A. Freeman, † 1892.
Three Historical Essays. Von Dr. *C. Balzer*. Br. ℳ 0,70. Kart. ℳ 0,80.

Bret Harte (Am.).
Tales of the Argonauts. Von Dr. *G. Tanger*. Br. ℳ 1,40. Kart. ℳ 1,50.

Nathaniel Hawthorne (Am.).
Wonder Book for Boys and Girls. Von *E. Ross*. Br. ℳ 0,70. Kart. ℳ 0,80. — Anmerkungen und Wörterbuch. Br. ℳ 0,40.

Thomas Hughes, † 1898.
Tom Brown's School Days. Von Dr. *I. Schmidt*. 2 Parts. Br. ℳ 3,00. Kart.

ℳ 3,20. Part I. apart. Br. ℳ 1,70. Kart. ℳ 1,80. Part. II. apart. Br. ℳ 1,30. Kart. ℳ 1,40.

Henry Wadsworth Longfellow (Am.), † 1882.

Tales of a Wayside Inn. Von Dr. *H. Varnhagen.* 2 Bände. Br. ℳ 2,00. Kart. ℳ 2,20. 1. Band apart. Br. ℳ 1,00. Kart. ℳ 1,10. 2. Band apart. Br. ℳ 1,00. Kart. ℳ 1,10.

Thomas Babington, Lord Macaulay, † 1859.

England before the Restoration. (History of England. Chapter I.) Von Dr. *W. Ihne.* Br. ℳ 0,70. Kart. ℳ 0,80.

England under Charles the Second. (History of England. Chapter II.) Von Dr. *W. Ihne.* Br. ℳ 1,00. Kart. ℳ 1,10.

The Rebellions of Argyle and Monmouth. (History of England. Chapter V.) Von Dr. *Immanuel Schmidt.* Br. ℳ 1,00. Kart. ℳ 1,10.

Lord Clive. (Histor. Essay.) Von Prof. Dr. *R. Thum.* Br. ℳ 1,40. Kart. ℳ 1,50.

Ranke's History of the Popes. (Historical Essay.) Von Prof. Dr. *R. Thum.* Br. ℳ 0,60. Kart. ℳ 0,70.

Warren Hastings. (Historical Essay.) Von Prof. Dr. *R. Thum.* Br. ℳ 1,50. Kart. ℳ 1,60.

Justin McCarthy.

The Indian Mutiny. (Chap. 32—35 of "A History of our own Times.") Von Dr. *A. Hamann.* Br. ℳ 0,60. Kart. ℳ 0,70. — Wörterbuch. Br. ℳ 0,20.

Florence Montgomery.

Misunderstood. Von Dr. *R. Palm.* Br. ℳ 1,60. Kart. ℳ 1,70.—Wörterbuch. Br. ℳ 0,40.

Sir Walter Scott, † 1832.

The Talisman. Von Dr. *R. Dressel.* Br. ℳ 1,60. Kart. ℳ 1,70.

Tales of a Grandfather. First Series. Von Dr. *H. Löschhorn.* Br. ℳ 1,50. Kart. ℳ 1,60. —Wörterbuch. Br. ℳ 0,50.

Tales of a Grandfather. Second Series. Von Dr. *H. Löschhorn.* Br. ℳ 1,70. Kart. ℳ 1,80.

William Shakespeare, † 1616.

Twelfth Night; or, What you will. Von Dr. *H. Conrad.* Br. ℳ 1,40. Kart. ℳ 1,50.

Julius Cæsar. Von Dr. *Immanuel Schmidt.* Br. ℳ 1,00. Kart. ℳ 1,10.

Macbeth. Von Dr. *Immanuel Schmidt.* Br. ℳ 1,00. Kart. ℳ 1,10.

Earl Stanhope (Lord Mahon), † 1875.

Prince Charles Stuart. (History of England from the Peace of Utrecht to the Peace of Versailles. 1713—1783.) Von Dr. *Martin Krummacher.* Br. ℳ 1,20. Kart. ℳ 1,30.

The Seven Years' War. Von Dr. *M. Krummacher.* Br. ℳ 1,20. Kart. ℳ 1,30.

Alfred Lord Tennyson, † 1892.

Enoch Arden and other Poems. Von Dr. *A. Hamann.* Br. ℳ 0,70. Kart. ℳ 0,80. — Wörterbuch. Br. ℳ 0,20.

W. M. Thackeray, † 1863.

Samuel Titmarsh and The great Hoggarty Diamond. Von *George Boyle.* Br. ℳ 1,20. Kart. ℳ 1,30.

Charlotte M. Yonge.

The Little Duke, or, Richard the Fearless. Von *E. Roos.* Br. ℳ 0,90. Kart. ℳ 1,00. — Wörterbuch. Br. ℳ 0,20.

Manuals of Conversation (same size as Tauchnitz Edition).

Each Volume, bound ℳ 2,25.

Für Deutsche.

Englische Conversationssprache von *A. Schlessing.*

Französische Conversationssprache von *L. Rollin.*

Russische Conversationssprache von Dr. *Z. Koiransky.*

For English students.

German Language of Conversation by *A. Schlessing.*

À l'usage des étudiants français.

Conversation Allemande par MM. *L. Rollin* et *Wolfgang Weber.*

Made in the USA